"[Do... creat... make... and ...

"The ultimate for fans of Sara Douglass. . . . [She] definitely has a gift for storytelling. . . . Eminently readable, with dramatic twists and turns all over the place."

Associated Press

"Tea...ing with cosmic plot... and high adventure...

"Sto...telling at its best, with... gritt...ful character... roma...

"Dou...s consistently demonstrates ... high...ered of sto...lling in the epic fantasy tradition...

"In a...ld, thrilling...

By Sara Douglass

THE
INFINITY
GATE

DarkGlass Mountain: Book Three

SARA
DOUGLASS

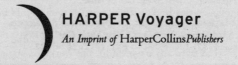

HARPER Voyager

An Imprint of HarperCollinsPublishers

8⁰⁰

03/12

Originally published in 2010 by HarperVoyager, an Imprint of Harper-
Collins*Publishers*, Australia Pty Limited.

HARPER Voyager
An Imprint of HarperCollins*Publishers*
10 East 53rd Street
New York, New York 10022-5299

Copyright © 2010 by Sara Douglass Enterprises Pty Ltd.
Map by Sara Douglass Enterprises
Cover art by Steve Stone
ISBN 978-0-06-088220-4
www.harpervoyagerbooks.com

First Harper Voyager mass market printing: August 2011
First Eos hardcover printing: June 2010

Harper Voyager and ❭ is a trademark of HCP LLC.

Printed in the U.S.A.

10 9 8 7 6 5 4 3 2 1

To all those who raked—
thank you.

CONTENTS

THE LANDS BEYOND TENCENDOR

PROLOGUE

My name is Veldmr. I understand that in your language it is not a beautiful name, but in my ancient language, now sadly lost, it had a particular musicality. Many parents were pleased to bestow it upon their sons.

I find it difficult to speak of my people. Their name cannot be translated out of our lost language, but the concept, perhaps, can. It comes close to 'river angel'. We once were the River Angels.

A long, long time ago.

We danced and sprang through the rivers and lakes of this world. Not the oceans—they were too tumultuous for us, and liked us not—but every body of water cradled within the landmass contained a number of our people. We were part spirit, part joy, part wraith, part flesh. We were formed in mystery and existed in enchantment.

We were truly astounding.

No other race who has come after can compare, although the Icarii now like to think *they* take the honours in mystery and musicality. Ha!

Ah, hark to my pride. I should learn to better subdue it.

For aeons we danced amid the waters, largely lost within ourselves, minding none of the other creatures which inhabited this world. Races like the Icarii or humans did not exist then. I speak of a time at the very beginning of the world, when mystery ruled triumphant and flesh and its continuance did not matter as it does now.

We danced, we sang, we explored countless secrets. We came to understand creation itself. We knew about Infinity.

We knew of it, but we did not care. Even Infinity was of no matter to us.

We were the River Angels.

Nothing mattered but ourselves and the waters which cradled us.

One day, another among our number decided that there was no other race or creature in this world that mattered, save us. Creation could never manage a more magnificent creature than ourselves.

We were the pinnacle of life, and of learning, and the culmination of all mysteries.

This creed spread rapidly throughout the River Angels. We believed it utterly, and it became part of the fabric of our existence. We pitied every other creature within and without water.

They had no matter in life. No point.

Then another one among us supposed that if they mattered not, and if they had no point, then they should be despised.

That idea, too, gained great currency among the River Angels, and soon we despised all creatures not of our number.

They were pointless, a drain on creation. They marred our world, our very existence.

They needed to go.

Thus began our campaign of murder. It is not what we called it, then, but I have enough wisdom and grace now to see it for what it was. Murder. Rampant massacre.

All other creatures depended on water. They needed to drink of it; they needed to eat the creatures within it; they needed it to dampen their roots.

Everyone came to water, sooner or later.

And, as they did so, we murdered them.

Insects; great hoofed creatures; birds of the sky. As soon as they bent to drink from the water, they were seized in our malicious, prideful hands and slaughtered.

We tore out plants, even great trees of the forests, and drowned them as soon as their roots touched our domain.

No one should be allowed to exist save us.

Oh, we were such disgusting creatures!

Naturally, such wholesale butchery did not go unnoticed. One day our god came to us and he asked us what we did.

We explained. We told him that none mattered save us, and that we intended to rid our world of all creatures that had no point to their existence.

Everyone save us.

And our god, of course. We could tolerate his presence.

Ah, I cannot explain to you the depth of our god's wrath. Initially, we could not understand it—unbelievable as that sounds—for were we not committed to the most practical of works?

His wrath deepened. He asked us to forbear our madness, but as we did not understand it as such, we could not comprehend our god's wrath (such shallow creatures we were!), and thus we could not acquiesce to his wishes.

More creatures and plants died.

Thus, our god destroyed us. Such a simple thing to say— four words to describe the most appalling time.

He destroyed us. The water was removed from us, and we could never more touch it. We were condemned to wander within the air, we were condemned to hate the element which had once cradled us and we were condemned to be hated and despised by all who met us.

We became The Hated, and we existed only in horror.

Worst of all, we lost our god, our beloved, and we have spent aeons looking for him again. Sometimes we think we have found him, or something, someone, who might replace him.

But they have never come close to he who we lost.

The god of the waters, who so long ago turned his back on us.

[Part One]

CHAPTER ONE

Elcho Falling

Elcho Falling lay quiet in the night. Its lord slept in the antechamber off the main command chamber, his lady wife by his side.

An hour or so ago he had been dead, murdered through the treachery of a woman he'd once taken to his bed, but now he lay whole and clean and breathing again due to the power and love of his wife, Ishbel.

They lay sleeping, Elcho Falling quiet about them.

All was still, save for the deeper treachery that was about to be enacted against them.

Go! *whispered the One, and in Elcho Falling Eleanon and his twelve thousand fighters picked up their weapons and dissolved into invisibility.*

A moment later and they were dispersing throughout the citadel, seeking out the units of the Strike Force, an unseen cloud of silent death.

Go! *whispered the One, and in the Twisted Tower Josia frowned at the scratching at the door.*

He opened it, and stared bemused at the red tabby cat that entered and wound its way about his ankles.

And now I! *whispered the One, and he stepped through Eleanon's Dark Spire, which the Lealfast man had placed in the very depths of Elcho Falling, flexed his shoulders, and began the long climb up into the heart of the citadel. As he rose, he began to sing, a triumphal chorus drawn from the depths of darkness.*

Infinity had come to claim Elcho Falling, and death its inhabitants.

* * *

Maximilian Persimius rolled out of the bed, hitting the floorboards with a thump.

For a moment he lay half crouched on the floor, his eyes keen, his head tipped very slightly to one side.

Then he rose in one fluid movement and grabbed the blood-stained breeches that had been tossed to one side of the bed.

"The One is here," he said, almost conversationally.

Ishbel rose from the bed, winding a sheet about her body. "Where?" she said, her voice and demeanour as calm as Maximilian's.

"Far below," said Maximilian, sliding his feet into his boots. "We have a little while. Some minutes, perhaps."

"How?" said Ishbel, and for the first time Maximilian displayed some emotion.

"We have been betrayed once more," he said, and strode for the door.

Axis and Inardle were on the stairs, walking down to the level which held their suite of chambers. They were still quiet, stunned into introspection by what Garth Baxtor had told them as he'd come from the antechamber which both Axis and Inardle had thought held only Maximilian's dead body.

"Ishbel healed him," Garth had said. "Now they sleep."

They rounded a corner and Axis stopped suddenly. He lifted his head, peering upward.

"What is it?" Inardle said.

Axis held up a hand for silence, then spoke after a moment's hesitation.

"I can hear the clash of swords," he said. "There is fighting somewhere."

His entire body tensed as he spoke, and now he peered about, listening intensely, not noticing that Inardle had gone utterly white.

"Treachery," whispered Axis, then he began to climb the stairs three at a time.

Inardle stared after him, then followed.

She didn't know what to do, or what to say. She knew what

had happened—her brother Eleanon would have launched an attack against the Strike Force—but what could she say to Axis?

As she trailed behind Axis, sick to her stomach, she used a discreet amount of her power to heal her wings.

Then she started to look for an open window.

Two turns of the stairs and Axis literally ran into Maximilian who was on his way down.

Axis grasped Maximilian by the shoulders. "Thank the stars you live," he muttered. "Maxel, there is treachery. I—"

"Indeed," Maximilian said. "There is fighting above us. And, worse, the One is in Elcho Falling's basement, rising up this very stairwell."

Before Axis had a chance to respond, one of the Strike Force members, StarHeaven, spoke into his mind.

StarMan, we are under attack. From the Lealfast, we think. They are invisible, appearing only if we can wound one through sheer luck. StarMan, we are desperate. BroadWing is dead. We are all dying . . .

"Dear Gods," Axis whispered. *Help is on its way,* he sent back to StarHeaven, although he had no idea *what* help could be of aid to them. "The Lealfast are attacking the Strike Force," he said to Maximilian. "They are invisible, and are murdering my fellows."

Then he spun about and seized Inardle by the wrist. *"What do you know of this?"* he hissed at her. He saw that her wings were healed and hatred filled him.

She had betrayed both him and Elcho Falling.

Inardle shrank back as far as she could. "I'm sorry, Axis. I couldn't tell you. I—"

Axis' hand jerked even tighter about Inardle's wrist, and she cried out in pain, half sinking to her knees. He opened his mouth to speak, to hiss at Inardle, to hurl abuse at her, but was forestalled by Ishbel's calm voice.

"I can help with the invisibleness," she said.

Axis whipped about.

Ishbel stood a few steps above Maximilian, garbed only in a sheet wound about her body.

In her hands she held the Goblet of the Frogs.

"This remains filled with Maximilian's blood," Ishbel said, her voice unnaturally calm given the circumstances. "It remains filled with the power of the murdered Lord of Elcho Falling."

She lifted one hand, dipped its fingers into the goblet, then flicked them out in a circle as she turned on her heel.

Blood droplets filled the space of the stairwell, hanging suspended in the air.

"Who plots treachery," Ishbel said, her voice thick with power, "must now be stained."

Then, all of a sudden, the droplets of blood flew outward, and abruptly disappeared.

The next moment, StarHeaven spoke again in Axis' mind. *My thanks to you, StarMan. The Lealfast are now visible, stained with blood.*

Not my doing, said Axis, *but that of the Lady of Elcho Falling. Stand fast, I shall be with you shortly.*

"I need a guard for Inardle," said Axis. "She has betrayed us, as have her fellows."

Inardle cringed at the flat coldness of Axis' voice.

"I shall take responsibility for her," said Ishbel. "All fighters are needed elsewhere."

"No," said Axis. "She needs swords and—"

"*I* shall take responsibility for her," Ishbel said again. "Go now, Axis, you are needed elsewhere desperately."

Still Axis held on to Inardle's wrist. "What about the One?" he said to Maximilian.

"The One is my battle alone," said Maximilian. "Axis, do as Ishbel says."

"Be careful of her," Axis said to Ishbel. He tipped his head at Inardle. "She deceived me too easily, the treacherous bitch. Trust not one word she utters."

Then he was gone, running upward past Ishbel and Maximilian, and vanishing down a side corridor. Inardle crouched on the stairs, her eyes wary as they followed Axis, then she looked at Ishbel, one hand rubbing at her bruised wrist.

Ishbel lifted the hand she'd used to scatter the blood

and laid it against Maximilian's cheek. "What can I do to aid you?" she said.

"Nothing," he said. "This must be my battle."

Ishbel nodded, accepting it. "Then be careful, and come back to me."

Maximilian kissed her cheek, and was gone down the stairs.

"Now there's just you and me," Ishbel said to Inardle. "What *shall* I do with you?"

Axis had taken two turns down the corridor, racing for the Strike Force's quarters, when StarDrifter appeared from a doorway.

"I have an idea," he said to Axis, taking his son's arm as he spoke low and rapid.

The One rose slowly through the stairwell that wound upward from the very pit of Elcho Falling. He was climbing with more caution than he had initially, and had stopped singing.

The Lord of Elcho Falling knew he was here. The element of surprise had vanished.

"I rise to greet you," the One whispered, his obsidian eyes gleaming.

Then he jumped in surprise as thick, dark blood spattered over his face, neck and chest.

CHAPTER TWO

The Twisted Tower

Within the Twisted Tower, Josia was horribly aware of the crisis in Elcho Falling, but he was so stunned by its sheer suddenness, as by the strange appearance of the cat, that momentarily he was incapable of rational thought, let alone action. He gaped at the open door of the tower, then he gaped at the red tabby cat, now investigating a table on the far side of the ground floor chamber, then he looked at the stairs rising upward.

He had to see what was happening. He needed to get to the window in the top chamber.

Josia closed the door, then tried to grab the cat. He had no idea what the cat represented, nor if it boded good or ill, but he didn't want to leave it on its own. He lunged once, then a second time, and a third, but the cat scampered out of his reach each time.

"Damn it," Josia muttered. He looked again at the stair-well, increasingly distraught at what he felt emanating from Elcho Falling, then made a decision.

The cat could wait.

Josia turned for the stairs.

"Stay," said a voice behind him.

Josia turned about, feeling as if his heart had literally thudded out of his chest into his throat.

A tall naked man stood behind one of the tables. He was an older man, having a strong beak-nosed face under grey-ing dark hair with intense deep-blue eyes that stared unwav-eringly at Josia. He radiated assured power, and Josia felt his knees weaken with despair.

"I am the One's companion," the man said. "I have been sent to murder you—yet once more—and to destroy this fabrication of memory." He waved a hand at the crowded interior of the Tower.

"Neither my death nor the Twisted Tower's destruction will harm Maximilian," Josia managed to say.

"Ah, but they will eat away at his confidence," said the man. "The One leaves no stone unturned. He is determined to destroy Maximilian and Elcho Falling completely this day."

"Who are you?" said Josia. His heart thudded less violently now, and he stared at the man, who was moving across to another table. There was something about him . . .

"You do not know?" the man said, lifting a bundle of folded linen from the table, shaking it out and winding it around his hips to cover his nakedness. "Ah, do not worry, Josia. I am sure that Maximilian has long retrieved the memory from this piece of linen. He shall not notice the cloth's absence."

The man gave a slight, secretive smile. "The memory involves the construction of the strange columns on the ground floor of Elcho Falling, if I am correct."

"Gods," Josia whispered, grasping at the edge of the nearest table for support as the realisation of what this man was flooded him. "You are a Persimius, come to betray Elcho Falling and its lord."

The man grinned. "Come to betray, yes, but not Elcho Falling, to which I owe my complete loyalty. And, yes, I am Persimius. You do not recognise me, Josia?"

He stepped forward, his handsome face still smiling widely, holding out his hand, and Josia forced himself not to shrink back. He still couldn't think—on the one hand he could sense the desperation inside Elcho Falling, could sense the *One* inside Elcho Falling, yet on the other he had this apparition advancing on him. Josia did not know what to think, nor know what action to take next.

The man stopped in front of Josia. "Oh for the gods' sakes, man! Come to your senses! You *must* know me! I am Avaldamon Persimius, father of Boaz, ancestor of Ishbel, former companion and now betrayer of the One, come to do what I can for Maximilian and Elcho Falling. Now, will you stop cringing against that table and give me your hand, to stand with me to save what we can of the situation?"

CHAPTER THREE

Elcho Falling

StarHeaven SpiralFlight shrank against the wall of the common room where the Strike Force had gathered late yesterday. She was half covered by the bodies of two of her Strike Force comrades, their blood soaking into her clothes and the feathers of her wings. She lay very still, the only sign of life her darting eyes.

One of the bodies lying heavily atop her was that of her commander and friend, BroadWing EvenBeat.

StarHeaven didn't know what to do.

The Strike Force had been awake and weaponed. The news of the disaster of Maximilian's death—on top of the continued apprehension caused by the arrival of Armat's massive army and its penetration into Elcho Falling—had dismayed everyone. BroadWing had expected Axis to launch an attack, or maybe mount a defence against Armat's attacking army, but since the time they'd been informed of the terrible news of Maximilian's death, there had been no further orders. They'd stayed gathered in the massive common room, talking, pacing, arguing now and again, wondering . . .

And then, literally out of thin air, they had started to die.

Bodies had sliced open, limbs were hacked free, heads tumbled from shoulders.

They were under attack by invisible assailants.

BroadWing had realised instantly it must be the Lealfast. He'd shouted at the Strike Force, trying to gather them into a defensive huddle in one corner of the common room. Everyone had grabbed at bows and swords, or whatever was to hand.

BroadWing's efforts, as those of his command, were

mostly in vain. The Strike Force had been scattered over the entire vast chamber when they were attacked, and now, impossibly, the Lealfast filled the air above and between them.

Stars, StarHeaven had thought, *there are well over ten thousand Lealfast within Elcho Falling, and barely a thousand of us.*

The Strike Force had fought back as best they could, striking out blindly into the air. Lealfast visibled as soon as they were wounded, and the air was so thick with them that the Strike Force managed to hit many with their arrows or swords even by aiming blind.

But as soon as one Lealfast was wounded, a score or more invisible ones took his or her place.

And they fought so well, so professionally. StarHeaven had thought them infantile amateurs previously, but now she realised they had been pretending; that everything the Lealfast had done and said had been meant to deceive Maximilian and Axis, and Elcho Falling itself, so that the Lealfast could accomplish this treachery.

It appeared nothing could be done to counter the Lealfast offensive, and nothing could save the Strike Force. StarHeaven had contacted Axis, although thinking he could do little, but then . . . then suddenly, strangely, the Lealfast had visibled, spattered with dark, stinking blood.

Yet visible was worse. Visible meant that now StarHeaven could see that the entire space just above head height in this great vaulted chamber was filled with Lealfast, that there was an entire nation of them here to murder every last Icarii.

It was worse being able to see them, because then StarHeaven could understand that there was no hope, and that all the Icarii would shortly be dead.

One of the Lealfast hovered directly above her, and saw that her eyes moved. His mouth curled into a smile as he recognised yet another target for his sword. He lowered a little closer to StarHeaven, who was now too numb even to cower, raised his sword arm . . . and then stopped, puzzlement and anger etched across his face. He stared at StarHeaven, then looked about.

"Where have they gone?" he called out, and StarHeaven saw that all the Lealfast looked about in confusion.

StarHeaven, Axis said in her mind, *do as I say, and do it now.*

Axis stood with his father StarDrifter on the floor below the chamber where the Strike Force were being slaughtered. He had his hand on his father's shoulder, sharing strength and support as both worked the enchantment which had confounded the Lealfast, but he was staring at Egalion, captain of the Emerald Guard.

"You have no idea what you go into," Axis said, glancing behind Egalion to where hundreds of the Emerald Guard stretched down the corridor. Axis didn't know much about the guardsmen, only that they were Maximilian's personal guard and that they had some vague connection to the gloam mines known as the Veins where Maximilian had spent seventeen years imprisoned during his youth and early manhood.

"I have *every* idea," Egalion said. "*You* have no idea where we came from and what we can do. You and your father cannot keep this enchantment going much longer by the look of you, and someone needs to deal with the Lealfast. I and mine stand here ready to do so. Let us."

Axis had no choice. Egalion was right, this was a horrendously difficult enchantment to keep going against a race of creatures who commanded the Star Dance in their own right, and who were likely to literally see right through it at any moment. And there was no one else . . . Georgdi and his men were fighting further down in Elcho Falling, where another contingent of Lealfast had attacked their quarters, as also those of the Isembaardians within the tower.

He gave a short nod. "Go. And for the stars' sakes, watch out for the Strike Force—they will be huddled against the walls."

StarHeaven had called with her power to the Enchanters still living among the Strike Force, telling them to have all Strike

Force members stay as close as possible to the walls of the chamber. She hoped most would manage it—they had been closely grouped against the walls anyway, in their pitiful defence.

She looked again at the Lealfast. They had drawn back a little on the air, still staring about, now very angry.

Axis and StarDrifter had used the Song of Mirrors against them. It meant that whatever the Lealfast looked at, all they saw were their own reflections mirrored back to them. It was disorientating and dangerous, as individual Lealfast could not even see each other, let alone the members of the Strike Force.

But the enchantment was a very difficult one, and Star-Heaven could sense StarDrifter and Axis struggling. She drew in her breath, then very quietly added her voice to those of the StarMan and his father.

Within moments she heard three other Enchanters among the Strike Force lift their voices as well.

There was a movement at the main door and the room filled with men in emerald jackets. Quite suddenly, the Lealfast were being cut from the air.

CHAPTER FOUR

Elcho Falling

The One grimaced at the blood spattered over his face and chest. He tried to flick it off, then to rub it away, but no matter what he did the One could not remove the bloodstains from his glassy flesh.

He resolved to put it from his mind, and continued his climb. Within minutes, he thought, he would leave the subterranean basement chambers behind and emerge onto the ground floor of Elcho Falling.

Then the One would see what was what.

He could sense the Leaffast deep within the citadel, and could sense the death that seeped down through the levels above him.

It was all very pleasing.

The One stepped up, turning a corner in the twisting stairwell . . . and walked directly into a wall.

He stopped, frowning. The stairs led directly into a wall? How could this be? The One glanced behind him.

There was a corridor running off to the left ten or twelve steps down.

It hadn't been there previously.

Now very, very cautious, his every sense alerted, the One stepped down to the corridor and peered along it.

It stretched for about twenty paces before it terminated in a closed door.

The One looked up at the wall closing off the stairwell, then back along the corridor.

Power was at work here.

He made his decision, and walked confidently along the corridor to the door.

He laid a hand to the handle, then opened it.

There was a stone wall behind it.

The One slammed the door shut, cursing. He turned on his heel, meaning to walk back to the stairs, then stopped in his tracks.

There was a strange creature standing halfway between the One and the stairwell. It had the appearance of a tall slim man, wearing simple breeches and a jerkin, but the creature radiated such an aura of otherworldliness about him that he was obviously not human.

"You are a part of Elcho Falling," the One said, realising what the creature was. "Flesh of its flesh."

The creature inclined his head and shoulders in a slight bow. "I am indeed, my lord. I am one of Elcho Falling's servants."

"Good," said the One. "You may escort me from this maze."

"I am afraid—" the servant began.

"Clear my passage!" the One said.

"I may not," said the servant.

"You may *not*?" the One asked, his voice dangerously quiet. He took a step forward. "You may not? Do you not, as does Elcho Falling, recognise my blood? I am of Elcho Falling itself, of its master's bloodlines, and I am bound to Elcho Falling in the same way as is its lord. Clear the way before me."

The servant's expression stayed bland, neutral, even though the One had now advanced within two paces.

"There has recently been some considerable trouble with the Lord of Elcho Falling's blood," said the servant. "The blood of his child, carried by Ravenna, was used to effect a betrayal of Maximilian and of Elcho Falling. We are now wary of Maximilian's bloodlines. They have been used for treachery once. They might be so used once more."

The One's eyes narrowed. '*We*'? And what in the world did the creature mean about blood effecting a betrayal?

There was a step behind the servant, and the One's focus shifted.

Maximilian Persimius was walking down the corridor toward the One.

StarHeaven, emotionally and psychologically battered by the events of the past quarter of an hour, spent several heartbeats just staring before she realised what was happening.

It was the Emerald Guard. Hundreds of them had filled the chamber and were attacking the Lealfast. In itself, that was hardly surprising, for Axis or Maximilian would have thrown whatever they could to the Strike Force's aid, but it was the manner in which the Emerald Guard fought which astonished StarHeaven. There were so many of them filling the floor of the chamber, fighting with the winged creatures in the air above them. By rights it should have been a debacle: guardsmen striking each other as often as they struck a Lealfast; stumbling over and into each other as they fought the enemy above, their arms and shoulders colliding; those who had bows unable to set arrow to string within the jumble of colliding bodies; those with swords unable to swing effectively for a strike; all horribly vulnerable to the marksmen in the air above them . . .

But it was not like that at all.

It was instead supernaturally graceful. Everything about the Emerald Guard's attack—their movements, their absolute uncanny certainty about where each of their encircling colleagues was and what he was doing and what he *would* be doing in two heartbeats time—was otherworldly. StarHeaven could scarcely credit the skill and coordination of it, and she was quick to realise that a supernatural skill of some kind lay behind it.

No ordinary human could move that instinctively, that surely, with such a degree of foreknowledge of the movements of everyone about him.

The Lealfast still held the advantage—they were airborne after all, and the Song of Mirrors that had blinded them had finally disintegrated enough that they could see their attackers—yet even so they could not hold their own against the Emerald Guard. Like the guardsmen, some of the Lealfast fought with the bow, some with the sword, but StarHeaven saw none of their arrows or sword strikes reach their targets.

There were so many Lealfast crowded into the chamber that they filled almost the entire airspace. That meant their lower ranks were within striking distance of the guardsmen's swords, while arrows shot from within the guardsmen's ranks reached the Lealfast in higher planes (and those very arrows seemingly shot with foreknowledge of where Lealfast bodies would be at any one instant, flying straight and true to their target through the jumble of bodies in the air).

StarHeaven's respect for the Emerald Guard, a cohort of men she had previously all but ignored, soared to celestial heights.

"You are amazing," she whispered.

Ishbel had taken Inardle back to the main command chamber. There, while Inardle had sat on a stool, casting occasional glances toward the windows and wondering if she dared make a dash for them, Ishbel had produced a clean gown from one of the antechambers and had re-clothed herself.

Then she sat down opposite Inardle.

"What is happening?" she asked Inardle.

Inardle took a deep breath, now studying her hands fidgeting in her lap.

"The Lealfast are attacking," she said.

"This was always planned?" Ishbel said.

"Yes," Inardle whispered.

"In concert with the One? You have always been in league with the One?"

Inardle's head came up at that. "No. Not I, nor the Lealfast, not always. They . . . we . . . Ishbel, I did not want to betray Maximilian, or Axis. I did nothing to—"

"You did nothing to warn us."

Inardle dropped her eyes once more.

"Inardle, I do not believe that you actively worked to betray Maxel, or else you would now be spattered with his murdered blood. But your silence itself is a form of betrayal."

Inardle said nothing, still looking down.

"Are you prepared to help us now?" Ishbel said.

"Yes," Inardle said.

"Betray your fellows, your blood, to help us?"

Inardle hesitated for a heartbeat. "Yes."

"I wonder," Ishbel said, "if either Maxel or Axis will believe that, now."

"Was Ravenna part of your machinations against me?" Maximilian said, coming to a halt just behind and to one side of the servant. "Was she your creature? If so, then you miscalculated, my friend. It appears that Elcho Falling has decided it needs to be more cautious of any who claim my blood."

"Is he a traitor, my lord?" the creature said, turning his head a little toward Maximilian, but not moving his eyes from the One.

"Does he wear my murdered blood over his flesh?" Maximilian said in a low tone. "Is not Elcho Falling filled with my murderers?"

The One took another half pace forward, his entire form quivering with power. He raised his hands, preparing to strike, but both Elcho Falling's servant and Maximilian ignored him.

"Should we—" the creature said.

"Reject them," Maximilian said, one hand now resting on the servant's shoulder as he stared at the One.

StarHeaven cried out, and even the guardsmen stumbled in surprise, their movements finally crashing into discord.

As one, the Lealfast appeared to have been grasped in a gigantic fist and hurled against the stone walls of the chamber.

There, instead of striking the stone, they vanished, and a heartbeat later StarHeaven heard someone by a window cry out that the Lealfast had reappeared far distant in the sky.

In the stairwell, just below the ground floor of Elcho Falling, Maximilian watched as the One suddenly vanished.

"Where has he gone?" Maximilian murmured.

"A very, very long way away," Elcho Falling replied.

* * *

In the very deepest subterranean chamber of Elcho Falling, the Dark Spire that Eleanon had placed there a day or so previously continued to throb with power.

The One was gone, but it was not perturbed. There was another close who could direct the spire and tell it what it needed to accomplish.

CHAPTER FIVE

Elcho Falling and the Twisted Tower

"What happened?" Axis shouldered his way past the first few guardsmen in the chamber where the Strike Force had been attacked. His jaw tightened as he looked beyond the Lealfast bodies in the centre of the room to the Icarii bodies piled up at the margins of the room.

"I am not sure, StarMan," one of the Emerald Guard said. "We were fighting the Lealfast, then . . ."

"Some power forced the Lealfast out," Egalion said, now pushing his way through to Axis, "but not before we whittled their numbers down satisfactorily. They are outside, now, I believe."

Axis managed to work his way to one of the windows. Egalion followed, muttering orders to the guardsmen that most of them should depart the chamber.

"Gods," Axis muttered as he stared out the window. The Lealfast, some eleven thousand of them, were now riding the winds beyond Elcho Falling. Every so often one or two made a foray closer to the citadel, but some fifty paces out it appeared as if they hit a barrier beyond which they could not fly.

"Elcho Falling has raised its defences," Egalion said.

"And yet the One is inside," said Axis. "Maximilian had gone to deal with him . . . Egalion, I have no idea what is going on. And—"

Axis broke off, muttering a curse.

"What is it?" Egalion said.

"Insharah!" Axis said, suddenly remembering that the Isembaardian army was camped on the shores of Elcho Falling's lake. He'd heard a whisper that Ishbel had somehow negated the general, Armat, and that Axis' once-friend Insharah

now led the army. "Does he know what is happening? And all
the Isembaardians . . . they are vulnerable to the Lealfast . . .
I have no idea what is happening, Egalion. What did Ishbel do
earlier? I know she went to see Armat and Ravenna, and that
she did something, but what?"

"Armat and Ravenna are negated," said Ishbel from behind them, making the two men turn to look at her. "Lister
is dead. Insharah now controls the Isembaardian army. And
you are right, Axis, they *are* in danger. We need to get them
inside Elcho Falling."

Axis's eyes narrowed in suspicion. *Invite them in?* Only an
hour or two ago the entire Isembaardian army had been their
enemy. "We have just repelled one lot of invaders and traitors,
Ishbel. I do not want to invite a new lot in. And where is Inardle? Were you not supposed to be guarding her?"

"Do not worry about Inardle," Ishbel said. "She is waiting in the command chamber. She will do no harm for the
moment. When this situation is a little settled we all need
to speak with her, but there are more important matters to
worry us."

"The One," Axis said.

Ishbel's face relaxed a little. "He is gone. He went at the
same time the Lealfast were expelled. Elcho Falling drove
them out. The One must have been marked with Maxel's murdered blood as well as the Lealfast. For the moment those
within Elcho Falling are safe, Axis."

"Unless we have further traitors among us," Axis muttered. "Maxel?"

"He is well. He said something about the Twisted Tower
and Josia needing to speak to him. I think he has gone there
for the moment. You and I, Axis, need to see Insharah and
determine what to do about the Isembaardian army."

Axis nodded, but he turned in to the room, now almost
emptied of the Emerald Guardsmen save for a score of so
standing as sentinels.

For a long moment Axis just stared. It was a disaster.
Bodies of Strike Force members, almost their entire number, lay strewn about the edges of the chamber, while in the

centre of the chamber lay the bodies of the Lealfast members the guardsmen had struck down. Those Icarii who had survived were struggling to their feet, aided here and there by Emerald Guardsmen; others lay moaning on the floor.

The physicians Garth Baxtor and Zeboath had entered the chamber and were moving among the wounded Icarii, bending down briefly to assess severity of injury before giving instructions to their assistants and then moving on, prioritising the injured as quickly as possible.

Lealfast corpses covered the major area of floor. There were, Axis estimated, probably about a thousand dead.

No Emerald Guardsmen lay among the dead or injured.

They had done a remarkable job, Axis thought and, like StarHeaven before him, his estimation of their worth as a fighting force rocketed up to vastly greater heights than previously.

"They came from the Veins," Ishbel murmured at his side. "Who knew what they learned down there? They had to fight with the blackness itself to survive."

"They closed their eyes to fight." It was StarHeaven, moving quietly over to Ishbel and Axis. "They fought instinctively. It was . . . extraordinary."

StarHeaven paused, taking a deep breath that trembled. "They shamed us."

Axis rested a hand on StarHeaven's shoulder. "You were attacked by those you trusted, and attacked invisibly. You did not for a moment expect that—"

"Damn it," StarHeaven said, "we *should* have expected it! And now . . ." She looked about, her eyes glistening with tears. "Now so many are dead, and BroadWing among them."

"You shall need to take command," Axis said.

"No!" StarHeaven said. "I cannot! I am not good enough! I—"

"You are all I have right now," said Axis. "You shall *need* to be good enough. We can discuss a permanent arrangement later, when we have the luxury of time and breath and the ability to sit down and sort everything out. For now, you take command. Find those who can still fight, and await my orders. Ishbel and I may need the Strike Force against the Lealfast outside. So, gather yourselves together, patch yourselves up and be ready. Yes?"

StarHeaven gave a nod, straightening her back, and Axis gave her a smile, pleased. Then he looked at Ishbel.

"Insharah," he said.

Maximilian stepped inside the Twisted Tower, and stopped immediately, staring at Avaldamon, recognising him from the time he had called Avaldamon's and Boaz's shades back from the dead.

Then he took a pace forward and touched the man's chest. "You are flesh!"

Avaldamon nodded. "Yes, and there is a tale to it, Maximilian, but not one I think I need waste time with here and now. The One?"

"Gone," said Maximilian, explaining how Elcho Falling had expelled the traitors marked with his blood. "To where, I do not know. Avaldamon, what are you doing here? How did you get here? Why the Twisted Tower?"

"He came," Josia said, in an ironic tone, "to destroy the Twisted Tower, apparently, and me with it. And he came as a cat."

Maximilian's eyebrows went up. "A cat?"

"It is part of the long and twisted tale," Avaldamon said. "I took the form of a cat and became the One's companion, and learned some of his secrets and vulnerabilities."

Maximilian's mouth dropped, just slightly. "You became the One's companion? You—"

"All this can wait," Avaldamon said. "You and I, Maximilian, and Ishbel too, shall have time enough later to discuss it. But for now . . . I take it Elcho Falling is relatively secure?"

"Relatively," Maximilian said. "The Lealfast have been expelled, along with the One. I cannot think of anything else within Elcho Falling that may prove an imminent threat." His mouth twisted a little. "Although, I have been wrong before. Avaldamon, why do you need to see me?"

"You and Ishbel," Avaldamon said, "need to retrieve something from within the heart of DarkGlass Mountain—the Infinity Chamber—and you have to destroy the pyramid. We need to get there within the day, before the One can get back to DarkGlass Mountain himself."

"We can't get to DarkGlass Mountain within the day," Maximilian said. *And destroy it? How?*

"Yes, we can," Avaldamon said. "There is a small trick you appear to have forgotten, which is not surprising given everything that has been happening over the past few weeks. Elcho Falling can aid us. I will remind you later how this can be done; it is something you learned on your way up through the Twisted Tower, but which you put aside to concentrate on raising Elcho Falling. But—ah yes, there is always a but, isn't there?—we cannot return so easily. I am afraid your days on the road are not yet over, Maximilian Persimius."

CHAPTER SIX

Elcho Falling

*W*hat has happened? Bingaleal cried into Eleanon's mind as Eleanon hovered with the rest of his fighters some hundred paces away from Elcho Falling. *I have felt something terrible!*

Where are you? Eleanon asked his brother, who had been commanding the other twenty thousand members of the Lealfast fighting force further south in Isembaard.

Perhaps half a day's flight away, maybe a little more. Eleanon? What has happened?

The One has been expelled from Elcho Falling, as have we.

But—

The One was not as prescient as he had thought. He has been outwitted.

Eleanon?

Eleanon could not for the moment respond any further. He was furious, the fury driven and deepened by the humiliation of what had happened to him and to his fighters. They should by now have been in control of Elcho Falling. Instead . . .

We have been tricked, brother, Eleanon finally responded, *and whether by the One or by Elcho Falling or by one among those inside I do not yet know. But once I know . . . once I know . . .*

The One? Where is he? Is he with you? What does he say?

Eleanon sent his power ranging out, searching for the One. For a long moment Eleanon could not feel any sense of the One, then he cursed as he realised where the One was. *He has been expelled by Elcho Falling! He is back in Isembaard!*

What?

Ah, what a rout, Bingaleal! What a catastrophe, and none of it our fault! We should never have trusted the One so implicitly. We had every advantage. Every *advantage. Our enemies should be lying slaughtered and Elcho Falling ours by now. Instead here we are, trapped beyond Elcho Falling, and the One in* Isembaard!

Eleanon suddenly realised that the Lealfast fighters were milling about uncoordinated and unsure in the sky. Gods, what a nightmare! Axis must be standing at some window laughing at him.

He shouted orders, grouping his fighters once more into their squads and setting them to patrolling the skies above Elcho Falling.

Once they were organised, Eleanon flew a short distance to a low hill just north of Elcho Falling. Here he alighted, standing with wings and arms folded, regarding Elcho Falling as Bingaleal still asked questions in his mind.

What happened to the One? Bingaleal said. *I do not understand how he could have—*

He has been outfoxed, Eleanon said, *as have we, and that only because we were so stupid as to place ourselves under the One's orders.*

You can't be implying that . . .

I am implying that perhaps we'd be better off looking after our own fortunes.

The One is a dangerous enemy to make, Eleanon.

Eleanon gave a little snort.

Eleanon . . . we are pledged to him.

He has broken his pledge to us, Eleanon said. *I doubt he can deliver a single one of his promises to the Lealfast, nor, perhaps, did he ever have any intention of doing so. Look, Bingaleal, we will be careful. We will not overtly alienate him, nor overtly disobey him. But I tell you, I no longer trust him nor his promises of Lealfast home and glory. I don't think he has the wit for it. Yes, he is powerful, but he is like the running-to-fat bully in the schoolyard, able to push around those too weak to resist, but toppled unceremoniously by the first opponent who knows what the word "tactic" means.*

And what do we have, Eleanon?

Eleanon realised for the first time that it was he who was the natural leader. Not Bingaleal.

What do we have? We have our cunning, we have the Leal-fast Nation winging its way to join us, we have our command of both Star Dance and Infinity and we have the Dark Spire. We don't need the One and his promises to attain Elcho Falling and Infinity. Not now.

Eleanon turned to look back at Elcho Falling. "Elcho Falling's destruction lies in its basement," he murmured, not sharing the words with Bingaleal. "Waiting for that word from me."

Where are the Isembaardians? Bingaleal asked.

Lost in his contemplation of the Dark Spire, Eleanon did not immediately know to what Bingaleal referred. *What?*

The Isembaardian army. Is it still camped at the lake?

Eleanon turned his regard to the sprawling encampment on the western shore of the lake.

His mouth curved in a slow smile.

I think they might provide us some fun, Bingaleal. Maybe I can retrieve something from this day, after all.

CHAPTER SEVEN

Elcho Falling and Sakkuth

"What has happened to Lister, Armat and Ravenna?" Axis said. He and Ishbel stood just inside the great arched entranceway of Elcho Falling, staring along the causeway that stretched over the lake toward the Isembaardian encampment. It was close to dawn now, and the lightening sky revealed the massive sprawl of tents and horse lines. Above them, the Lealfast rode the thermals high in the air.

They were biding their time. Waiting.

"Lister is dead," Ishbel said. "Slaughtered in the same manner as the many men he sent me to slaughter as Archpriestess of the Coil. Armat has become a witless puppet, with Insharah his master. I thought he might prove useful in that capacity, given that the general Kezial is still out there, somewhere. Ravenna . . . she I cursed with Maximilian's blood. Her child has been disinherited, and Ravenna condemned to wander friendless and alone." Ishbel paused. "I would have killed her, save for the child."

"Is she dangerous?"

Ishbel gave a small shrug. "Less so than formerly."

Axis grunted, wishing Ishbel had not left Ravenna alive. He could see movement in the Isembaardian camp now and, with his excellent Icarii vision, could see Insharah standing by one of the tents closest to Elcho Falling's lake. Axis didn't know how to feel about Insharah. For a long time he had been a close and trusted companion of Axis. When they were in Isembaard they had travelled and fought together. Axis had liked him immensely.

Then Insharah had decided to abandon Maximilian for

the rebel general Armat, taking with him the majority of Isembaardian forces who had been with Maximilian.

It had been a foolish decision, and had lowered Insharah in Axis' estimation.

Now Insharah had command of Armat's army. Three hundred thousand men, give or take a few ten thousand.

Axis did not know if he could trust Insharah, yet at the same time neither did he want to abandon him to possible—probable—attack from the Lealfast.

He glanced up again, more nervously now. *StarHeaven?* Axis said, sending out the query with his power.

Yes, StarMan, the Enchanter replied.

What strength are you?

Perhaps two hundred who are fully fit, StarMan.

Axis winced. Two hundred *only* left? What a disaster this treacherous night had been! *You are ready to fight?* Axis asked StarHeaven.

There was no hesitation. *Yes.*

She sounded strong and in control of herself, and Axis found some satisfaction in that. *Elcho Falling is encircled by a defensive cordon, perhaps fifty paces or so. Stay within it. With your numbers there is no means by which you can take on the entire Lealfast force, but you should be able to shoot through it.*

Axis looked at Ishbel. "Can you hear my conversation with StarHeaven?"

"Yes," Ishbel said, and Axis realised just how strong her power had grown in recent days.

Can the Lealfast shoot their arrows through to the Strike Force, if it stays within the defensive cordon? Axis asked Ishbel, sharing also with StarHeaven.

No, Ishbel said, and Axis nodded.

Good, he said. *Weapon and array yourselves, StarHeaven.*

He returned to his speaking voice. "They cannot give us much protection, Ishbel. This is going to be a bloodbath."

"Then a bloodbath it must needs be, Axis. But we do need to get as many of those Isembaardians inside as possible. Elcho Falling can absorb them easily."

Axis sighed. "Yes, I suppose you are right. Ishbel, I can

use the Song of Mirrors that I used previously to help the Strike Force . . . it should take the Lealfast a few minutes to realise it is being used and where we are, given that we are so far below them. We should make it across to Insharah well enough."

StarHeaven, he said, *show yourselves, and distract the Lealfast.*

Then he took Ishbel's arm and, humming the Song of Mirrors under his breath, started across the causeway toward Insharah.

The One screamed with frustration and sheer anger. Such a chance to take Elcho Falling and Maximilian, and it had been wasted, all wasted!

Elcho Falling had expelled him. The One could not believe it. He had been inside—*inside!*—and then Elcho Falling had spat him out.

The One could not understand what had gone so wrong. Elcho Falling rejected him because of the blood he carried, the blood of Maximilian and Ishbel's dead daughter? Some problem with treacherous heirs and Ravenna?

The One knew he should have slaughtered her years ago. Cursed be her name! She had failed, and thus *he* had failed.

But, oh, of everything, the One blamed Maximilian and Elcho Falling most of all.

He would destroy them both for this.

He had not a thought for the Lealfast; to the One they were such minor players in this battle between himself and the Lord of Elcho Falling that he could not afford to waste a single thought on them right now.

The One looked about, wondering for the first time where he was. Elcho Falling had expelled him with great power and the One knew he had come a vast distance, but where . . .

He moved in a slow circle, looking at the lightening landscape with narrowed eyes.

Where was he?

Ah . . . there. What remained of Sakkuth after the Skraelings had been through it. He was in the north of Isembaard, then.

Why had Elcho Falling sent him here? What purpose?

The One furrowed his brow, thinking. Why not send him back to DarkGlass Mountain?

He stilled, very suddenly, his gaze flattening.

Elcho Falling did not want him at DarkGlass Mountain. Instead, it had sent him to a point halfway between Elcho Falling and DarkGlass Mountain.

It did not want him at DarkGlass Mountain just as badly as it did not want him at Elcho Falling.

The One roared, then summoned forth the power of Infinity so that he might transfer himself instantly back to Dark-Glass Mountain.

But . . . Infinity came forth jumbled and confused, and the One clenched his fists and shook them at the dawn sky.

Whatever had happened in his transfer here had disorientated his power. It was not gone, nor even permanently impaired. Just . . . damaged, for the moment.

The One roared once more, shaking his fists until the distant stones of Sakkuth trembled. Presently, he strode southwestward, heading for DarkGlass Mountain.

He could not transfer himself there instantly, but the One could still eat up the distance with his unnatural strides, and it would take him but a short time to reach DarkGlass Mountain.

"Axis," Insharah said as Axis and Ishbel came up to him.

Axis saw the man's head tremble very slightly, as if he had started to incline it, then had stopped himself.

"How do you, Insharah?" Ishbel said brightly. "It has been a long night and many things have happened of which we need to appraise you. But not here in the open. Where is a suitable tent? This? Good, let us enter."

"What is going on?" Insharah said as soon as they were inside and the tent flap fallen closed behind them. "There has been fighting in Elcho Falling. Maximilian? He *is* alive, yes? Ishbel?"

"Maxel is alive and well, Insharah," Ishbel said, "as you so rightly expected. But there has indeed been bother in Elcho Falling. The Lealfast—"

"The Lealfast have proved true traitors," Axis said, looking Insharah directly in the eye. "They have ever been allied with the One—with DarkGlass Mountain. They, as the One, want Elcho Falling for themselves. Just like Armat and his companions, eh?"

"Armat has been dealt with," Insharah said, his eyes angry at the implied condemnation in Axis' voice and words.

"But not by you!" Axis snapped. "It took Ishbel to focus your loyalties, did it not? It would be good to see you choose a cause and stick to it, Insharah!"

"You two can sort this out later," Ishbel said. "Right now, Insharah, you and your men are in terrible danger. You have seen the Lealfast in the air—Elcho Falling has expelled them—and I have no doubt that they will have no compunction about attacking you."

StarMan, StarHeaven said, *the Lealfast have vanished.*

"And then there are the Skraelings—" Ishbel said, then stopped as she, too, caught StarHeaven's message. She looked at Axis, who had drawn his sword and was now staring about the tent.

"Then there are the Skraelings, indeed," said Eleanon, materialising to one side of the three.

Axis lifted his sword arm, then froze, his face registering both surprise and horror as he discovered his arm no longer responded to his commands.

The Lealfast commander smiled, his entire form frosting in pleasure. "I am sick to death of you, Axis," Eleanon said. "For weeks I've had to put up with your snide remarks and your insufferable superior swagger. You insulted me, you insulted every last one of the Lealfast, and for that, one day, you will pay."

"Not today," said Ishbel. She looked at Eleanon very carefully. "No doubt this tent is full of your comrades?"

"At least five others," said Eleanon. "None of whom you can see."

"Then neither Axis, nor Insharah, will be so stupid as to strike at you," Ishbel said. "I am sure you can release Axis from whatever enchantment you have cast upon him."

Eleanon gave a small shrug, and the next moment Axis

found his arm once more under control. He glared at Eleanon, glanced at Insharah, who was standing very slightly back, regarding the other three with an intense wariness, then lowered his sword arm.

"You have learned interesting new tricks, Eleanon," Ishbel said.

"You fought—betrayed—the Strike Force while invisible," Axis said. "You were not able to do that before."

Again that indifferent shrug from Eleanon. "We have changed, StarMan. We have touched Infinity and bonded with it and are the better for it."

He turned, speaking to Insharah. "Which brings me to the point of my visit. Greetings, Insharah, we have not had the pleasure of direct speech previously."

Eleanon inclined his head and upper body in an elegant bow, his wings sweeping out behind him.

Insharah gave the Lealfast man a careful nod.

Eleanon straightened. "I am come to speak with you about what approaches and about your course of action. You now command the Isembaardian soldiers?"

Another nod from Insharah.

"A goodly army, then," Eleanon said. "Many hundreds of thousands strong. You command great power, Insharah, and you have my respect."

Insharah glanced at Axis, then returned his regard to Eleanon.

"I wonder if you have had time to reconsider your allegiances," Eleanon said.

"Insharah *always* has the time to reconsider his allegiances," Axis muttered.

That earned a very small smile from Eleanon, but no other reaction. "My friend," Eleanon said to Insharah, "troubled times lie ahead. I command a group of fighters who are, in fact, a great deal more skilled than Axis ever gave us credit. If you want proof of that, then you need only glance outside to see the pitiful remains of the oh-so-vaunted Strike Force, now too scared to venture further than a wingspan from the comforting bricks and mortar of Elcho Falling. You have seen this, yes?"

"Yes," Insharah said.

"I command currently some twelve thousand fighters—"

"A few less, now," Axis said *sotto voce*.

Eleanon ignored him. "Another twenty-odd thousand fighters will be with me within, oh, half a day, and the rest of the Lealfast Nation also, travelling behind them. You know how fast we can travel. You know that we can invisible ourselves, and you have just learned that we can fight in that state, too. It is how we decimated the pitiful Strike Force."

"Where is all this leading, Eleanon?" Axis said.

"I am merely demonstrating to Insharah what good allies we might be for him," Eleanon said. "And I should mention . . . and it is good that you, Axis, and Ishbel hear this . . . that some several millions—after all, who has ever done an actual head count—of by now supernaturally-enhanced Skraelings are seething this very way. They, too, shall be under my command."

Axis' mouth lifted in a slight sneer.

"Thus you can understand, Insharah," Eleanon said, "what a bad enemy I might be. I offer you, however, my alliance, my friendship—"

"And we all know how much that is worth," Axis said.

Eleanon whipped about to him. "You are *surrounded* by people who betray you, Axis! Have you never once considered why that is so? Your very nature attracts it! Your sons— who can forget what they did—"

Axis, Ishbel said to him, *don't let him needle you. Let it go.*

"—and not forgetting your current lover, who has told me everything, Axis. *Everything.* You are not such a good lover by Lealfast standards, you know."

Ishbel reached out a hand, certain that Eleanon had by now said enough to goad Axis into attack, but Axis simply stepped back, folded his arms, and regarded Eleanon with a slight smile.

"Your attack failed," Axis said. "You need to learn to accept your defeats. The One has been repelled. *You* have been repelled. Elcho Falling is stronger than it has ever been. Go back to chasing your snow rabbits through the frozen north, Eleanon. It is really all you are good for."

Ishbel fought to stop herself rolling her eyes. *Men!*

"Elcho Falling is stronger than ever, Axis?" Eleanon's mouth quirked. "Really?" His eyes glittered with genuine amusement as he held Axis' stare, then Eleanon returned his attention to Insharah. "I give you the chance to ally yourself with me, Insharah. Elcho Falling has no hope, nor does Isembaard, without my aid or the One's. There is no reason to be afraid of the One, he—"

"My wife was in Aqhat," said Insharah. "My children, too. Prove to me that they are alive, as also the families of all my men awaiting outside, and I am for you and for the One."

"Everyone rests safe and sound within Hairekeep," Eleanon said. "There is no need to worry."

"StarHeaven informed me," Axis said very quietly, "that Isaiah told her that Hairekeep was a dark mass of tortured souls. If they are there, Insharah, then they are not in any manner 'safe'."

"I have twelve thousand fighters, here and now," Eleanon said, holding Insharah's eyes, "and they are all unseeable, and they are all *scattered among your men*, Insharah. Choose unwisely and many of your men will be dead and shall thus never see their families again."

"And there you have the true Eleanon," said Axis, his voice still calm. "Do you really believe it when he says your wife and children are safe? Maybe they are, but only if they managed to *escape* Lealfast 'protection'."

"You have twelve thousand fighters invisibled among my men?" Insharah said to Eleanon.

The Lealfast man gave a nod. "I needed some insurance," he said. "Some form of persuasion. Come join with me, Insharah. You will only gain by doing so."

"Twelve thousand men among my three hundred thousand?" said Insharah, then he chuckled. "I think I prefer *my* odds."

With that, he drew his sword and lunged toward Eleanon.

Axis moved instantly. As Insharah stepped forward, he could *feel* the movement as Eleanon's invisible companions moved in to kill himself, Ishbel and Insharah. He moved instinctively, in somewhat the same manner as the Emerald

Guardsmen had moved in their battle with the Lealfast, and in one single arc of his sword he sliced through three Lealfast.

"There," Ishbel said to Insharah, "and there." She pointed, and suddenly the blood she had caused to spatter over the Lealfast a few hours earlier reappeared, glowing in space. The Lealfast may have been invisible, but the glowing splotches of blood betrayed their presence.

Axis recovered from that single deadly arc of his sword, taking a step toward Eleanon, who had managed to drive Insharah back.

The Lealfast stood his ground for a heartbeat, then he vanished entirely.

"We need to get you and your army inside Elcho Falling," Axis said to Insharah.

"The citadel will take us all?" Insharah said, incredulous.

"Aye," Axis said, "and protect you against both Lealfast and the approaching Skraelings."

Insharah opened his mouth to say something, but was forestalled by the sound of fighting outside.

"We need to move," said Ishbel. "*Now.* Insharah, get your men moving toward the causeway, in whatever manner you may."

CHAPTER EIGHT

Elcho Falling

The battle to get the Isembaardian army inside Elcho Falling was a bloody, terrible nightmare, and without Ishbel it could easily have turned into a rout.

The sudden visibling of the spatters of blood over the Lealfast saved hundreds, if not thousands, of Isembaardian lives. The Lealfast remained invisible, but the blood glowed, betraying their presence. While the Isembaardian army had no warning of the attack, they had been armed and ready to fight: initially, under Armat's command, to attack Elcho Falling, but now, under Insharah, as a precaution against the power and treachery of the previous night. The surprise attack by the twelve thousand Lealfast killed many, but the Isembaardians were skilled and practised soldiers, and it took them but heartbeats to realise that the glowing blood revealed their enemy.

On the ground the Lealfast had no chance against the sheer numbers of Isembaardians, especially if they were trapped inside tents when the blood glowed to betray them. They soon lifted into the air, and there they did hold the edge. Not merely did they hold a height advantage, but the Isembaardians, now organised into the move to Elcho Falling, were trapped in a bottleneck—the causeway was narrow and the army needed to be guided across it by Ishbel, for otherwise Elcho Falling would not have accepted the foreign soldiers. Everyone was frighteningly vulnerable on that causeway, and it was to the causeway that the Lealfast directed their most murderous efforts.

In the air the Lealfast maintained their invisibility. Above two or three paces high the glowing spatters of blood became indistinct and at ten paces high few ground soldiers could see them at all. The Strike Force members with their enhanced Icarii sight could see the spatters of blood well enough from even a hundred paces distant, but the Isembaardian archers could only shoot blindly into the air, and while doing so could not protect themselves. The Strike Force's arrows caused some casualties among the Lealfast, but mostly the Lealfast stayed out of arrow range of the Icarii, who were tied to their narrow protective airspace about Elcho Falling.

The ground forces used their shields, raised above their heads, to create a defensive roof between themselves and the Lealfast arrows. But arms grew tired and it was hard to keep shields perfectly aligned to maintain an impenetrable roof. All too often arrows penetrated through widening gaps in the shield roof and struck soldiers beneath.

Many Isembaardians died. Within an hour of the army starting its painfully slow way into Elcho Falling, the turquoise waters of the lake surrounding the citadel were thick with floating bodies feathered with arrows.

Axis spent most of his time either protecting Ishbel, or organising protection for her. Nothing could be allowed to harm her. His task was made easier by Egalion who, understanding what was needed, sent a squad of Emerald Guardsmen out to protect her. They surrounded Ishbel on all sides, using their uncanny ability to deflect arrows from above with their shields.

Without them, Axis thought Ishbel may well have been dead within a few minutes.

It took the entire day to get the Isembaardians inside Elcho Falling, and all day they were subjected to attack. Tens of thousands died, but the number would have been hundreds of thousands had it not been for Ishbel, for the Emerald Guardsmen, for the Isembaardians themselves who put up their own spirited defence and had it not been for the remnants of the Strike Force, who, while they did not venture far from Elcho Falling's protection, nonetheless managed to make the final third of the journey across the causeway safer for the Isembaardians.

Axis did what he could, but in the end it was not much

more than providing a little guidance and an extra sword. He tried using the Star Dance to aid the Isembaardians, but his powers were either blocked, or somehow subdued. It was irritating—and frightening. He and StarDrifter had managed to use the Song of Mirrors against the Lealfast earlier, but now it appeared that the Lealfast were using something else against him, something that made it difficult for any Icarii Enchanter to raise the Star Dance against the Lealfast.

Was it the Lealfast's own command of the Star Dance . . . or something else? Was it Elcho Falling itself? Why had Axis been able to use the Star Dance against the Lealfast inside Elcho Falling, but not outside?

Whatever it was, Axis did not have the luxury of solving the mystery during this day. There was nothing but fighting and pushing and shoving and shouting, and desperation to get everyone possible inside Elcho Falling.

Every so often, when he was on the south side of the causeway, Axis would pause to glance over his shoulder, looking further south.

Looking for the Skraelings.

Gods, to have those creatures coming back . . .

By mid-afternoon Axis was stumbling in weariness, as was Ishbel, but both worked relentlessly on the causeway, guiding, shouting, cajoling, pushing men on, on, on, and trying not to fall away from the protection of the covering shields of the Emerald Guardsmen, wincing whenever an arrow penetrated the shield layer and struck a nearby soldier.

"How many more?" Ishbel said to Axis when they met halfway along the causeway. Her voice was toneless with exhaustion, and dark shadows ringed her eyes.

Axis pulled her close to him, and closer under the shields their guardsmen escort held over them. "Go inside, Ishbel. You have done enough."

She shook her head. "I cannot, you know that. Elcho Falling knows it is under attack. It wants to close the entrance . . . only I or Maxel can at this moment persuade it to remain open *and* to accept the Isembaardians."

"Have you heard anything from Maxel?"

Another tired shake of her head. "Nothing, he has been

in the Twisted Tower all day, I think." She gave a tiny smile. "I envy him."

"Is he in any danger?"

"I have no idea."

"Ishbel, I think we ought to—"

Axis broke off. There had come a cry above him—not of horror or despair or even anger, but of sheer exultation.

It hadn't come from any member of the Strike Force.

Axis risked a glance upward through a break in the shield canopy. It was getting dark now, darker than he would have expected for this time of afternoon.

"Stars . . ." he muttered.

"What is it?" Ishbel said.

Death came a whisper, and then laughter.

"The rest of the Lealfast have arrived," Axis said, grabbing Ishbel by the upper arm and pushing her forward as fast as he could. "Bingaleal and his fighters. Twenty thousand at least, unless he lost a few thousand somewhere. Shit, Ishbel. *Shit.* We can't withstand the kind of barrage they can direct down on us. We have to get inside. *Now.*"

"But there are still many thousands of Isembaardians waiting to cross into Elcho Falling, Axis! We can't abandon them!"

"We must," Axis said. "We can't save them, Ishbel." He was pushing her forward now, despite her protests, and shouting orders at the Emerald Guardsmen to cover them.

"I'll get you inside, Ishbel," Axis said, "then I'll do what I can for those remaining. *You* can't be lost."

"Don't be ridiculous, Axis. We can't lose you, either!"

"For all the gods' sakes, woman," Axis muttered, *"get moving!"*

He pushed her bodily through the men in front of them, not caring who he shouldered aside.

The next moment they were cringing close to the ground, pushed there by their Emerald Guard escort as a torrent of arrows stormed down. Axis tried to move, to say something, but then two of the guardsmen collapsed on top of him, dead, and Axis had to struggle to try to dislodge their weight.

Stars! They were still eighty or ninety paces from the entrance to Elcho Falling!

Men were screaming, shouting, dying all about them.

Then, suddenly, stunningly, silence.

Axis dared to push the dead guardsman on top of him to one side and look around, staring in wonder.

All the shields of the soldiers on the causeway, and of those waiting on the shores of the lake, had wondrously lifted into the air and were welded together, with what looked like bands of glowing turquoise, to form an impenetrable canopy above the Isembaardians.

Axis struggled up on one elbow, as did most of the men around him who were left alive.

"Maxel," Ishbel said, sitting up.

"What?" Axis said. "How?"

"This is Maxel's doing," said Ishbel. "He is back from the Twisted Tower."

"*This*," said an Emerald Guardsman close by, now rising to his feet, "is a memory from the Veins. Lord Maximilian once did something similar there."

"*This*," said Maximilian, stepping through the scores of men now rising to their feet, "is an adaptation of a trick that Drava, Lord of Dreams, taught me a long, long time ago. Quick now, Axis, look lively. I cannot hold this forever and it will take a good hour to get the rest of the Isembaardians inside."

Axis looked at Maximilian, quelling the urge to ask a multitude of questions, then gave a nod and moved back down the causeway, urging men forward. They could move much faster now that they did not have to try and shelter from arrows at the same time, and within minutes, once the injured and dead had been carried inside Elcho Falling, Isembaardians were trotting six abreast along the causeway.

Insharah appeared by Axis' side, and together they helped the remaining Isembaardians to reach Elcho Falling, with no further losses.

The final few score men had brought horses with them, dragging the terrified animals by the reins along the causeway. They must have cut the horse lines before they'd left the encampment, because the mass of Isembaardian horses from the camp followed their companions into the tunnelled archway, forcing both Axis and Insharah to flatten themselves against the walls to avoid the stampede.

"Are you *sure* Elcho Falling can take all these?" Insharah said.

"Elcho Falling is an amazing place," Axis replied.

CHAPTER NINE

Elcho Falling

At the sound of Elcho Falling's massive portal closing behind him, Axis sank down on his haunches, resting his back against one of the giant columns of the vast ground floor chamber. He was exhausted. He had not slept in almost two days, he had been driven to the edge both physically and emotionally, and he simply had no strength left with which to think, or plan, or solve.

And yet he had to do all three.

Somehow.

There were men and horses milling about, but they were gradually being sorted and redirected by Emerald Guardsmen, some of Georgdi's Outlander men and by the citadel's silent servants.

Axis closed his eyes, wondering if he could snatch just a few minutes sleep before he had to attend to that one thing that had been nibbling away at the back of his mind all day.

Inardle.

"Axis?"

He opened his eyes wearily. Maximilian and Ishbel stood before him, Ishbel leaning on her husband's arm for support.

"Come up to the command chamber," Maximilian said. "We need to talk." He offered his free hand and Axis sighed, took it, and allowed Maximilian to pull him to his feet.

They filed into the command chamber where, so it felt to Axis, this current crisis had begun over a thousand years ago—and he'd been awake for all of it. Was it only a day since Maximilian had been murdered; only a day since he'd thought Inardle trustworthy, since he'd thought he'd loved her?

She was sitting in here now, on a stool against a far wall, her hands folded in her lap, her eyes downcast.

The perfect pose for the repentant traitoress.

Axis couldn't look at her. He averted his face, choosing to move to a chair as far distant from her as possible.

The Outlander general Georgdi was here, too, as was Insharah, Egalion, StarDrifter, StarHeaven and a dark, handsome man Axis did not recognise but who he supposed must be somehow associated with the Isembaardians, perhaps a commander under Insharah.

He didn't care, he was too fatigued. Axis exchanged a brief word with StarHeaven and then his father, then slumped down in the chair.

Maximilian and Ishbel sat down where they had a clear view of everyone else, and Maximilian gestured at those few still standing to take seats as well.

"We are safe enough for the moment," Maximilian said, "although I cannot guarantee the morrow." He gave a brief smile. "The moment shall have to do for now. There is something I need to tell you, but first, perhaps, we need to review what has happened here, Georgdi, Egalion, how stands security within Elcho Falling?"

"Good, so far as I can tell," Georgdi said. "But who is to know what other traitors lurk in the shadows?" He glanced at Inardle as he spoke.

"Everyone who has entered Elcho Falling has been assigned quarters," Egalion said. "Garth and Zeboath are attending the wounded as best they can, but many more will die from their wounds."

"For your part this night," Maximilian said, "I need to thank you, Egalion, and your guardsmen. We may all have been lost, had it not been for you."

Egalion nodded, like so many others, too tired to waste energy on unnecessary words.

"What other threats lurk, Axis?" Maximilian said.

"The Skraelings are coming," Axis said, rubbing at his eyes with one hand, "and they will be here as soon as they may. Eleanon has been reinforced with Bingaleal and his twenty thousand." Axis sighed, thinking. "Kezial and some few score thousand Isembaardian soldiers are roaming the Outlands *somewhere*, but who knows if they are a threat or if they'll be overwhelmed by the approaching tide of the Skraelings. But who am I to talk of what threats and treacheries we face? For that we have Inardle to ask."

He looked at her then and she raised her eyes and caught his gaze. Inardle's eyes were distraught, and Axis thought her a most talented actor. He hoped everyone else in the chamber saw through to the treacherous soul that she tried to hide.

"I will speak here," Ishbel said. "Inardle is no traitor, not to Elcho Falling. If she had been, she would have been spattered with the blood—the blood of murdered Maxel—that I cast from the Goblet of the Frogs. It did not stick to her. She did not betray Elcho Falling."

Axis banged his fist on the table, his exhaustion forgotten. "*What?* Have you not seen the murdered bodies of the Strike Force, Ishbel? Did you not see Isembaardian after Isembaardian cast down into death from the causeway? Could you walk the few paces to the window and look out on the waters which surround us and not see the corpses floating so thick the water is hid? Is Inardle not responsible for all—"

"No," Ishbel said.

"She *knew* this was going to happen!" Axis shouted as he rose to his feet, now joined by StarDrifter, who had leapt to his feet also, sending Inardle a look of implacable hatred as he did so.

"She *knew* it," Axis said, "and she said nothing."

"She was torn by twin loyalties," Ishbel said. "She was—"

"Sent here to betray us," StarDrifter said, "and this she did perfectly."

"Sit *down*, StarDrifter," Maximilian said, his tone moderate. "Both of you. And Axis, take a deep breath and calm yourself. I understand your anger, everyone here does—"

"Don't patronise me," Axis snapped, remaining on his feet.

"I am not patronising you!" Maximilian said. "I just want you to calm down so that we can hear what Inardle has to say! None of us has the energy to deflect such bitter anger,

Axis. Please, just calm down and let myself and Ishbel talk to Inardle."

"I am not allowed to challenge her?" Axis said, his eyebrows raising.

"Not in the mood you are in now," Maximilian said. "Be quiet for the moment, Axis."

Axis hesitated, then gave a curt nod, sitting down and gesturing to his father to do the same.

"I think Inardle has a great deal to tell us," Ishbel said, "and I think she will. Inardle, you must have felt yourself in an impossible position."

Inardle looked at Ishbel, fighting back the tears. That single phrase of sympathetic understanding on Ishbel's part almost undid her. She had kept herself under such tight control from the moment she'd seen Axis walk into the chamber . . .

"Inardle?" Ishbel prompted.

"I was sent by Eleanon and Bingaleal to spy on Axis," Inardle said, her voice brittle and hard as she tried to stop herself from weeping.

"You put yourself through the horror at Armat's camp deliberately?" Axis said. "You allowed Armat to cripple you, and Risdon to rape you . . . all to get into my bed and my trust?"

Inardle could not look at him. She swallowed, then gave a tight nod.

"And look at her now," Axis said, his voice hard with hatred. "Her wings healed perfectly. Doubtless she could have healed herself any time she wanted, but no, she played the cripple well enough to engage our sympathies, and played BroadWing so that I would trust her above him. You are loathsome to me, Inardle."

She flushed and her entire body tensed.

"Leave it for the time being, Axis," Maximilian said. "For now it is information we need, not recrimination."

Axis grunted in disagreement, but he leaned back a little in his chair and stared studiously at the far wall, and the mood in the chamber eased a fraction.

"The Lealfast always meant to betray Axis, and Maximilian?" Ishbel said to Inardle.

"No," Inardle said, then cleared her throat to speak more clearly. "No. We were always undecided whether to offer our loyalty to you, Maximilian Persimius, as Lord of Elcho Falling, or to the One in DarkGlass Mountain."

"You knew of the One," Maximilian said.

"Yes," Inardle said. "Always. We have known of the pyramid since the Magi first began its construction."

At the back of the room the dark, handsome man who Axis had noticed earlier, leaned forward very slightly, his eyes intense.

"We, the Lealfast," Inardle continued, "wanted power and we did not know who could best offer us that."

"Just power?" Maximilian said.

"We wanted also, *want* also, more than anything else, to be free of our half and half heritage," Inardle said. "Always we were half Skraeling and half Icarii, and both the Skraelings and the Icarii loathed us for it. We wanted our own identity and purpose, not our half and half hatefulness. We wanted our own home, far away from the frozen northern wastes. We did not know who could best offer us all that we wished, Maximilian or the One."

"*How* did you know of the pyramid, and the One?" Ishbel asked.

"Two thousand years ago, give or take," Inardle said, "the pyramid known as Threshold, which you know today as DarkGlass Mountain, was dismantled under the orders of the Magus Boaz and his half-brother Chad Zabryze, ruler of Ashdod. The glass was taken from its surface, the Infinity Chamber dismantled. Everything was buried, even the stone carcass of the pyramid itself. Worship of the One was forbidden and his Magi were disbanded. The libraries of the Magi were burned."

Inardle's voice strengthened, and she looked about the room with far more courage than previously.

"But not everything in the libraries was burned and not all former Magi forgot their loyalty to the One, nor their learning and training. Five escaped northward. They travelled fast, and they travelled far, fearful always that somehow the soldiers of Zabryze would find them, or cause others to apprehend them.

"With them they carried the few scrolls and books pertaining to the One and Infinity that they had managed to save from the hateful fires of Boaz and his brother."

"I am descended from Boaz," said Ishbel. "You know this, yes?"

"I know this," Inardle said. "We were always wary of you."

"The Magi travelled northward," said the handsome stranger, "to your frozen wastelands? To the Lealfast?"

"Yes," said Inardle. *And think not that you are a stranger to me, Avaldamon.*

Avaldamon's mouth curved slightly as he recognised the power behind that thought, but he did not respond, allowing Ishbel to continue to question Inardle.

"The Magi travelled northward to the frozen wastes," said Ishbel, "and there they met with the Lealfast. I imagine a deal was brokered, Inardle, for the Magi taught the Lealfast a great deal, didn't they?"

"They taught us everything," said Inardle. "They taught us the way of the One and the secrets of the Magi."

"You control the power of the Magi?" StarDrifter asked.

"Yes," Inardle said. "Not all of us, but many of us. I control a little of this power, but nowhere near as much as Eleanon and Bingaleal, who are the most powerful Magi among us. Now that they have combined with the One and have pledged him their utter allegiance, their ability to touch Infinity and to use its power must be a hundredfold to what it was a few short months ago. My own command of the power of the One is much poorer—I am female, and the One despises females for our power to subdivide the One."

"The ability to give birth," Avaldamon said, "and thus subdivide the One."

Many in the chamber now looked at Avaldamon curiously, wondering at him, but Maximilian still chose not to reveal his identity.

"You combine the power of the One with the Star Dance," Maximilian said, and Inardle nodded.

"It was how our forbears made the spires, which Lister

gave to Isaiah and others to enable them to communicate over vast distances."

Stars, Axis thought, *Isaiah! Amid the chaos I had forgotten about him!*

He would be travelling north toward Elcho Falling, by now somewhere between Margalit and the citadel.

And the Lealfast were in the air, and the Skraelings fast approaching from the south. Oh, stars, stars . . .

Axis almost opened his mouth to say something, but kept it closed. He would mention Isaiah's plight to Maximilian as soon as he had a chance.

"So the Lealfast have the ability to use the power of the One," said StarDrifter. "Wonderful."

"Jealous, StarDrifter?" Inardle said softly.

"Why are you still here, Inardle?" Maximilian said abruptly. "You could have left hours ago. You can leave *now*," he waved a hand at the windows, "for none here would stop you."

"Perhaps she stays to spread the treachery a little deeper," StarDrifter said. "Taunt us a little longer, work the Lealfast's purpose a little more accurately."

"Inardle?" Maximilian said.

"I stay," she said, "because I think Eleanon and Bingaleal chose wrongly when they chose the way of the One over you, Maximilian Persimius, Lord of Elcho Falling."

"And you expect us to believe *that*?" Axis said. "If you had decided that Eleanon and Bingaleal had chosen wrongly, why did you not tell me or Maxel what the Lealfast had done, and what they planned? Why did you leave it until so many lay dead?"

"How easy do you think it, StarMan, to abandon the loyalties of a lifetime for a new set?" Inardle said. "And how easy do you truly believe it could have been, to have come to you, and said, 'Oh Axis, all I have told you has been lies, but I am sorry for it, and as proof I shall tell you some secrets'? You would have hated me instantly, as you have now, and refused to listen to a word I said. I was trapped, trapped by conflicting loyalties and loves. There was nowhere for me to turn, and no one to believe me."

"*I* abandoned the loyalties of a lifetime for a 'new set'," Axis said softly, "when I abandoned the Seneschal for the way of the Forbidden—the Icarii, I found my conscience a good guide. I suggest you might like to try that, too, one day. *If* you have a conscience."

Inardle stared at him, her face losing its colour. "I stayed for love of you, Axis. That's why I stayed. A bitter choice, I am sure you will agree."

Then she sighed, and looked at Maximilian. "I do not blame any of you for not believing me. Nor for your distrust of me now. So, in order to alleviate just a little of that distrust, I shall tell you a secret, that when Eleanon or Bingaleal discovers I have spoken it, will be my death sentence."

"Then speak it," Axis snapped, "and earn your death sentence."

Maximilian thought about reprimanding Axis, but decided that the man had good enough reason to be bitter. Inardle had truly played to all his weaknesses, as all his strengths, in gaining his trust.

He raised an eyebrow at Inardle. "And your secret is . . . ?"

"Elcho Falling is *not* secure," Inardle said. "You know of the rose-coloured spires. But there is one other, made of pure magic and the power of Infinity, and perhaps beyond Infinity for all I know. It is what we know as the Dark Spire and it is a thing of great bleakness, of frightening potency. I believe that it is now somewhere within Elcho Falling. It is the only way the One could have gained access. Eleanon would have placed it here to aid and guide the One.

"And as long as it stays here, then we are all corpses walking. None of us can combat it."

Eleanon and Bingaleal sat on the small hill north of Elcho Falling, arms resting on raised knees, chins resting on arms.

"There is nothing from the One," Eleanon said. "Nothing. Whatever consumes his interest in Isembaard, it is not worry about us."

"Do you mind overmuch?" Bingaleal said.

Eleanon's mouth curved slightly. "No. But I'd like to know where he is and what he does. He's moving south-west through Isembaard, probably to reach DarkGlass Mountain. Why, I wonder?"

"He feels safe there, perhaps," Bingaleal said.

Eleanon grunted. "So he runs away, eh? Of what use is he to us now?"

"We do need to be careful, Eleanon."

"We will be careful, brother."

"What do you plan for the Dark Spire, Eleanon?"

Eleanon took a deep breath, and told him.

Bingaleal's eyes widened progressively as Eleanon spoke. "Is this possible?"

"I believe so," Eleanon said. "I do not know how I can get inside Elcho Falling again to do what I must . . . but if I can work that out, then, yes, it is possible. I have spoken to the Dark Spire, and it is ready. It has . . . grown."

"The One will not object?"

Eleanon shrugged. "As I said, he appears to have lost interest in us for the moment. In any case, it will serve his purpose as well as ours."

"And the Lealfast Nation?"

"They will need to come here. We seem to have acquired an empty encampment of thousands of tents for their comfort."

"I will send word," Bingaleal said, and Eleanon nodded.

"There is a prize sitting there," he said, looking at Elcho Falling. "A portal into all the power we could ever want. A home that is more than we could ever want. The One had promised to achieve it for us, but now I doubt he could achieve the barbecuing of a small frog without someone holding his hand for the entire procedure. This is up to us, now, brother."

CHAPTER TEN

Elcho Falling

"Where is this Dark Spire?" Maximilian said, his voice edgy for the first time.

"I don't know," said Inardle. "I am almost certain it is here, but I do not know where."

Maximilian was not sure whether to believe her or not. Did this Dark Spire exist? If so, did Inardle actually know its location? Did she think to amuse herself watching them panic?

She doesn't know, Maxel, Ishbel said to him, and Maximilian gave a nod.

"Very well," he said. "Georgdi, Egalion, StarHeaven, organise a search. Inardle, what should they look for?"

"A dark, almost black, corkscrewed spire about so tall," said Inardle, holding one hand above the other.

"Is it dangerous?" Maximilian said.

"They shouldn't touch it," Inardle said, "nor approach it too closely. If it doesn't feel threatened it likely will not lash out."

Maximilian looked at the three he'd entrusted with the search, already on their feet and by the door. "Be careful," he said, and they nodded, and left.

His gaze returned to Inardle. "I didn't need this, Inardle."

"I'm sorry, my lord."

"Is there anything *else* you think you should tell us?"

"No. Eleanon didn't trust me enough to confide in me once I had become Axis' lover. All I know is that he probably placed the Dark Spire within Elcho Falling and that he, and Bingaleal, and likely all of the Lealfast, are now much changed to what once they were."

She gave a short, bitter laugh. "I think I must be the only original Lealfast remaining, the only one torn between her twin heritages."

"Are we going to be able to remove the Dark Spire when we discover it?" Maximilian asked.

"No," Inardle said, "none of you will be able to touch it."

"What can it do?" Axis said.

"It can reach into Infinity, Axis," Inardle said. "What can it *not* do? But . . . I do not know what its instructions are. I am sorry."

Maximilian looked at Avaldamon, then to those remaining at the table. "It is time to introduce you to my friend, I think, and explain to you what I learned from the Twisted Tower. Ishbel," he took her hand, "do you know this man?"

She smiled. "He is Persimius, and . . . familiar, but I cannot name him."

Avaldamon rose at that, walking over to Ishbel. He dropped to a knee before her and took the hand that Maximilian relinquished.

"I am Boaz's father, Ishbel. Your ancestor. Avaldamon."

Ishbel stared at him, then her mouth moved in a broad smile. She leaned down and embraced him.

"What do you here?" she said. "Oh, what legends I have heard of you!"

"Really?" Avaldamon said. "From who? You have long been distanced from your real heritage."

"From your daughter-in-law's cup, the Goblet of the Frogs. It talked of you a great deal."

Avaldamon laughed, kissing Ishbel's cheek, then rose to take a nearby chair that Georgdi had vacated for him. "Do I have time to tell my story, Maxel?" Avaldamon said.

"Until someone returns with news of the Dark Spire's location," Maximilian said.

"You all know of Josia?" Avaldamon said to the rest of the gathering, and everyone nodded.

"Josia's return was planned many thousands of years ago," said Avaldamon, "and so also was mine. Let me tell you a little of my background. I am a Persimius prince, younger brother to one of the Lords of Elcho Falling." His mouth twisted wryly. "As happens with many younger Persimius sons I think, I, like Josia, was given a task to accomplish that lay beyond Elcho Falling. Something that would have a great impact on the future."

He sat back in the chair, crossing his legs. "News of the construction of Threshold had reached Elcho Falling. My brother and I, as our advisers, were deeply concerned about both the cult of the One and the rise of Threshold itself. The ability of the Magi to touch Infinity? It was a nightmare. So . . . I was sent on the long journey to Ashdod, what you now know as Isembaard. My task?" He gave a small smile. "To sire a son on an Ashdodian princess. This would combine the blood of Ashdod with that of Elcho Falling, in an effort, should it be needed, to secure the destruction of Threshold and the cult of the One. Marry a princess I did and sire that son I did also, on the first night of our marriage—then, disaster.

"Within days of our marriage, while I was stupidly cavorting on a river boat trying to make my new bride laugh, I fell overboard, and was consumed by one of the Lhyl's great river lizards. It was not a pleasant death."

He fell silent, and no one spoke.

"I was not supposed to die so soon," Avaldamon continued after a time. "I was supposed to watch my son grow, to teach him and raise him in the skills of Elcho Falling. Instead, my son Boaz fell into the clutches of the Magi, and became one of their number, indoctrinated in the way of the One.

"Then Fate took a hand. A slave, bought in one of the foreign markets, came to Threshold as a glass worker. She was a Vilander and may even have had some long-distant glimmer of Elcho Falling within her, for she had powerful abilities. She was no plan of ours, nor of Elcho Falling's. Tirzah, or Ygraine, as she was originally known, was simply Fate. She came to Threshold and, to cut this story short, for I fear we have not much time, she drew Boaz away from the way of the One and back into his elemental powers. Between them, they managed to stop Threshold from attaining its true power and to effect its dismantling."

"Were you always meant to come back, like Josia?" Axis said.

"No," Avaldamon said. "I am back because I had not finished my task. I was always going to be drawn back."

"Not Boaz?" Maximilian said.

Avaldamon shook his head. "Not Boaz. Boaz never knew the power of Elcho Falling, and it is Elcho Falling which will cause the destruction of DarkGlass Mountain. If I had remained alive, I would have taught my son the ways of Elcho Falling, but I died and he did not do what was necessary to destroy the power of the pyramid. Thus I have returned rather than my son." He nodded at Maximilian, and smiled. "A new prince has risen, and his lady wife, both of whom can rally Elcho Falling against Infinity. My purpose remains: to show the Persimius blood how to destroy the hateful glass pyramid and, now, the One with it."

"You can't do this yourself?" asked Axis. "You are a Persimius prince, after all."

"I am nowhere near as powerful as Maximilian or Ishbel," said Avaldamon. "I can guide them, but I cannot be them."

Ishbel took a deep breath, catching Maximilian's eyes. "It can be done?" she said.

"So Avaldamon tells me," Maximilian said, "but the catch is that we likely have only a day or so in which to do it."

He turned to Axis. "Axis. I am afraid I am going to leave you in charge of Elcho Falling, as well as all the mess of the Lealfast and the Skraelings. Ishbel, Avaldamon and myself need to return to DarkGlass Mountain within the next few hours."

"Oh, for the stars' sakes!" Axis said. "You can't think I am willing to—"

He broke off as StarHeaven spoke in his mind.

We have found it, StarMan. It stands in the lowest basement of Elcho Falling. And . . .

And?

And . . . it has grown.

CHAPTER ELEVEN

Elcho Falling

"StarHeaven has found the spire," Axis said, interrupting Maximilian, who had been about to speak.

"Where?" several people said at once.

"In a chamber in the lowest basement level," Axis said. "Wait, there is more . . . let me speak with her."

The others waited, shifting impatiently on chairs and exchanging glances, before Axis spoke again.

"It has grown," he said. "It now stands just above the height of a man. And StarHeaven says it has set roots into Elcho Falling. She won't go closer to it than the head of the steps which lead down into the chamber where it rests . . . even now she waits several levels above it. Maxel, you can't leave. Not with this."

"I must," Maximilian said. "Avaldamon says that Ishbel and I have but one chance at DarkGlass Mountain and it must be soon. Today, or tomorrow at the latest."

"Oh, rubbish," Axis said. "It's been standing there for millennia and I am sure it can—"

"It is not so much DarkGlass Mountain," Avaldamon said, "but what it hides within the Infinity Chamber. When I first travelled from Elcho Falling to Ashdod to marry my princess, I brought with me one of Elcho Falling's greatest treasures, the *Book of the Soulenai*. I died, and Boaz—thank every god in existence—actually kept it, and it has rested within the land of Ashdod, now Isembaard, ever since. It has fallen into the hands of the One, who understands its power if not its purpose, and he left it in the Infinity Chamber. Maximilian and Ishbel need to get to it before the One storms back there and either destroys it, or uses it himself. Axis, they as

I, need to go soon. We have no real idea where the One is, although all three of us sense that he is not at DarkGlass Mountain. Yet."

"For the moment, Axis," Maximilian said, "I must leave Elcho Falling in your hands. I am sorry, but this cannot wait."

Axis rose, intending to argue the matter, but Maximilian ignored him, rising to his feet himself and holding out a hand for Ishbel.

"Come," Maximilian said. "We need to see this Dark Spire."

They gathered where StarHeaven waited, in the third lowest of the nine basement levels. Georgdi was there, as well as Egalion.

Everyone from the command chamber had come down, including Inardle.

"I can feel it," Ishbel said, rubbing her shoulders as if she were cold.

Most of the others murmured assent. The air was cold here, as you might expect so far below ground, but there was something else. Axis thought it an otherworldly chill. He looked at his father, seeing the strain on his face.

He shifted his gaze to Inardle. She stood slightly apart from the rest of the group, her wings close to her side as if she tried to shelter within them.

Stars, she had betrayed them all . . . whimpering about her injuries when she could have healed them herself within an instant, playing on all their sympathies and emotions, reporting to her brothers his every move and thought . . .

I never did that, Axis, she said to him, holding his eyes, although with some apparent effort. *I did not betray—*

He turned his back and walked over to Maximilian who was standing at the steps leading down.

"What do you feel?" he asked Maximilian.

"Enough to know I should have picked up something *else* was in Elcho Falling," Maximilian said. "But with everything that has been happening, its 'wrongness' was lost amid the turmoil."

He stepped down, then turned and looked around. "Ishbel, Avaldamon, Axis, StarDrifter, Inardle . . . if you please."

And with that he was running lightly down the steps.

Axis let the others go down before him, then he brought up the rear.

He wanted to keep a close eye on Inardle.

They stopped halfway down the stairs into the chamber in the lowest basement, staring at the corkscrewed dark spire in the centre of the floor.

"Inardle?" Maximilian said. "How greatly has it changed?"

"Hugely so, my lord," she said softly, coming down to stand beside him. "It *has* grown. Previously I could hold it easily in my hands. Now . . ."

Now the spire stood well above the height of a man. It was not perceptibly throbbing or moving, but everyone who looked upon it could sense that it lived. No one had any doubt that if they stepped up and laid a hand to it, the spire would be warm to the touch.

No one wanted to test this belief.

It was dark, as Inardle had said, almost black, but shot through with lines of bright blue and a dark red. Its corkscrews twisted wildly, asymmetrically, to the point of the spire which looked wickedly sharp.

At its base, thick roots had grown into the stone flooring, twisting and upsetting the flagging across virtually the entire basement. A tip of one root had crawled up the lowest stair, sitting there as if to survey the journey upward but also as if to trip up any who were foolhardy enough to try to approach the spire.

As they watched, the tip of the root waggled slightly, searching about for a crack to invade.

"Can anyone here understand it?" StarDrifter said, standing by his son. "I cannot . . . it is entirely foreign to me."

"As it is to me," said Axis. "Avaldamon? Maxel? Ishbel?"

"It feeds from the cold winds of Infinity," said Avaldamon. "*That* I can sense and only because I spent time with the Magi who worshipped the One, who used its power. I'll

wager some of those roots touch Infinity itself. It sends a
chill down my spine."

Maximilian looked at Inardle, and raised an eyebrow.
"Tell us everything you know about it, Inardle."

She sighed, wrapping her arms about her shoulders as
Ishbel had earlier.

"It was made with the aid of the original Magi who had
come north from Ashdod," she said. "They had knowledge
that we didn't. Not at that stage. They said it was a gift to us.
Who knows. Maybe the One suggested its crafting."

Not at that stage, Axis thought, and shuddered at the
remembrance of sharing his bed and body with this bleak
witch.

"You used no Star Dance in its making?" StarDrifter
said, and Inardle glanced at him as she replied.

"A little, I believe," she said. "The Lealfast who sat with
the Magi and who helped in its construction drew on the
power of the Star Dance to create the Dark Spire, but the
Star Dance did not go into the Dark Spire's flesh, as it were.
That was all the power of Infinity."

"Do you know how to use it, how to *negate* it?" Axis
asked.

"Not really," Inardle replied, and Axis made a noise of
disbelief.

"You cannot expect us to believe that!" Axis said. "You—"

"Only those Lealfast completely indoctrinated into the
highest levels of the Magi could use it properly," Inardle said.
"And among the Lealfast now living, that was only Eleanon
and Bingaleal. I would help on those few occasions we used
it, but that was merely a courtesy on their part. They did not
truly need me, nor any of my power."

"You *are* a Magus?" Ishbel asked.

"I have been trained in some aspects of a Magus," Inardle said, "but never truly accepted into its brotherhood. The
Magi can only be a brotherhood. Women corrupt the One by
subdividing it, by carrying within them the potential to give
birth . . . it is amazing that Eleanon and Bingaleal allowed
me even a glimpse into the arts of the One."

"And they did that because . . . ?" Axis said.

Again she met his eyes. "Because, at times in the past, I have been the lover of both of them. There was affection and respect between us, and thus they drew me a little distance into the way of the One."

"Inardle," Maximilian asked, "what can we do about this?" He waved a hand at the Dark Spire.

"I don't know," she said softly, and Axis made another impatient noise.

"The rose spires," he said. "They were made by your people as well. Surely they can be used in some manner to understand or affect their dark brother?"

Inardle shook her head. "They are foreign to each other, Axis. I am sorry. The rose spires are of no use against this."

"What exactly can this Dark Spire *do*?" Ishbel asked.

"It channels the power of Infinity," said Inardle. "This," now it was she who waved a hand at the spire, "is like nothing I could have accomplished. *This* is the touch of Infinity."

She paused, thinking. "It is a cancer at the very heart of Elcho Falling. I do not know if it can destroy the citadel completely. But it can aid the One, and Eleanon and Bingaleal, in whatever they plan. And no," she glanced at Axis, "I do not know what that might be."

"Well," said Maximilian, "whatever that might be, I am afraid you will need to deal with it for the moment, Axis. I leave you in complete charge of Elcho Falling. You may do whatever you need to in order to ensure—"

"I cannot believe this!" Axis said, almost shouting. "How dare you just wander off! I don't care how important Dark-Glass Mountain is . . . *this*, Elcho Falling, is vastly *more* important! Have you no sense of duty? Of responsibility? Do you think you can just walk away from this utter mess? Do you think that—"

"Axis," Maximilian said.

"—you have any *right* to just walk away and—"

"*Axis!*"

Axis stopped, half turning away from Maximilian in his anger.

"Axis, I am sorry, but Ishbel and I *must* go. We—"

"You abandon every kingdom you inherit," Axis said.

"Escator and now Elcho Falling. The responsibility is obviously far too much for you."

That stung, and Maximilian flushed. Ishbel moved closer to him, placing a hand on his shoulder, but before she could speak she was forestalled by Georgdi who, accompanied by Insharah, had walked down the steps and now stood just behind Axis and StarDrifter.

"I think I speak for most of the people sequestered within Elcho Falling," Georgdi said, "when I say that we would all prefer that Axis led us through this time of crisis than Maximilian. We wish you well, Maximilian, Ishbel, but the disaster that Elcho Falling now finds itself in requires a war leader and that you are not. It is *my* country, the Outlands, which is overrun by armies of every ilk and by ghostly monsters now surging up from the south. You are a good man, Maximilian, but I want Axis, not you. Safe travelling."

Axis opened his mouth, then shut it again, not sure what to say.

Maximilian stared at Georgdi a moment, then laughed softly. "You say it bluntly, Georgdi, but you say it well . . . as did Axis. I am not the man Elcho Falling or this land needs in this moment. That man is Axis. Elcho Falling was never a mountain of war, and its lords not trained in the arts of war or defence or strategy. Ishbel and I can close off, we hope, the main gateway into Infinity, but that may not do a damn thing to save Elcho Falling from its current crisis."

He smiled then, his charming, infectious smile. "I am sorry, Axis. You must rue the day that Isaiah dragged you back from the Otherworld. Hopefully he shall be here soon enough, and safely enough, for you to tell him so yourself. But . . . please, Axis, I beg you, do this, if not for me, for all those who want to live."

Axis rubbed a hand over his eyes, his shoulders tensing as if he tried to force all the tightness out of them.

"And to think," he muttered, "that I had been foolhardy enough to once thank the stars that it was not meant to be me to save everyone this time. Fool that I am, I spoke far too soon."

CHAPTER TWELVE

Elcho Falling

"I am sorry, Axis," Maximilian said. "You of all people do not need this thrust upon you. But—"

"I am not ready to hear the 'but' yet," Axis said.

They sat alone in the command chamber, everyone else gone to snatch a few hours sleep, a meal, or to check on defences. Maximilian had left some of the Emerald Guard minding the Dark Spire; there was little else he could do about it at this stage.

"There is no one else, Axis," Maximilian said.

Axis did not reply. He was staring toward the windows, his face lined with exhaustion, his skin almost grey.

"You are the best—"

"Don't," Axis said, and Maximilian sighed and studied his hands. He didn't blame Axis for being angry, but at the same time he was growing tired of it. Axis was still furious at Inardle and was projecting that fury on to everything and everyone else.

"I will keep in contact," Maximilian said.

"How?" Axis said, looking at Maximilian for the first time. "DarkGlass Mountain is far, far away. Do either of us have enough power to communicate over that distance?"

Maximilian nodded at the window, and Axis looked that way once again. He straightened in his chair in surprise, then rose. "Who is that?"

"Josia," Maximilian said, walking with Axis to the window.

Instead of space and sky beyond the balcony, there appeared another window some two or three paces away. In that window stood a young, dark-haired man.

Josia Persimius, the soul who had inhabited the Weeper, and who now existed only within the Twisted Tower.

"Josia," Axis said.

Josia made a small bow of respect from his window. "Axis SunSoar. Maxel suggested you use me as a go-between. Maxel can access the Twisted Tower from anywhere. I can speak to you from my window at the top of the tower. If you need to speak to me, just call my name and go to the nearest window."

"Ishbel had told me that to look from the window at the top of the Twisted Tower was death," Axis said.

Josia gave a small smile. "Ah, but I have already died, and have no body to die again. Such restrictions are meaningless to me."

"It will at least give us something," Maximilian said, and Axis sighed, and nodded, finally willing to relent.

"Yes. It will give us something. Thank you, Josia."

Josia bowed once more, and the window faded.

"A neat trick, Maxel," Axis said as they walked back to their chairs.

"I have a few left, Axis," Maximilian said.

They sat down, and Axis rubbed at his eyes, his shoulders slumping.

"You need to rest," Maximilian said.

"Thirty thousand Lealfast fighters are outside, millions of Skraelings approach and we have some dark finger of Infinity sitting in the basement. *Rest?*"

"Nonetheless . . ."

"What do you want me to do, Maxel? What is your point putting me in charge? What do you want me to achieve for you?"

"To save as many lives as you can; to keep intact as much of Elcho Falling as you can."

"And defeat the Lealfast and the Skraeling hordes. And the One, should he decide to pop back for a visit."

Maximilian risked a smile. "That would help, Axis."

Axis didn't return the smile. "And how long do you expect me to hold all this together?"

"We can reach DarkGlass Mountain quickly through

Elcho Falling's graces, but we cannot return the same way. Even Elcho Falling has its limitations. So . . . we reach Dark-Glass Mountain within the day, spend, oh, perhaps a week there at most, then return the slow way via our feet, or horses, through to the east coast of Isembaard. Hopefully, there will still be vessels on the coast willing to carry us north to Elcho Falling."

"I will speak to Georgdi. He may be able to organise to have something waiting for you."

"That would be a help. Thank you."

They fell into silence for a few minutes. It stretched awkwardly, Axis' continued ill-temper creating a chasm between them.

"I know nothing about Elcho Falling," Axis said eventually. "Nothing of its power, of its lore, of how it works. I am not its lord. How will it respond to me? How can I defend it when—"

Maximilian nodded to a point at Axis' side, and Axis broke off as he saw one of Elcho Falling's servants standing there.

"You shall not be our lord," the servant said, "but we shall be allies, you and I. Whenever you need to speak, then I shall be here."

"You speak for Elcho Falling?" Axis said.

Something crossed the servant's face, a strange wild look. "As if I were Elcho Falling," he said.

Axis looked at Maximilian in astonishment, but when he looked back to the servant to speak to him, he was gone.

"Elcho Falling will listen to you, and will offer advice if needed," Maximilian said. "It will recognise you almost as if you were me. There may be some constraints, but I doubt they will be too restrictive."

"And the Dark Spire? What do you expect me to do about that? What shall I do when it grows through all of Elcho Falling?"

"I am sorry, Axis. I do not know. I *hope* that when Ishbel and I manage to destroy DarkGlass Mountain, then we will either destroy the One or remove his access to the power of Infinity. Maybe, with the One gone, then the Dark Spire will fade and die, too. Maybe. If not, then we can tackle the Dark Spire together, Axis."

"Hope is an insubstantial thing," Axis said, "for something of such cold dark magic as that spire."

"It is all I have to offer you." Maximilian paused. "Axis, talk to Inardle. I know you think she has betrayed you—"

Axis sent him a bleak look.

"—but I do not think her the utter traitor that you do. She can help. I think all she wants is for you to ask her."

Axis grunted in dismissal.

"Axis, she stayed here because she loves you. That's what kept her here. Not me, not Elcho Falling. You."

"If she had truly loved me then she would have told me—"

"For you to do what? React precisely as you have now? She knows you too well, Axis, but still she stayed."

"How many have died because of her silence?"

"Talk to her, Axis."

Axis made a gesture with a hand, dismissing the subject. "Do you know how close Isaiah is?"

"I don't know. Your guess is as good as mine."

"Isaiah travels with the Isembaardian general, Lamiah—at least we don't have to worry about that general as we do Kezial—and, what, some hundred thousand Isembaardians. They are horribly exposed to both the Lealfast and the Skraelings."

"I know, Axis. I know." Maximilian sighed. "If I could do something . . . you can't send out some of the Strike Force?"

"They'd be slaughtered by the Lealfast as soon as they left Elcho Falling's protection, Maxel. I am worried that the Lealfast might turn their attention to Isaiah. And if he approaches Elcho Falling . . . how to get him and his army inside without loss of life . . . if the Skraelings have left any army *to* get inside, of course."

Axis paused. "I am trapped inside this great big bloody citadel, Maxel. I hate being trapped. I *hate* it."

To that Maximilian had nothing to say.

It was deep night and Maximilian and Ishbel had said their farewells. They stood now with Avaldamon in a small chamber in the heart of Elcho Falling, small packs lying at their heels.

They were not alone.

"No," said Maximilian, looking sternly at Serge and Doyle. The two Emerald Guardsmen, former assassins, had accompanied him on his journey from Escator into the heart of Isembaard to rescue Ishbel from Isaiah.

That all seemed so long ago.

"Egalion sent us," Doyle said.

"I had told him, *no*," Maximilian said, knowing he would lose this battle as he'd lost it previously.

"Two extra swords are always handy," said Serge. "Well, two swords only, as I see that none of you are armed."

Ishbel laughed. "Oh, Maxel, let them come. I assume it will be all right, Avaldamon?"

"Two more won't matter," Avaldamon said.

Maximilian shrugged, then smiled. "I am sure I shall not be sorry to have you."

Then he turned to Avaldamon. "Avaldamon, how precisely does Elcho Falling transfer us? Will it eject us like it did the One and the Lealfast?"

"No," said Avaldamon. "Tonight we use a gentler method, one that can deliver us precisely to the place we want, if it can't actually get us back again."

"I learned of this only briefly in the Twisted Tower," Maximilian said. "Mostly I concentrated on the knowledge I needed to raise Elcho Falling."

"This method is just one of Elcho Falling's lesser known abilities. All you need do, Maxel, is ask of it what you need, and it shall provide. But—"

"Ah," Maximilian and Ishbel said together, and Avaldamon chuckled.

"*But*," he said, "there is a small price, if you can call it that. It is a matter of balances. Elcho Falling can transfer us to DarkGlass Mountain, but it will need to transfer something back. It will need to know what you want as a counterbalance, Maxel."

Maximilian frowned. "What did the One counterbalance with in transferring here?"

"He used the Dark Spire, not Elcho Falling," Avaldamon said. "He needed no counterbalance."

"I need to pick something at DarkGlass Mountain? In the immediate area?"

"Something reasonably close by, but not perhaps in the immediate area."

"Does it need to come directly here to Elcho Falling?" Ishbel said. "Or just somewhere 'reasonably close by'?"

"What are you thinking, Ishbel?" Maximilian said.

"Avaldamon?" Ishbel said.

"Reasonably close by would do it," Avaldamon said.

"How close is 'reasonably'?" Ishbel said.

"For the gods' sakes," Avaldamon said. "I don't know what you mean!"

"Somewhere between Elcho Falling and, say, Margalit," Ishbel said.

Maximilian's mouth curved up in a slow smile. "Isaiah."

"Yes," said Ishbel, returning his smile. "Isaiah. I think I have thought of a way to aid him. There is something I had heard from the Goblet of the Frogs. Something about Lake Juit."

She looked again at Avaldamon. "Is it possible?"

"Yes," he said, "I know what you want to do, and yes, it is possible. I think Elcho Falling might rather enjoy it." Again he chuckled. "As would the inhabitants of Lake Juit."

"We should perhaps warn Axis, as well as Isaiah," Ishbel said.

"Axis can find out in his own good time," Maximilian said, "and Isaiah . . . well . . . I am sure Isaiah has had to cope with worse surprises in his past."

"Lake Juit it shall be then," Avaldamon said.

"Do you think they are actually speaking a different language," Serge remarked to Doyle, "or is it just me who cannot fathom a word of what they say?"

CHAPTER THIRTEEN

Lake Juit and Aqhat

For aeons the River Lhyl had wended its way down from the FarReach Mountains, through the lands now called Isembaard, to Lake Juit, the stretch of water in the far south of Isembaard.

Now, of course, the river was nothing but glass, having succumbed to the One's malevolent sorceries, but the lake itself was alive and vibrant.

Not even the One could touch Lake Juit, if he even knew of its existence.

Few people had ever lived near the lake. Ever since man had first come to this land, the lake had been reserved for the pleasure of, first, the Chads of Ashdod, then the Tyrants of Isembaard. A few servants lived at the beautiful royal house on its eastern shore and a few watermen trawled its surface and reed banks, but they did so only at the pleasure of the current ruler of the land, to serve his purpose.

Mostly the lake was left to its own devices.

It was a massive body of water, almost a world within itself. For all any Ashdodian or Isembaardian had ever known, it continued south into eternity. Chads and Tyrants too numerous to number had sent expeditions south to map the lake and to discover the lands beyond it, but somehow none of these expeditions ever returned and the curiosities of Chad and Tyrant alike had to remain unsatisfied.

Legend had it that the far southern waters of Lake Juit tipped over a cliff at the edge of the world.

The central portions of the lake were deep, but its shores were bordered with reed beds that stretched for hundreds if not thousands of paces into the lake. These shallows were full of mystery, and known by some to touch the border-lands of other worlds from time to time.

The reed beds were not a place for any to travel unless they were very, very sure of what they were doing. Isaiah had used the reed beds and the lake when he hauled Axis back from the Otherworld, but Isaiah had been a powerful god then, and there were few others who could ever hope to manage such a feat.

Mostly, the reed beds were left to the current inhabitants, millions upon millions of pink-feathered juit birds.

They were ungainly creatures, plump of body with long, spindly necks and legs, and oversized beaks. They fed on the grasses and waterweed that tangled about the reeds and squabbled among themselves for entertainment.

These past months they had been unusually quiet.

One day the River Lhyl had died. Very suddenly, within the space of a single breath. The river entered at the lake's northern border in a great marshy swathe ninety paces wide. Normally the river flowed into the lake strongly, rippling the reeds about its mouth and lifting juit birds' nests up and down in a soothing rocking motion day and night.

On this day, however, everything had stopped. The river had turned in a moment to glass and a clearly defined edge was created: a small cliff of glass, standing half the height of a man, stretching ninety paces east to west. Occasionally, glass beads that once had been water droplets strained out of the glass, held back by a tiny sliver of hopelessness. A single moment more and they would have dropped to freedom and life within the lake, but they had been a splinter in time too late.

The water of the lake lapped disconsolately at this edge of glass, caressing it, murmuring to it, but there was no re-sponse. The river was dead.

The juit birds stayed well away from the glass river. Those who'd had their nests close to the mouth of the river moved them away, cradling either chicks or eggs in their over-sized beaks as they stalked awkward-limbed through the shallows to safer abodes. No juit bird would come to within

two hundred paces of the dead river and, in their daily me-
andering through the reed beds, constantly kept their backs
to the north and the glass.

The juit birds knew what had caused this calamity and
they cursed, not the One, but the Magi who had, so many
thousands of years ago, raised the glass pyramid from the
desert floor.

If it had not been for Threshold . . .

On this night the reed banks were quiet, as usual. There
was occasional movement as birds resettled themselves in
their roosts among the reed beds, or snapped sleepily at a
neighbour, but mostly there was calm and stillness throughout the millions of juit birds who populated the lake.

Then, suddenly, every bird jerked its head upward, bright
black eyes fully awake and aware.

Someone called.

"Ah!" Maximilian felt the breath pushed from his chest as
he staggered against a stone wall, and he scraped several
fingertips as his hand scrabbled for purchase.

He heard movement about him, felt other bodies stumble
momentarily against his, heard others gasping for breath.

"We're here," Avaldamon said.

"Where?" Maximilian managed to get out, momentarily
disorientated and forgetting what it was he did, stumbling
about in the unknown.

"Aqhat, I hope," Avaldamon said. "Are we all here? Ishbel? Scrgc? Doylc?"

Voices murmured assent, and Maximilian reached out
for Ishbel's hand. She gripped it tightly, moving against him
for reassurance.

Maximilian looked around, his eyes becoming more
used to the dark. "We're in a courtyard."

"In the great courtyard, to be precise," said Ishbel.
"There is a gate over there . . . see it? It leads down to the
river. DarkGlass Mountain is in that direction," she nodded
to the west, "over the river. It cannot see us here if we stay
close to the wall."

Serge and Doyle had their swords drawn and had positioned themselves on the outside of the small group, looking for any danger.

"There is no one else," Ishbel said. "Not even an owl. Nothing."

"Everything would have been eaten by the Skraelings," Doyle said. "At least there don't seem to be any of the loathsome wraiths here."

"They're likely all headed for Elcho Falling," Maximilian said dryly.

"We need to find some shelter," said Avaldamon. "Then we need to talk while we wait for the dawn."

The One lay flat on his back in the middle of the desert, halfway between Sakkuth and Aqhat. His limbs were spreadeagled, and his obsidian eyes were wide, staring unblinking at the starry night sky.

The starlight twinkled deep within his glass flesh.

The One was not happy. He could feel *movement* and *power* and understood that the Lord of Elcho Falling and his bride from hell had somehow transported themselves far south.

South to DarkGlass Mountain.

"No!" the One whispered.

He knew what they wanted.

They wanted to destroy the pyramid.

And him.

They had their pretty tricky magics at their fingertips and they were going to walk into the Infinity Chamber and—

Suddenly the One remembered what he'd left in the Infinity Chamber.

The Book of the Soulenai.

He hissed, and all the sand surrounding his body began to roll and jump, as if it were being heated on a giant griddle.

Leaving that book had been an enormous tactical error.

"But not one that can't be fixed," the One said, leaping to his feet. He stretched out his arms to either side, straining them until the tendons and muscles bulged.

Then, with a slightly worrying creak, the One began to grow.

On Lake Juit, the birds stared into the night.

Then, in the same instant, the entire population of juit birds lifted screaming into the air.

CHAPTER FOURTEEN

The Outlands

Once river god and former Tyrant of Isembaard, Isaiah now led some one hundred thousand Isembaardian soldiers north from the Salamaan Pass, heading for Elcho Falling to aid its lord. Each night, with well-honed practice, the Isembaardians established a camp and settled down to sleep, either in tents or on bedrolls under the stars. This night, Isaiah moved restlessly about on a camp bed in his tent, the blanket twisting this way and that until it tangled uncomfortably around his legs. Finally he gave up. Pushing aside the blanket, he swung his legs over the side of the bed and sat up.

He shivered a little in the cold air, then reached for his clothes.

There was no point in staying abed and, with any luck, one or two of the cooks would be up and have prodded a cooking fire into life somewhere among the myriad tents.

Isaiah looked to see if the manservant sleeping at the back of the tent had wakened—he hadn't—then he pushed aside the tent flap and walked outside.

It was very quiet.

Armed sentries, scores of them, patrolled the outer rim of the sprawling encampment. They walked slowly, but they looked alert, and Isaiah breathed a sigh of relief. These past several days he had been filled with such a sense of dread . . . he'd never missed his power so much as he did at this point.

If only he could scry out with his senses and feel what had gone so wrong.

It could be anything—Armat, the One, Maximilian, the Lealfast . . .

What was happening? What was wrong?

Isaiah's power was gone, consumed by the One. If Isaiah had still had his power, understanding what was happening would have been easy.

But now . . .

There was only one thing Isaiah thought he knew for sure, and that was that Lister was dead. He knew it instinctively, having shared companionship with Lister over so many tens of thousands of years. Now the companionship was gone. Lister was dead.

Isaiah wondered who had done the deed, and hoped it had been either Ishbel or Maximilian.

Gods alone knew, both had had reason enough.

Isaiah was not terribly upset by the loss of Lister; they had never been close emotionally, but he was wracked with concern about what else might be happening up north.

None of the Icarii had stayed with Isaiah and the hundred thousand men he commanded (the former renegade general, Lamiah, being pragmatic enough to return to the role of second-in-command fairly happily) and Isaiah regretted this. If the Icarii had stayed, then maybe he could have sent them scouting, or maybe, maybe, if one of them had been an Enchanter, he could have communicated directly with Axis, or StarDrifter, and discovered intelligence.

But no, here he was, left with only mortal ability, and Isaiah resented it now more than ever before.

He looked toward the tent where slept Hereward, the former kitchen steward from Isaiah's palace of Aqhat. He'd hardly had any discourse with her on this hard ride north toward Elcho Falling. Isaiah still harboured some bitterness toward her for the loss of his power, despite what he might say to her. If it hadn't been for Hereward . . . if he hadn't surrendered his powers in order to save her life . . . well, then both he and everyone else would have had a far better chance at life than they did now.

Was it better to save Hereward and lose a hundred thousand because of it?

"What is wrong?" Isaiah muttered, tearing himself away from thoughts of Hereward and staring into the dark sky for some inspiration. *What is wrong?*

They were so vulnerable here. There was no terrain they could hide in or exploit for defensive (or even offensive) purposes. There were no trees to hide behind.

There was scarcely even a shrub to piss behind.

Just gently undulating, grass covered plains.

They were north of Margalit now, and Isaiah and Lamiah had sat down last night to estimate how long it would be before they reached Elcho Falling. Without any distractions— attacks from forces far more powerful than they, which was, considering the circumstances, more than likely—they had perhaps two weeks of hard riding to get there.

Two weeks, and gods knew what might happen to them in that time.

Isaiah also wished he knew what had happened at Elcho Falling. Something had happened; he was sure he could sense some disturbance, but *what?*

"Damn it," Isaiah said, and started to look for any camp-fires that burned brighter than usual, which would indicate— hopefully—the start of breakfast.

Before he could move to take a step in any direction, Isaiah found himself suddenly crouched in a defensive huddle on the ground. The air above him, and on all sides, suddenly seemed to be filled with noise and the warmth of thousands upon thousands of bodies . . . and feathers.

Feathers.

Everywhere.

Isaiah thought he would choke on them.

Lealfast! It was his first thought and automatically he reached for the dagger on his hip.

Something thudded into him and reflexively he grabbed at it, trying to wrestle it to the ground so he could stab it in the—

Something rather large, and very irritated, pecked him viciously in the upper arm.

"Ommph!" Isaiah said, spitting out feathers. He recognised the peculiar musty smell of the creature now stalking in a tight circle around him, looking for an opening to strike again, but his mind simply refused to accept it.

Isaiah could hear men stumbling from tents, crying out in surprise.

The bird pecked again at his arm, but with less intent this time.

Isaiah held out his hands in supplication. "I am Isaiah," he said. *"Isaiah!"*

The juit bird fluffed out its feathers in affront and looked away.

"Shoo," Isaiah said, rising carefully to his feet and flapping at the bird with his hands. "Shoo!"

The juit bird took several high-stepping paces away, looking at him carefully with its large red-rimmed eyes.

Men were rushing everywhere now, and Isaiah risked shouting to them (heavens forbid if he set the birds off!). "Shoo them to the perimeter of the camp! It is all right, they will not harm us—"

Much.

"—just shoo them to the perimeter of the camp! They are juit birds . . . *juit birds*!"

Initial panic now gave way to muted laughter. Most of the Isembaardians had heard of the juit birds, if not seen them firsthand. Now they began carefully to herd the creatures toward the outer edges of the camp.

Lamiah had by now appeared at Isaiah's side, still blinking sleep and confusion from his eyes.

"What the fuck . . . ?" he said.

Isaiah raised his hands. "I have no idea, Lamiah. I am as stunned as you. But . . . it appears as if the entire population of Isembaard's juit birds have just appeared in our camp.

"How?" Lamiah said.

"Magic . . . power . . . luck . . . a sudden southerly gust of wind . . . who knows? They are just now . . . here."

"There must be . . ." Lamiah stopped, peering through the slowly lightening sky.

"Millions of them," Isaiah said, chuckling. "Look, the entire encampment is coated with pink feathers. They must have just fallen straight down from the sky."

"But . . . but . . ." Lamiah was still struggling to accept the fact that a few million juit birds had suddenly appeared in camp.

Isaiah laughed. "Shall we not be a sight, Lamiah, marching

north in all our arrogant militancy, surrounded by squabbling pink birds."

"They are not going to stay with us, surely?"

"I very much doubt they are going to leave, Lamiah. I think they are here for a reason."

Lamiah grunted, watching in silence as soldiers everywhere tried to direct reluctant juit birds out of tents, beyond the range of cooking fires, away from the lines of half-panicked horses, and toward the perimeter of the camp.

"What reason?" Lamiah said finally.

"Gods alone know," Isaiah said, "for I have no idea at all."

CHAPTER FIFTEEN

Elcho Falling

It was almost dawn, and Ravenna could pick her way through the deserted Isembaardian camp easily enough in the faint light. There was food aplenty here, and blankets and gear: enough to keep her fed and warm for months if not years.

She suffered terribly from Ishbel's curses. Not only had Ishbel cut Ravenna's unborn son from his rightful inheritance to Elcho Falling, and Ravenna from her powers as a marsh witch, Ishbel had cut Ravenna entirely from the aid and succour of any person left on this world.

No man, no people, and no country shall ever love or offer you safe harbour again, Ravenna, Ishbel had said. *Go now from this tent and from this land. Go and bear your child in agony and sorrow, and weep that you have so thoughtlessly murdered those who loved you.*

When Ishbel uttered that curse in Armat's tent, Ravenna had struggled, but had been unable to resist the curse's urging. She'd half stumbled, half crawled from the tent and into the night. For that night and much of the next day she had walked aimlessly, wandering hither and thither, one hand constantly moving protectively over her pregnant belly. The few people she'd come across—some Outlanders driving a flock of sheep south—had avoided her, even though she had called to them most piteously.

Ishbel's curse: no one might aid her. She was an outcast, completely and forever.

Thus Ravenna had wandered, but, halfway through the day, she had become aware that all was not well at Elcho

Falling. In fact, all was very bad at Elcho Falling. She was too far distant to understand precisely what was happening, but she could *feel* it. Her powers as marsh witch might be gone, but not those powers of common sense and intuition.

Something was happening at Elcho Falling.

Ravenna hoped Maximilian and Ishbel were being slowly stripped of all their flesh by crows of gigantic magnitude. Her hatred of the pair of them had festered over the past day into something so frightful that *had* Ravenna still enjoyed her powers, Ravenna was certain she would have cursed them both into the Land of Nightmares.

For several more hours Ravenna had wandered, her sense of something *happening* at Elcho Falling growing stronger and stronger, and finally she had started back toward the citadel, her feet dragging through mud and slush, the hem of her skirts stained and sodden, her flesh shivering in the chill, her hair hanging unkempt about her face.

Ishbel's curse should rightfully have kept her away, but Ravenna gritted her teeth and ignored the nauseous feeling that grew stronger the closer she drew to Elcho Falling.

She would find out what was happening.

There might be an opportunity awaiting her.

So she slogged onward, one foot in front of the other, until she stopped in the late afternoon, gazing open-mouthed at the scene.

Isembaardian soldiers fleeing across the causeway into Elcho Falling, under attack from Lealfast fighters in the air.

Ravenna stood and watched for hours, arms hugged about herself, until that moment when Maximilian came out and worked his magic to ensure the last of the Isembaardians (and Ishbel, the bitch) managed to escape into Elcho Falling.

She watched as the Lealfast veered away in frustration, watched as the archway into Elcho Falling clanged closed, watched until late in the night when there was nothing left to watch any more, save the cold wind rippling over the waters surrounding Elcho Falling.

Then she moved into the deserted camp.

If there had been a soul left in it Ravenna did not think the curse would have allowed her to stay. She had pushed it too far already and was feeling a terrible urge to move away, move out of this land to wander, wander, wander . . . but for the time being she resisted as well as she could and scrabbled about the abandoned campsite for food and warmth. She even managed a few hours of fitful sleep, curled up in a ball under a pile of blankets in the corner of a tent.

The tent stank of men and armour, but she hadn't cared. Ravenna was supremely grateful for just those few hours of snatched sleep—grateful because she shouldn't have been able to settle, the curse should have driven her away. If she could resist the curse this much . . . then might she not eventually be able to break it completely?

Where there was even the smallest resistance, there was hope.

Hope for revenge.

At dawn Ravenna rose and started to scavenge anew, trying to find something she could use as a sled to drag behind her. Then she could haul away as much in the way of supplies as she could manage.

She was investigating a pile of abandoned horse gear, so engrossed in turning aside the heavy leather harness and horse collars that she failed to realise for a long moment the presence of someone standing behind her.

When finally she did, Ravenna spun around so precipitously she fell backward in an inelegant heap on the pile of tangled harness.

"Such a fall from grace, Ravenna," Eleanon said, "although I remember when first I met you that Ishbel had the better of you then, too. It comes as little surprise to me that you find yourself here now, a beggar among the remnants of Isembaard's pride."

Ravenna stared at the beautiful birdman, hating him for what he'd said and for his beauty and because now Ravenna reflexively hated anything that lived.

The entire world was hateful to her.

"What do *you* out here," she said. "I'd thought you inside, closeted tight with your lord and master."

Eleanon waved a hand airily. "You will have noticed the small altercation here yesterday, yes?"

Ravenna gave a nod.

Eleanon squatted down so he could stare Ravenna directly in the face. He radiated threat, and she shrank further into the tangled harness.

"I no longer work Maximilian's will, Ravenna, but mine only." Now Eleanon's hand moved directly in front of Ravenna's face, and she flinched.

But Eleanon did not touch her. Instead Ravenna found herself staring as if through a window at a blue-green glass pyramid, gleaming in a cloudless sky. As she watched, a beam of light shone from the golden capstone at the very summit of the pyramid, directly toward the sun. Higher and higher climbed this beam of light, until Ravenna gasped.

The light struck the sun, and obliterated it.

"Hark the power of Infinity," Eleanon whispered, and he clicked his fingers, and the vision vanished. "That power is mine now."

"How so?"

"The One shared Infinity with the Lealfast."

"For what price?"

Eleanon laughed. "The price is of no matter now, for the One is gone, far, far away, and now I must do what I can for my people."

"Which is . . ."

"To destroy the Lord of Elcho Falling," said Eleanon, "and to take Elcho Falling as our home."

"And the stars might fall from the skies and coat your foreheads in glory, too," Ravenna said.

Eleanon smiled coldly. "You are a stupid little woman, Ravenna. You thought to play at power, yet you had no head nor skill for it. I smell a curse about you. What is it? Tell me."

Now, finally, Eleanon touched Ravenna, his hands taking a strong grip of her head, and Ravenna felt power worm its way into her mind.

Ravenna did not want to tell him, but the words tumbled from her mouth nonetheless, pulled by Eleanon's power.

"Ishbel cursed me. She has disinherited my son from his

natural birthright, she has cut me from my power as a marsh witch by isolating me from the Land of Dream and she has cursed me to wander friendless and alone and to give birth in pain and agony with no one to aid me."

"Then Ishbel is a silly sad excuse for a witch as well," Eleanon said, "for I would have done much, much worse. But tell me, how did she do this?"

"Armat and I had murdered Maxel—at least we thought we had, but Ishbel must somehow have contrived to save him. Ishbel had Maximilian's murdered blood in a magical goblet of power which I have never seen before. She used it to kill Lister—"

Eleanon laughed in merriment at this snippet of information.

"—and to turn Armat into a puppet, and to curse me."

"An interesting tale." Eleanon paused, considering Ravenna. He did not know her well, but he understood that perhaps she could be very, very useful to him. She hated Ishbel and Maximilian . . . no doubt Elcho Falling as well . . . mayhap he could use that.

Perhaps he could use Ravenna to do what was needed within Elcho Falling, rather than risk it himself.

Yes. That would work well. Risk Ravenna, not himself.

But then there was Ishbel's curse, which made it difficult for Ravenna to stay within close range of any other living person . . . Eleanon wondered if the curse could be altered, even broken. If so, then Ravenna would prove very, very useful indeed.

Eleanon's hands suddenly tightened in their grip about Ravenna's head. She struggled and cried out, but she could not free herself.

"Stay still, you stupid woman," Eleanon muttered. His grip tightened yet further, and Ravenna cried out, twisting under his hands. Suddenly Eleanon pulled his hands away.

"I cannot undo her curse," he said, "not entirely, but I think you will find your stay here a little easier for the next few days, at the least. Your urge to wander off will not be as strong. And *do* stay here, Ravenna. I think we shall need to speak again. I am, I believe, going to find you somewhat useful."

Then, quite suddenly, he was gone.

High in the air, Eleanon punched into the sky in triumph.
He had his entry into Elcho Falling!

CHAPTER SIXTEEN

Elcho Falling

A xis sat at the table, his breakfast sitting uneaten and cold before him, one hand rubbing at the side of his forehead, regarding Inardle.

She looked worse than what he imagined he did. Axis had managed to snatch a few hours sleep last night.

Inardle looked like she'd had none.

Axis was not looking forward to this interview. If he were truthful with himself, all he wanted to do was to walk away from her and forget she'd ever existed. Forget everything that had been between them. Forget how he'd begun to feel about her.

How he'd trusted her.

StarDrifter had warned him about Inardle, but, no, Axis had refused to listen. He'd simply wanted her, and had shoved to one side all the problems associated with trying to bring a Lealfast into his bed and into the heart of the inner circle about Maximilian.

He'd believed her before BroadWing and before his father. He'd humiliated BroadWing and his father because of her.

And look what she had done to them.

"What a traitorous bitch you truly are," Axis said softly.

It wasn't how he'd meant to begin this conversation, but it was what he was feeling.

"And what an unfeeling, unapproachable, arrogant son of a bitch you are," she snapped back.

He hadn't expected that, attack instead of tearful defence, and his anger roared to the surface yet once more.

He half stood, sending his plate of food flying, hoping to see her at least flinch, but she did not move, or otherwise react.

For a moment Axis hovered in his half-standing, half-sitting posture, hating her that she had him at this disadvantage, then he completed standing in a smooth movement and wandered over to a side table, fiddling with a decanter of water, as if it might serve him some purpose.

"There can be nothing to excuse the fact you did nothing to warn us," he said.

"Who would have listened? *You?* You know that I could never have approached you with this, and there was no one else."

"Ishbel? She would have listened."

Inardle dropped her eyes at that. "I did not think of her."

"Ha!" Axis walked back to the table and sat once again. "What the hell do you want, Inardle? Why are you still here? What further treachery do you plan?"

"What do I here? Stars alone know! *I* don't!" She took a deep breath. "I stayed because there is nowhere for me to go, Axis. Look . . . I am sorry for what I have done. I wish I never had deceived you, or BroadWing, or any other that I have hurt or—"

"Murdered. Many hundred members of the Strike Force died in your brother's attack. Almost two hundred other men from among the forces gathered within Elcho Falling also died. A single word from you could have prevented their deaths."

"I am *sorry*, Axis."

"Sorry? Sorry? What an abysmal word with which to attempt amends!"

Inardle looked away, her face flushed, a muscle in her jaw twitching.

"I now control Elcho Falling and all who shelter within its walls," Axis said, his voice soft. "Your continued life or your death are now at my whim, Inardle. It is my decision. What should it be?"

"Whatever you want. I am too tired of this life, and of you, to care."

Axis wanted to scream, to pick up his chair and smash it against either the table or Inardle. His need to do something violent was so overwhelming that he had to close his eyes and clench both fists in order to fight it off.

He didn't want her to drive him to this.

Oh stars, what was he supposed to do with her? He was so angry and so hurt and so damned cursed furious at himself for trusting her, for allowing himself to start to fall in love with her, that—

"Let me stay, and help you now," Inardle said. "Let me make amends, Axis."

"I thought you were too tired of life to want to continue breathing."

"Axis, let me make some tiny recompense by helping."

"How?"

"By telling you now all I know about the Lealfast, about the power they command, about what they might do. There must be something I can tell you that will prove useful!"

"And I should trust this?"

Tears sprang into her eyes, and she flung an arm toward the window. "I could fly out there in an instant, Axis, and what would happen? My beloved brothers would murder me within a heartbeat! They no longer trust me, they no longer need me, and—"

"Ah, so you are more interested in saving your own skin than in making any kind of recompense for the deaths you have caused."

"Well," Inardle said, "surely that motivation at the least should make you more inclined to trust me." She paused. "If that is what you prefer to believe, then so be it. Yes. My only chance of living is to remain within Elcho Falling, thus I am willing to aid you in return for the chance to stay here. Will that do?"

Again she paused, taking a deep, shuddery breath. "Stars, Axis, *I told you about the Dark Spire!* I didn't have to do that! If I had kept silent, how many weeks would it have taken you to discover it? It would have sat there, doing its malignant work for the One and you would never have known!"

"Then tell me how to counter it."

"I can't," she said. "I am sorry, Axis, but I truly do not know how to counter it."

Axis took a deep breath. "Then I for one am sorry I ever saw your face."

Inardle's eyes widened, then she slapped both hands down on the table and rose abruptly.

"Oh, that is enough! I am *sick* of your melodrama! Ask yourself, if you dare, why you were stupid enough to trust the Lealfast in the first instance. It was your lust only that made you elevate me to your second-in-command, it was BroadWing's lack of thought that saw him confess every Strike Force strategy to Eleanon and, overall, it was your overweening arrogance that made it impossible for me to come to you and betray my own kin! By the heavens, Axis, you might as well have opened your shirt, painted a red cross on your chest and followed Eleanon about, hoping he'd put an arrow into it and put you out of your misery! I have had enough of all the blame being heaped about my shoulders. Shoulder some of it yourself, if you dare."

The door opened behind them, but neither noticed.

Axis was on his feet now, too. "I have no idea why you are still here, Inardle. I cannot think why you are not back with your kith and kin whom you were so loath to betray. There is nothing for you here."

"I remain only because I still—*stupidly!*—seem to believe more in Maximilian than I do in the One!"

"You can contribute nothing. Get out. You are useless to me."

"You fool," Inardle hissed. "I can hand you the Skraelings. You think they're your enemy . . . but what if they can be turned into your allies? How would you like that then, Axis, eh? A new and pretty title to add to your vast collection. Axis, Lord of the Skraelings!"

"*Get out!* Get out before I—"

"Leave, Inardle. I will speak with you later." Georgdi had come up, unnoticed by either Axis or Inardle. He took Axis by the elbow and pulled him back a pace or two as Inardle glared a final moment at him, shot Georgdi a black look, then stalked from the room.

"How dare you—" Axis began as he wrenched his elbow from Georgdi's grip.

"I dare very easily," Georgdi said. "Don't be a fool, Axis. All this condemnation of Inardle is driven almost entirely by your frustrated desire for her. She is guilty only of keeping her mouth shut when she might have spoken, and I can actually understand why she didn't feel able to speak to you. She also spoke a great deal of truth just now, Axis. You're a brilliant commander, but you are as flawed as any other man alive or dead. Get some distance, get some perspective and get some sense.

"And while you're in the get-some-sense mode, think about what Inardle just said. I'd like to hear more about 'handing us the Skraelings'. Wouldn't you?"

With that, Georgdi stalked from the room, slamming the door behind him.

Axis clenched his hands, taking several deep lungfuls of air, furious: at Inardle, at Georgdi, at himself, at the circumstances surrounding them all.

He muttered an obscenity, pacing about the room, trying to calm himself down.

Stars, what a mess.

Axis?

Axis spun about.

There was no one else in the chamber, and that had not been an Icarii voice.

Axis? It is I, Josia.

Axis hoped Josia hadn't witnessed that little scene. He walked to the window, opening it.

About three paces away, suspended in the air, Axis saw the partial wall of what must be the Twisted Tower. In the centre of the wall was an open window, and a young dark-haired man sat in the window, one leg idly swinging over the windowsill.

"Axis?" he said.

"Josia. You have news?"

"Are you well, Axis? You are flushed and appear—"

"I am well, Josia. Do you have news?"

Josia studied Axis briefly, then gave a small smile and

nodded. "Maxel, Ishbel, Avaldamon and their two companions have arrived at DarkGlass Mountain. They are well enough for the moment."

"For the moment. Will you know if . . ."

"If they succeed? If they fail? Yes, I will. And I will be sure to let you know as soon as I might."

Axis nodded, and as he did so Josia smiled, more widely this time, then he and the window faded from view, and Axis was left to stare at nothing but the view beyond Elcho Falling.

CHAPTER SEVENTEEN

Darkglass Mountain

Maximilian and his company settled in a room that ran off the courtyard. It had been the grooms' common room in happier times, and it was equipped with tables and chairs and even several daybeds.

There was no food left, for the Skraelings had been through here and had eaten anything they could find, turning over the furniture and breaking doors from cupboards in the doing. They had also defecated throughout the room. Ishbel and Doyle had grimaced and taken upon themselves the task of cleaning away the foulness. By morning it was done, and the tumbled furniture rearranged. They did not expect to be here long, but while they were here they needed a base.

Out of sight of the pyramid.

They had been aware of it through the night. It had been a sense in every one of them, a subtle twisting of their nerves so that none of them could truly relax. The pyramid was probing, testing.

It knew they were here.

"Does DarkGlass Mountain exist only as an extension of the One?" Serge asked Avaldamon as they sat eating an abstemious breakfast.

"No. Two thousand years ago, the pyramid seemed to have a power and purpose of its own. My son Boaz told me how it murdered at will. He said that he could feel its consciousness with him, following him everywhere. The One is Infinity, come to flesh within the pyramid. They are close, entwined even, but the pyramid has its own consciousness. It regrew itself, not through the agency, or at the behest, of any other power. It is greatly to be feared."

"Which is why we sit in this room," said Maximilian. "It has no windows to the west, so we are not in its direct line of sight. That affords us some protection."

"Then the pyramid will be difficult to destroy," Doyle said. "How will Maxel manage it?"

Avaldamon, Maximilian and Ishbel shared a look, then Avaldamon took a deep breath.

"Maximilian will not be the one to destroy DarkGlass Mountain," Avaldamon said.

"I will have to do it," Ishbel said.

"My lady?" Serge said.

"But . . ." Doyle added, his face as aghast as that of his friend.

"I have spoken of this briefly with Ishbel and Maximilian," said Avaldamon, "but it is good we talk of it now and go into some detail. Ishbel is descended from the eldest child of Boaz, my son, and his wife Tirzah. When Boaz did battle with Threshold, as the pyramid was then known, and the entity which inhabited it—Nzame—Tirzah was present. She was also pregnant with their first child, the girl who would later found the line which culminated in Ishbel. Something happened during that battle. We know that both Tirzah and the child were touched by Threshold and we now know that something happened . . . some knowledge was passed to the child. A power . . . an understanding, if you will, of the very nature of the pyramid itself."

"Ishbel is also of the bloodline of Persimius," said Maximilian. "Furthermore, she took many of the powers and abilities of the Lords of Elcho Falling during those few hours when I lay dead and she wore the ring of Persimius. Although I again breathe and wear the title of Lord of Elcho Falling, Ishbel retains much of the power. She is as much Elcho Falling's lord as I."

"And," Ishbel said, "I carry the abilities of the Coil within me. I was its Archpriestess and the best the Coil ever produced."

"Ishbel is the culmination of much accidental, as well as planned, contrivances," Avaldamon said. "She carries many abilities."

"And," Ishbel said, giving Maximilian an ironic smile, "while Avaldamon may not say this, none of us can risk Maximilian going into the pyramid. No one can risk losing him again."

"But you are not expendable either, my lady!" Serge said.

"No," Maximilian said very quietly, taking Ishbel's hand. "She is not."

"I am slightly *more* expendable," said Ishbel. "And this needs to be done."

"There is a book . . ." Doyle said. "Someone mentioned a book of power."

"The *Book of the Soulenai*," said Avaldamon. "It is an ancient Elcho Falling treasure. It has been sitting inside Elcho Falling for these past months, together with its special guardian—"

Ishbel and Maximilian looked oddly at Avaldamon at that.

"—who will serve to show Ishbel the way."

"Guardian?" Ishbel said.

"You will know more," said Avaldamon, "when you meet him."

Ishbel gave him an irritated look, but questioned him no more.

"When?" said Maximilian.

"Tonight," said Avaldamon. "Until then we wait."

They sat in silence, eating the last of their breakfast. Serge eventually rose, pacing about the room until he halted before the room's single window and looked toward the now rapidly rising sun.

"Maximilian!" Serge said. "Look! Look at this great foulness!"

Everyone leapt to their feet and came to the window. It faced east, yet they could see a triangular shadow moving over the courtyard . . . eastward, *toward* the sun.

DarkGlass Mountain.

Probing.

It moved across to the far side of the courtyard, then began to fall backward, closer and closer to the window.

Everyone reflexively stepped away.

The shadow crept to the wall, then they could feel it rising up the wall toward the windowsill.

Maximilian stepped forward and slammed shut the interior shutters, bolting them securely.

"It knows we are here," he said.

CHAPTER EIGHTEEN

Elcho Falling

Axis met with Georgdi, Egalion, Insharah, StarHeaven, StarDrifter and the Isembaardian general, Ezekiel. Garth Baxtor and Zeboath, the two senior physicians, were in attendance as well. Ezekiel had positioned himself slightly apart from the others and looked unhappy. A few months ago he had been the most senior general in the Tyrant Isaiah's massive invading army. Now here he was, largely irrelevant, under the command of the Tencendorian StarMan, Axis SunSoar. Invited to this gathering, he believed, only as a courtesy.

Everyone looked tired, if not completely exhausted.

"Garth, Zeboath," Axis said, not even bothering to welcome everyone or make any kind of statement, "a report?"

"Everyone who was likely to die has done so," Garth said. "We have—" he looked at Zeboath for confirmation "—perhaps some forty wounded Strike Force members in conditions ranging from the bothersome to the severe, but none now likely to succumb from their injuries, and . . ." He trailed off, trying to recall the numbers from his fatigued mind.

"Another hundred and fifty or so," said Zeboath. "Mostly Isembaardians caught by Lealfast arrows on their escape into Elcho Falling. A few Outlanders injured when the Lealfast had attacked within Elcho Falling. Again, their injuries range from the least to the severe, but again, no more are likely to die."

Axis nodded his thanks, then looked at StarHeaven. "The condition of the Strike Force?"

"We have two hundred and three left available and fit to fight, StarMan."

Axis repressed a wince. The Lealfast had been deadly, indeed. "But on the other hand," he said, "we have . . . scores of thousands of Outlanders, several thousands of the Emerald Guard," Axis glanced at Egalion as he said this, remembering with admiration what the Emerald Guardsmen had achieved the night of the Lealfast attack, "and at least two hundred thousand Isembaardians. A not inconsiderable force."

"And yet not one of which dares leaves Elcho Falling for fear of attack by the Lealfast," Insharah said.

This time Axis could not repress a wince. That was just too painful a truth. "And our threats?" he said.

"The Lealfast," said StarHeaven.

"A few million Skraelings headed our way," said Georgdi.

"And the Dark Spire, eating its cancerous way through the only thing keeping us safe," said Axis' father, StarDrifter.

"Have you had time to study it?" Axis asked StarDrifter.

His father nodded. "But for little enlightenment. It is dark and it is powerful and I cannot understand it, Axis. Every Enchanter within Elcho Falling has studied it . . . to no avail. It is of Infinity, not the stars, and beyond our comprehension. It was a bad day, Axis, when the Lealfast were admitted into Elcho Falling."

"And for that I take responsibility," Axis said, his voice soft. It had been a long and exhausting night and day, even more emotionally than physically, and he had no strength left to prevaricate.

He sighed, leaning a little over the table to look at the others. "I hope that Maxel and Ishbel can do something for us. I hope that if they manage to destroy DarkGlass Mountain then suddenly, miraculously, good times shall arrive for us. But, in the meantime . . . thoughts?"

"Isaiah is headed our way," Insharah said. "We need to think about aiding him."

Axis nodded. "I know. But we can come back to this, for there are closer problems. What else?"

"Kezial is also out there," Insharah said, referring to another renegade Isembaardian general who had fled Isaiah's army and then gathered a rebellious army about him. They knew where the other renegade generals were: the witless

Armat was now within Elcho Falling, and of no danger, and Lamiah was with Isaiah.

"And Ravenna," Insharah continued. "Both of them are unknowns."

"I take your point regarding Kezial," said Axis, "but I doubt he has enough men to threaten Elcho Falling. And he'd also have to contend with the Lealfast, unless, of course, he decides to join them. But for the moment he is the least of my concerns. Ravenna? Did not Ishbel strip Ravenna of her power and banish her?"

"Don't underestimate Ravenna," Garth said. "Maybe she will be no problem . . . but don't underestimate her. She has surprised us before."

"Until she *becomes* a problem," Axis said, "I will set worry about her aside. I—"

"Isn't that what you did with the Lealfast?" Ezekiel said.

Axis had to fight to restrain his temper, which he did only by reminding himself that Ezekiel was right.

"Which is what I said about the Lealfast," Axis said. "Garth, I want you and Insharah to tackle the problem of Ravenna. You both know her, probably best among us. You are the only ones likely to be able to forecast any threat from her. If you can think of any way she may be a danger, then let me know."

Both men nodded.

"We need to do something about the Dark Spire," Star-Drifter said.

"I know that, StarDrifter!" Axis said. "Look, unless we can understand it, we can do nothing about it."

"Can we try force?" Georgdi said. "I mean, has anyone actually tried taking an axe to it? Set a torch to it?"

"Not a torch!" several people said at once.

"We can't risk the thing going up like a bonfire and setting Elcho Falling ablaze," Axis added. "But force . . . I doubt it will make a difference, but . . . Ezekiel, perhaps you might like to take a squad of men down there and try it?"

It was not a request and Ezekiel gave a nod, rose, and left the room.

Axis watched him go, only speaking once the general

had left the room. "I doubt it will make much difference," Axis said. "The Dark Spire is a thing of power . . . I do not think either wishes or axes shall make it shatter."

"There is someone," Georgdi said, and Axis' face hardened, "who can help us."

Everyone save Axis looked at the Outlander general.

"Inardle," Georgdi said. "She spoke with Axis earlier. She said that she could bring us the Skraelings as allies."

"What?" StarDrifter said. "You cannot trust her! The *Skraelings* as allies? That is the stuff of nightmares."

Thank the stars, Axis thought, *that I will have one ally in this, at least.*

"How can she bring us the Skraelings?" said Insharah. He looked at Axis for a reply, but it was Georgdi who answered.

"She is half Skraeling," he said. "She, as all the Lealfast, have lived among them for millennia. There must be some sense of kinship there."

"The Lealfast loathe the Skraelings, and the Skraelings loathe them," Axis said. "I cannot think how she can 'bring us' the Skraelings."

"You cannot sit there," Georgdi said, "and refuse to consider Inardle. Elcho Falling did not brand her a traitor, she has stayed when she could easily have left, she—"

"She could have saved the Strike Force," Axis said, "but she did not!"

"And you know full well why she did not dare to approach you, Axis!" Georgdi said.

"*What*? Now the decimation of the Strike Force is *my* fault?"

"Cease this!" Insharah said, striking the table with the flat of his hand. "We do not need to rest all our trust in Inardle, but we *do* need to consider her, the knowledge she can offer us, and what she has said about the Skraelings."

The mood about the table now was tense. Eyes shifted carefully, and each individual wondered if the alliance within Elcho Falling was about to crumble into disarray.

"I apologise," Axis said. "My reaction to Inardle is skewed by the fact that I had—" *loved* "—trusted her intimately." He paused. "Yes, we should talk to her and see precisely what it is she has to offer. But maybe not me, not right now. There is too much bad feeling between us and that will skew anything that is said or decided. Insharah, will you and Georgdi talk with her? You have level heads and," Axis' mouth quirked, "no personal history with her to bias your decisions."

Both men nodded, and the mood about the room relaxed a little, although StarDrifter looked unhappy at the thought of trusting Inardle again.

"Isaiah," Axis said. "I worry about him. His knowledge and skills are invaluable, yet he is so exposed. We need to talk about what we can do to help Isaiah."

"Maybe Inardle will know something," Georgdi said.

Ezekiel ordered his men back from the Dark Spire, his voice harsh with frustration. They had tried axes and spades, and whatever other weapon came to hand, against it, but any blade or implement touching the spire would burst into flames, making the man who held it drop its handle and flinch back in shock.

There was nothing he, nor any man, could raise against it.

A half hour's flight away, Eleanon sat on a patch of grass-land, wrapped in wings and power and invisibility and a broad smile.

He had been communing with the Dark Spire, and it with him, when Ezekiel's men had attacked it.

Their frustrated efforts had barely intruded upon the Dark Spire's consciousness, which had given Eleanon his day's smile.

He rose, stretching his wings, still grinning.

There was nothing Axis nor any who stood with him could do against the Dark Spire.

Just as there would be nothing Axis could do against Eleanon.

CHAPTER NINETEEN

The Outlands

The soldiers were striking camp, readying for the day's ride northward.

Isaiah paced impatiently at the edge of the camp, looking at the sea of juit birds beyond. They were generally quiet save for a few squabbles, most contenting themselves with stretching and pruning.

None looked particularly discomforted to be here.

Isaiah knew relatively little about the birds. He had spent aeons as the god of the river, but the birds of Lake Juit? A mystery not even he could plumb. They simply existed, but had inhabited the reed beds of Lake Juit for so long, that Isaiah could not help but wonder if they had absorbed the mystery and magic of those borderlands into their very blood.

"What are they doing here, Isaiah?"

Isaiah turned, startled by Hereward's appearance. He had seen little of his former palace kitchen steward, and reluctant companion, in the weeks since he'd joined up with Lamiah. She'd dined with himself and Lamiah on one or two occasions, but both men felt a little uncomfortable in her presence and she'd known it. Isaiah and Hereward's companionship had never been easy, and both had grabbed the chance to go their separate ways the moment the opportunity arose.

Thinking about it, Isaiah realised this was the first time he'd seen her in two weeks, at least.

She looked well, far better than at any period since he'd met up with her on the banks of the Lhyl. She'd changed from her previous gauntness to a far more pleasant slimness, her hair was carefully dressed and the lines of pain around her eyes had all but vanished.

Isaiah glanced at her neck, where a Skraeling had sunk its claw under the One's direction. The coin-shaped scar was still there, but it was fading, and soon would barely be noticeable at all.

"They have a purpose," Isaiah said, "and I cannot help but think that purpose shall be good for us, but as to what it is . . ." He shrugged. "I have no idea."

"Have you heard any news from Elcho Falling?"

"No, and it worries me."

"No news from any of the forward scouts?"

"Where did you learn to interrogate so forcefully?"

"Any news?"

He sighed. "No. Hereward, surely you should be packing?"

"I am packed already, thank you. I am sorry to have taken up your time."

Isaiah repressed another sigh. Always their relationship was fraught with so much tension and simmering dislike.

He wondered if Elcho Falling had any kitchens where Hereward would feel at home, then berated himself for the ungenerous thought.

"Isaiah?"

"Hmm?" Isaiah had been so lost in his thoughts it took him a moment to refocus on Hereward.

"What is that bird doing?"

Isaiah turned to look.

One of the juit birds had walked away from the vast pack toward Isaiah. There was an open space of some ten paces between the birds and the border of the camp, and the bird crossed to within two paces of Isaiah.

There it stopped.

It turned its head, very deliberately, and looked south.

Then, as deliberately, it turned its head and looked north.

Then it looked directly at Isaiah as if he should by now be getting the message.

Isaiah frowned.

"It is trying to tell you something," Hereward said.

"I know that," Isaiah snapped.

The bird went through the procedure again, looking south, then north, then at Isaiah.

Isaiah's frown deepened.

Then suddenly the bird's form blurred, and Isaiah thought he was looking at . . . at . . .

"Oh no!" Hereward wailed, and it was the fear in her voice that snapped Isaiah into full alert.

"*Shetzah!*" he said. "The Skraelings are moving north!"

They must be seething up from Isembaard toward Elcho Falling, and his army would be standing in their way.

Isaiah turned on his heel and ran back through the camp, shouting orders as he went.

The juit bird fluffed out its feathers, gave Hereward a cool look, then stalked back to the company of its fellows.

They rode through the day as hard as they could. Isaiah spent half his time reining in his horse at the rear of the column to stare south, and half the time spurring his horse forward to urge the men onward.

The force was mounted, for which Isaiah was unendingly grateful, for it meant they could push north fast, but that positive was countered by the fact that feeding for the horses was poor at this time of the year and if he pushed too hard the animals would begin to founder in exhaustion.

How far to Elcho Falling? Too far. Isaiah knew the Skraelings would catch them and that they would need to battle it out.

How many men did he have? A little under one hundred thousand. Not enough to counter the millions of wraiths he knew must be surging northward.

Oh, and a flock of several million juit birds.

Isaiah had no idea what they would do, what they could do, but he feared it might not be enough against the sheer weight of the Skraeling numbers.

On those occasions when Isaiah stopped his horse to stare south, he thought he could just distinguish a brown haze at the limits of his vision.

Dust thrown up by the racing feet of the Skraelings?

It was tempting to march through the night. Isaiah knew

he could not do that, but they camped late, resting uneasily, and Isaiah meant to push on well before dawn the next day.

That night, he quadrupled the sentries, and bade all who slept to keep their swords unsheathed at their sides.

To the south the Skraelings surged forward, intent on their purpose. They were to get to Elcho Falling and they were to eat everything in their path.

The One had instructed them, and they were as one with the One. They could feel his presence, strong and powerful, and they knew what they had to do.

Get to Elcho Falling. Eat anything in their way.

The instructions were simple enough, even for Skraelings.

There was something up ahead, they could smell it. A mass of men, trying to flee. They could smell the stink of fear.

The Skraelings smiled as they ran.

They would catch this great mass of men soon, and then life would be good.

CHAPTER TWENTY

Isembaard

Ishbel and Maximilian sat alone among the reeds on the eastern side of what had once been the River Lhyl. It was dusk. They had moved here in the late afternoon, not caring that DarkGlass Mountain's shadow tracked them the entire way.

The pyramid knew they were here. There was no point in hiding.

For a long time they had been silent. They had held hands, leaned close to each other, occasionally kissed.

"Ishbel—"

"Don't say it, Maxel."

"Ishbel, you found the unwinding of the Weeper difficult. What you face here is so infinitely worse."

"I don't have Ravenna here to try and murder me on the way in."

"What you do have is—"

"Infinitely worse, I know. But I have more power now and, I think, a few more friends. And this guardian, about whom Avaldamon is so mysterious."

"Likely because he has no bloody idea."

Ishbel laughed. "Likely. But still, this needs to be done, Maxel. The pyramid must die, if this world is to survive in anything resembling freedom. We need to be rid of it."

Maximilian sighed. "Ishbel—"

"Shush," she said, and leaned over to kiss him lingeringly. "Shush. Wait here for me among the reeds, and believe, and I will return."

* * *

The One strode toward DarkGlass Mountain. He was not far away now, but he feared even that short distance might be too great.

Elcho Falling was at DarkGlass Mountain.

"I am going to *eat* you!" he whispered, increasing yet again both the rate and length of his step until he was jogging in long, thundering strides.

The One was half the height of DarkGlass Mountain itself, and growing a hand's-breadth with every pace.

Ishbel walked across the glass river, her strides slow but sure. The light breeze lifted her loosened fair hair and twisted her long skirts about her legs, but Ishbel paid no mind.

Her eyes were fixed on the pyramid.

It took her until almost full dark to walk along the causeway to the pyramid, and in that time light started to flash and fork underneath its glass skin. The static electricity raised goosebumps on Ishbel's arms, but she did not hesitate, nor lower her eyes from DarkGlass Mountain.

She was concentrating, very hard, on something the Goblet of the Frogs had told her.

Glass is liquid.

Glass is liquid. As she drew to within twenty paces of its eastern wall, the pyramid looming and throbbing high over her, Ishbel began a great unwinding.

Pace after pace she drew closer, then, ignoring the gaping black hole of the door she and Isaiah had once used to enter, and without any hesitation, Ishbel walked straight into the glass wall.

And vanished.

The One broke into a run, his mighty arms pumping at his sides, his eyes fixed on the horizon, over which, just over, lay his purpose.

Now invaded by that witch . . .

Ishbel took a deep breath, feeling herself merge with both stone and glass, and then she was in the Infinity Chamber.

She blinked. It was lit, but not from any internal light. Instead, she found herself looking at a large rat, holding up a candle.

It was sitting on a very large book that looked as though it had recently been scorched with fire.

Hello, the rat said.

Ishbel considered that. She had not heard the rat, either with her ears or her mind voice. The greeting simply "was".

"Hello," she said. "Who are you?"

I am your courage.

Ishbel frowned a little.

When Josia died, it took many hours for him to pass. It took enormous courage for him to endure. Magnificent courage. Too good to be wasted. I was the one who took his life and with it I took his courage. Now it is yours.

That was something Ishbel knew she'd need to spend a little time thinking about later, if she were fortunate enough to enjoy a "later". But for now she let it go. "Is that the *Book of the Soulenai*?"

Yes. It has been waiting for you as well. Would you like to read it?

"I think I should."

Ishbel moved toward the rat and the book, glancing about her as she went. The candlelight glimmered off the golden glass and Ishbel thought the glass was moving, almost as water, but she was not sure.

For now, the book.

Ishbel knelt down, and the rat moved to one side, helpfully holding up the candle.

Ishbel turned the cover, then the first few blank, creamy pages until she came to an index page.

It contained a list of stories.

The tale of the Magus Ta'uz and his lover Raguel.

The tale of Druse and of how he was turned to stone and then crumbled into the river.

The tale of the little girl, Ishbel, and how she was burned alive in her family house when it was overcome by pestilence.

Ishbel drew in a sharp breath, and her fingers trembled where they rested on the page. Then she read on.

The tale of all those murdered by the pyramid's malice.
The tale of how they shall all aid you, Tirzah's child, to murder Threshold.

The rat used its spare forepaw to touch Ishbel's arm gently.

The One comes, he said.

Maximilian stood on the river bank, staring at DarkGlass Mountain. It still throbbed and sparked with light.

What was happening to Ishbel inside?

He was undecided whether to go to her or not. Surely he could help her . . . surely he could provide some assistance, surely . . .

His head jerked to the north. The ground beneath him had started to shake, as if by the footfalls of a giant's feet.

Thud.
Thud.
Thud.

"Oh merciful gods!" Maximilian said, looking on with absolute horror as the enormous form of the One appeared, quite suddenly, out of the darkness.

He was flailing his arms in a windmill motion, as if to propel himself forward, and he was running straight for Dark-Glass Mountain.

Without any hesitation, and before Maximilian could even think about what action to take, let alone enact, the One ran straight into the side of DarkGlass Mountain and vanished without trace.

CHAPTER TWENTY-ONE

Darkglass Mountain

Ishbel rose to her feet, turning in alarm.

The One!

She could feel him crashing through the pyramid toward her, feel his anger, feel his murderous need to wrap his gigantic hands about her throat and—

Ishbel, the rat said. He raised up the candle, and Ishbel turned to him . . . and cried out in horror.

Just as the rat pulled the candle close to blow it out, Ishbel saw hundreds of black hands rise up behind the golden glass of the Infinity Chamber and then reach through it, reaching for her.

Before she could react, even move a muscle, she was caught fast and dragged into the pyramid.

Ishbel found herself in a strange place that she could only comprehend as thick light. She could breathe, if she concentrated on it, but movement was difficult.

She could sense many, many others close, pressing in so that they almost touched her.

At her feet sat the rat, atop the *Book of the Soulenai*.

A man emerged before her. He was tall with a lined face, as if he had suffered greatly, and his dark hair was slicked back into a club at the base of his neck.

"Did you read the first tale in the Book?" he said.

Ishbel opened her mouth to say "No, I had no time", but in that instant she realised she *knew* the first tale.

Long, long ago, a Magus named Ta'uz took as his mistress a slave from the camp that surrounded Threshold, and which housed its enslaved builders. This Magus, Ta'uz, affected great disdain for his mistress, whose name was Raguel. When she bore their child he murdered it, for Threshold, and the Way of the One, demanded its death.

No Magus was permitted to subdivide away from the One.

But Ta'uz continued his affair with Raguel, even though it took many months before she could bear to go back to his bed. Despite what had happened between them, despite the murder of their daughter, and despite the fact that Ta'uz was a Magus and Raguel a slave, they became close and eventually came to love each other.

They edged close to happiness, and Threshold was displeased.

One day it took them.

A great sheet of glass slid from its upper walls, slicing through the air, and before either Ta'uz or Raguel could move it speared them on the jagged edge of the glass and they died.

The pyramid did not like their closeness, which drew the Magus away from his devotion to the One.

"Yes," said Ishbel. "I know who you are. Ta'uz, why is the light here so thick?"

"Because it is crowded with the souls of those the pyramid has murdered over the years," Ta'uz replied.

"Why are you here?"

"Because I am going to aid you. I am going to show you the first step you must take within this intricate puzzle of a pyramid, the first stone you must unwind to open up the pyramid's deepest vulnerabilities."

"Thank you," Ishbel said. "I must start soon, for the One is here, and searching for me. He has great hands, I fear, and he has grown them for me."

"Indeed. Ishbel, do you know the second story in the list?"
Ishbel thought.

The tale of Druse, and of how he was turned to stone and then crumbled into the river.

"Yes," she said, smiling.

Druse was Tirzah's father, sent into slavery with her, and like her, a glass worker, although nowhere near as magical as his daughter.

Druse had also been slaughtered by the pyramid, turned to stone before Tirzah's eyes in an effort to punish her, and then his body was taken to the river and its stone remains crumbled to lie scattered along its muddy bed.

"Why do I need to know that story?" she asked Ta'uz.

"So that you will know that not all your family died in the charnel house you once called home."

Ishbel did not know what to make of that.

"If you know these two stories," said Ta'uz, "then I can show you the stone that, if overturned, will lead to the unwinding of the entire pyramid. But, beware, Ishbel, for both the pyramid and the One will fight back. They will give no quarter. Do you dare this?"

Ishbel thought, and as she did so, the rat left his perch on the *Book of the Soulenai* and tugged at Ishbel's skirts. She lifted him up, amazed by his warmth and the dark beauty of his eyes, and he scrambled onto her shoulder.

"I am ready," said Ishbel, knowing that the rat would be her courage.

"Good," said Ta'uz. "See."

He moved his hand and the light shifted, and Ishbel saw set out before her a flat piece of land shimmering under the desert sun. To one side lay a deep and winding river, encased by thick reed banks.

The River Lhyl, as it had once lived.

This piece of land was marked out with pegs and stretches of creamy cord were tied between the pegs. The cords and pegs described an intricate pattern on the ground.

Ishbel could see that this pattern described power.

Magi walked about, stepping carefully over the cords and pegs. They were dressed in long robes of blue, over white under-robes. Their movements were measured, their arms folded with their hands secreted away in the voluminous sleeves of their blue robes.

"Their movements describe a pattern," said Ta'uz. "A mathematical formula."

"An enchantment," Ishbel said.

"If you like," Ta'uz said. "A set dance to garner power, if you will. Look."

Now Ishbel saw slaves, hundreds of them, hauling with ropes many huge blocks of stone. She saw, as though many months passed in a moment, the slaves begin to construct the foundations of what would grow to be Threshold, later called DarkGlass Mountain.

Many slaves died, crushed when the blocks of stone slipped and fell.

"Do you see?" said Ta'uz. "Do you understand?"

He pointed to a single block of stone, one among hundreds now laid into courses, and apparently innocuous in its similarity to its fellows.

"Yes," Ishbel murmured. "I see. I understand."

"Unsat that stone, and the entire edifice of the pyramid, all that it is, has been or could ever be, will unwind to dust. You will need to find this stone, and you will need to unseat it. Can you do this?"

Ishbel looked into Ta'uz's eyes, and saw increasing anxiety there.

"I can do this," she said.

"It will take great fortitude and courage for I feel the One thunder close, and I feel the pyramid's malice tighten about you like a fist about a gnat."

"I have fortitude," said Ishbel, "and," she lifted a hand to touch the rat, "I have courage."

"Remember the story of Druse," said Ta'uz. Ishbel leaned close, kissed his cheek, and turned away.

She took a deep breath, then a big step forward . . .

. . . and stepped out of the dense light and into one of the black-glassed internal corridors of DarkGlass Mountain.

She could hear the pounding of feet and knew that it was the One, coming for her.

"This way," she said to the rat and walked down the corridor without hesitation, taking the first turn on the right, and then the third on the left.

Ishbel stopped, staring about her, unable to comprehend for the moment what had happened.

The pyramid had vanished, and she was now standing in the hallway that led to the kitchen in her parents' home in Margalit.

She could hear the faint sounds of a crowd outside, cries that the house be burned to save the rest of the city from the pestilence within the Brunelle residence.

I can smell corpses, said the rat.

"I can hear the crackle of flames," Ishbel said, so horrified her voice cracked from the dryness in her throat and mouth.

CHAPTER TWENTY-TWO

The Brunelle House, Margalit

Ishbel was eight, trapped in her parents' house in Margalit. The bodies of her parents and aunts and cousins and all their servants lay strewn about the house, decomposing into noxious heaps of whispering blackened flesh.

She stood at the top of the staircase, both hands clutching white-knuckled at the newel posts, listening to the crowds at the front doors.

There is plague inside!

All are dead!

Burn the house! Burn the house, so that we might live!

"No!" Ishbel cried, her hands now shaking, her voice quavering in fear. "No! I am alive! I am alive!"

She raced down the stairs, tripping once and rolling four or five steps to a landing, before picking herself up, bruised and scraped, and racing downward again.

Watch out, Ishbel. They are lighting the faggots right now.

Ishbel fell again in her terror, cringing against a wall.

The whisper had come from the body of a servant girl who lay in a doorway. Her name was Maria and she had always been kind to Ishbel. But now she was dead, her face half rotted away, her teeth poking out all green-stained and oddly angled. What was left of her face rippled, and Ishbel saw that the movement had been caused by maggots feeding deep within the girl's cheeks.

Watch out, Ishbel, the faggots are burning well, now.

It was not the corpse that whispered, but the silvered hoops in Marla's ears.

Watch out, Ishbel. It is getting awfully *hot.*

"No," Ishbel whispered, backing away on her hands and knees, then turning so she could continue down the stairs on her bottom, too shaken to try to get to her feet, her breath jerking from her throat in terrified, tiny sobbing hiccups.

She slid down the stairs, her skirts tangling with her thighs and hips, one shoe half falling off.

Someone pounded on the front door, and Ishbel tried to call out, to let the crowd know that she was alive, that they must not set fire to the house, but as she opened her mouth she slid another turn of the staircase, and instead of words, nothing came from her mouth but a terrified squeal.

A man of glass stood four or five steps down. His flesh was formed of a pliable, and utterly beautiful, blue-green glass. Deep within the creature's chest a golden pyramid slowly rotated and pulsed.

His head was glass-like as well, his features beautifully formed, and his eyes large round wells of darkness.

They were staring at Ishbel with dark, malicious humour.

"I am the Lord of Elcho Falling," the glass man said, "and I am come to save you."

He took a step upward, and Ishbel screamed, turning to scramble away as fast as she might.

"I am come to save you," the glass man whispered, and Ishbel felt his hand close about her ankle.

She almost blacked out in her terrified panic, but just as the darkness was closing about the edge of her vision, a new voice spoke in her mind.

Courage, Ishbel. Remember who you are, and where you have been, and what your purpose is this day.

The glass man firmed his grip about Ishbel's ankle, and she knew that at any moment he would haul her down the stairs . . . but she tried to concentrate . . .

The glass man was not the Lord of Elcho Falling. He was the One.

Maximilian was the Lord of Elcho Falling.

Suddenly Ishbel was not eight, but thirty, and she rolled over onto her back and thrust her foot as hard as she could into the face of the One.

She did not manage to touch him, but he reeled back in surprise, and his grip on her ankle loosened.

Twist it, Ishbel! the rat said, scrambling for purchase on her shoulder.

"Oh, be quiet," Ishbel muttered, and jerked her ankle free of the One's grip.

The One regained his balance and reached once more for Ishbel, still scrambling to get to her feet, but as he did so the stairs under his feet warped and curled, and he was no longer there.

What happened? said the rat.

"I unwound the staircase from beneath his feet," Ishbel said. "Now he's above us."

Then she was on her feet and hurrying down the stairs, trying to get to the front door before the crowd outside set fire to the house.

Her terror had abated somewhat, but it was still there. The month she had spent among the rotting corpses of her family when she was eight had left an indelible scar on Ishbel's psyche. To merely recall the memory was unbearably painful.

To find herself back in the house, even knowing it was a construct of the One's power, was almost too much for her, even as an adult.

She wished Maximilian were here.

The crowd outside had quietened and that caused Ishbel more concern than had they been vociferous.

What were they doing?

She could hear the One pounding down the stairs, but she was almost at the front door, and if she could open that and escape the house, then Ishbel knew she'd be back in Dark-Glass Mountain, at the place within its structure where that single key foundation stone lay . . .

Ishbel reached the foot of the stairs and dashed across the foyer toward the door.

But just as she reached it, the door exploded in flames, and Ishbel reeled back, crying out in horror as the heat scorched her face and hair and clothing.

She realised her dress was afire in several spots and she beat at the flames, terrified, unable to reason her way out of it, sure that, this time, she was going to burn to death within the charnel house of her father's abode.

Then, before she could successfully beat out her flaming skirts, the walls burst into fire.

CHAPTER TWENTY-THREE

The Brunelle House, Margalit, and Darkglass Mountain

Ishbel could not think. She was caught, back in her parents' house, but this time she was caught in the hell she had always feared—the crowd outside had set fire to the house, and she was trapped.

No one can save you now, Ishbel, the One said in her mind.

She was going to burn, this time.

All your family are dead. All the servants rot. No one can save you now, Ishbel.

Ishbel was crying, her hands beating futilely at the flames on her skirts, beating out one fire only to find that another had sprung up in a different place. There was no time to think. She could feel the rat scrambling about on her shoulders, whispering away in her mind, but Ishbel was so terrified that she paid it no attention.

What use courage now, when she was going to die? Ishbel had always feared death by burning . . . it had been her lifelong worst nightmare, and that terror now so overwhelmed her that she was incapable of thinking—

Gods, even the stone flagging was now alight!

Courage! the rat screamed in her mind.

It is pointless, Ishbel responded. *Look, my hands are blackened now. I will burn, and you with me.*

She could not speak, for the air was now so overheated it had burned her throat and lungs.

Her legs were now enveloped in pain as her skirts roared into full flame, and Ishbel held out her arms, knowing that in another moment she would be a pillar of fire.

Courage, the rat whispered, and Ishbel thought she would

take a bit of that courage, just so that she would die more easily. She calmed her mind and shut out the sound of the One's laughter—

There is no one left here for you, the One said. *No member of your family left alive to aid you. Die, Ishbel. Die.*

No member of her family left to aid her? The words tumbled about in Ishbel's now calmer mind. She could feel her flesh burning, smell its stink, but she put the agony to one side and thought about it.

No family left alive?

"Yes," Ishbel managed to croak out of her burning throat, the sound only a harsh cackle to anyone who might have been standing close. "Yes, there is."

And then, taking all the courage the rat had to offer, Ishbel said, "Druse? Druse? Come aid me, Druse. Please."

Druse, Tirzah's father, still trapped within the pyramid. Her ancestor. Her family.

"Ishbel, my dear," Druse said, throwing a blanket about her and smothering the flames. "I didn't think you would ever call."

"Druse . . ." Ishbel said, startled to find that her voice sounded normal, and then blinking in surprise as Druse lifted away the blanket to discover that her flesh and clothes were unmarked.

All the agony had vanished.

"It was but a ruse, Ishbel," Druse said, smiling at her. "Now, do what you must to tear this horror down and free all of us who remain trapped within its vileness."

He nodded at the door and Ishbel saw that it was unmarked.

And that the key sat in the lock, as her mother had always left it.

So that we might escape the faster, my dear, her mother had always said, *if there were a fire.*

Ishbel squeezed Druse's hand, then she stepped toward the door.

High above, she heard the One shout.

Ishbel turned the key, and opened the door.

She found herself deep within DarkGlass Mountain once again.

Maximilian paced back and forth on the banks of the glass river, staring at the pyramid. He was desperately worried. Ishbel had been inside the pyramid for hours, *hours*. What was she doing? The One had vanished inside, and the pyramid had suddenly quietened. The lights had died, the pyramid had sunk back into darkness. Maximilian could see it now only as a great triangular blackness rearing into the night sky, blotting out the stars.

What should he do? Go after her? *What was happening?*

"Ishbel?" he said.

Ishbel heard him, but could not respond. She could only hope that Maximilian would stay where he was. To try and enter DarkGlass Mountain now would be death for him.

She stood deep within the glass and stone pyramid. In actuality she knew she would be standing within solid rock, but wrapped in power as she was, it appeared to Ishbel as if she stood in a chamber composed of black glass. The chamber was filled with floor-to-ceiling columns which shifted constantly. These columns were so crowded together and moved so abruptly that Ishbel found herself constantly having to move to avoid being crushed.

It was if she were inside a gigantic puzzle.

Every now and then Ishbel caught sight of the stone she was after—the foundation stone of the pyramid, and the stone which, if broken, would begin the unwinding of the mathematical formula that had constructed the pyramid.

With the unwinding of that formula, so would the pyramid itself unwind and be destroyed into dust.

The stone sat about twenty paces away, its location revealed every so often by the movement of the black columns. Unlike the rest of the chamber, this stone looked very ordinary . . . just plain sandstone, marked here and there with the chisels of the slave stonemasons, and speckled with their blood.

Courage in the dance, Ishbel, the rat whispered, and Ishbel almost jumped, for she had forgotten its presence. *Courage in the dance.*

The One was here, too. Ishbel saw him from the corner of her eye moving to her right some distance away, hiding among the columns.

Then again, closer now.

Ishbel began to slip in and out of the columns, using her power and intuition to understand which way they might shift at any given moment. Now and again they brushed at her skin, and Ishbel felt them rasp away the very top layer of her flesh whenever they touched her.

If she emerged out of this, then she would emerge scraped and bloodied.

Ishbel tried to move closer to the foundation stone, but, oh, it was so difficult. The columns themselves shifted so that she was constantly cut off, while the One seemed to glide among them as if they were his friends.

As likely they were.

Ishbel kept moving, one eye on the One, one on the stone.

The One was silent now, his eyes keen on Ishbel, moving as smoothly as she.

Ishbel slipped behind one pillar, then another. She felt as if she were a thread in a weaver's loom, being twisted this way and that, never proceeding forward, only ever sideways.

She moved again, ignoring the sudden scrape of pain along her left arm where a column had caught her.

The only sound was the slight noise the columns made as they shifted, like leaves rustling in the breeze.

But these were not leaves and Ishbel knew if she made a misstep then she would be dead.

Yet even knowing this, Ishbel was calm. She was being tracked through the dancing columns by the One as Ravenna had once tracked her down into the Weeper's soul, but this time Ishbel was stronger. She had survived Ravenna's attempt on her life. She had survived her worst nightmare trapped burning to death in her father's house.

This was nothing.

The One was very, very close now. Ishbel imagined she could feel his warmth as he neared.

Was he warm? Yes, he was. Ishbel remembered that his hand had felt hot against the clammy skin of her ankle.

Now and again Ishbel saw his hand slink out from behind a column and snatch at her.

But always she glided out of his reach a moment before.

The One was not using his powers here; Ishbel suspected it was because it would be too dangerous. They were within the living heart of DarkGlass Mountain, and Ishbel thought the One must be so tied to the pyramid that to use his power would be to risk the entire structure.

She thought he must be panicking and wondered to what that panic might drive him.

The rat gripped tight to her shoulder, and Ishbel thought that if she ever emerged from this she would do so bruised and bloody both from the constant scrape of the columns and the claws of the rat.

The One's fingers grazed her flesh, just for an instant. Ishbel moved too quickly, scraping her right shoulder and arm badly on a shifting column.

Courage, Ishbel, the rat said.

Ishbel wanted to swat the thing against the nearest column, but managed to quash the urge.

Courage be damned. All she wanted was that stone, now so tantalisingly close.

She shifted twice more, then a third time, and suddenly she was beside the stone and looking at the One standing on the other side of it.

"I hope you enjoy your unravelling," Ishbel said, and she dropped to her knees before the stone, placing both hands flat upon it.

Ishbel heard the sound of distant laughter and knew it to be her ancient forbears, Boaz and Tirzah, and with that sound Ishbel remembered what knowledge it was that Tirzah's baby had imbibed from the pyramid when Boaz had done his terrible battle with it.

Then she knew what she could do with that knowledge

when combined with her training as the Archpriestess of the Coil.

Ishbel's hand moved in a complex tangle of movements over the stone and the One cried out.

Black inky writing appeared on the stone—hundreds of strange numerals and symbols that began to move and then lift off the stone to float in the air between the One and Ishbel.

She moved her hand again, and the symbols whirled upward.

Then Ishbel spoke a word that she had never heard before, but which now seemed to her as familiar as her own name. "Numestos."

The One cried out again, utterly panicked, and lunged across the stone toward Ishbel.

She evaded him easily, concentrating completely on the task at hand. "Numestos!"

The symbols flew about the chamber, a thick ribbon of black twisting characters that moved about the shifting columns.

"Numestos!" Ishbel cried a third time, then ducked as the ribbon flowed over her head to spin upward through the pyramid.

Be careful, she heard Ta'uz's voice say in her mind.

Maximilian was frantic. He'd decided he had to do something—that he could not leave it a moment longer—when suddenly the pyramid glowed with a soft green light.

He stopped dead, his mouth slightly agape as he stared. DarkGlass Mountain looked stunningly beautiful, illuminating the nearby landscape with its soft light.

Then, as suddenly as the appearance of the light, inky black numbers and symbols started to race across the glass surface of the pyramid, winding up from its base toward the golden capstone.

Maximilian took a step forward, moving from the river bank onto the glass of the Lhyl, then another, then stopped, stunned by what was happening.

The symbols continued to wind up, up, up around the entire pyramid, drawing ever closer to the capstone.

They reached it.

There was a heartbeat where nothing happened.

Then the capstone went black . . . another heartbeat . . .

It exploded into countless pieces of glass, and Maximilian instinctively ducked as deadly shards rained down over a wide area.

CHAPTER TWENTY-FOUR

Darkglass Mountain

Careful, Ta'uz whispered, and Ishbel ducked as a column four or five away from her began to crumble.

The One was shouting, incomprehensible words that made little sense to Ishbel. He was finally bringing the power of Infinity to bear against what Ishbel had worked, but it appeared to be making the situation worse rather than better.

More and more columns were crumbling.

Then Ishbel heard a tremendous explosion far above.

The One screamed.

Careful, said the rat.

A torrent of symbols continued to flow out of the stone, winding up in a never ending ribbon through the pyramid. Now Ishbel heard other voices, unknown voices, murmuring in excitement.

All those the pyramid had destroyed over the millennia.

Suddenly something grabbed at Ishbel's hand. It was the One, staring at her maniacally.

His grip tightened into a vice, and Ishbel cried out and tried to pull away.

"Don't think this is the end of it, bitch," the One rasped.

Ishbel stared at him in fright. Black fault lines were spreading through his flesh—she could almost *hear* them spread, as if cloth were being ripped into shreds.

"Don't think this is the end of it," the One said again, and his words terrified Ishbel for all the malice had gone from his voice and instead there was only cold certainty.

Then, horribly, he started to break apart. The process was aided by the collapse of a column of stone next to him that sheared away half of his head.

For an instant Ishbel was staring at a single black eye that returned her gaze unblinkingly, then another column collapsed and the One shattered into a thousand pieces.

Ishbel fell backward as the One's grip vanished. She felt herself caught between two crumbling columns, then everything went dark and unknowing.

Maximilian paced back and forth, back and forth on the glassy river staring at the disintegrating pyramid. He'd been cut by several shards of glass from the exploding capstone, but had escaped serious injury.

The pyramid collapsed into itself, sending a dust-and-debris cloud flying upward and outward, although it stopped short of the far river bank and didn't threaten Maximilian.

Where was Ishbel? Maximilian did not know if she had escaped the pyramid but was hidden by the debris cloud, if she was still inside but was protected by her power, or if she was still inside and *not* protected.

Anything but the third, please gods, anything but the third.

The continuing destruction of the pyramid was now almost overwhelming. It had been a massive structure, virtually solid stone and glass and it made a thunderous roar as it came down.

Maximilian stood helpless, not knowing what to do. He wondered if Avaldamon, Serge and Doyle had come out from their hiding hole and were watching this from the safety of the great courtyard of the palace of Aqhat.

They had been caught within the pyramid for what seemed to them an eternity. Their bodies had long been disposed of, but their souls had remained trapped within the entity that had murdered them.

There had been nothing but bleakness and hopelessness for them.

But now, feel the bonds unravel!

Now! *cried the one who had once been Ta'uz.* Go now! *And as one the thousands of the murdered stood and shook off their bonds and walked out of the pyramid.*

* * *

Maximilian saw them in the debris cloud, walking toward the river. They were not solid, not flesh, just disturbances within the dust that appeared as human shapes. As they drew closer to the edge of the debris cloud, so they began to dissipate.

But one remained visible long enough to make it halfway across the river.

The dust shape smiled at Maximilian. *Thank her for us*, it said. *And tell her that Druse is finally on his way home to his family*.

With that, the dust fell apart and Maximilian stood alone in the centre of the glass river.

Isaiah sat at his campfire with Lamiah, Hereward and several of the senior captains within the force. The mood was subdued, only the occasional word being spoken. Everyone was on edge both with the arrival of the juit birds (not dangerous within themselves, but hardly a sign of confidence in what might be happening in Isembaard) and Isaiah's belief that a horde of millions of Skraelings was headed their way.

Isaiah's sense of unease had been growing all day. For most of the day, into the early evening, that had been attributable to the approaching threat of the Skraelings, but now Isaiah believed there was something *else* happening.

He had not been this nervous and this jumpy, well . . . not in his very considerable life span thus far.

Something bad was happening.

Or maybe good. Isaiah simply could not decide.

Hereward looked over the fire at him, then cleared her throat to say something.

Before she could speak, however, she suddenly gasped, her eyes wide, and clamped both hands to her throat.

Blood was pumping forth, drenching the front of her robe.

Maximilian was still pacing when, in one startling, stunning moment, he found himself being driven down through water.

For a moment he was so stunned he could not react, then he was trying to fight his way up through the water, struggling with the sudden, terrifying current, desperate for breath. Something seemed to be keeping him down; he didn't know what it was, but it was starting to panic him.

Then suddenly he was free of whatever force held him and he was gasping for breath at the surface.

The Lhyl had returned to water.

The current was fierce, fiercer than Maximilian expected, and he wondered if the sudden release of the water meant it flowed far more violently than usual. He started to swim for the eastern shore, desperate to get to land and look back to see what had become of the pyramid, when he became aware that a rat was swimming in circles about him.

Watch out, said the rat, and suddenly Maximilian was hit from below by a large, solid object. It grabbed at his legs, then his hips, pulling him under, and as Maximilian sank yet once more, he found himself staring through the water into Ishbel's eyes.

One more time, Isaiah found himself leaping about a fire and clamping his hands about Hereward's neck.

What the fuck is happening?

She stared at him with wild eyes, her expression half of bewilderment and half of deep anger.

"Stay away from me!" she hissed, managing to get to her feet, both her hands still held tight against the spot where, many months ago, the Skraeling had dug its claw deep into her flesh.

"Stay away!" she said once more, then stumbled away from Isaiah forcing him to release his hold.

Lamiah and the other men were on their feet by this stage.

"What—" Lamiah began.

"I have no idea," Isaiah said, his eyes following Hereward as she walked unsteadily away into the night. "I have no idea at all."

"Grab my hands!" Avaldamon shouted, and Maximilian and Ishbel spat out water, shaking their heads, reaching for Avaldamon's, and Serge's and Doyle's, hands.

"The river!" Ishbel said as she managed to find firm footing.

"Ishbel!" Maximilian said, and wrapped his wife in an embrace so tight that she laughed in protest.

Everyone was laughing and hugging each other.

"You did it!" Avaldamon said, trying to prise Ishbel away from Maximilian and not succeeding. "The pyramid is gone . . . gone!"

They all turned to look over the river. There was nothing where DarkGlass Mountain had been save a low cloud of drifting dust. No stones, no glass.

Nothing.

"Are you all right, Ishbel?" Maximilian said. "You're bruised . . . and cut . . ."

"I am well enough," she said. "They are just scrapes. Oh, I have so much to tell you!"

"The One?" Maximilian said.

"Gone, I think," Ishbel said. "I saw him crumble before my eyes. He tried to use the power of Infinity within the very machinery of DarkGlass Mountain and it only accelerated his own destruction. Can you feel him? Avaldamon?"

Both men shook their heads.

"Nothing," Maximilian said. "What did—"

"Look!" Ishbel said, laughing anew. She reached into the water, searching with her hands, then she straightened, holding up the *Book of the Soulenai*. It dripped water everywhere, but looked otherwise undamaged.

"I am well, the Book is returned, the river is made water once more, the pyramid is destroyed, and the One with it," Ishbel said. She grinned wildly, looking about the group. "Is this it? Can we go home now? Are we done?"

Maximilian kissed her. "We are done, Ishbel. We can go home."

Neither of them saw the shadow of worry in Avaldamon's eyes, but he smiled when they turned to him, and nodded.

"Yes, we can go home."

In the Outlands, the Skraeling surge northward faltered suddenly.

The One's presence had abruptly faded.

I think, said the leader among them, *that we ought to proceed with a little more caution. Just until we hear from the One again.*

[Part Two]

CHAPTER ONE

The Outlands

Isaiah walked through the camp, looking for Hereward, when suddenly he stopped. His eyes stared, his mouth opencd. He felt . . .

Whole.

He bent over, resting his hands on his knees.

His power was filtering back!

Isaiah could hardly believe it. He had thought he was reconciled to a mortal life without power, but now . . .

Was this a trick of the One?

Taking a deep breath and straightening up, Isaiah tested himself (hardly daring to, in case it *was* a trick!) by sending out a probe, trying to scry out the One.

His power worked perfectly, but he could feel nothing of the One. Nothing.

Nothing.

And the river was back! Isaiah could sense it flowing in delight, full of life as it swept down from the FarReach Mountains toward Lake Juit.

The River Lhyl flowed again.

Isaiah sank down and sat in the dirt. All about him the camp was rousing for the day, but he just sat there in the dirt, his eyes gleaming, ignoring the curious looks sent his way.

The water was back.

His power was back.

He was *whole*.

The river was back.

He was *whole*.

DarkGlass Mountain was gone. Every sense of it had vanished. It was *gone*.

And the One . . . Isaiah could not feel him at all.

He, too, was gone.

Isaiah gave himself one moment of sheer happiness, then he rose to his feet. It must have been Maximilian or Ishbel, or both. Nothing else could have managed the destruction of the One or of DarkGlass Mountain.

Isaiah chuckled. "I had not thought either of you capable of managing it," he said softly, "but I am more than glad to be proved wrong."

He couldn't decide what to do next. Talk to Hereward? To Lamiah? To the damned juit birds and find out why they were here and what they knew? Try to communicate with Axis, or Maximilian, or Ishbel?

Out of all those possibilities, Hereward was coming a distant last, but as he turned to retrace his steps Isaiah saw her tent and decided he might as well speak with her while he was here.

Besides, she would be pleased to learn he had his power back.

Smiling happily (and drawing strange looks from the soldiers for that smile), Isaiah walked over to Hereward's tent.

"Hereward?" Isaiah lifted the flap and looked inside.

Hereward was sitting on her camp bed and looked at him irritably when he came in.

"I do not need you," she said.

"Nonetheless," Isaiah said. He came over and sat down beside her, then carefully lifted away the linen she had pressed against her neck.

"Be careful!" she snapped.

"I will be careful," Isaiah said. The wound had started to coagulate—it had not been as bad or as deep as the original had been, although frightening enough—and was only seeping a pinkish fluid now.

Isaiah wondered why it had reopened. What did it signify? Was it just another effect of the destruction of the pyramid and the One, and the rebirth of the River Lhyl?

Or was there some darker mystery behind it?

His fingers probed at Hereward's neck and she hissed at him, making Isaiah look at her sharply.

"Don't touch it, Isaiah," she said. "There is nothing you can do to—"

Isaiah's fingers ran over the soft scab, just lightly, and suddenly it was healed, completely sealed over.

Hereward twisted her face about to stare at him. She lifted her own fingers to her neck, and her eyes widened. "What did you do? How . . . ?"

"I have my power back, Hereward. I am whole."

Hereward stared at him uncomprehendingly. "Whole?"

Isaiah laughed, softly at first, then louder in sheer joy. "The river god is back, Hereward. What say you?"

"That I preferred the man," she said, and her tone was so dismissive that Isaiah's laughter died, and he rose and left the tent.

Isaiah walked to the edge of the encampment, irritated at Hereward. Once again he thought how good it would be to leave her behind.

Or to hand her over to her father Ezekiel at Elcho Falling.

"She has never been anything but trouble," Isaiah muttered to himself.

He reached the edge of the camp, walked about ten paces toward the juit birds, then sat down, bowing his head as he did so.

Isaiah may have had his powers as river god restored, but the juit birds were so magical as to be barely of this world. They deserved his respect.

The birds turned to regard him with their bright black eyes, then one walked forward and, a pace away from Isaiah, fluffed out its feathers and sank to the ground.

You have returned to us, Mighty One, said the bird. *We thought to have lost you forever.*

I thought to have lost myself, Isaiah said. *Tell me, what brings you here?*

A great transference of power. Something came down from this land to the glass obscenity—

Isaiah had to restrain a smile at the bird's description of the pyramid.

—and in return, here we are. There was a balance required.

Isaiah nodded, understanding. *It was the Lord of Elcho Falling who came to the pyramid?*

We do not know who it was.

It must have been Maximilian, likely with Ishbel, Isaiah thought, and then did smile, thinking that they were working very hard to avoid him!

What can you tell me, bright-feathered one?

That the mass of grey wraiths approach, Isaiah. They are, perhaps, but three hours away. Are you ready?

Eleanon and Bingaleal sat on a mountain top several hours' flight from Elcho Falling.

They had flown there this very morning in the space of just three breaths. For a long time they sat in silence, revelling in the growth of their potential, in their union with Infinity which had brought them so much power—ever-increasing—and at the sight of Elcho Falling in the far distance which they could just pick out in the darkness.

As they cast their gaze about, both Lealfast men could see as far as Escator to the west, to Elcho Falling in the east and to the foothills of the FarReach Mountains in the south.

They did not cast their eyes northward. They never wanted to see the frozen wastes again. It had been a prison for too long.

"Interesting times," Bingaleal said eventually, and his brother sighed and stretched his arms.

Frost crackled and fell from his skin, which gleamed a soft ivory in the morning light.

"DarkGlass Mountain is no more," Bingaleal said.

Eleanon shrugged, now rubbing the last of the frost from his biceps. "It was an aberration," he said, "whichever way you look at it. I am surprised it lasted this long."

"Ishbel did it."

Eleanon bared his teeth, just a little. "She thinks to be so clever. One day *she* will be unwound."

"And the One . . . ?"

Now Eleanon smiled genuinely. "Ah, the One. They have no idea. Likely they celebrate, thinking him gone."

"Will he be a trouble to *us* where he is?"

Eleanon thought a little. "I doubt it. I think he has almost forgotten us. After what has happened at DarkGlass Mountain, his attention will be entirely and absolutely on Ishbel and Maximilian. For the One, Elcho Falling can wait. This is personal for him, now."

"He hasn't been in touch."

Eleanon chuckled. "Would you? With all that has happened this night? No, of course he has not thought to speak with us. He would not, in any case, as it might well reveal his presence to those inside Elcho Falling. So we will be careful, Bingaleal. We shall continue on with our plan. Everything we do appears to be in his favour, too. The One shall not trouble us."

"I like the idea very much that it is the StarMan from whom we must wrest Elcho Falling," Bingaleal said. "Maximilian was never the real enemy. Never a challenging enemy. Axis is. *StarMan*." He said that last with a curl of his lip.

"I felt his fear and frustration when we attacked."

They both sighed, remembering, revelling.

"We must be careful," Eleanon said after a moment.

"Inardle. We can no longer trust her."

Eleanon looked at Bingaleal. "Did you ever? You must have known that the instant she went to Axis' bed she was compromised. She was useful for only a short while." He shrugged.

"She could be dangerous."

"Then we must fix that."

"She knows a little too much, Eleanon."

"Then we will fix that, too."

Bingaleal nodded, then changed the subject. "The Dark Spire?"

"It continues to grow. It waits. For Ravenna. Once she enters Elcho Falling, then it will become what we need."

"Do you have any idea how you will get her inside?"

"Not yet. But when the chance arrives, I will seize it."

"And Ravenna?"

"She needs a little . . . work," Eleanon said. "I need to alter Ishbel's curse. But there is no rush. No need for us to show our hand just yet."

He paused, thinking, then resumed speaking. "Isaiah is coming. The Skraelings are coming—I can just see them, in the far distance, the revolting little sprites. Axis will want to save Isaiah from the Skraelings and from us . . . and Inardle may well suggest the way. Bingaleal . . . I suggest it might be foolish to try and stop them just yet. It might be best to allow—"

"Axis and Inardle to escape. To actually *save* Isaiah?"

"Yes."

Both grinned simultaneously.

"Axis will not be able to resist the saving of Isaiah," said Eleanon. "And it will be the death of him, and of Elcho Falling."

"And of, finally, every last remaining Icarii. It is time they were wiped from the face of this world and from all memory, brother. Time, indeed."

The two Lealfast sat on that mountain top until late morning, in silent accord, rejoicing in the certainty that soon they would be masters of the world.

CHAPTER TWO

Elcho Falling

A xis received the summons from Josia just as he was running down the stairs to find Georgdi, who was currently reviewing security in the lower reaches of Elcho Falling.

Axis moved to the nearest window. "Josia?"

Josia sat there in his window a few paces away, hovering in the clear air, as he had been the last time he had talked to Axis.

"Good news, Axis. Maximilian and Ishbel have succeeded. DarkGlass Mountain is destroyed. Gone. No more."

"Ah, thank the stars!" Axis felt relief flood through him. Finally, *good* news! "They are well?"

"Yes. Both are well."

Axis grinned, the day suddenly bright. "And the One?"

"Gone. Dead, they say."

"Is that possible? He drew on the power of Infinity itself."

Josia shrugged disinterestedly. "It is what Maximilian told me to tell you."

"Well, then, if Maxel said it was so, then it is so. I thank you, Josia. This is blessed news indeed. Are Maxel and Ishbel on their way home now?"

"Where else?"

Axis ran lightly down the stairs, whistling under his breath, all his other troubles forgotten in the face of this bright news. He saw Georgdi in the spacious foyer of Elcho Falling and stopped for a brief chat.

"DarkGlass Mountain is *gone*?" Georgdi said.

Axis was still grinning. "Aye, and Ishbel and Maxel safe.

Georgdi, we need to send a boat to them. Do you have any means of contacting any boatmen, or ships? It should be such an easy thing, yet we are bottled up here in Elcho Falling with no means of communication with the outside world."

"Not quite no means," Georgdi said. "I have men roaming the Outlands. Give me a day or two and I can pass a message to a band of them and—"

"How?"

Georgdi gave a small shrug. "The sun. A small mirror. It can be done. They can contact a boatman in Margalit or one of the smaller ports south. Someone will be able to sail to pick them up."

"Good." Axis clapped Georgdi on the shoulder. They talked a few more minutes about security issues then Axis continued his way down the stairs.

He wanted to see what was happening with the Dark Spire now that DarkGlass Mountain was gone and the One with it.

With any luck the spire would have withered into the size and threat of a sausage left for eight weeks in the sun.

He reached a chamber just above the lowest basement which contained the Dark Spire. StarDrifter was there, conferring in close whispers with several other Enchanters.

StarDrifter turned and Axis was surprised to see deep worry in his face.

"Good news, StarDrifter," Axis said. "DarkGlass Mountain is destroyed. The One with it. Maximilian and Ishbel are on their way home. How . . ." he paused, wondering why there was no expression of relief or joy on StarDrifter's face. "How goes the Dark Spire?"

"Badly, Axis," StarDrifter said. "In the past hour it has grown remarkably. None of us can enter the lowest basement level now, for the spire's dark tentacles reach everywhere."

He stepped aside, and indicated the floor. "Look. This happened just before you arrived."

Axis looked to where StarDrifter pointed, and all his happiness faded.

There was a dark streak spreading across the floor.

A crack.

As he watched, the floor began to break wide open, and everyone hastened for the stairs.

The Dark Spire was ascending.

CHAPTER THREE

Aqhat

They sat on the river bank in the morning light, a fire blazing, eating a meal. Their mood was jovial and there was much shared laughter. Every so often one or the other would turn their head to look across the river to the great emptiness where once DarkGlass Mountain had stood.

Avaldamon watched Ishbel turn and look one more time, and he smiled.

"Boaz and Tirzah would be proud of you," he said. "That was one almighty achievement, Ishbel."

Maximilian smiled, reaching to squeeze his wife's hand. "Indeed it was."

"Did Josia say anything about Axis?" Ishbel said. Earlier, Maximilian had spent a little time in the Twisted Tower, talking with Josia.

"No news," Maximilian said. "All Josia wanted to talk about was how you had managed the destruction of the pyramid and the One, Ishbel. But I imagine that this news will lighten Axis' heart."

The mood sobered. "Mayhap the One is gone, and the pyramid," said Serge, "but the Lealfast and the Skraelings still thrive. I wish I were there to help." He grinned. "I came down here expecting a decent fight . . . and look what I got. Nothing!"

Again they laughed together.

"Ishbel," Avaldamon said as the laughter died, "what did you find in the Infinity Chamber?"

Ishbel told them about the *Book of the Soulenai*, and the rat. "He was my courage, the courage taken from Josia as he died so many years ago. Has anyone set eyes on this rat since the pyramid collapsed?"

"He surfaced just before you," said Maximilian, "but I have not seen him since."

Avaldamon nodded at the book lying by Ishbel's side. "What does it say now, Ishbel?"

She picked it up and opened it, turning over the pages, a frown deepening. "Nothing, Avaldamon. Its pages are blank. It tells me nothing."

"Then perhaps its task is done," Avaldamon said. "We should not worry."

"*Is* there something to worry about?" Ishbel said. "You have appeared sombre at times . . ."

Avaldamon studied his hands, fiddling with a piece of uneaten bread. "I worry about the One," he said finally, looking up.

"That he is not dead?" Maximilian said.

Avaldamon nodded. "I cannot sense him—"

"As neither can I," Maximilian said.

"Nor I," Ishbel said.

"—but," Avaldamon continued, "yes, I do fret about it. The One touched the power of Infinity. That is immensely strong. Immensely durable. *Infinitely* so. Would the mere collapse of a building, even one so immense and arcane as DarkGlass Mountain," he waved a hand across the river, "actually destroy him? I don't know. Yes, it may have destroyed his body . . . but the One himself? He had already learned the trick of jumping into a new existence, and once learned that trick is not easily forgotten. Ishbel, tell me again what happened when you say he crumbled."

Ishbel described once more how the One had disintegrated before her eyes. "He was terrified, Avaldamon. I am sure I could see knowledge of his own doom written in his expression. He was so frightened he brought the power of Infinity to bear where previously he had been too cautious. He—"

Ishbel suddenly stopped.

"What?" Maximilian and Avaldamon said together.

"He said . . . he said that I should not think that this was the end to it."

Avaldamon and Maximilian exchanged a glance.

"If he only used the power of Infinity at the very end," Maximilian said, "then perhaps he was using it to do something *other* than try and save DarkGlass Mountain. Perhaps he had been saving it to . . ."

"Move elsewhere," said Avaldamon. "Into another existence."

"Where's that rat now?" said Doyle, drawing his sword.

There was a long silence.

"Into *what* existence?" Ishbel finally said.

"Where least we expect it," Avaldamon said. "We should rest here for today, but tomorrow we must be prepared to move north as fast as possible. I think the One is no longer in Isembaard . . . he will have gone back to Elcho Falling, or as close to it as he could manage."

"You don't think it is the rat?" Doyle said.

"The rat would be too easy," Avaldamon said. "Unfortunately."

"Nonetheless," Doyle said, "I might kill that rat if it strays across my path."

They spent the morning searching through what remained of Aqhat to see what they could find to aid them in their journey north. Everyone now wanted to return to Elcho Falling as fast as possible.

"Fast", unfortunately, was going to be difficult to accomplish. There were no horses left to ride, and little in the way of stores (apart from some mouldy grain the Skraelings hadn't wanted to touch, and some hard cheese that had been so thoroughly wrapped, and sealed inside pots, that the Skraelings had not discovered it).

"There will be fish in the river," Avaldamon said, and Maximilian grinned at him.

"*And* giant river lizards," Maximilian said. "We shall have to keep a leash on you."

The one item of real use that Serge discovered in the mid-afternoon was a nearly completed reed boat sitting in one of the boat sheds close to the river. It was not very large, and still lacked seating and the final installation of its rudder, left lying nearby, but it was a welcome find and everyone clapped Serge on the shoulder in relief.

"Serge and I will have this ready within a day," Doyle said. "If the rest of you find whatever stores you can, then we should be able to leave tomorrow afternoon at the latest."

"The Lord of Elcho Falling has many skills," Maximilian said, "but boating isn't one of them. I don't suppose . . ."

Avaldamon gave him a smile. "I became well acquainted with the art of river boating while I lived in Ashdod, my friend."

"Until you fell off one," Serge muttered.

"And the art and craft of sailing a reed boat are simple enough that within a day of sailing all of you shall have become experts as well," Avaldamon continued. "Come now, Ishbel, Maxel, let us find a prodigious quantity of stores still secreted about, so that Serge and Doyle may not look down their noses at us."

CHAPTER FOUR

Elcho Falling

Inardle sat on the railing of a balcony high in Elcho Falling. It had been some days now since Eleanon's attack on the Citadel and her level of wretchedness had not abated in any degree.

What else could she have done?

Told Axis beforehand? Even now Inardle closed her eyes momentarily in horror at the thought. She simply could not have gone to Axis.

Fled to Eleanon?

No, not that, either. Inardle hated what he and the rest of her brethren had become, and she knew she had no place with them.

And now they would kill her if she went back. She was not at one with the One, and they would not trust her.

Her only option lay within herself. Inardle looked out to the country stretching beyond Elcho Falling. Could she survive on her own? Oh, she would be able to find enough sustenance, and shelter too, if it came to that, but could she survive the utter isolation? She had no kin left, no brethren.

Axis had been her lifeline, and now that lifeline was irreparably frayed and the ends lost to opposite shores of a vast ocean.

Inardle had healed her wings in the heat and panic of the moment on the night of Eleanon's attack, but still she had to fly. Now she looked into the air, wondering, yearning. It would take but a moment to launch herself from the balcony, and then she could soar to her heart's content . . .

Until she was cut down either by one of the Lealfast or a

member of the Strike Force who, never having trusted her, now outright loathed her.

Still . . . Inardle unconsciously edged further into the space beyond the railing, her wings lifting fractionally from her back, her eyes gleaming as she stared upward.

Perhaps, if she took her chances, if she cloaked herself in invisibility, even the Lealfast would miss her slipping between their number.

"Inardle?"

She teetered on the railing, almost overbalancing into the air, until a hand grabbed her by the elbow.

For a heartbeat Inardle could not look. Thus had Axis, in concern and love, once grabbed for her, believing she would die if she had fallen.

"Inardle?"

It was not Axis. Inardle turned her head. It was the Outlander general, Georgdi.

"Don't, Inardle," he said, and his voice was gentle, and his eyes full of understanding.

She sighed, blinked, then readjusted her weight so that she was once more balanced within the balcony rather than out of it.

Inardle did not know Georgdi well, although as Axis' second-in-command she'd always had a reasonable amount of contact with him.

Georgdi had shared that pit in Armat's camp with her, Axis and Zeboath.

What Inardle did know of Georgdi she liked and trusted, and at least he did not look at her with eyes of judgement.

"Inardle, come down and talk to us—"

Inardle looked behind him, and saw the warier form of Insharah.

"Come down and talk to us, Inardle."

Inardle had so nearly flown away that it was an almost impossible step for her to readjust her mentality to staying.

"Come down, Inardle."

She twisted her head a little, looking once more to the sky.

"Please, Inardle."

Now she sighed once again and, feeling more wretched than ever, slid down from the railing so she stood on the balcony floor. "What do you want, Georgdi?"

"Insharah and I would like to speak to you about what you said to Axis. That you could deliver him the Skraelings."

"Does Axis know you are here?"

"Yes."

"Yet he does not come." Inardle felt even more wretched. She brushed past Georgdi and Insharah and walked into the room, sitting on a stool and spreading her wings behind her.

Both men followed her and sat on chairs. Georgdi still looked open and friendly, but Insharah looked more uncomfortable than ever.

"I will not bite, Insharah," Inardle said. "And, surely, you and I have much in common . . . all this swapping about of allegiances and such."

The two men were silent a moment, then both chuckled and the mood between the three relaxed. Even Inardle dared a small smile—that comment had been an enormous risk, but ultimately worth it.

"I think we are a tower of mismatched allegiances," Insharah said. "I have never before met a more disparate grouping of loyalties, ambitions and races in one sad, besieged tower."

"I am sorry for the way Axis has been treating you, Inardle," Georgdi said.

She waved a hand, dismissing it.

"Georgdi says that you told Axis you could bring him the Skraelings," Insharah said.

Inardle gave a very small smile. "I was furious with him."

"Inardle," said Georgdi, "*can* you bring him the Skraelings?"

"Do I *want* to?" Inardle said, then apologised. "Look, I am half Skraeling, something StarDrifter never fails to remind everyone, so I do have some kinship with them. On the other hand, the Skraelings have always disliked the Lealfast as we have tended to look down our long, long Icarii noses at them. I suspect the Skraelings also resent and hate the Lealfast for their alliance with the One. The Skraelings are jealous creatures and I think that they like to think themselves as the senior partners in any alliance with the One."

"How does this help Axis?" Georgdi said.

Inardle considered a little before continuing. "They may be turned against the Lealfast."

"To ally with *Axis*?" Insharah said. "They loathe Axis!"

Inardle now grinned. "They curse with his name! So, yes, this might be difficult—but hear me out. The Skraelings have ever looked for their own lord. They are servile creatures, and naturally gravitate to any who proclaims dominance over them in return for a homeland and lots of eating."

"Thus Gorgracl so many years ago?" Insharah said, who had spent his youth listening to tales of Axis' battles with his half-brother, the Lord of the Skraelings.

"Yes, as with Gorgracl," Inardle said. "And as also with Kanubai, and later with the One. The Skraelings are habituated to servility—"

"But to *Axis*?" Georgdi said.

"Were not Kanubai and the One equally preposterous choices?" Inardle said. "I believe that all someone has to do to win the Skraelings' loyalty is to offer them something bigger and better than their last master. That, coupled with their deep instinctive need to actually have a master—a Lord of the Skraelings—and even an ant with a deep enough promise bag and enough pretty tricks could win them over. It is worth a try, anyway. Better to have the Skraelings on our side rather than on someone else's."

Georgdi and Insharah exchanged a glance.

"But *Axis*?" Georgdi said once again.

"Is not the line between love and hate a thin one?" Inardle said. "Am I not enough example of that? One moment Axis' favoured commander and the next his most reviled enemy. It swings back the other way as easily, believe it or not. Axis only has to offer them enough and they will suddenly proclaim Axis their new master." She gave a chuckle. "Axis, Lord of the Skraelings."

Both men smiled. The title did have a distinctive ring to it.

"Would Axis agree?" Insharah said.

Inardle shrugged.

"And what could he promise them?" Georgdi said.

"Axis would need to decide that," Inardle said. "I am sure he could invent something."

"We'll take this back to Axis," Georgdi said. "But I cannot promise that he will accept it."

"Tell him he does not have much time," Inardle said.

Georgdi frowned in question.

"The rest of the Lealfast Nation is undoubtedly on their way here," Inardle said. "I am a little surprised they are not here already . . . but I can sense them approaching. They will be here by morning, and I doubt we can escape the cordon after their arrival. It must be tonight."

"Wait," said Georgdi. "I don't follow. Who is this 'we'? And you will need to leave Elcho Falling?"

"No one can afford for the Skraelings to get to Elcho Falling," said Inardle, "where we will have almost no chance at all of deflecting their current loyalties. No doubt Axis will need to tell them some solid lies in order to swing their love toward him. He won't be able to do that with the Lealfast—" *Strange*, Inardle thought, *how she spoke of her brethren as if they were no relation at all* "—so close and able to disprove any artifice Axis comes up with. And as to the 'we'— Axis and myself. Axis because he *needs* to be there to persuade the Skraelings to their new master, and I because . . . well, because the only way I can get Axis away from Elcho Falling is through the use of my Lealfast ability to invisible myself . . . I can take just one person with me and cloak them as well. I cannot take more than one. So it has to be Axis and myself only, and it must be soon, no later than tonight. Even then it will be a dangerous task to slip through the Lealfast cordon. Tell Axis this. He must decide if he wants to dare it, and whether or not the dare is worth the risk.

"But," Inardle finished, "it might just save Isaiah."

CHAPTER FIVE

The Outlands

The Skraelings had been approaching since dawn. Isaiah had expected a great wave of them to wash over the Isembaardians . . . but instead the Skraelings had crept closer and closer, never rushing, always cautious.

Now, at noon, there was an undulating wave of grey wraiths to the south, perhaps thirty paces from the edge of the juit birds, which had gathered in one great flock, putting themselves between the Skraelings and the Isembaardians.

Lamiah and Isaiah stood, surrounded by birds, at the southern edge of the flock, alternately looking south to the Skraelings or at the birds.

Isaiah was more concerned with the Skraelings, Lamiah with the birds.

"Do you think the juit birds might be any aid against the Skraelings?" Lamiah said.

Isaiah gave a small shrug. "Maybe."

Lamiah looked at him then again at the birds.

As one they had fluffed out their pink feathers and were weaving their beaks to and fro toward the Skraelings. They looked very, very angry, and every so often each bird would hiss.

"Perhaps save us?" Lamiah said, then grunted dismissively. "I suppose they could fluff out their feathers and hiss and look very, very angry."

Isaiah grinned. "Hasn't your wife ever done that to you, and haven't you backed down every single time she has done it?"

Lamiah chuckled. "But, seriously . . ."

"But seriously," Isaiah said, now returning his gaze to the

distant line of Skraelings, "I have no idea what is happening.
I wish Axis were here so he could advise us. I had thought
the Skraelings might attack . . . what are they doing just *gathering*?"

"They look different to what I expected," Lamiah said.

"They *are* different," Isaiah said.

Very different. He had seen them in Isembaard, and they'd
each had long thin limbs terminating in heavily clawed hands
and feet, with the head of a jackal atop their grey, wraith-
like bodies. Although many still looked like that, others
had grown into half-wraith, half-great cat forms; others looked
like the gryphons from the legendary tales of Tencendor and
others had become all jackal; others still were misshapen
lumps of creatures for which Isaiah could assign no descrip-
tive name.

The Skraelings also appeared to have leaders, for some
of the larger and more misshapen of the Skraelings moved
about the greater mass, directing and ordering.

Isaiah shivered. *What was happening?* Were they now
directionless for want of the One?

"The army is ready?" he asked Lamiah for the sixteenth
time.

"Yes," Lamiah replied patiently, knowing the worry that
underscored Isaiah's repetitive questioning. "They are ready.
Every man armed and in place."

And little good that would do, both men thought, *if this
massive army of wraiths attacked.*

The Skraelings stretched south as far as any eye could
see, a mass of million upon million, undulating slightly in
the clear noon sunshine.

"Look!" Lamiah said, and Isaiah nodded.

One of the Skraelings, among the largest of the misshapen
leaders, had left the main pack and now walked across the
open space between the Skraelings and the Isembaardians.

Lamiah turned and shouted some orders, but Isaiah did
not shift his eyes from the creature.

It was just one.

But, oh, what a one.

The Skraeling stood about the height of a very large bear

walking on its hind limbs, and even looked slightly like a bear in the shape of its lumbering body. But its head looked like a piece of dough that a cook had crumpled in her hands until it bulged unevenly.

It had two silvered orbs, smaller than the usual enormous eyes of the Skraelings, tucked away in the left side of its face. Instead of being side by side, they were arranged one above the other . . . the lower one slightly skewed to the right.

It had a slit for a mouth . . . and clawed hands and feet at the extremities of its body.

That, at least, was normal for a Skraeling, as also the constant grey shifting nature of its body so that it faded in and out of view as it shuffled forward, the mass of its comrades often appearing in perfect focus through its body.

Of all its loathsomeness, Isaiah found its unbalanced eyes the most troubling.

"I have men coming to aid us," Lamiah said softly.

"Tell them to stay back," Isaiah said.

Lamiah stared at Isaiah a moment, then turned and waved to a halt the squad of men moving through the birds.

Isaiah moved forward.

"Be careful!" Lamiah hissed, and Isaiah paused to turn and grin.

"Was there not a time you could not wait to be rid of me?" Isaiah said.

"Once upon a time," said Lamiah, "when I was lost in fairytale ambitions."

Isaiah nodded, then his grin faded, and he turned back to wade forward through the hissing birds.

He walked to some five paces past them, and stopped.

The Skraeling had halted another three paces away. Its silver orbs, so obscenely unbalanced, watched him unblinkingly.

It looked very sure of itself.

In reality, the Skraeling was extremely unsettled.

The One, who had guided the Skraelings to this point with clear instructions and purpose, had vanished. His presence was no longer apparent to the wraiths. They could no longer sense him, although they did not quite believe him dead.

Just gone.

Off somewhere.

And he'd forgotten to tell them about it.

This was not only deeply hurtful to the Skraelings, it was highly unsettling. It made them nervous.

Worse, this army they had suddenly happened upon was led by Isaiah.

God of the waters.

The Skraelings hated water, and they hated and feared Isaiah because of who he was. When the One had been with them and had wrapped them in his power, they had been able to ignore Isaiah, even approach him.

But now, with the One vanished . . .

The Skraelings did not like Isaiah. He made them feel not only uncomfortable, but also ashamed of themselves, and they could not understand why.

Thus they had slowed as they approached Isaiah's army, and now they prevaricated, and sent ahead this Skraeling, one of their leaders, the most courageous of them, to see what they could discover.

The Skraeling decided to bluff, to see if he could startle Isaiah into revealing some information.

"We demand to speak to the One," the Skraeling said, wishing he didn't slaver so when he spoke. "Now."

"The One is gone," Isaiah said. He was watching the Skraeling carefully, and the Skraeling was feeling more uncomfortable than ever.

"We know you're hiding him," he said. "We'd like to speak to him." He only barely stopped himself from saying "please".

Isaiah narrowed his eyes, and didn't speak.

"Please," the Skraeling finally blurted. He was beginning to wish he hadn't started on this conversation.

"The One is dead," Isaiah said.

The Skraeling grinned, now feeling more sure of himself. "No," he said, "the One is not dead. Only . . ." he stopped, adopting what he hoped was a sly expression. "We know you have him. We'd like to speak with him. Now."

The tip of Isaiah's tongue emerged, touching his upper lip, and the Skraeling understood that Isaiah was himself uncertain and unsettled, and so the Skraeling felt more comfortable.

"The One is within my camp?" Isaiah said.

The Skraeling, who had no idea at all, suddenly saw the means to create mischief.

"Yes," he said, "and we'd like to speak—"

But Isaiah was gone, striding back through the sea of pink birds, and the Skraeling was left standing, staring after him, wondering what it had accomplished.

Isaiah strode back to Lamiah.

"We need to go back to camp," he said. He paused, staring toward his army. "We need to speak with Hereward."

CHAPTER SIX

Elcho Falling

Axis sat, elbows on the table, leaning his head in his hands.

At the other end of the table StarDrifter was giving his opinion—loudly and very volubly—of Inardle's proposal that she and Axis go to the Skraelings.

Egalion, Garth Baxtor, Georgdi and Insharah sat, utterly silent, watching Axis and listening (as if they had a choice) to StarDrifter's thoughts on the matter.

The worst thing, Axis decided, was that whatever Star-Drifter said it would make no difference. He had seen from the faces of the other four men that they were all in favour.

Stars, how had Inardle won their support?

No, that wasn't the worst thing. The worst thing was that he could feel, deep deep down within himself, a bright flame of interest in the idea.

Oh, how good it would be to get out of this cursed beautiful prison of a citadel and be doing *instead of always* reacting!

The idea of looking danger in the face and slipping underneath the cordon of Lealfast who besieged the tower appealed to Axis; the idea of riding wild across the plains in an attempt to save Isaiah appealed to Axis, and the idea that he could soon meet with the friend he had thought dead was even more appealing. Even the idea of trying to outwit the loathsome Skraelings appealed to Axis, although he shuddered at the title of Lord of the Skraelings for himself.

And, above all, he could leave behind the problem of the Dark Spire, which had now broken through into the next basement level and was growing ever upward. No one had a way of stopping it and Axis was beyond frustration in trying to find a solution. *Damn it! If Maximilian could escape, then why couldn't he?*

If only Inardle hadn't been the one to suggest it.

If only it didn't depend almost wholly on Inardle for its success.

If only it wasn't Inardle who Axis would have to ride wild with across the plains.

He'd much prefer Georgdi. Why in all stars' names didn't Georgdi have some magical affiliation with the Skraelings?

Suddenly Axis had a thought . . . ride . . . horses . . .

"The plan can't succeed," he said, raising his head out of his hands.

"It has problems, yes," Georgdi said, "but—"

"Inardle said she could get just one person and one person only out of Elcho Falling with her, yes?" Axis said, waving StarDrifter into silence.

Georgdi nodded slowly, wondering where lay the trap.

"No one else?" Axis said.

"No," Georgdi said slowly, exchanging an anxious glance with Insharah.

"We won't be able to get horses out," Axis said. "If Inardle's power is so weak—" he could not resist the jibe, even though she was not present to hear it "—then she certainly cannot spirit out horses for us as well. Oh yes, she can fly, but I can't. I, at least, will need a horse . . . more than one if we are to travel fast. So you suggest it is feasible that—" Georgdi was starting to smile, which worried Axis, but he ploughed on regardless "—I somehow manage to walk all the scores of leagues to wherever Isaiah is before the Skraelings eat him into the dust? The plan doesn't make sense, Georgdi. It is an enjoyable fantasy, nothing more."

Now Georgdi was leaning back in his chair, grinning widely, his fingers laced across his chest. Suddenly he took a deep breath and let out a piercing, three-toned whistle.

Everyone in the room jumped, and Georgdi laughed.

"Learn that whistle, Axis," he said.

Axis just glared at him.

Georgdi was clearly enjoying himself hugely. "Outlanders always plan for the loss of horses. We leave horses to run freely across the plains, and, in the event that we lose our own mounts, all we need do is whistle that pretty little ditty and, if any horses are in the vicinity, they will come. Those tones carry long distances. Sit and wait an hour or two and you never know what will turn up. Just take a couple of bridles with you—if Inardle wants to ride instead of fly—and you will have your horses. I am certain there will still be many left roaming the plains. When I was riding to meet with you at Elcho Falling we left scores of them behind. They'll still be about. Shall I tell Inardle that you'll be leaving in an hour or two, then?"

CHAPTER SEVEN

The Outlands

Isaiah marched through the camp to Hereward's tent, Lamiah a step or two behind him.

He couldn't get out of his mind the image of the blood spurting out of the healed scar on her neck at the same time as the One had vanished.

That had to be of some significance.

Hereward was standing outside her tent. Her face was white and strained and she had her arms crossed protectively in front of her.

She kept glancing in the direction where the Skraelings were gathered, and she looked very, very scared.

But was she truly? Isaiah wondered.

"I need you to come forward with me," he said.

"Why?" Hereward said.

"I need you to come closer to where the Skraelings are. I want them to see you."

"No! *Why?*"

Isaiah studied Hereward. She looked terrified—as a normal Hereward should, having previously almost lost her life at the claws of a Skraeling.

But *was* she a "normal" Hereward?

Isaiah was still not as powerful as he had been once—it seemed his abilities were returning at their own sweet pace—but, still, he should have been able to scry out whether or not Hereward was other than what she should be.

He should have been able to scry out the One's presence in her.

What if the One hadn't died? What if he had simply

shifted existences? And if it wasn't Hereward, then who else within this vast army?

Isaiah could ascertain nothing about Hereward. It was as if his power probed at a brick wall. He couldn't even tell if she were a mere woman, let alone the One in disguise.

That worried him more than ever. She was a kitchen steward, in the name of the gods. She shouldn't have the ability to resist Isaiah's probing.

"Why do you want me closer to the Skraelings?" Hereward said, and Isaiah could hear the fear in her voice.

"Because they have asked to see you," Isaiah said, and took her by the elbow.

"Isaiah?" Lamiah said.

"No!" Hereward tried to pull out of Isaiah's grip, but he was too strong and, ignoring both her cries and Lamiah's puzzled expression, Isaiah pulled Hereward forward, closer to the southern border of the camp.

She protested all the way and as they drew close her protests gave way to tearful entreaties, but Isaiah closed his ears to her. He dragged her all the way through the juit birds, stopping just inside their southernmost edge.

The Skraeling still stood a little distance away.

"Well," Isaiah said to it. "Is this what you wanted?"

"I have no idea what you mean," the Skraeling said, his face all creased in what appeared to be puzzlement. Then his face cleared a little. "Would you like me to eat her?"

Hereward wailed, clearly terrified.

"No!" Isaiah hissed at the Skraeling. "I thought you wanted to talk with . . . her."

"And make friends?" said the Skraeling, now apparently enjoying himself enormously.

"No!" Isaiah hissed, and the Skraeling grinned hugely, then turned about and shuffled back to the mass of his fellows.

"What is going on?" Lamiah said to Isaiah, who still gripped the elbow of a fear-stricken Hereward.

"I don't know," Isaiah said, looking at Hereward. "I just don't know."

Hereward finally jerked away from Isaiah and, moving as

fast as she could, pushed her way through the birds toward the camp.

Isaiah watched her go, his face hard. "I want a guard put on her, Lamiah. I want no one to speak to her or go near her apart from giving her food."

"Isaiah—"

"I don't *know* what is happening here, Lamiah. I don't know what the Skraelings are doing, or what they want. I do not know why they haven't attacked."

"Why Hereward?"

"I have told you about the One."

"Yes, yes."

"I have told you that DarkGlass Mountain has been destroyed and the One along with it."

"Yes. Isaiah—"

"The Skraeling told me the One was still alive. It intimated the One is now in our camp. I think the One may be residing in Hereward."

Lamiah now shifted his gaze to the retreating form of Hereward. "How sure are you?"

"There *is* something wrong about her, Lamiah, but I cannot scry it out. It is a 'new' wrong, and dates from the moment of DarkGlass Mountain's destruction."

"Then as you order," said Lamiah, "so shall it be."

He set off after Hereward, and Isaiah turned one more time to watch the Skraelings. They were still waiting, watching, and Isaiah thought he would give his right arm right then and there to have his questions answered.

"Well?" said the several other Skraelings as they milled about the one they had sent out to talk with Isaiah. "What should we do? Attack? Eat? Go around them?"

The Skraeling who had spoken with Isaiah shook his head. "Just wait. There is something happening. Something coming. We wait. If Isaiah moves, then we follow."

"Did Isaiah know where the One is?"

The Skraeling grinned. "He has no idea."

The other Skraelings did not share his amusement. "Then what are we to do? The One has gone, we have no direction.

No one to tell us where to go and what to do. Should we go home? Home to the frozen northern wastes?"

A great murmuring arose among the Skraelings.

Home to the frozen northern wastes.

"No," said the Skraeling. "We wait a while, and watch, and see. I think . . ."

"What?"

"I think there is something coming."

CHAPTER EIGHT

Elcho Falling

"The last thing you need to do," Georgdi said as he rubbed a little more dirt into the lines of Axis's newly shaved face, "is to look like the StarMan setting off to save the world. The Lealfast are sure to see you wandering along, so you need to look as much like a shepherd as possible."

Axis did not reply. He was already in a foul mood, and the fact that Georgdi remained resolutely cheerful was driving him even further into ill-temper. He'd had his hair dirtied and dyed so it looked a faded brown, his beard was gone, he'd been forced to dress in clothes that bore more than a passing resemblance to rags, he had no weapon apart from a small eating knife, and Inardle was leaning against the far wall watching him with an expressionless face that Axis was sure hid amusement.

"You do realise you won't be able to use your power, don't you?" she said.

Axis glared at her.

"Any Lealfast within a league will feel it," Inardle said. "Don't use your power, don't touch the Star Dance."

"I understood you the first time," Axis said. "But I still am not sure how you can hide us from the Lealfast. I thought you could still see each other when invisible."

"There are two ways of invisibling," Inardle said. "The second way will also hide us from Lealfast sight. It is difficult to accomplish; thus, the reason I can only take one other with me."

Axis gave a small shrug, as if indifferent to her response.

"Be careful, Axis," Georgdi said, the humour gone from his face and voice.

Axis nodded. "And you be careful of Elcho Falling, Georgdi. Don't take any nonsense from your underlings."

The others in the room—StarDrifter, Egalion, Star-Heaven and Insharah—managed to smile at that, although their humour faded quickly in the tense atmosphere.

"Travel down the coast to begin with," said Georgdi, "then strike inland. Hopefully, you will run across Isaiah and his army soon enough."

"And, hopefully, it is before you run into Kezial," Insharah said. "Maybe stick to the coast for four or five days, Axis. Kezial will be inland." He looked at Inardle. "You will stay invisible?"

"For the most part," she said. "I can hide myself better from my fellows that way . . . materialising to walk with Axis would be catastrophic."

Thank the stars for that, Axis thought. At least he'd be travelling virtually on his own. There would be little opportunity for them to ever speak, let alone look into each other's eyes.

"It is dusk," Georgdi said, glancing at the window. "Time to go, soon."

"The Strike Force are ready with a diversion to take the Lealfast's attention from the entrance to Elcho Falling and its causeway," StarHeaven said.

"Just remember that it can't *look* like a diversion," Axis said. "Otherwise the Lealfast will be ignoring you and feeling their way along the causeway with their fingertips to discover what is trying to escape from this damned tower."

Axis had not felt this edgy for an extremely long time. Trying to escape Elcho Falling under the noses of the Lealfast was a massive risk, and one which could easily see him dead.

He didn't care a jot about Inardle. If it came to it, Axis knew he'd have no problem tossing her to the Lealfast and escaping while she was being torn apart.

That made him remember how his daughter Zenith had died, and he looked at his father, knowing that the connection with StarDrifter was so close that StarDrifter would catch his thoughts.

StarDrifter gave a small nod, then came over and embraced his son. "Stars shine on you, Axis."

"I have talked to Josia," Axis said, "and he will contact Georgdi or you if there is anything you need to know."

StarDrifter nodded. "I have got used to the idea of having two sons, Axis. Make sure you *do* come back."

Axis and Inardle stood just inside the great arched entrance to Elcho Falling. They were very close, and Axis was extremely tense. He hated that all he could think about was Inardle when all he should be thinking about was how to survive the next few minutes and then hours.

Egalion and Georgdi stood to one side. The Strike Force were due to stage a distraction in the next few minutes—but as none of the Enchanters risked using their mind voices lest the Lealfast pick up their thoughts, Axis needed to depend on others to let him know the best time to leave.

He looked at Georgdi, who looked toward one of his men positioned on the great staircase.

"Not yet, StarMan," Georgdi said, looking back to Axis.

Axis repressed a sigh, shifting the pack he had on his back. It didn't contain much—a bit of food, a rough bridle, a bed roll, a few coins, flints to make a fire should he be fortunate enough to find fuel . . .

Nothing else to aid him or to identify him.

Suddenly the man on the staircase looked upward, then turned to Georgdi and gave a signal.

"Now!" said Georgdi.

Axis wanted to say something, share one last moment with Georgdi, but Inardle grasped his wrist and Axis gasped as frost penetrated deep into his arm until it felt as if the bones had been frozen.

"Now," Inardle whispered, and pulled Axis forward.

Axis found it difficult to do anything but think about the pain in his arm. He stumbled slightly, then found his footing.

Everything about him seemed grey. Even Georgdi, staring in his general direction with a surprised expression, seemed cloaked in grey hues. Axis looked at Inardle, and found that he could barely make her out. There was a faint gleam from her eyes, and he thought he could see the rime of frost on one shoulder, but if it had not been for her painful grip around his wrist, Axis thought he'd miss her completely with any stray glance.

"Move!" she hissed, and Axis started forward.

They slunk out a side door set deep into the arch—not even the keenest eye would see it open briefly before closing again. There was a sound from high above, some mocking laughter, the beat of wings, which Axis assumed was one or two members of the Strike Force hovering close to the boundary of Elcho Falling's protection zone and taunting the Lealfast.

It was almost full night outside and Axis and Inardle started their way down the causeway, sliding their feet through the thin covering of water over the causeway's surface so that splashes would not attract any attention. They remained very close. Axis could feel Inardle with every move, feel her hand on his arm (and, stars, now that cold ache was gnawing into his shoulder), feel her hip brush against his, feel her breath from time to time across his cheek.

There was movement in the air above them, a Lealfast swooping low, and Axis' heart lurched in his chest.

Inardle's hand tightened even more—if that were possible—and Axis felt understanding seep into his mind. Not words, just understanding. *Don't look up. Don't use your power.*

Axis wanted to hiss and snap at her, but couldn't, so he kept on grimly, one careful slide of foot through water after another, every muscle in his body tense, his heart thudding in his chest.

And again, the feel of another winged creature in the air above him, the sweep of wings, the swish of their passing.

Axis could feel Inardle growing ever more panicky. There was something happening that he could not discern, something going wrong that she understood, but could not (or would not) share with him.

Damn it! Axis wanted to shout his frustration, or at least ask Inardle what had gone so wrong, but he could do nothing.

They were halfway across the causeway now, drawing closer to the deserted Isembaardian camp.

Then Axis saw a figure walk out from behind one of the tents, and stand, looking down the causeway toward Elcho Falling.

It was Ravenna.

Axis prayed to every god he had ever known or had heard vague rumour of, that Ishbel had indeed stripped Ravenna of her power, because otherwise Ravenna would be able to see them as clear as day. He glanced at Inardle, wondering if she had spotted Ravenna, but saw by the gleam of her eyes that she was staring into the southern skies. She intuited Axis' look and caught his eye, then tipped her head once, twice, to the sky in the south.

Axis had no idea what she was trying to say. He wished she would communicate with him as she had a few minutes ago, but apparently Inardle was too scared to even use that means.

Again she tipped her head south and now Axis thought he could see pure panic in her eyes.

He stared south, hating to take his eyes off Ravenna, and suddenly his stomach dropped away in horror.

The stars in the southern sky were obscured by a moving cloud.

Oh dear gods! It was the Lealfast Nation about to arrive!

Then that horror was eclipsed by a sudden rush of wings as Eleanon alighted on the causeway some ten paces in front of Inardle and Axis.

They stopped dead, staring at him, barely able to breathe.

Eleanon turned about slowly, his eyes narrowed, looking about.

Axis held his breath, fighting pure panic at Eleanon's arrival, and the sudden dramatic increase of pain in his arm as Inardle intensified the power she used to cloak them.

Axis hoped Eleanon could not see through it.

Then he thought . . . what if he *can* see through, but will pretend not to? What if this is all a fabrication on Inardle's part? *What if this is all a plan she and Eleanon had devised long before to trap me?*

But Axis could feel Inardle trembling and feel her heart beating alarmingly fast through the touch of her hand on his arm. If she could pretend this level of terror, then she was far better than Axis thought.

Before them Eleanon had stopped to look south. He raised his arms, waving them slowly, and sent out a long, soft undulating call to his approaching fellows.

That call prompted Inardle into action. She started forward again, slowly pulling Axis with her.

She wanted to get past Eleanon and through the camp on the other side of the causeway before the might of the Leal-fast Nation dropped down around them.

Axis knew their disguise was good, but it would not save them amongst a quarter of a million bodies bumping about the Isembaardian camp—and Axis had no doubt the approaching Lealfast were heading straight for it.

Why not? It had all the tents and beds and cooking equipment they could need.

Axis and Inardle were very close to Eleanon now. The causeway was not particularly wide and they shrank together as they drew level with him.

He moved, turning slightly, and from the corner of his eye Axis saw Inardle look downward, removing the gleam of her eyes from possible detection.

Axis hurriedly did the same.

Stars, if Eleanon reached out now he would touch them.

They edged past, every movement minutely careful, and so terribly, terribly slow. Eleanon was looking just to their left, when his eyes began to slide their way . . . and then, so suddenly it made both Axis and Inardle jump slightly, there was the rush of wings overhead and Bingaleal landed in the spot where Axis and Inardle had been standing just a moment previously.

Inardle's grip tightened more, and Axis had to bite his lip to avoid groaning with the pain of it. It felt as if the bones of his entire arm, shoulder and now some of his upper ribs had frozen solid. Even breathing was painful.

"They are almost here," Eleanon said, and Axis had to

remind himself that Eleanon was speaking to Bingaleal, and not to himself or Inardle.

"It is a shame they will not arrive in the daylight," Bingaleal said. Both of the Lealfast men were turning to stare south again, and Axis allowed himself a small measure of relief as he and Inardle picked up their pace.

"It would make a grand showing for Axis if they had," Eleanon said. Then, "What was the fuss with the Strike Force . . . or whatever happens to be left of it."

Bingaleal laughed. "Several of the Icarii came out to taunt us . . . and then one of the stupid arrogant idiots got caught within one of the revolving rings . . . she was lucky she didn't get herself killed."

Axis made a mental note to reward the Strike Force member who had been that brave. StarHeaven, he thought.

He and Inardle were moving faster now, drawing away from Eleanon and Bingaleal and close to the shoreline. Ravenna still stood waiting by one of the tents, but all her attention was on the sky rather than the causeway.

Then, gratefully, they were on firm ground and able to move faster. Her power still cloaking them, Inardle pulled Axis into a half trot, leading him through the deserted encampment on an angle to take them southward.

There was a heaviness in the air. Axis could almost feel the weight of the Lealfast Nation approaching, and could also sense Inardle's increasing anxiety.

"My arm," Axis risked murmuring. It now felt as if it were on fire, and he did not think he could bear the pain for much longer.

"Not yet!" Inardle hissed. They were running now, almost at the boundary of the camp, and it was not a moment too soon, for behind them Axis heard a soft roar of beating wings and excited greetings.

The Lealfast Nation had arrived at Elcho Falling.

CHAPTER NINE

The Outlands and Isembaard

Isaiah sat cross-legged before Hereward. He held her chin in his hand with a tight grip and her eyes with his own fierce gaze.

Did Hereward harbour the One?

Hereward stared back, both with anger and with fright. Isaiah had retreated into his full aloofness and power as god-Tyrant—any closeness they had once shared was completely gone and utterly forgotten.

Would he kill her?

Isaiah could see that Hereward thought he would. There was terror and resignation in her eyes, along with all that anger, and he didn't know what to make of it. He tightened his fingers slightly, sending his power deeper and deeper into her being . . . and yet still he encountered nothing but un-broachable walls and dead ends.

Was she hiding something? Or was it that Hereward had somehow managed to block him out through sheer force of will? Heavens alone knew she disliked him enough for such to be the case.

There were others in the tent: Lamiah and several of his senior captains. They stood restlessly, shifting occasionally from foot to foot, glancing among themselves before look-ing back at Isaiah and Hereward sitting close together. They, too, thought Isaiah would likely kill her.

They wanted it over and done with, so they could go back to the business of rallying the army against the Skraelings massing to the south. Hereward wasn't worth the trouble . . . if Isaiah wanted her dead, so be it.

"She's Ezekiel's daughter," Isaiah said, quite suddenly, and Lamiah and the other men blinked.

Ah, no wonder he hesitated . . . or was it due to something that had grown between them on their journey from the Lhyl into the Salamaan Pass?

Isaiah simply did not know what to do. He was now certain the One had escaped whatever destruction Ishbel and Maximilian had wrought at DarkGlass Mountain . . . and the Skraeling seemed to believe that the One had taken up residence within Hereward. There had been that strange re-opening of Hereward's neck wound at a particularly crucial moment, and her tarter-than-normal demeanour afterward.

Did that mean the One had taken refuge within her, or were all of these clues a subterfuge? Did the One simply want Isaiah to believe he'd taken up residence within Hereward? Wanted Isaiah to waste his time on the woman while the One lurked elsewhere?

Isaiah hissed in exasperation, and released Hereward's chin with a little shake.

She leaned back from him, trembling in a release of tension.

Isaiah rose to his feet in a fluid movement and turned to Lamiah. "Guard her with several men. She is not to be left alone at any point. She is to have no privacy afforded her, and every word she says is to be reported to me. Tell those men who guard her to do so as if their lives depended on it, for well they might."

With that he was gone.

Maximilian rose toward wakefulness, enough to feel Ishbel beside him and tighten his arm about her so that they cuddled tighter together. The reed boat rocked gently in the night breeze and Maximilian spared a thought for Serge whose turn it was to sit by the tiller and watch their way upriver.

He sighed, comfortably warm, and sank deeper into sleep.

After a few minutes he began to dream.

Maximilian found himself walking atop a cliff. To one side the cliff plummeted down into a placid sea, to the other, hills rolled away into infinity. Grass and meadow flowers cushioned the passage of his feet.

Maximilian walked on, enjoying the breeze and the scent, but feeling a trace of anxiety which he could not define.

Time passed.

As he walked, so his anxiety levels increased. Now he could recognise the feeling. He was here to meet someone, but they were out of reach.

Not yet here.

But coming.

Maximilian began to feel ever more fretful. He sensed no danger from this person, but he did understand that he needed to meet with him (*him, it was a man*) as soon as possible.

The man had a message of great import for Maximilian.

Maximilian began to toss and turn in his sleep, finally jerking fully awake.

He lay on his back for a long time, staring at the beams of the deck above him.

He did not sleep again that night.

In the morning Maximilian sat by Avaldamon as they ate breakfast. He waited until the others were chatting between themselves, then, in low tones, told Avaldamon of what he had dreamed.

Avaldamon frowned. "You dreamed of the Otherworld," he said. "Someone who has passed over needs to speak with you."

"But they could not reach me," Maximilian said. "I felt they were struggling to do so, but could not. What does that mean?"

Avaldamon thought for a moment. "Possibly that they have not yet completed their journey into the Otherworld. It takes a while, sometimes. Nonetheless they are terribly anxious to meet with you, and it is their tension that has pulled you into the Otherworld to wait for them in your dreams."

Maximilian sat, his empty bowl held loosely in his hands, watching the land slip past. They still had not seen any live animals or people on the land, although the river was full of frogs and fish and eels, and even one or two of the great water lizards.

"Who has died and wants to contact me?" he said, softly. "Why?"

"Someone with a powerful reason," Avaldamon said. "This is not ever done lightly."

CHAPTER TEN

Elcho Falling

The Lealfast Nation landed in a massive swarm of wings and greetings and drifting frost. They revisibled themselves a few paces above the ground so that it appeared to anyone watching (and that was most of those within Elcho Falling) as if a great wave of snowy wings suddenly appeared rolling and breaking along the far shore of the lake surrounding the citadel. There were hundreds of thousands of them, almost a quarter of a million, and within an hour of the first one landing the Lealfast Nation took up the entire western shore of the lake where the abandoned camp of Armat's army stood.

"How much gear and food did you bring in with you?" Georgdi asked Insharah as they stood on a balcony watching.

"Absolutely none of it," Insharah said.

"Then the Lealfast will be well fed," Georgdi said dryly, and Insharah nodded in agreement. "What did you leave behind that can be used against us?"

Insharah thought a moment. "We brought in most of our hand weapons . . . but there are engines of siege there, Georgdi, and military supplies . . . gods alone know what they can find useful."

Georgdi sighed.

Eleanon and Bingaleal spent most of the first part of the night in greeting their fellows and helping to organise them into the abandoned encampment. They had recognised its potential and, while the Lealfast could indeed live on wing and air for extended periods, they vastly preferred more corporeal accommodations and comforts.

And comforts they had aplenty. There were tens of thousands of tents fully equipped with bedding, supply dumps of food and clothing and medicines and other sundries, stocks of fuel and water. Neither Bingaleal nor Eleanon felt there was any real threat from Elcho Falling: after the debacle of the Strike Force, and after that the horror and deaths in getting the Isembaardian army inside Elcho Falling, both felt it was highly unlikely either of those forces might assay back *out* of Elcho Falling in the near future.

Not against the Lealfast.

Everyone within Elcho Falling was well and truly trapped.

Late in the night, a few hours before dawn, Eleanon and Bingaleal were sprawled before a large fire with several other of the most senior Lealfast. They had eaten well, and were getting slightly inebriated on some of the liquor that the Isembaardians had left behind.

The Lealfast rarely drank alcohol, and when they did it did not make them drunk in the same manner as humans or the Icarii. Rather, it gave them a sense akin to sexual arousal—a mildly erotic sensation that tingled up and down their nerves and left thick trails of frost over their bodies.

Eleanon was feeling very mellow, pleased with himself and the situation. He and Bingaleal had told their fellows—Falayal, Sonorai and Kalanute—what had transpired since last they met, and Sonorai had told them what news the Nation had, as well.

"Have you heard from the One?" Falayal asked Eleanon and Bingaleal.

Both birdmen narrowed their eyes, then Eleanon spoke. "No. He remains quiet . . . lest he be discovered, I suppose."

"What should we do?" Kalanute said, his words very slightly thickened with alcohol-induced arousal.

"As we always planned," Eleanon said. "Within Elcho Falling rests the Dark Spire." He held out his hands, and for a moment an image of the crazed twisted form of the Dark Spire appeared between them. "We can use it to destroy the citadel—if we wish—or to take it for ourselves . . . and the One, of course. The spire is growing with the power of Infinity, but under my direction."

It wasn't quite what Eleanon had planned for the Dark Spire, but it was enough for his fellows. He could take them further into his confidence later.

"And when will we be taking Elcho Falling?" Sonorai said. He spoke this with no impatience or ill-will, merely a languid curiosity.

"When we can be utterly certain of victory," Eleanon said. "We tried once and failed . . . Elcho Falling even rejected the One. The next time we attempt to take the citadel, we must be certain of victory. The One, even now, works his way with the unwitting occupants of Elcho Falling. We will take our time, brothers, but we will succeed."

"And where is our dear sister, Inardle?" Kalanute asked. "I miss her and this wine," he made a lewd gesture, "is making me think most ardently of her."

"Inardle preferred to throw in her lot with the StarMan and Lord of Elcho Falling," Bingaleal said. "She is lost to us. You must sate your desire on another of our sisters this night, Kalanute."

Kalanute laughed softly, now stretching a little. "Such a shame, for I particularly desired Inardle . . . but, as you say, there are others."

"Then perhaps Inardle is inside Elcho Falling slaking *her* lust with the StarMan," Sonorai said.

Eleanon and Bingaleal exchanged a glance and a small smile.

"What?" Sonorai said. "A secret? Share, do!"

"Inardle and Axis may well be slaking their lust somewhere—although personally I think they might still be trembling in too much fear to even think of it—but I can assure you they are not doing it inside Elcho Falling," Eleanon said.

Falayal, Sonorai and Kalanute all raised their eyebrows.

Eleanon gave a soft laugh. "Axis and Inardle 'escaped' Elcho Falling this evening, slipping out under the cloak of Inardle's power. She thought I could not see through it . . .

but I am aided by the power of Infinity, and they were immediately apparent to me. The moment they left Elcho Falling I knew of their presence."

"You allowed them to escape?" Kalanute said, all amorous thoughts driven from his mind.

"Why not?" Eleanon said. "I am curious as to what they might do . . . although I, as Bingaleal, am certain where they go."

"And that is . . . ?" Sonorai said.

"To offer their aid to Isaiah," Bingaleal said. "Isaiah and his army are two weeks or so distant. Isaiah leads them straight for Elcho Falling, believing he can be of some assistance." He uttered a soft, mocking laugh. "Our 'allies', the Skraelings—" everyone smiled derisively "—are with him now, although they seem to be dilly-dallying in some confusion. Isaiah has many things to worry him."

"We saw the Skraelings on our flight here," said Falayal. "I have no idea why they don't attack. They must outnumber the Isembaardians ten to one."

"They are likely missing the direction of the One," said Bingaleal; and the others nodded.

The Skraelings would have no idea what to do now that their master had fallen silent.

"I am assuming you will keep Axis and Inardle under observation," Kalanute said to Eleanon.

"Naturally," Eleanon replied, and the conversation drifted on to other matters.

Eleanon leaned back against the pile of blankets he was using as a cushion and tuned out the conversation. He was feeling mellow indeed: happy to have the Lealfast Nation here, happy that Axis and Inardle—the fools—had had no idea he was aware of them the entire time (stars, Eleanon did not know how he had not burst out laughing while they were edging around behind his back), and just happy with the entire situation. The One was safe in his hidey hole where he could work the most damage (and yet not interfere with Eleanon's plans), the Dark Spire still throbbed in the heart of Elcho Falling and all would be well in time.

Then Eleanon's senses sharpened as he saw a movement at the corner of his eye.

He rose, drawing queries from the others about the fire.

"It is nothing to be worried about," Eleanon said. "Forgive my absence for an hour or two."

Then he was gone, skirting the fire as he stared intently at something at the edge of the camp and walking into the night.

CHAPTER ELEVEN

Elcho Falling

Eleanon reached out and caught at Ravenna's elbow. "My dear," he said.

She tried, and failed, to pull away from him. "Leave me be."

"No. You fascinate me," As indeed she did, although Eleanon was aware that currently his fascination was due more to the effects of the alcohol than anything else.

They were just outside the camp, and Eleanon led Ravenna further into the night, putting distance between them and the Lealfast Nation.

"What do you want?" she said.

"To talk. To investigate a little more deeply this curse Ishbel has cast on you. If I know how it works, then I understand Ishbel a little better."

What he wanted, of course, was to alter it slightly, turn it to his own use.

"I want to go."

"Nonetheless you keep trailing about Elcho Falling, drawn to it like a moth to the fire. Or is it Maximilian you lust for? He has gone now, I believe. I have heard that he and his lovely, lovely wife have been up to some mischief at DarkGlass Mountain."

Eleanon turned Ravenna so that she faced him, and took both her shoulders in his hands. "You yearn for Elcho Falling, yet your curse keeps you distant from everyone. How is the baby, Ravenna?"

She blinked, confused by the sudden change of subject and made anxious by the pressure of his hands on her shoulders.

"I . . . I am not sure," she said. "I suppose he is well enough."

"Not sure? Truly? This is your child, the heir to Elcho Falling! And you are not sure?"

"Ishbel made it that he is no longer heir to—"

"Ah, but this is still Maximilian's child, yes? Of course. Then this baby still has some connection to him and his pretty citadel. Besides, what can be wound can also be unwound. It is, after all, what Ishbel specialises in."

"You can unwind this curse?"

"That is not what I said . . . but, well, who knows." Eleanon pulled Ravenna closer despite her reluctance, pressing her body against his and running his hands over her shoulders and down her back.

"It is so strange to feel a woman with no wings," he murmured. "How can you bear it?"

She struggled. "Let me go."

"Stay." Eleanon was pressing her more tightly against him now.

"I don't want to . . ."

"What? What don't you want?" He tried to kiss her, but Ravenna twisted her face out of the way.

"Don't do this to me."

"Are you not glad that I *can* stay this close to you? That I *can* touch you? That I *can* subvert Ishbel's curse to this extent?"

"I am glad—now leave me alone."

Eleanon hated the arrogance in her voice. Ravenna's haughty contempt, particularly given her current circumstances, could well outdo even the self-importance of the hated Icarii.

It made him want to hurt her, just a little bit.

And he knew precisely how to do it.

"You could be useful to me, Ravenna."

"Leave me—"

Eleanon grabbed her face with a hand, twisting his fingers in cruelly deep, then kissed her as hard as he could. There was no passion or comfort or even much arousal in his kiss—it was meant purely to humiliate.

"You do not respond," he said when he finally raised his mouth. "Am I not as good as the Lord of Elcho Falling?"

"Get away from me!" she hissed, and Eleanon smiled. There was fear in her voice now, stronger than her arrogance.

"I mean to investigate this curse of Ishbel's," he said, "as closely as I might."

And twist it to what I want.

Ravenna was fighting back, but Eleanon still held her easily. He lifted a leg and kneed her violently in her groin, bringing her struggles to an abrupt halt as she bent double, gasping for breath, both arms now wrapped protectively about her pregnant abdomen.

He hit her again, this time using his fist to punch her in the side of her head.

Ravenna fell to the ground, moaning, half senseless, and Eleanon knelt beside her. He bent over, running his hands up and down her body, feeling her both physically and with his power, scrying out the twists and turns of Ishbel's curse.

It was powerful. Eleanon felt it as dark bands of some gruesome material . . . *blood, it was blood!* . . . that wrapped about her body like a cocoon. He could slip his hands between them here and there, finding Ravenna's vulnerable flesh, but he could not unwrap them.

No matter. He could *isolate* them.

"You are very lovely," he murmured, now using a knee to prise her legs apart, "even with this cumbersome belly of yours."

Ravenna cried out, struggling weakly, but it was of no use against Eleanon's strength. He penetrated her body and mind, using spiteful fingers of power to probe deep into her thoughts as he also moved his body inside hers, leaving long agonising trails of hurt wherever he went.

Ravenna screamed, then again, and then yet again, unable to bear the pain.

Eleanon smiled. He enjoyed her agony and was glad it was necessary in order to freeze a little bit of Ishbel's curse into uselessness.

"You think Ishbel your enemy," he said, finally rising

from her body, "but she is nothing compared to the enemy I will become if you do not do as I command."

He stood, adjusting his clothing and looking at Ravenna as she wrapped herself about her belly, sobbing.

"I have frozen the part of Ishbel's curse that isolated you from others," Eleanon said conversationally. "People will still feel uncomfortable about you and wish to move away from you, but you will be able to stay in their presence. The other aspects of her curse—your isolation from the Land of Dreams and the disinheritance of your son—remain in place."

Eleanon paused. "Don't wander too far away, Ravenna. Sooner or later I am going to be needing you. Who knows, you may get the chance to see your true love once again. Maybe he'll reconsider this time."

CHAPTER TWELVE

Elcho Falling

Georgdi stood on the balcony, bathed in the mid-morning sun. Across the lake, Armat's former military camp seethed with Lealfast. They glinted in the sun, the lines of frost on their eyebrows and on the ridges of their wings sending shimmers of light sparking into the air and surrounding countryside.

It was a stunning spectacle, but it did nothing to lighten Georgdi's mood.

Then he tensed in alarm, straightening his back and sliding his hand down to the knife in his belt.

A window had appeared in the air some two or three paces out from the edge of the balcony. In that window sat a young dark-haired man, regarding Georgdi with considerable amusement.

Georgdi allowed himself to relax slightly, although he rested his hand on his hip, close to the knife.

"You must be Josia," he said.

"Indeed," said Josia, "and it is with you I must chat now that Axis has vanished." Something crossed Josia's face, almost irritation, but then the smile returned. "Do things go well in Elcho Falling, Georgdi?"

Georgdi gave a short laugh. "We eat, dance and are merry," he said. "Light entertainments are all that is left to us now that we lie under such heavy siege."

"It must be galling to you, sir, to be so confined."

"I am an adaptable man." Georgdi injected a light tone into his voice, wondering what Josia wanted. There was something about the man that riled Georgdi, but he couldn't put a name to it, and he thought it must be just a projection of his frustration at being, indeed, so confined within Elcho Falling.

He was an Outlander, born and bred for the vast open spaces of the plains, and house confinement of any description abraded his nerves.

"Do you have any news of Maximilian and Ishbel?" Georgdi said.

"Axis told you of their success at DarkGlass Mountain?"

"Yes."

"The One is gone and all Maxel and Axis need to fret about are the approaching Skraelings and," Josia waved a hand behind him, "these winged creatures. I am sure Axis can—"

"Do you have any news of Maximilian and Ishbel?" Georgdi asked again. Josia was really starting to irritate him, and Georgdi knew now it wasn't just frustration at his own confinement.

He didn't like the man.

"None interesting enough to relay," Josia said. "They have begun their journey home, which shall take them a good few weeks as I am sure you realise."

"Then is there *anything* you need to discuss with me?"

Josia's mouth curved in a very small smile. "No. Not really, Georgdi. I just wanted to get your measure."

He was gone, then, before Georgdi could even open his mouth to reply.

Gods, that man was annoying! Georgdi had no idea why Maximilian and Ishbel seemed to think him such a friend and confidante. He turned to walk back into the command chamber then he stopped suddenly, his heart thumping.

Two surprises in just a few minutes. Georgdi didn't think he could take much more of an escalation in surprises this day.

One of Elcho Falling's servants stood just inside the doorway. He was half shrouded in shadow so that Georgdi could not see him clearly, but he could easily make out his form.

As soon as the servant saw Georgdi react he stepped into the light, bowing his head slightly in greeting.

"And what can I do for *you*?" Georgdi said.

"We, too, make ourselves known to you," said the servant. "You need only to think your need of us and we shall be here."

"You speak for Elcho Falling itself, do you not?"

The servant bowed his head again.

"What do you think of Josia?" said Georgdi.

"We are glad he resides only in his Twisted Tower," said the servant.

Georgdi grunted in amusement. "I had not thought of it that way, but yes . . ."

"Just remember that words can often be as harmful as weapons or power."

"Is that a warning?"

Again the servant inclined his head, but in a manner that could have meant anything.

"Well," Georgdi said, "thank you . . . I suppose." He paused. "May I ask something? Is there any way in and out of this fortress other than by the front door?"

The servant smiled.

"There *are* chambers as yet undiscovered," he said.

The servant leaned closer to Geordi and the two spoke quietly for some time.

An hour later Georgdi met with Egalion, Insharah and Ezekiel. Neither Maximilian nor Axis had consulted much with the once most senior of Isaiah's generals, but Georgdi liked Ezekiel and valued his opinion.

"I am tired of all this sitting about," Georgdi said, lacing his hands over his chest as he leaned back in his chair and looked at the other three.

Both Ezekiel and Insharah grinned, and Egalion narrowed his eyes thoughtfully.

"And what do you plan to do about it?" Egalion said.

"I have heard so much about the Isembaardian military prowess," Georgdi said, "and yet I have not had an opportunity to view it firsthand. You've done a great deal of moving from place to place—and in *my* land, may I point out—but little to demonstrate your great reputation."

"Are you about to give us a chance to demonstrate it, then?" Ezekiel said, leaning forward a little, his eyes bright.

"And you and your Emerald Guard," Georgdi said to Egalion, ignoring Ezekiel for the moment. "What you did that night the Lealfast attacked was extraordinary. I'm betting Maximilian has never allowed you very far off the leash in all the time you have trotted about in pretty green columns at his back."

Egalion chuckled. "Either you are trying to make us angry, or you have a plan, Georgdi. I think the latter."

"I have always been a great fan of the unexpected," Georgdi said. "Axis expects us to sit here and hold the fort for him. Maximilian expects everyone to sit and twiddle their thumbs awaiting his glorious return. The Lealfast think to have us trapped impotent in this citadel. No doubt the Skraelings scampering their way toward us also think we sit around dreading their arrival. Well, I am sick of all this sitting. I'd like to see what you and your commands can do, and I'd like the chance to show you what the Outlanders can do."

"Not the Strike Force?" Ezekiel said.

"The Strike Force can sit this one out," Georgdi said. "They've had their chance."

"And you think to . . ." Insharah said.

"Look," Georgdi said, finally unlacing his fingers and sitting up straight, "we cannot free ourselves from the Lealfast siege, but I see no reason why we cannot make things uncomfortable for them. I think some niggling, embarrassing action could unsettle them enough to make them do something stupid. They do have an awful lot of Icarii blood in them, after all."

"Never say that in front of Axis, or StarDrifter or Star-Heaven," Insharah said.

"*Am* I saying it in front of Axis, or StarDrifter or Star-Heaven?" Georgdi said. "No? Then don't worry about it. Any of those three would want to plan some grand—and no doubt foolish—action which would see too many of our friends dead. I don't want to do that. I'd rather see none of our friends dead. Just a *little* bit of action is all I ask for."

Georgdi smiled as he reached into the leather pocket of his jerkin and pulled out a small square block of brown fibrous material.

"Do any of you know what this is?" he said.

His smile broadened at the looks of puzzlement on the faces of the other three.

"It is a block of pressed seed pods from the falamax plant," Georgdi said. "Falamax grows fairly widely on the Outlands' plains and our people often carry a small block like this on their persons. Many of my warriors here do. The falamax plant is a fairly innocuous shrubby perennial that is remarkable for one thing only—the value of the spores contained within its seed pod. Mostly we use it for cooking purposes." Georgdi turned the block over in his fingers. "A tiny bit of this crumbled into our food gives flavour along with a mild intoxicating and warming effect."

Georgdi paused. "But if this is crumbled and blown into the wind, and if someone *inhales* it, well then . . . then the falamax spores become a powerful hallucinogen."

"Ah . . ." Ezekiel said, and he grinned.

CHAPTER THIRTEEN

Elcho Falling

StarDrifter stood with Georgdi, Insharah and Egalion on the balcony where earlier in the day Georgdi had conversed with Josia. It was almost full night and across the lake the Lealfast were settled in front of fires, drinking what was left of the Isembaardian wine. There were a hundred or so in the air, barely visible, but the majority were in the former Isembaardian military camp.

"I don't understand," StarDrifter said, "why you don't use this trick to mount a full-scale military assault on the Lealfast?"

"Because I am not completely sure how this will affect the Lealfast," Georgdi said, "or how long any effect will last, or even if I have enough of the falamax pods to affect *all* of the Lealfast. I am not going to commit every man in this citadel to action, without knowing if I may lose every last one of them."

He pointed down to the causeway. "The only viable way we can exit and re-enter is via that causeway." Georgdi *had* heard of another possibility from Elcho Falling's servant, but it was even more unfeasible than the causeway. "It is narrow. To start with, I can't get many men out without everything becoming congested or taking six weeks to accomplish, nor can we retreat without the same problem. I take sixty men with me and sixty only. I just want to make a point, StarDrifter, but it is going to be a damned good point."

"And you're going to have some fun," Insharah said. He was a little out of sorts because he was to be left behind, but Georgdi hadn't wanted to risk every commander they had in the citadel. Georgdi and Ezekiel would be going with the sixty men—comprising twenty Isembaardians, twenty Outlanders and twenty Emerald Guard—but Insharah and Egalion would remain within Elcho Falling.

"*And* I am going to have some fun," Georgdi said. "StarDrifter? Can you do this?"

StarDrifter glanced at Georgdi disbelievingly. "Of course I can do this. But won't the spores affect you as well, when you go into the Lealfast camp?"

Georgdi shook his head. "We'll give it two hours . . . the spores do not last long in the open air and will disintegrate. By the time we sally forth it will be safe."

StarDrifter picked up a large wickerwork basket full of crushed and crumbled squares of falamax pods. Georgdi had earlier collected the squares from his men . . . now it was up to StarDrifter.

"Just be careful you don't inhale any of it," Georgdi said, taking a precautionary step back.

StarDrifter closed his eyes and counted to ten, finding within himself the means to ignore that unnecessary remark.

Then he fixed his eyes on the basket and began to weave magic out of the air.

It took a moment or two, but soon a ribbon of spores rose slowly from the basket, higher and higher into the air. Gradually, the ribbon of falamax spores broadened and moved over the lake toward the Lealfast encampment.

There the ribbon widened and thinned until it covered the entire camp, then, infinitely gently, the spores drifted downward.

Eleanon lay slouched about the fire, as he had the previous night. He felt warm and content, and slightly inebriated once again.

He wondered if Ravenna was anywhere close, and was vaguely thinking he might go look for her when, close by, Bingaleal looked into the air in terror.

"We're under attack by gryphons!" Bingaleal shrieked, pointing upward.

Eleanon took a moment to ponder the fact that he didn't feel like reacting very energetically to this pronouncement despite the terror and urgency in his brother's voice, before, equally unsurprised, he saw one of the Lealfast who had been patrolling the skies about Elcho Falling fall directly into the fire.

Bingaleal was on his feet, shrieking over and over that it was a gryphon.

The Lealfast in the fire was writhing and shrieking, too (not particularly surprising, Eleanon thought, again somewhat amazed at the tranquillity of his thoughts), and shouting something about misshapen giants attacking the outer perimitter of the camp.

Misshapen giants, Eleanon thought. *How ridiculous. He has been drinking too heavily of the wine.*

Still, he supposed he should do something about the situation. He yawned and stretched, rising to his feet to watch, puzzled, as something bulbous and warty (the ghastly result of a mating between a warthog and a bull?) stepped up behind Bingaleal, then gutted him with its horns.

Bingaleal staggered a few paces away, clutching at his belly. He dropped to the ground with a nauseating wet thump.

"Oh," said Eleanon.

The creature then turned to Kalanute and Sonorai, standing to one side observing Bingaleal's misfortune with wide, glazed eyes, and gutted them as well.

Then it turned to Eleanon, and for the first time Eleanon felt terror.

The creature waved its bloodied and gore-streaked horns at Eleanon, and spoke. "I might come back, Eleanon. One day, when you are asleep. Do you *dare* sleep ever again, do you think?"

Georgdi looked at Eleanon who had, finally, begun to shriek in horror. Then Georgdi laughed as Eleanon pissed himself.

"I hope you remember *that* in the morning," Georgdi said, waving his bloodied sword at the dark stain running down Eleanon's breeches, then he turned and shouted the order for his men to retreat into Elcho Falling.

As he jogged toward the causeway, Georgdi began to

laugh. The entire encampment of Lealfast was in turmoil. The spores had tumbled those Lealfast in the air straight down onto the encampment as they forgot to fly amid their hallucinations—at least thirty had burned to death on camp fires. Meanwhile, Georgdi, Ezekiel and his men had run amok through that area of the camp closest to the causeway. Georgdi had personally killed a score of Lealfast, and thought most of the others had managed a similar feat.

Georgdi reached the start of the causeway then stood, counting the men who now headed back into Elcho Falling.

Fifty-eight . . . fifty-nine . . . sixty . . . and now Ezekiel, bringing up the rear.

Not a single loss.

Ezekiel was laughing as well, and Georgdi thought the man looked thirty years younger. Georgdi clapped his hand on the man's shoulder, and together they jogged back to Elcho Falling.

At dawn, Eleanon stood on the shore of the lake, staring at Elcho Falling and nursing a raging headache. He had used his power to wrap the Lealfast camp in an invisible, thin barrier—not enough to repel an arrow or even a bird, but enough to keep out whatever airborne hallucinogen had been directed at them last night.

They would not be caught out again.

Eleanon's headache was currently being made worse by the fact that the One had decided to make contact and was screaming into his mind.

Fool! Fool! Did you not for a single moment think they might try something like this?

"Shut up," Eleanon said, very quietly. He wanted silence, so he could concentrate his hate.

They had killed Bingaleal.

Fool, I say it again, and again! Fool! How could you not have anticipated—

And you did not *anticipate, did you?* Eleanon shot back at the One. *You did not know what was happening. Do you not have Georgdi's ear, then? You were as fooled as I.*

I wanted to see if you had the skills at hand to manage even this. I wanted to see if you could pass this one single test. I wanted to see if—

Eleanon shut the One out. He'd had enough of the One and he'd had enough of doing the One's bidding. Fuck him.

He was going to take revenge for last night, and he was going to damn well do it on his own terms.

"You think to humiliate *me*?" Eleanon whispered to Elcho Falling and all its inhabitants.

Not today. Not tomorrow. Maybe not even next week.

But not too far away, either.

They would all die now, and Elcho Falling would be torn down and trampled into the dust.

Meanwhile, there were Inardle and Axis.

Eleanon had to vent his fury somewhere, and his curiosity about what they might do with Isaiah was now at an utter end.

CHAPTER FOURTEEN

The Outlands

A xis kept his heels close to the flanks of the horse, moving it at a slow canter, riding ever further south. He'd found the horse about noon on the first day out from Elcho Falling by using Georgdi's whistle. Now, two days after his escape with Inardle, Axis had a small collection of horses trailing along behind him, enough that he could change mounts several times a day and keep pushing the pace.

He was relaxed but watchful. He enjoyed *doing* something, but he was very aware that danger lay all about. Yesterday evening Inardle told him that Kezial's army rode just to the west, moving toward Elcho Falling. They would be there very soon. Axis hadn't seen them himself, but he kept an eye out for any scouts.

And then there was the possibility of the Lealfast. Axis still couldn't believe that he and Inardle had escaped from Elcho Falling unnoticed—whatever Inardle said, Axis preferred to keep his options open as to whether or not Eleanon had realised their presence. Lealfast treachery was always a possibility, and every few minutes Axis would raise his eyes and scout the sky—a fairly useless activity since the Lealfast could travel virtually invisible. He knew he'd never spot an individual Lealfast.

There was something niggling at the back of Axis' mind, something that made him believe there were Lealfast following him. Axis couldn't define the feeling and this close to Elcho Falling he didn't want to use his power lest Eleanon pick it up, but he tried to reason to himself that Eleanon would normally have scouts patrolling and that they'd be curious about any activity . . . even what appeared to be a lone goat or sheep herder.

Axis was a little less worried about Isaiah's situation. According to Inardle, Isaiah was at least a week ahead. She had told Axis the previous night that the Skraeling army had caught up with Isaiah, but had not yet attacked.

That was good news, but it also concerned Axis. He wondered why they'd not attacked.

It wasn't like the Skraelings. What were they planning?

Inardle had asked if he wanted her to contact Isaiah, but Axis had said no.

He didn't want Inardle engaged in any conversation with Isaiah of which he was not a part. Of course, Axis had no way of knowing if Inardle had or had not talked to Isaiah . . . with her abilities, she could certainly have travelled the distance to meet with him . . . so Axis contented himself with the thought that if he found out she had disobeyed him and contacted Isaiah, he would kill her.

It would be reason enough.

Axis had not actually seen Inardle since their escape. Shortly after they'd escaped the descending Lealfast, Inardle had taken to the sky. Now she travelled high above him, as would any Lealfast who wanted to remain unobserved. She did not join his small campfire at night.

Instead, the only contact Axis had with her was when she invaded his dreams as he slept. He hated this so much that he had tried to stay awake these past two nights, even though he'd needed his rest, but he never succeeded and always drifted into sleep at some point.

Axis would feel her before he ever heard her voice—a disturbing presence at the edge of his mind. Inardle would slip into his dreams coyly, Axis glimpsing her in the shadows of whatever dream had engaged him, passing back and forth, back and forth; she came forward only when he'd reached a point of such exasperation that he was close to waking.

I have news, she would say, and Axis would grind his teeth, even in sleep, and be forced to ask her to speak it. And so Inardle would relate whatever it was she had seen from her vantage point high in the sky that day, and then she would ask how he was, and then Axis would dismiss her.

Often the only way he could do this was to force himself awake. He'd lie there in his blanket, cold even though the fire would always be stoked (*had she done that just before she'd entered his dreams?*), and tremble with anger.

Axis just wanted to reach Isaiah . . . although it didn't sound as if Isaiah still needed his help.

If nothing else, Axis was enjoying the ride. The horses were good—strong obedient animals fit enough to keep up a canter for many hours at a time—and the scenery was spectacular. For the time being Axis was keeping to the coast, as it was easier to avoid any scouts Kezial might have out and about. Later, when he was certain Kezial's army was well behind him, Axis meant to angle inland so he could intercept Isaiah.

The land in the northern coastal Outlands consisted of low, rolling grassy hills above steep cliffs that plummeted a hundred paces down to the pounding surf of the Infinity Sea. It was easy going for the horses, and pleasing for their rider. The weather was mild now that the seasons had turned away from winter and into spring, the air fresh. The constant low roar of the surf and the cries of the sea birds wheeling overhead calmed Axis' nerves.

The only thing he missed was company. Axis was not a loner by nature, always enjoying the company of good friends . . . either in a fight or a journey.

Here he had only Inardle.

That night Axis established a camp in the lee of a rocky formation some fifty paces back from the cliffs. He used the carcass of a long-dead tree for wood and started a roaring fire, not particularly caring who could see it. His disguise lay in his visibility. He ate a simple meal from the diminishing supplies he carried with him in his pack, replenished the supply of wood he had to one side for the fire, then unrolled his sleeping blanket and prepared to settle for the night.

Just as Axis was stretching out though, Inardle suddenly appeared, fully visible, on the other side of the fire.

Axis was so startled—and so angry at her incaution—that he jerked to his feet.

"What are you doing?" he hissed. "If anyone sees you they will—"

"Bingaleal is dead," Inardle said, then stunned Axis by starting to cry silently.

"What?" Axis said. "How?"

"I don't know the details, but I felt his death. It was last night. I have been heavy with grief all day. I—"

"Inardle, what are you doing so visible? Someone can easily see you . . . I have felt other Lealfast about and—"

"They have gone, recalled to Elcho Falling by Eleanon. Axis, I do not know the details, but there was deceit and murder, and it involved Georgdi."

Axis grinned, all his humour returning. Trust Georgdi to come up with some scheme to create mayhem among the Lealfast. Axis wished, very deeply, that he'd been there to take part.

Inardle's face tightened at Axis' smile. "He was my brother!"

"Forgive me if I do not share your grief. Besides, have you not spent hours telling me how the other Lealfast are lost to you now? I do not understand these tears."

"That is because you have no understanding of love, Axis."

Now Axis lost his humour. "I am glad he is dead. I am not even going to pretend any sorrow or concern for your grief. I hope Georgdi managed to take a few more of your fellows out as well. Now, is there any other news you wish to share? You threaten me by appearing about my campfire, and I am not sure I should believe you when you say that our Lealfast watchers have gone. If Bingaleal can be so easily tricked into death, then you can just as easily be tricked into believing whatever our watchers want you to believe."

Inardle rose to her feet. "I have no idea why I stay with you."

"Because you have nowhere else to go, and no one else who wants you. Inardle . . . do you still believe Eleanon did not know of our presence when we left Elcho Falling?"

"If he had he would have killed us."

"Maybe so and maybe not. I am keeping on alert none-theless."

"I would not weep for you, Axis, if you died."

Axis sighed. "How far is Isaiah now? How long before I reach him? And what is happening with the Skraelings who trail him? Or have you been too lost in your grief today to take note of any of these matters?"

Inardle took a step back from the fire, her form beginning to frost over and then fade.

"Four or five more days of riding should bring you to Isaiah. Angle inland on the day after tomorrow. Maybe you will hit his force at the wrong spot, Axis, and find the trailing Skraeling gaggle instead. I hope to the stars they eat you."

With those words, Inardle vanished completely.

CHAPTER FIFTEEN

Elcho Falling

Kezial reined in his horse, raising his fist to shoulder height to bring the column behind him to a halt.

He'd watched as Elcho Falling had risen—he'd been able to see it on the horizon—and his sense of awe had not abated one bit as he'd ridden closer.

Neither had his sense of danger.

Everything was wrong about this.

Armat should have sent riders with messages (orders, knowing Armat) many days ago.

There should have been Isembaardian scouts everywhere.

Nothing.

There had been some Lealfast overhead, but they had not deigned to descend to speak to him, and even if they had, Kezial would not have trusted them. He'd heard from Armat's messengers (before they all became strangely absent) that Armat had humiliated the Lealfast in a battle in the central Outlands and that they had joined Maximilian in Elcho Falling when that weakling had raised the citadel.

But now . . . everything felt wrong.

The column behind him, sixty thousand men strong, was fully armed and battle ready. Kezial had his own scouts reconnoitring, and knew that a great mass of Lealfast, hundreds of thousands of the creatures, were camped about the shores of Elcho Falling.

Why were they not inside the citadel if they were Maximilian's toys?

And where was Armat? Where his army?

And why were there no Icarii around? Kezial had expected to see them in the skies above.

At least the Lealfast hadn't attacked Kezial or his forward scouts, but again that fact made Kezial nervous.

If the Lealfast were allied with Maximilian, then rightfully they should have attacked his scouts. If the Lealfast were not allied with Maximilian, but now committed to their own cause, then they should still have attacked Kezial's scouts . . . if for no other reason than they had no cause to love any Isembaardian after what Armat had done to them.

That left the possibility that the Lealfast were now allied with Armat.

But if that was so, *then where was Armat?*

Kezial could make no sense of it at all.

Everything made his tightly drawn nerves vibrate, sensing danger.

He currently sat his horse perhaps an hour's ride from Elcho Falling. He could see it clearly: the walls rising as water and then crystal and then stone, high into the sky, the three golden rings revolving slowly about its peak, the lake of turquoise water surrounding the citadel . . . and the enormous encampment of Lealfast that Kezial could now see through his eyeglass and who, to his dismay, were occupying Isembaardian tents.

Kezial sat his horse and wondered if he should simply turn around his army and ride away while he still could.

But ride to where? His homeland was gone, and what else was there of any worth in this godforsaken land save this extraordinary citadel?

Then Kezial tensed even further.

There was a Lealfast approaching in the sky, and, much further back, a rider coming forth from Elcho Falling.

Armat.

The Lealfast man held back until Armat had come close to Kezial (now on full alert and with armed men twenty thick behind and to each side of him), then landed a few paces out from Kezial.

He held out his hands to show that he wasn't armed, which did not relax or impress Kezial greatly. He knew the Lealfast had powers beyond that wielded by any sword or dagger.

"Who are you?" Kezial said.

"My name is Eleanon, and I speak for the Lealfast," the man said. "Perchance you have heard of me?"

Kezial grunted. Indeed he had heard of Eleanon. "Were you not the one in charge of that rout when Armat—who I see is but a moment's ride away now—skewered tens of thousands of you out of the sky?"

The pleasant smile on Eleanon's face did not slip. "It was but four or five thousand, and it was done to my purpose at the time."

"Which was?"

"To make Axis StarMan think us fools."

"And I should somehow believe that you are not?"

"I hope to convince you of that," Eleanon said. He looked behind him as the sound of hooves grew loud and stepped very slightly to one side as Armat reined in his horse.

"Armat," Kezial said, very carefully. He did not like the look on Armat's face. He could not put a name to his concern . . . but Armat did not look himself.

"My friend," Armat said, and smiled broadly.

Both words and expression sounded and looked so false that Kezial actually reined back his horse a step or two. He noticed also that Eleanon's smile had broadened a little at Armat's words.

"What is happening here?" said Kezial. "Speak quickly and plainly, one or both of you, for I am feeling too nervous to rest here for hours listening to involved histories of the past weeks."

"I have allied with Maximilian," Armat said, and Kezial gawped at him.

"*What?*" he said.

"I ride forth to show my goodwill and to ask that you, too, ally with Maximilian within Elcho Falling and—"

"Neither Maximilian Persimius nor his wife, nor even Axis StarMan, remain in Elcho Falling any longer," Eleanon said. "Elcho Falling is left under the command of a group of sub-lieutenants. Armat speaks false words."

"I speak truth!" Armat said, and for an instant Kezial thought that sounded more like the real Armat.

"Armat is a puppet," said Eleanon. "He has been cursed by Ishbel Persimius so that he speaks only the words of his puppet-master, which is why he sounds so false. His puppet-master is, I believe, Insharah. What you hear issuing from Armat's mouth is not what Armat wants to say to you—undoubtedly those words are seething, trapped beneath the surface of the curse—but what the traitor Insharah wants you to hear."

Now Kezial was more confused than ever. "Insharah? I do not understand . . ."

"Let me explain," Eleanon began, and Kezial thought that he was starting to sound the more genuine of the two by far.

"If you listen to Eleanon then you will die," Armat said. "He is allied to the very darkness issuing forth from Infinity itself. He—"

Eleanon roared with laughter. "Oh, come now, Insharah—for I shall not pander any more to the pretence that this is Armat who speaks. That is too implausible to convince even a toddler."

He turned to look Kezial fully in the eye. "I and the Leal-fast are the only things of truth and good heart left standing in this mess, Kezial. The Outlander general Georgdi has assumed command of Elcho Falling after Maximilian, Ishbel and Axis departed for better climes, or should I say, fled in the face of the Skraeling invasion that approaches and which they fear greatly. Elcho Falling has been abandoned to fools and traitors."

"But Armat's army . . ." Kezial said, looking between the two of them and not knowing what to think.

"Mostly dead," said Eleanon. "Killed by treachery."

"False!" Armat said. "Kezial, it is *I* who speaks to you now, and *I* say to you that my army is now inside Elcho Falling and mostly intact save for those that this creature—" he flung a hand out at Eleanon "—murdered on their way in. If you see the Lealfast now encamped in what had been *my* encampment, then know they do so only through the spilling of good Isembaardian blood."

Lord gods, Kezial thought, *I am sure I can hear truth in those words.*

"I am the way forward," Armat said. "Ally with me, Kezial, and with Elcho Falling, and you will live."

Kezial looked at Elcho Falling, and wondered how, if this was so, Armat expected him to get through the several hundred thousand Lealfast huddled about what appeared to be a single entrance, without a bloody and debilitating battle.

"Let me show you how false are Armat's words," Eleanon said, and he lifted both hands.

The next moment Kezial gasped. Black bands of dried blood appeared, wrapped about Armat's body.

"This is the curse with which Ishbel wrapped Armat," Eleanon said. "Armat is virtually dead. He commands no power and can offer you no alliance. He speaks only what the traitor Insharah—who you can blame almost completely for the slaughter of Armat's men and your comrades—"

Kezial remembered how Armat's messengers had mentioned that Insharah had abandoned Maximilian for Armat.

Insharah must have meant to betray Armat and his army all the while.

Eleanon looked at the expression on Kezial's face, and knew he had won. He stepped forward, lifted his sword and, as Kezial and his men raised their own swords at this sudden threat, ran Armat through so that he toppled from his horse.

"If that *had* been Armat," Eleanon said as he ran his sword over a tussock of grass to clean it, "then he would have defended himself. As it was, a mere puppet, his master could not get the words to him quickly enough to save his life. Now, Kezial, let me speak plain and true to you. Between us, we can win Elcho Falling. The force that is inside—consisting of a few hundred Icarii, some renegade Outlanders and the pitiful remnants of the Isembaardians now under Insharah's control—cannot hope to hold it for much longer. Why don't you join me, Kezial, and partake of the riches of power and glory that Elcho Falling contains?"

"Why ask me to ally with you?" Kezial said. "Why not take it for yourself?"

"Because you will be useful," Eleanon said.

Kezial looked at Eleanon, and knew he was looking at a murderous and treacherous liar. He did not trust a single word the Lealfast man said.

Nonetheless . . . Kezial raised his gaze and looked up at Elcho Falling in the distance. The one thing Eleanon did not lie about was the power and glory and potential of Elcho Falling. As Armat had before him, Kezial sat there and lusted.

He was also not sure he could defeat the Lealfast in any confrontation. Best to ally with them, for the moment, and learn their strengths and weaknesses.

Then he lowered his eyes to Eleanon. "Shall we discuss terms?" he said.

Very late that night Eleanon walked out beyond the Lealfast camp.

In one hand he held a bag.

He walked for a while, then stopped, his teeth flashing momentarily in the darkness. "Come, come now, Ravenna. Did you think I wouldn't find you?"

She sighed, barely audible, then walked a little closer to Eleanon. Her steps were hesitant and her face gaunt and lined.

"You look terrible," Eleanon said.

Ravenna didn't respond.

Now it was Eleanon who sighed. He tossed the bag toward her, and she flinched as it landed to one side of her feet.

"Food," said Eleanon. "I thought you might be grateful."

"Thank you," she whispered.

"I have a new ally," Eleanon said.

"I saw."

"Ah, nothing escapes you, does it? I doubt Kezial will be very useful, but one mustn't turn away allies when they appear. Did you see what happened to Armat? Your friend?"

She stared at him, silent.

"I ran my sword through him. He was but a puppet, anyway. Useless. I am sure that Insharah must be grateful he doesn't have to feed him any longer. So, out of the three of you that Ishbel cursed, why, there is only little Ravenna left."

"I wish I were dead, too."

"Doubtless, but wishes are not going to do you any good. Now, we need to discuss something."

Ravenna tried to take a step back, but Eleanon closed the distance between them and grabbed her wrist, making Ravenna gasp in fear.

"You will go nowhere," Eleanon hissed, "until I command it of you! You live and breathe only at my wish, Ravenna."

She stared at him, then dropped her eyes, and Eleanon's grip loosened fractionally.

"Good girl," he said. "I have some work to do here, Ravenna, to make you the best servant possible, and it may hurt a little. Do try not to scream. My people sleep close by."

Ravenna tried to pull away, but Eleanon was too strong. He dragged her very, very close and grabbed her face with his other hand.

"Don't worry," he said, grinning at the horror in her eyes, "you won't feel the caress of my loving this time. You might wish you did, though. It might have been preferable to what I am going to do."

He altered his grip on her face, digging his fingers deep. "Do you know what I command, Ravenna?" he said softly, so softly Ravenna could almost not hear his words over the sound of her own harsh, terrified breathing. "Do you know what I command? A magic, Ravenna, such as you have never seen, not even in your Land of Nightmares. A magic and an object, and tonight I am going to introduce you to it. The Dark Spire. You are going to get to know it intimately, Ravenna, because you are going to midwive its children. You'd like that, wouldn't you, Ravenna? It will give you fine practice for when you birth your own child . . . should it survive."

Eleanon grabbed her consciousness then, as he had grabbed her face, and he wound it with his and with that of the Dark Spire so that the three of them danced together in a nightmarish communion.

Feel it, Ravenna, touch it, know it, and allow it to touch you, and to know you.

Ravenna screamed, her body jerking, but she could escape neither Eleanon's grip nor the embrace of the Dark Spire.

Do you see it, Ravenna? Do you understand what you must do?

"Yes! Yes!" she screamed, wanting only to be allowed escape from both Eleanon and the Dark Spire before either harmed her baby.

Are you sure you understand, Ravenna?

"Yes! Yes! Yes!"

There was but one more thing to do. Eleanon used some of his power, melded with that of the Dark Spire, to endow Ravenna with the Lealfast invisibility. He wouldn't use it now, but when Eleanon sent Ravenna inside Elcho Falling he would enable it so that no one inside would be able to see her.

At least while she had a task to do. After she'd completed that, Eleanon didn't care who saw the sad witch.

Finally, satisfied, Eleanon let Ravenna go, breaking the connection with the Dark Spire as he did so.

Ravenna fell to the ground, white and shaking and moaning.

"You will be able to enter Elcho Falling," Eleanon said. "Not even the citadel will realise your presence. So now, Ravenna, you are perfectly suited to my purpose. To enter Elcho Falling and to midwive the Dark Spire's babies."

CHAPTER SIXTEEN

The River Lhyl, Isembaard

Maximilian jerked awake. Above his head the stars whirled through the velvet blackness of the sky, beside him Ishbel lay warm and completely relaxed in sleep. Behind him, at the tiller, Maximilian could hear Avaldamon draw in a deep breath, then resettle his weight.

This would be their last night in the boat. Tomorrow they should reach that part of the Lhyl where they would abandon the water for the long trek eastward toward the coast and, hopefully, a waiting vessel to take them back north to Elcho Falling.

Maximilian lay, staring at the stars. He'd had the dream again, drawn into the Otherworld by someone's desperate need to speak to him.

Yet still he did not know who, or, more worryingly, what was so important that Maximilian was being drawn into the Otherworld to discover it.

He was wide awake now, with no hope of slipping back into sleep for the remainder of the night. Maximilian drew in a small sigh, letting it out silently, not wanting to alert Avaldamon to his wakefulness, then closed his eyes, and travelled the eighty-six steps to the door of the Twisted Tower.

Perhaps Josia might have some clue.

"It has been a long time, Maxel," Josia said as Maximilian opened the door and entered the tower. "I had thought you to have forgotten me."

Maximilian tipped his head in apology. "I am sorry, Josia. To be honest, I have been enjoying the first relaxing period of time since . . . gods alone know when. Just drifting northward in our small riverboat, with nothing to occupy me save drawing Ishbel close at night and watching the countryside drift past during the daylight hours, has been refreshing. What news from Axis and all at Elcho Falling?"

"Ah, well, Axis has left Elcho Falling. He—"

"*What?*"

"You should have come sooner, Maxel. Yes, Axis and Inardle have left Elcho Falling on some foolhardy mission to save Isaiah from the Skraeling advance. I do not know the full details." Josia turned about, fiddling with an item on one of the crowded tables. "Georgdi is left in charge of Elcho Falling. I do not like him as well as Axis."

Maximilian chewed his lip, wishing desperately that Axis had not left Elcho Falling. Georgdi was a good man, but . . . "Any other news?"

Josia turned back to face him. "The Lealfast Nation have arrived at Elcho Falling, and have taken up their residence in Armat's old camp. Kezial and some sixty thousand men have now allied with Eleanon, who leads the Lealfast. Elcho Falling lies under tight siege."

So much for his unworried days, Maximilian thought. He'd spend the rest of the time before he reached Elcho Falling in a state of sick anxiety.

"Any news of Ravenna?" he asked, and Josia shook his head.

"I have not noticed her," he said.

Maximilian sighed. "Well, that at least is some good news."

"What brings you here now, Maxel?"

Maximilian perched on the end of one of the tables. "I have been having dreams."

"Dreams?"

Maximilian told Josia about his dreams of the Otherworld, of his sense that someone wanted to meet with him quite desperately. "Avaldamon says it must be important, that someone needs to tell me something, warn me of something, very badly."

"Ah," Josia waved a hand dismissively. "It is likely little more than a remnant of the time you spent dead, Maxel. How many hours was that? Two? Three? You hovered at the very border of the Otherworld until Ishbel pulled you back.

I think the dreams are little more than that. Just a shadow of the time you began the journey."

"You think? If so that would be a relief."

"Maxel, I am glad that you found the time to visit with me tonight. I need to see both you and Ishbel urgently."

"Why?"

"You are about to set off on your journey eastward?"

Maximilian nodded.

"Then you will come across Hairekeep."

"Yes," Maximilian said. "The fort sits just beneath the southern approaches to the Salamaan Pass. We'll pass by it on our way to the ports of the eastern coast of Isembaard."

"Hairekeep is stuffed full of Isembaardians, Maxel. You and Ishbel can rescue them. It will be something you can do for this land. I have been watching the fort from the window atop this tower. I can see it, and I think I know how you can free those trapped inside."

Maximilian nodded. "Does Ishbel need to be involved? I feared for her so much in DarkGlass Mountain."

"This task will need both you and Ishbel. Both of you to unwind the One's power and release the tortured souls from their imprisonment. Bring Ishbel back with you the next time you visit and make it soon. I will explain more then."

"And the One? Avaldamon postulates, and Ishbel and I are inclined to believe him, that the One was not destroyed during the obliteration of DarkGlass Mountain, but escaped elsewhere. Do you have any thoughts on the matter?"

"I agree, Maxel. The One is too powerful to have been killed by Ishbel. But as to the where . . . I have no idea. I am sorry."

CHAPTER SEVENTEEN

The Outlands

Axis had been riding for six days and thought he must be close to Isaiah. He'd angled inland as Inardle had told him, riding as hard as he could, using every minute of light available in the lengthening days to push forward.

He had not seen Inardle since that night she'd told him of Bingaleal's death. He did not care. Axis was utterly done with her. He hoped she drifted off somewhere and he would not have to think about her again.

He had not seen Inardle and was happy for that, but Axis *was* growing weary of the lonely ride. He'd always had a companion—someone . . . Belial, Azhure, any number of Axe Wielders, other companions, Star Gods, more recently Insharah or Georgdi.

Now there was no one save himself, and Axis did not always find too much of his own company a good thing.

He was truly looking forward to meeting with Isaiah again.

It was well after noon and Axis was hoping that soon he'd see a smudge on the horizon that would tell him a large army was moving ahead. If luck was with him, if he saw that smudge, then maybe he'd be sitting with Isaiah about a campfire tonight.

Axis' heart lifted at the thought.

He pushed his horse a little harder, his eyes scanning the horizon as carefully as he could. His Icarii blood gave him excellent vision, far better than any pure human, but even so . . .

Damn Inardle for not being here and sharing with him her elevated view.

Axis glanced upward, vaguely hoping that she might

materialise above him and tell him that Isaiah was, indeed, only just over the horizon.

But there were only a few scattered birds, high in the sky.

No Lealfast to be seen.

Of course, Inardle could be invisible and just above him anyway.

"Inardle?" Axis called.

There was nothing but the gentle breeze and the sound of the horse's hooves.

Axis silently cursed her. Inardle was likely hovering directly overhead, knowing precisely where Isaiah was, but refusing to communicate with him out of spite because he had not shared her tears at Bingaleal's death.

Axis rode for a few more minutes. Now he was beginning to obsess about Inardle's lack of response and the fact she likely knew just how much further he had to ride.

Curse her!

For perhaps the first time in his life Axis began to wish he had not refused StarDrifter's offer to coax out his wing buds. It was all very well to refuse when you thought you would always have winged companions who would be true to you and who would always provide you with as much information as they knew, but when you had to depend on someone like Inardle . . .

Winged companions who were always true, and who always provided information . . .

Axis suddenly smiled, looking up into the sky again.

There! An eagle, soaring high above him.

When Axis had been the StarMan of Tencendor, he'd had a venerable eagle often serve as his eyes in the sky. Would this one be as amenable?

My friend eagle? Axis used his power to call out to it, even though he knew such use of the Star Dance would light him up like a candle in a dark cave for any Lealfast about. *My friend eagle?*

The bird said nothing, but it tipped it wings and spiralled down closer to Axis.

My friend eagle, I crave your aid.

You are the StarMan. I know you.

I am indeed, but how can you possibly know me?

My venerable father's aunt had a mate who came from Tencendor. That eagle knew of you and spread word among the eagles of this land of your name and accomplishments.

Then I thank him. Friend eagle, I have need to see through your eyes. May I do so?

It is of no matter or risk to me. You may do so.

The next moment Axis found himself looking, not at the rolling plains before him, but at the world from several hundred paces in the air.

It took him a moment or two to orientate himself, then he began to scan the way ahead.

There was the green smudge he'd been wondering about for an hour or so. It was a small, low-lying wood, mostly thick shrubs with a few trees, and all probably grouped about a spring. Beyond the trees was a vast herd of sheep, perhaps several thousand strong, and their shepherds, who were grouped about four or five horsemen. Axis thought he would instruct the eagle to look closer at that group, but for the moment he wanted to try and spot Isaiah's army.

He focussed beyond the sheep and the trees, the eagle's eyesight now running further and further over that vast expanse of plain beyond the trees . . . and there . . . the smudge that Axis had been looking for. It was many hours away, perhaps not reachable until well after nightfall, but reach it tonight he would.

Axis grinned. Isaiah!

StarMan, the eagle said.

Yes, my friend eagle?

Look with me now behind you, there . . . there . . . not five hundred paces behind you . . .

Axis saw Inardle first. She was invisible, but the eagle's vision picked her up as a distortion in the air that was so detailed Axis could actually see the features of her face.

Damn, he had never realised eagles could see so finely!

Look, StarMan.

Axis could now see behind Inardle, another forty or fifty

paces, and saw a group of about fifteen Lealfast. They were approaching very fast, and they had their bows set with arrows.

Inardle had no idea they were there.

For an instant Axis thought the arrows were meant for him, then he realised the Lealfast were focussed on Inardle, not on him.

Axis reacted instantly. *Inardle!* Axis called, and she looked at him.

Inardle! Behind you!

She looked over her shoulder, and Axis, through the eagle's vision, saw her expression turn from one of mild annoyance to outright fear.

"Shit!" Axis murmured, withdrawing his eyesight from the eagle and reining his horse in before turning it about and booting it back toward Inardle's position.

She became suddenly visible—probably, Axis thought, in order to assist him in aiding her rather than in any attempt to evade the Lealfast behind her—and tilted her wings so that she angled down toward the ground.

Damn it! Axis had no weapons save for a knife. There was nothing he could do to—

An arrow, then five, arced out of the air behind Inardle. She cried out, twisting away so that they all fell useless to the earth, but then came another volley, fifteen arrows this time; and then yet another volley, and then another, all aimed at different points to either side of her.

Axis saw Inardle panic. She didn't know which way to turn and, in her hesitation, left herself open to the arrows.

Two of them thudded into her left wing, and Axis was now close enough to hear her cry of shock.

Inardle tumbled downward, then managed to regain some control of her flight.

Inardle! Get down to me! Axis cried. *To me!*

She heard and angled herself toward him. She was very close now, a moment away . . . more arrows flew around her.

One more hit her left wing, then one to her right.

Just before she hit him, Axis wrenched the horse about so that Inardle thudded into his back.

"Hang on as tight as you can," Axis cried, then booted the by now terrified horse—stars alone knew how fast it could go with the double load—into a gallop.

If only he could get to that stand of low trees.

At the same time, he used the Song of Mirrors to cloak himself and Inardle and the horse in reflections.

With any luck these would be Bingaleal's fighters coming along behind them, and would not realise the deception until Axis and Inardle had managed to reach the stand of trees.

There they might have a chance.

Several arrows thudded into the ground directly in front of the horse, making it swerve in fright. Axis felt himself being dragged to one side by an unbalanced Inardle, and for one terrible moment thought they would both fall to the ground, but at the last possible heartbeat, he managed to pull both of them upright.

The horse was now running wild with fear for the trees.

Stars, give them enough time to make it!

Axis heard the beat of wings directly behind them, even above the pounding of the horse's hooves, and knew they were doomed. The Lealfast were not being deceived by the reflections.

He heard the twanging of bowstrings, then an instant later both he and Inardle cried out as they fell forward over the horse's neck with the impact of an arrow.

Inardle had been clasping Axis about the shoulders, and the arrow had gone through her right hand and into Axis' shoulder, pinning them together.

The pain and shock of impact was momentarily blinding. Axis had dropped the reins in shock, and now attempted to fumble for them again.

His right arm was almost useless.

The beating of Lealfast wings was directly overhead, he could hear them clearly, and Axis was sure they were dead with the next volley of arrows.

Then, stunningly, the scream of an eagle.

Axis couldn't see, he was concentrating too hard on the ever-nearing line of trees, but he heard the *thump, thump,*

thump of impact, and knew the eagle had careened through the group of Lealfast fighters.

Suddenly there was an almighty thud five or six paces to the right of the horse and Axis saw that two Lealfast fighters had hit the ground.

They were not moving.

I thank you, my friend! Axis said to the eagle, hoping it had survived its attack. The sound of Lealfast wings overhead had faded . . . the surviving fighters had likely scattered with the eagle's attack and were now reforming.

The line of trees was finally very close, five or six heartbeats away, and Axis knew what he had to do.

It might kill them both—at best it had the potential to seriously injure them—but he had no choice. It was their only chance.

"Inardle," he gasped. "When we reach the trees, we need to tumble off this horse and burrow as deep as we can under the shrubbery."

"We *can't* . . . the arrow—"

"I know about the damn arrow!" Axis said. "Listen, we have to do this any moment. Just do it! Understand?"

There was no more time for her to complain. The horse had plunged into the line of trees and shrubs and low branches were whipping and catching their legs and bodies.

"Axis!" Inardle wailed, and he felt her tilt to the right, he with her.

"Damn!" Axis had time to mutter before letting himself slide, giving the horse as hard a boot as he could as they crashed to the ground.

The impact was so painful Axis almost blacked out. He felt the arrow tear through the flesh of his shoulder as they tumbled over and over, and then suddenly Inardle's hand was freed and they were separate.

Axis grabbed at one of her arms, pulling her deeper under a dense shrub.

At the same time he reformed the Song of Mirrors wrapped about the horse that was now almost at the other side of the stand of trees and ready, so far as Axis knew, to plunge into the undoubtedly startled sheep and shepherds.

There were cries and the continuing, if fading, sound of the horse's hooves.

Then Axis heard the sound of arrows impacting flesh and he assumed the Lealfast had killed his horse in their belief that the riders still clung to it under the cloaking enchantment.

Then a thump as the horse hit the ground.

Then another thump.

Then several more.

Axis frowned, trying to make sense of it. Was the horse's corpse jittering all over the ground?

Inardle was curled in a ball, moaning in pain to one side, but Axis ignored her.

He was fighting to retain consciousness, fighting to cut through the pain and shock of tumbling off the horse as well as the agony in his shoulder, and couldn't make sense of what he had just heard.

Why had the horse fallen to the ground many times over?

It made no sense, and Axis realised they were still in grave danger. He grabbed at Inardle, trying to get her to her feet so they could run—*Stars, there were footsteps running toward them!*—but she could not even rise to her knees. Axis found himself sinking to the ground again as blackness threatened to overwhelm him.

There was the sound of men, many men, surrounding the shrub under which Axis and Inardle crouched.

Then, impossibly, the sound of soft laughter as someone pushed aside the shrubbery.

"By the gods, Axis," Isaiah said, "I never thought to find the great StarMan himself loitering under a bush!"

CHAPTER EIGHTEEN

The Outlands

The shepherds had built a fire and Axis sank down before it, shaking both from the pain in his shoulder and from the aftermath of the fight. Isaiah had extracted Inardle from the shrubbery, and now helped her to sit beside Axis.

"Isaiah," Axis said. "How . . . what are you doing here?"

"Let me see to your wounds first, Axis, then we can talk," Isaiah said.

"Don't bother with her," Axis said as Isaiah bent closer over Inardle. "She can heal herself."

Isaiah gave him an odd look at that. "Inardle is—"

"She can heal herself," Axis said again, his tone harder. "Waste no pity on her." He looked at Inardle, huddled into herself, her wings and one arm covered in blood, and despised her. Was she going to use this trick on Isaiah, now?

"Normally I could," Inardle said, "but those arrows were poisoned, Axis. They wanted to make sure they killed me. The arrows were tipped with senzial, a poison made from a fungus grown on rocks in the high mountains. It negates any ability a Lealfast has to heal themselves."

Axis grunted, not believing her. He wanted to get Isaiah alone, that he might fully convey the depth of treachery of which Inardle was capable.

"The poison won't affect you in any significant way," Inardle said, and Axis grunted again.

"But it will kill me within the day," Inardle finished, softly.

Axis did not respond.

"Perhaps—" Isaiah said, looking between the two of them at this exchange, then said nothing more as one of the shepherds came up with bowls of herbs steeped in warm water and clean rags so that he could clean the pair's wounds.

"The Lealfast will come back," Axis said. "You'll need to keep an eye out—"

"The Lealfast are dead," Isaiah said, gently lifting out one of Inardle's wings, despite her moans, so that the shepherd might attend to its wounds.

"Dead?" Axis said.

Isaiah nodded to the west, and Axis rose so he could see.

There, some distance from the camp and to one side of the flock of sheep, lay a pile of several Lealfast bodies. Four of Isaiah's men were dragging further corpses over to the pile and gathering faggots so they could burn them.

"They were invisible!" Axis said. "How did you . . ."

Isaiah's twinkling eyes caught Axis' at that moment, and Axis stared. "You have your power back?"

"Every last wonderful piece of it," Isaiah said. "You know that Ishbel and Maxel succeeded at DarkGlass Mountain?"

Axis nodded as he sat down once more.

"Well, the River Lhyl runs again," said Isaiah, "and so also does my power. The One's defeat freed both of us. You shall need to be polite to me again."

Axis laughed softly. "You could see the Lealfast."

"Yes. I used your friend eagle . . . he has been anxious about you, Axis. Anyway, I saw them, and took my bow and my arrow, and directed my men to do likewise, and I allowed them to see with my eyes the vision I received from the eagle, and so the Lealfast died."

"And you are *here* because . . ."

"I could feel you approach. I left the army early this morning to intercept you. And thank the gods I did, eh?"

"At least *this* god I shall thank indeed," Axis said. "You saved my life, Isaiah. Thank you."

"As you did your best to save Inardle's," Isaiah said, finally letting her wing go as the shepherd finished. He sank down before the fire, crossing his legs and looking between the two of them. "There is a story to be told, I think."

"And much news to tell you," Axis said, then winced as the shepherd began to clean his shoulder.

"Then we shall eat and rest, and in the doing you may tell me," Isaiah said, and as he spoke one of his men set a burning faggot to the funeral pyre of the Lealfast and it burst into flame.

CHAPTER NINETEEN

The Outlands

Isaiah sat thinking as he watched Axis and Inardle sitting distanced about the fire. They had talked while they ate (well, while Isaiah and Axis ate, Inardle took nothing), all three sharing news, and now Isaiah was not quite sure what to say. He felt sorry for both of them, but at the same time was angry . . . more at Axis than at Inardle.

Still, their personal relationship was not his problem.

"You actually think," he said to Axis, "to ally with the Skraelings as their lord?"

"What we actually *thought*," Axis said, "was to ride to your rescue. The alliance with the Skraelings was an added attraction."

Isaiah chuckled. "I simply cannot imagine you allying with the Skraelings, Axis. How could it possibly work?"

"Inardle says she can manage it," Axis said.

Isaiah glanced at Inardle. He did not think she would be managing very much at any time in the near future.

It will kill me within the day, she had said, and Isaiah supposed he should see if he could do anything for her . . . but what? He was no god of healing, not of deadly wounds.

Hereward had been simple, but poison? Isaiah decided that Inardle was a beautiful creature who had made some hard and perhaps foolish decisions in the past weeks, and if she was going to die . . . well . . . better her than Axis.

Isaiah decided that the one thing the Lealfast were good at was causing problems.

"You think that the One did not die at DarkGlass Mountain?" Axis said. "That he exists elsewhere?"

Isaiah nodded. "The Skraeling implied that he still lived,

that he transferred elsewhere, and I suspect Hereward if only for the simple reason that her neck wound reopened at the same time I felt the One vanish. I imagine he has taken residence within someone else . . . whether they know it or not. But who? I don't know."

"But you still suspect Hereward," Axis said, and Isaiah nodded again.

They were silent for some minutes, before Isaiah spoke. "We may as well spend the night here, then ride for the army in the morning. There is no point in arriving late at night and Lamiah surely is enjoying the chance to resume complete command."

"We are going to need to think about what happens when we near Elcho Falling," Axis said, for the moment putting to one side the problem of the Skraelings. "Kezial and his army are undoubtedly there by now. They may or may not have allied with the Lealfast, and they may or may not be dead, but whichever way their fate has fallen we are going to face a formidable force. A deadly force."

"Eleanon must control, what, thirty or thirty-five thousand fighters, Inardle?" Isaiah said.

She nodded, clearly in pain, her face drawn and a sickly yellow.

"And the rest of the Lealfast Nation," Isaiah said. "Can they fight?"

Inardle had to clear her throat twice in order to speak. "Many of them, yes. As, I believe, happens with the Icarii, all Lealfast men and women in their youth go through training. They will not be as sharp as the force currently about Elcho Falling—"

Axis winced at that.

"—but they will still be very good. And you must not forget they are now changed by the One. They fought while invisible within Elcho Falling and that was not something my brothers and sisters could do previously."

"If the Skraelings are still in league with the One by the time we get to the citadel," Axis said, "we are going to be in deadly trouble. From what you tell me, it sounds very much as if they are herding you into a trap."

Now it was Isaiah who winced. "Perhaps we will all have clearer wits by morning. Axis, how is your shoulder?"

"Well enough," Axis said. "The shepherd cleaned and stitched it tidily. I am grateful." He nodded toward the second fire, where sat Isaiah's men and the three shepherds. "The Outlanders are good men."

"Indeed," said Isaiah. He rose and moved over to Inardle. He might as well have a look at her wounds, if only to say that he *had* tried. With the way she looked now, he didn't expect her to be alive by morning.

He squatted beside the Lealfast woman. She flinched as he laid a hand to her shoulder, but did not resist while he ran his hand down her arm and lifted her injured hand, unwrapping the bandage the shepherd had placed about its wound.

The arrow had gone through the back of her hand, emerging from her palm. When she and Axis had rolled from the horse, the arrow had ripped its way free, completely tearing through the section of her hand from central palm to thumb. It was a bad injury under any circumstances, worse when it had spread poison through Inardle's system.

The edges of the wound looked inflamed, even green in places, and oozed a vile black muck.

Isaiah put it down, then looked at the other wounds on her wings and shoulders. They were not as bad in terms of initial injury, but they, too, were inflamed and oozed the same muck. Isaiah could feel the heat pumping out from them and realised Inardle must be in considerable pain.

"I am sorry, Inardle," Isaiah said, now placing both hands on her shoulders as he squatted behind her. "I wish I could do something for you, but—"

Isaiah broke off abruptly, frowning. His hands tightened on Inardle's shoulders, the fingers digging into her flesh. She cried out softly, and Axis looked concerned.

"What are you doing, Isaiah?" he said.

"Wait," Isaiah said, his hands moving over Inardle. "Inardle, I am sorry, but this will hurt a little. Just bear with me." One of Isaiah's hands now rested at the nape of Inardle's neck, the other on her chest just above her breasts.

They were pressed against and into her flesh.

Inardle cried out, louder this time, trying to free herself
from Isaiah's grip.

Isaiah sat back, lifting his hands, and Inardle gave a single
sob, choking back tears.

"Isaiah?" Axis said.

Isaiah was staring at Inardle. Then he blinked. "Axis,
may I examine you for a moment? This is an intrusion, for I
am likely to cause you as much discomfort as I just caused
Inardle . . . it is important, more than you can know. Please."

Axis looked at him, then gave a single nod.

Isaiah moved about the fire and placed his hands on Axis as
he had on Inardle. They rested on nape and chest lightly, then
Isaiah pressed hard against Axis' flesh.

Axis had to restrain himself from crying out, too. It was
the most uncomfortable experience, part pain, part fear . . .
the sense of someone else within his body, probing, probing,
probing.

Just when Axis thought he could bear it no more, Isaiah
sat back, lifting his hands.

"Amazing," he murmured.

"*What* is amazing?" Axis ground out through clenched
teeth. He had had to endure Inardle almost freezing off his
arm; now Isaiah was biting his power deep into Axis' body.
Axis felt he'd had enough for this current month.

"Inardle's Skraeling blood," Isaiah said, moving again
to sit behind her. She cringed as she felt his hands on her
once more. "I just felt something deep within her. It was
either her Icarii blood, or her Skraeling blood. I had to examine you to see if you had it in you, but no. It must be her
Skraeling blood."

"*What?*" Axis said.

"Water," Isaiah murmured. "She has a great affinity with
water within her, bequeathed by her Skraeling blood. Inardle, I can help you, after all, but what I will do in drawing
the poison from your body is going to pain you like nothing
you have ever felt before. I am so sorry for this, but I know
of no other way to manage it. But it does mean that you will
live."

"Then do it," she said. "Do it."

* * *

Axis watched, appalled.

Isaiah sat behind Inardle, his legs sprawled to either side of her. His hands rested as they had initially and again they pressed into Inardle's flesh, but deeper this time, the expression on Isaiah's face one of intense concentration.

It caused Inardle to cry out immediately, twisting under Isaiah's hands, but his grip was so tight, so profound, nothing she did could free her of him.

Axis stayed where he was, only moving to give a calming sign to the soldiers and shepherds, who had risen, concerned, at Inardle's first loud cry.

He knew better than to interfere.

Isaiah kept his hands pressed against Inardle's neck and chest for several long minutes, then he moved them, running them all over her body. His hands and fingers pressed deep into her flesh wherever they travelled; occasionally they paused so that he could sink the heels of his hands in as deeply as possible, as if he were collecting great pools of poison beneath them.

Then, very gradually, he began shifting the poison up Inardle's body, from her toes into her torso and toward her shoulders.

All the time Inardle wept and twisted. Axis understood it was not the pressure of Isaiah's hands that caused her so much pain: partly, it was the poison Isaiah shifted through her body, and partly the deep intrusion into Inardle's body of Isaiah's power. Axis thought that he must have endured only a fraction of the discomfort that Inardle must be feeling.

He was shifting water. He was using the water within Inardle to flow the poison back toward the puncture wounds.

Axis was not sure at what point he realised this, but somehow he did. Isaiah was using his own deep affinity with water to manipulate this mysterious water element within Inardle's body, to remove the poison from her system.

Isaiah's hands travelled faster now, from toes to hips, from hips to belly, from belly to breasts and thence to shoulders; and from her fingers all the way up her arms, over the elbows, to shoulders again.

There Axis saw blackness pouring forth from the wounds, more of it than he would have thought, a vile flood of poisonous substances that actually steamed in the cool night air.

It stank, too, and Axis had to swallow on several occasions in order to keep his bile down.

Praise the stars this poison had no effect on him.

As he watched, Axis began to feel guilty about his hard words earlier, insisting that Inardle could heal herself. He wished he hadn't said them, although he reasoned he had actually been entitled to speak them.

Inardle had, after all, very effectively tricked him with her previous, healable, wounds.

Damn it. He wanted to continue to be angry with her, but right at the moment he could feel only sympathy.

Isaiah sat back, finally done. Inardle lay before him, crying softly, arms outstretched, pools of vileness collecting under her shoulders.

"I'll find some water," Axis said quietly, "and some wash cloths." Isaiah nodded at him, and gave him a small smile.

He looked very weary.

Later, when Inardle had been washed, and her wounds bound loosely to collect the last of the poison as it drained forth, Isaiah came to sit with Axis.

"She will be better when she wakes," Isaiah said, keeping his voice low so as not to disturb Inardle's sleep. "Tired, exhausted even, for a few days. But she will recover. She will be able to close over her wounds herself when she wakes."

"Good," Axis said.

"Good?" Isaiah said, a glint of humour in his eyes.

Axis gave a small, indifferent shrug of his shoulders, and Isaiah repressed a wider smile.

"What is this strange 'water' you found within her?" Axis said. "What is its importance? And it came from her Skraeling blood?"

Isaiah took a long time to answer, and when he did it was no answer at all.

"I think maybe this Skraeling alliance is a good idea, after all," he said. "We should meet with them, you and I and In-ardle. But when we do, there shall be one slight change to your plan. I should be their Lord, not you." He grinned. "Isaiah, Lord of the Skraelings. It has a nice ring to it, yes?"

CHAPTER TWENTY

The Twisted Tower

"Maxel, Ishbel, I am glad to see you." Josia beckoned them up to the fifth level of the Twisted Tower where he had managed to clear a space and find some chairs for them to sit on. "Ishbel, Maxel told you why I wanted to see you?"

"Yes," Ishbel said, seating herself. "Hairekeep is stuffed full of souls, whom we need to release. Or are they as yet alive, Josia?"

"Alive," Josia said, giving a smile that lightened his normally serious face. "They are people still alive. In torment of spirit, but alive. Many, many tens of thousands of them."

"In Hairekeep?" Maximilian said. "It is big, yes, but—"

"It has altered, grossly so," Josia said. "It now pulsates with the power of the One. Nothing you could do would ever murder him, Ishbel. He lives. Where, I have no idea. But he lives, and doubtless spends his time plotting your own murders."

Ishbel bridled a little at the "nothing you could do would ever murder him, Ishbel", but let it go. Josia had reason enough not to have kept up with the social niceties after his time spent locked inside the Weeper.

"What can we do, Josia?" she said.

"Look," Josia said. "I have done a rough sketch of the fort as I have seen it from the window on the top level. I could take you there, but . . ."

"We would die, I know that, Josia," Ishbel said, bending forward to look at the paper Josia had produced. "Maxel! That looks a little like the Twisted Tower!"

"A parody of the Twisted Tower," Maximilian said. "It is black, and vile."

Josia nodded. "As is the One. This drawing is bad, I know, but it gives you some idea. The 'fort' is perhaps five times as large as what you saw when riding past it on your way out of Isembaard, Maxel."

"What do we do, Josia?" Ishbel said.

"You unwind it, as you did DarkGlass Mountain," Josia said. "Look," he drew out another page of sketches and plans, "this is where the key foundation stone lies. Unwind that, and the entire edifice falls apart, freeing those trapped inside."

"I can't do it by myself?" Ishbel said.

"For this you will need Maximilian and his power," Josia said. "You complement each other perfectly. And . . . it may be that the One has reinforced Hairckeep since the destruction of his pyramid. It is better you both enter."

"Well," Maximilian said, smiling and squeezing Ishbel's hand, "I for one am happy enough about that. I thought I would die of fear for Ishbel while waiting for her outside DarkGlass Mountain."

"Good, then," Josia said. "How goes your journey eastward?"

"We have left the boat," Maximilian said, "and had thought we'd need to walk the entire distance to the east coast of Isembaard. But a day into our journey we found a small herd of horses who were as happy to see us as we them. So now we ride, and make good time. Can you imagine such luck?"

Josia beamed. "You must truly be blessed by the gods."

CHAPTER TWENTY-ONE

The Outlands

Axis sat sipping the cup of tea one of the shepherds had given him, watching Inardle as she pushed away her blanket and slowly managed to sit up. She was obviously very stiff and, from her numerous winces, still in a fair amount of pain. Axis said nothing, lowering his eyes when she glanced his way, and waited until she, too, had accepted with thanks a cup of tea. He remembered how once he'd had to remind her to thank his body servant, Yysell, for making her a cup of tea, and reflected that at least she'd learned some manners since then.

Then Axis considered what an ungenerous thought that had been. "You are still very sore," he said.

She glanced at him, rapidly dropping her eyes to her tea. "Yes."

"But better?"

"Yes." A hesitation. "I will be able to close the wounds myself now."

Axis bit back a grin at the tightness in her voice. "Is the poison all gone?"

"Yes. Isaiah . . . I don't know how he managed what he did. Or why he wanted to."

"Not everyone hates you, Inardle."

That produced a long awkward silence, and Axis berated himself for his words.

"Inardle . . ."

"Yes?"

"Inardle, I am sorry for what I said yesterday. About you being able to heal yourself."

"You did not know about the poison." Another pause.

"And you had every right to say that, based on my previous behaviour."

Axis drank another mouthful of tea, grateful for the prop. Had any conversation with Azhure ever been this awkward? It was too long ago to remember.

"I am famous for my inability to apologise gracefully, Inardle."

"We both have a great deal to apologise for, perhaps, Axis. But I do not want to start a score sheet."

Axis almost remarked on why he could understand *her* not wanting to start a score sheet on their various wrongdoings, but managed to stop himself. "I already have enough women keeping score sheets against me, Inardle. Please don't add yours to the crowd."

She smiled. It was a slow thing, but genuine, and it relaxed her entire body. "No score sheet, then."

They descended into yet another clumsy silence, saved only by Isaiah who wandered up looking overly fit, handsome and altogether too pleased with himself.

"We should start as soon as you are ready," he said. "Inardle . . . you cannot fly, not yet."

"I can heal myself now, Isaiah. A moment's work only, once I have finished my tea."

"Nonetheless you are still very weak from the poison. You'll need to share Axis' horse as we do not have a spare. Most of your horses scattered during the Lealfast attack, Axis, and we only managed to catch the one you were riding. So I am afraid it means you'll have to share a horse . . . unless you want to borrow a sheep from the shepherds."

Then, bestowing his broadest grin on both Inardle and Axis, he walked off again.

They rode for three hours before they caught up with Isaiah's army and the following Skraeling horde. The ride, at least for Axis and Inardle, was as awkward as their morning conversation had been. They did not speak a word throughout it, Inardle keeping her hands light on Axis' waist, and her body leaning back so that they touched as little as possible.

By the time they sighted the army, Axis had vowed to

himself a thousand times over that he must *always* keep at least one spare horse on hand.

When they were some three hundred paces away, Isaiah signalled them to slow back to a walk.

"I want to talk to the Skraelings first. Axis, let me take the lead here."

Axis had no problems with that. This was the first time he'd seen Skraelings since he'd battled them so long ago when they were vowed to his ghastly half-brother, Gorgrael.

Then they had been so vile, so hated . . . such a nightmare. They had wreaked havoc and murdered too many of his friends and people.

Axis found his stomach clenching, his entire body tensing, as they approached the wraith army trailing the Isembaardians.

Stars, they looked so different. Most of them sported jackal heads, while others had malformed into grotesque horrors.

And half of Inardle's blood was this . . .

"I dislike being their kin too, Axis," Inardle murmured behind him, and he gave a curt nod. He was glad he didn't have to speak to them.

Isaiah signalled the group to a halt as one of the Skraelings peeled away from the horde and made his way toward them. "Just myself, Axis and Inardle will talk with the Skraeling," he said. "The rest of you can rejoin your units."

His men nodded, peeling off to canter toward the Isembaardians.

Isaiah watched them go, then looked at Axis and Inardle. "Whatever happens here," he said, "let me do the talking. It may seem strange to you, but I have my reasons."

Axis and Inardle nodded.

The creature approached with a lumbering gait, and Axis' face twisted in revulsion. It was huge, twice as large as any Skraeling he'd ever seen before, and its swollen, lumpy face was so grossly misshapen that its silver eyes, sitting on one side of its face, were actually set one above the other.

It is repulsive, Inardle said in his mind, and he gave another nod, not daring, or trusting himself, to speak.

The Skraeling stopped a good ten paces away, looking at Axis rather than Isaiah.

"You bring the *StarMan*?" it hissed from the slit of its mouth, spittle oozing down in a winding rope from one corner.

"And you will note he brings no army with him," Isaiah said. "Surely you cannot be afraid of just one StarMan. He will not harm you. He answers to me."

Axis closed his eyes briefly at that. Oh, how the Skraeling would rejoice, thinking the StarMan was now under the command of another.

"We have come with a proposition for you," Isaiah said, and the Skraeling grinned.

"You want to surrender?" he said.

"You think *I* would surrender to *you*?" Isaiah said, and something either in Isaiah's voice or in his face made the Skraeling, literally, cringe.

"Do you know who I am?" Isaiah said to the Skraeling.

"You are Isaiah, once Tyrant of Isembaard, once ally of our Lord, Lister."

"Now long gone and well forgotten," said Isaiah. "But, yes, mostly you are correct. One or two omissions but we can skip past those for now. My friend Skraeling . . . ah, I cannot keep calling you that. You know my name, now I crave to know yours. I would parley and for that I need your name."

"My name?" Momentarily taken aback, the Skraeling blinked slowly, a bulbous blue-tinged tongue rolling out to lick its lips.

"Your name, friend," said Isaiah.

"Well," said the Skraeling, "you may call me—"

"Your *mystery* name," said Isaiah, and Axis felt Inardle tense and draw in a sharp breath.

What is it? Axis said to her.

How does Isaiah know of the Skraelings' mystery names? What are—

I will explain later. Listen, for now.

The Skraeling cringed back a step. Then he straightened and stared defiantly at Isaiah. "I shall not give it," he said.

"Friend," Isaiah said, "I ask in Veldmr's name and with

an authority far greater than his. Tell me your mystery name.
I command it."

Axis thought the Skraeling boggled so hard at Isaiah that
his silver orbs would actually detach themselves from their
sockets and fall to the ground.

Who was Veldmr? Axis wondered.

"It . . ." the Skraeling whispered. "It is . . ."

"Yes?" Isaiah said.

"It is . . ." The Skraeling glanced at Axis and Inardle.

"Neither Axis nor Inardle will speak it without my permission," Isaiah said. "Tell me."

"It is Ozll," the Skraeling whispered, and Isaiah smiled.

"Friend Ozll, then. We shall meet this evening, when I
have eaten and refreshed myself. I am sure we shall have
much to discuss."

Without another word, or even a glance at the Skraeling
standing staring at him, Isaiah waved for Axis and Inardle
to follow him, then kicked his horse toward his army.

"What is this mystery name thing?" Axis said to Inardle
as he pushed their horse after Isaiah.

"All the Skraelings have what they call mystery names,"
she said. "They never told them to the Lealfast and, frankly,
I thought it was just some means they had dreamed up to
make themselves feel important. Every time they wanted to
appear enigmatic and self-important, they'd carry on about
their 'mystery names'. I have no idea how Isaiah knew about
them. I also had no idea the damned creatures actually did
have them."

"Maybe friend Ozll made it up on the spot."

"Maybe," Inardle said, her voice doubtful.

They rode another few minutes, then Axis began to
chuckle. "By the stars, Inardle, look what Isaiah has collected about himself. Such flummery!"

"What are they?"

"Juit birds," Axis said. "I remember them from the time
when Isaiah pulled me from the Otherworld. Not everything,
but I do remember those birds." He chuckled again. "Stars
alone knows what they are doing keeping company with
Isaiah, but suddenly I feel a great deal more cheerful."

* * *

Ozll stood and watched them ride away, his mind and heart in turmoil.

Why had the water god wanted to know his mystery name?

Ozll quite suddenly felt they'd made a major mistake in not simply overwhelming the Isembaardian force and eating them to the ground before carrying on to Elcho Falling and whatever awaited there.

It had been a bad miscalculation to worry that the One might have secreted himself within the army. If the One *had* been within the Isembaardian army, then he would have made himself known to the Skraelings by now.

Nonetheless, when Ozll returned to his comrades, and they asked him what was happening, he replied simply, "Isaiah will speak with us this evening."

He did not tell them that Isaiah had asked his mystery name, nor that Isaiah had invoked the name of Veldmr. None of the Skraelings could remember quite who Veldmr was, only that he was a great and revered figure from their past.

A past, some among the Skraeling whispered, that had had some beauty and power to it.

A past of mystery.

CHAPTER TWENTY-TWO

The Outlands

That evening, Isaiah, Axis and Inardle gathered at the
boundary of the Isembaardian camp. Isaiah had been
busy all day and neither of the other two had had a chance to
talk with him. Now they were full of questions.

"Enough!" Isaiah said, raising his hands in self-defence.
He was looking his majestic best. His long black hair had
been washed and rebraided with hundreds of glittering crystal beads (it would not have surprised Axis to have learned
they were diamonds) that jingled whenever he moved his
head. He had abandoned his usual riding attire of leather
trousers and jerkin for an all-black close-fitting ensemble
that highlighted his musculature and strength.

From somewhere, possibly Lamiah who may have liber-
ated it from one of Isaiah's original invading supply wagons,
Isaiah had found one of his extraordinary jewelled collars. It
hung about his upper chest and draped over his shoulders in
a blaze of diamonds, sapphires and emeralds, which, along
with the jewels in his braids, caught every glint of light.

Axis thought the Skraelings would be salivating in envy.

Isaiah sighed, thinking about what he could, or wanted, to
say. "All I want to say for now is that when we talk with the
Skraelings, I will probably take us back to almost the beginning of time when this world was very new. I lived then, as
did Lister, and we each had many adventures and made many
decisions that have long, long been forgotten.

"At least, I thought they had been forgotten. When I
touched you yesterday, Inardle, one of those decisions, one
of my ancient secrets, reared up and told me in no uncertain
tones that it still lived, and that the consequences of a rash

action tens of thousands of years ago have now come back to haunt me." He paused. "As they have haunted you, Axis, and this land. I made a grave mistake many, many aeons ago, and I had no idea . . . no idea at all . . ."

He managed a small smile. "Perhaps that mistake can be revealed, and maybe I can have a chance to make right for the future a wrong that is anciently old. Maybe the Skraelings can have a chance, too. And, Axis," Isaiah's smile grew a little broader, a little more genuine, "maybe you will understand why the Skraelings loathe water so much. Gods, that alone should have given it away to me . . . oh, well, no matter now. Are you ready?"

That little speech hadn't enlightened either Axis or Inardle, and it had made Axis feel a great deal more uneasy. He wasn't happy at all about walking toward a throng of millions of Skraelings, even with Isaiah at his side, and from what Isaiah was saying . . .

"Come, Axis," Isaiah said. "It will be an adventure, and you like adventures."

"I gave up admiring adventures a long time ago," Axis muttered, but Isaiah pretended not to hear him, and together the three began the journey across the no-man's land between the two armies.

The juit birds had preferred to make their roost elsewhere this night.

They walked in silence toward the Skraeling mass which opened up as they approached, forming an avenue toward their centre.

Axis began to feel very nervous . . . he had expected to meet with a delegation somewhere *other* than surrounded by several million Skraelings.

It will be all right, Axis, Isaiah said, and with that Axis had to content himself.

He glanced at Inardle. She was walking to his side, outwardly calm, but he could tell by the way she held her wings and the tight skin about her eyes that she was also very tense.

Isaiah strode without hesitation into the midst of the Skraelings, Axis and Inardle a half step behind him.

None of the Skraeling had eyes for any other than Isaiah, and Axis thought that whatever Isaiah had said to Ozll earlier had so impressed or otherwise astounded the Skraelings they could now completely ignore the fact the StarMan walked within their midst.

Under any other circumstances Axis thought they would not have hesitated to tear him to pieces.

The entire mass was utterly silent, staring at Isaiah.

The man glittered as he walked. Axis had to admire his sense of style—something Axis had never really exploited when he was StarMan. Isaiah strode forth as if he owned the very ground on which he walked, radiating majesty and serenity and confidence, and everyone either stared silently or followed meekly.

Eventually Isaiah, Axis and Inardle came to a small circular area, delineated by the standing, crammed Skraelings. In the centre of this circle stood Ozll and two other Skraelings, both as hideously malformed as Ozll.

Isaiah walked to within three paces of them, then sat cross-legged in one graceful, elegant move.

He gestured to Axis and Inardle to do likewise (who managed it smoothly if not with as much elegance as Isaiah), then spoke to the Skraelings. "You may sit, also."

He had, in an instant, taken total command of the meeting.

"You know me as Isaiah," he said, "and you likely all know my companion, Axis SunSoar, StarMan, and perhaps even Inardle, who as a Lealfast has been a companion to many of you. I know I address Ozll, but I wonder who else sits with you, Ozll. How may I call them?"

Ozll hesitated.

"Their mystery names, I think," Isaiah said, "for this grand parley."

Another slight hesitation, then the two Skraeling spoke in turn.

"Mallx," said one.

"Pannh," said the other. Then, "How did you know of Veldmr?"

"The question is," Isaiah said, "how do *you* know of him? But, we'll get to that. May I begin? There are many things we need to discuss, and the night promises to be cold, and I and my friends would like to return to my campfire as soon as we may.

"Now, here is the situation as I understand it. I am leading this army toward Elcho Falling so that I may assist my friends within to dislodge their besiegers, the Lealfast led by Eleanon. Eleanon may or may not—I have no intelligence on this—be allied with my former general, Kezial, and his army. You, on the other hand, are allied with the One, and are marching behind us with an uncertain purpose in mind. I don't suppose you would care to elaborate?"

None of the three Skraelings spoke, and Isaiah continued.

"Ah, well, then, perhaps we can cover that later. The One has an uncertain location at the moment . . . you don't wish to disclose this . . . no? Perhaps you don't actually know? Well, never mind, we can leave that for later, as well. Now, to my purpose in meeting with you. I propose an alliance between you," a wave of the hand indicated all the Skraelings, "and I, against the Lealfast and against the One."

Ozll sniggered and a low wave of laughter twittered through the ranks of the Skraelings. Axis thought it sounded like an axe being grated slowly over a flagstoned floor.

Isaiah smiled slowly. "You ask yourselves why . . . well, may I relate to you something I have learned over the past day?"

"We are hungry," Ozll said. "It has been a long time since our last eating. I hope you make this story a short one."

The threat was clear, but Isaiah ignored it. "I shall make this story an entertaining one," he said, "and revealing. Indeed, eventually I shall reveal to you how you came by your mystery names and what purpose they serve."

"Speak no more of our mystery names!" Mallx said. "You have no—"

"I have every right," Isaiah said, and now the threat had moved to his voice. Then he softened his tone. "And I am going to talk about water—a great deal. This also is my right. But first . . .

"Inardle here, whom you know, was injured recently. I had cause to examine her wounds. She had been attacked by her fellow Lealfast . . . well, not quite fellows, as they—as you—had been altered by their association with the One. Inardle's attackers had tipped their arrows with poison, so that even if the strike did not kill her, the poison surely would within the day.

"At first, when I came to examine her, I thought I could do little for Inardle. But then . . . then . . . tell me, Ozll, you do know who I am . . . yes?"

Ozll stared at him. "You're a god. Was . . . until the One stripped you of your powers."

"*Am* a god," Isaiah said, holding Ozll's gaze, "for even the One could not strip me of my power permanently."

Ozll's thin strip of a mouth—as those of his companions— began to lift in a sneer, but Isaiah moved his hand over the ground between them.

It changed into a small pool of green water.

Ozll, Mallx and Pannh all leaped to their feet, stumbling backward, their faces contorted in horror, and the entire mass of Skraelings hissed and shifted.

Isaiah waved his hand again and the water vanished.

"I am water," he said. "I am the essence of this element. Call me a god if you wish. But whatever you call me, I must be everything you hate and fear most."

"Be rid of him!" someone hissed from the surrounding mass of Skraelings, and the cry was taken up among the multitude.

Be rid of him! Be rid of him!

Axis tensed, glancing at Inardle, and wondering if they would survive long if they made a run for it. *Damn Isaiah! What was he doing!*

"Raise one finger against me or my two companions," Isaiah said quietly, "and I swear to the very heavens I will turn the ground beneath you into water."

The Skraelings quietened, although they still moved restlessly.

And I would do it, Isaiah said to Axis, keeping the thought closed to all others, *and if I did you would be astounded at what would happen, Axis.*

Isaiah—

Trust me, Axis. When we leave here—

If we leave here.

—I will explain all. Just wait.

"Sit," Isaiah said to the three leading Skraelings, and, very warily, they once again sat before Isaiah, Axis and Inardle.

"I was talking about Inardle," Isaiah said. "I need to explain this to you, so please be patient. The sooner I can say what I need to, the sooner I can go home and eat. So . . . I was examining Inardle, thinking I could do nothing for her, when I realised that Inardle was quite special. She has much water within her. Not physical water as such, but the spiritual manifestation of water. Water has somehow been at the very essence of her creation—far, far back in time, through many tens of thousands of generations. So, as Water itself, I was able to heal her. I used the essence of water deep within Inardle to remove the poison from her body.

"Inardle is a very special woman. Very mystical, very magical. Axis, tell our assembled friends just how special."

Axis wasted a moment gaping at Isaiah, then collected himself enough to speak.

"Isaiah is right," he said, carefully not looking at Inardle. "Inardle is very special. She . . . she *flows*."

To one side Isaiah gave a small smile, and nodded.

"Inardle, like all Lealfast, can flow through the air," Axis continued. "Almost become one with it. Vaporous. She frosts," now he did glance at Inardle, "when she is in pain or when she is, ah, excited. Water coats her flesh in ice crystals. She has magic that I cannot understand. It does not come from the Icarii."

"No," said Isaiah. "What makes Inardle so very, very special does not come from her Icarii heritage, but from her Skraeling heritage. From *you*."

Now the Skraelings stared at Isaiah, puzzled, their malformed faces creased by lines of doubt. They could not fathom that Isaiah might be about to make some positive statement about them.

No one ever did that.

"It is why you have mystery names," Isaiah said, "from

your mystery past. Tell me, my friends, from where did the Skraelings originate?"

"From the frozen northern wastes," Pannh said.

"But from *whom*?" Isaiah said. "Who were the ancestors of the Skraelings? The Icarii boast a sparrow," Isaiah threw a smile at Axis, "and the Lealfast can say that they resulted from a mating between an Icarii and a Skraeling, but from whom did *you* spring?"

"I am certain you must think it was something hateful," Mallx said.

Then Isaiah spoke, and it was in a language that Axis had never heard before. It was the most beautiful sound he'd ever heard issue from someone's mouth—liquid, lilting phrases that were almost, but not quite, the sound of woodland song-birds at dawn.

It absolutely captivated every last single Skraeling. The entire mass froze solid in surprise, or perhaps yearning.

Axis glanced at Inardle, to share his wonder with her, and was stunned to see the same astonishment, almost hunger, on her face as on the Skraelings'.

"Did you know what I just said?" Isaiah said.

Every Skraeling, as well as Inardle, shook their heads slowly. Axis had no idea what was happening, but he had never, in all his time, seen Skraelings so still and so captivated as he did now. He thought that if he had known whatever it was that Isaiah had just said, and spake it to the Skraeling hordes who had invaded and destroyed so much of Tencendor, then he could have stilled an entire army of them in an instant.

"Isaiah?" Inardle said, and there was deep hunger in her voice.

"I said, 'Welcome home, my friends.' I spoke in one of the most ancient languages of our world. Water."

"What do you want?" Ozll almost growled. "Why do you taunt us?"

"I do not taunt you," said Isaiah. "I am currently sitting here feeling the weight of aeons of guilt piling about my shoulders, because once I did you a great wrong, and it was simply that I forgot about you. I am going to right that wrong today, if you will allow me."

"You owe us something?" Ozll said, more puzzled than ever.

"Yes," Isaiah said. "I owe you something. Now, do not be afraid, for I am going to cast over everyone here a mild enchantment which will enable you to see back into the distant past. Do not fear. I do not mean to entrap you. Any of you can leave the enchantment at any time, by simply uttering a word. Any word, but it will still be enough to break the enchantment. Would you like to proceed?"

"It will not harm us?" Ozll said, and Isaiah shook his head, making his braids ripple in light and sound.

Axis thought the Skraeling would ask for more reassurance, but Ozll merely nodded.

"Go ahead," he said.

"Imagine," Isaiah said, "a time before there were any men or any Icarii or any Skraelings."

His voice was soft, reassuring, though commanding, and Axis found himself looking into a landscape so foreign it appeared to be of a different world. Every Skraeling had vanished, and instead he saw a land of gently rolling low hills stretching into the horizon. The hills were carpeted in deep green moss, broken here and there with huddles of tiny cream and pink flowers. Breaking up this verdant landscape were myriad streams and rivers, glinting silver in the soft light.

"There were no trees in this early world," Isaiah continued, his voice flowing softly, hypnotically, through everyone's mind. "No great herds of beasts as we know them now. No cities, no towns, no quests, no wars. Just peace. You see that there were many creatures—"

And Axis did see that this land of emerald-carpeted hills was dotted here and there with small animals, not one of them much larger than a hare, and all grazing the moss and occasional stand of low plants. They were many and varied in shape and hue, but they all moved peaceably with each other and about the landscape.

"—but they lived in harmony and contentment. Such is the way, always, in the beginning of new worlds. Now, let us look in the streams and rivers. No, do not fret, I shall not drop you in. Be still my friends, we shall just peer, briefly."

Axis found his vision being drawn down to a small river, tumbling its way along a rocky bed. For a moment he saw nothing in the water, then he gasped, and heard everyone about him gasp, as a face floated up from the river bottom and stared at them.

The face almost had no features at all—just eyes, the hint of a nose and mouth, and the ethereal shape of cheek and forehead—for all was distorted by the water. There was a body there, too, but Axis could barely make it out.

All he knew was that, firstly, this was the most beautiful creature he had ever seen in his life, and, secondly, it was among the most magical.

The creature spoke, its words lifting from the water, and it spoke in the language Isaiah had used earlier.

Water.

"She is a River Angel," Isaiah said. "See how glorious she is?"

He paused, allowing everyone to drink their fill of the beautiful creature, then he drew their vision back once more until they overlooked the wider landscape.

"For many thousands of years," Isaiah continued, "the River Angels existed in harmony with their fellow creatures. Then, over the space of a few years, they developed a creed which supposed that no other creature dared to exist, given the overwhelming superiority of the River Angels. So they began to destroy them."

Now the vision showed watery hands emerging from the streams and rivers to seize the necks of all the creatures lowering their heads to drink and twisting, ripping off those heads.

"It was appalling," Isaiah said, his voice soft. "And so, if I may cut this story short to save the pain, I destroyed the River Angels before they could destroy the rest of the world's living creatures."

The vision ended abruptly, and Axis found himself blinking as he looked once more at the encircling Skraelings. They also were blinking, their faces a mix of emotions and confusions. He looked at Inardle.

She felt his gaze and returned his gaze, and Axis saw that

she was weeping. She looked devastated and Axis wondered what she had realised that had as yet escaped him.

Axis returned his attention to Isaiah. "You 'destroyed' them?"

"I took them from the water," said Isaiah, his quiet voice carrying over the entire horde, "and I made them to hate and fear it. I took from them the one thing they adored above all else. Water. Then I set them to wandering and I cursed them that they would become the most hated and reviled creatures that existed. I was so angry. I needed to punish their arrogance and cruelty.

"Then, to my eternal shame, I forgot them. Light and I became embroiled in our battles with Kanubai, with chaos, and then other matters came up, and aeons passed . . . and, my friends, I am afraid I forgot you. If I had thought of you then I supposed that you had all perished. I had not thought . . ."

Axis' mouth was actually gaping open. He stared at Isaiah, then at Inardle who looked utterly shocked—then about at Ozll and the other Skraelings.

He could see that they did not yet fully comprehend. They were struggling, *trying* to make the connection, but so many, so many *countless* generations had passed that the Skraelings had lost most of their intuitive and intellectual powers.

They had descended into the abyss of brutality and ignorance and stupidity, and there they had stayed, in terror of the element which had once nurtured them.

Hating that which they had lost.

Constantly looking for a leader. Perhaps, unknowingly, wanting someone who could lead them back to the world they had lost.

"My friends," Isaiah said, his voice full of pity, "you are the lost River Angels."

CHAPTER TWENTY-THREE

The Outlands

The Skraelings still could not grasp the enormity of what Isaiah was telling them, and Axis thought that he, too, might have trouble were he in their position.

But then, he had been through similar, hadn't he? But never had he descended to the level of the Skraelings, creatures universally reviled and hated for their stupidity and the brutality of their existence.

Now, Isaiah was telling them that, in truth, they were probably the most wondrous and enchanted creatures this world had ever produced: more mysterious than the Icarii; more magical than the Lealfast; stunning creatures who had emerged from the mystical birth pangs of the world itself. Glorious.

Axis wondered, cruelly, if they still had the intellect to grasp it.

He looked again at Inardle. She had her hands over her mouth, her eyes wide, and was rocking backward and forward very slightly.

It is why you frost, he said to her. *That is your River Angel magic.*

She stared at him with those wide eyes, but Axis was not even sure if she had actually heard him.

"I have left you alone for far too long," Isaiah said to the Skraelings. "I had forgot you and, lo, look to what mischief you descended. Even cursed you tried to ruin the world."

Isaiah sighed. "I have many choices before me. I could destroy you utterly and, yes, I have the power, for I am Water and you are descended of water." His voice turned bitter. "If *only* I had realised all this earlier. I could have saved this land, and saved Isembaard, so much trouble. So much slaughter. Right now, my friends, I loathe myself quite terribly. But I have a decision to make, and so also do you. Here is what I propose. I have the means to destroy you completely. I have, likewise, the means to restore you to your full heritage. I can turn you from the ugly vile creatures you are now, back to the magical, beautiful creatures you once were. Or, I can give to you that responsibility—the decision as to whether to go back or not—in your hands. I can give you the power to restore yourselves if you want.

"But . . . which choice of those three should I make? Both River Angels and Skraelings have created havoc. They have murdered and slaughtered. Perhaps destroying you completely and putting a final end to the nightmare that you are and that you have caused this world would be the best thing."

"No," said Ozll.

Isaiah ignored him. "I don't know what to do and I don't know if I have the right to make that choice, given that I am almost as culpable as you. So . . . I am going to leave the decision to you. I, and Axis and Inardle, are going to return to our camp, and there we will rest. Tomorrow we shall meet with you and you shall tell me what you think best for yourselves. There are no conditions attached to this. And if you choose either the second or third options—that I, or you yourselves, restore you to full River Angel status—I will not demand that you ally with either myself or my friends against the One."

Axis hissed, trying to grab Isaiah's attention, unable to believe he was giving the Skraelings this much power and freedom. Stars, they would destroy the world in a minute if they took back the power of the River Angels!

The Skraelings were, to a single one of them, staring at Isaiah in total disbelief.

"I am going to put my trust in you," Isaiah said softly. "Consider well overnight. We will meet again tomorrow, at noon."

Then he rose, indicating to Axis and Inardle they should do likewise, and he walked back to the Isembaardian camp, head high, braids jingling, jewels gleaming in the faint light of a multitude of campfires.

"Are you *mad*?" Axis hissed as they neared the edges of the Isembaardian camp. "What have you done? Stars, Isaiah, if you have the means to destroy them then just—"

Isaiah turned on him. "I have as much blame to bear for the actions of the Skraelings as they themselves. *I* forgot about them, assumed they had all died, and how many millions have suffered because of it? This is my recompense to the Skraelings for—"

"What about recompense to all the people who have been slaughtered by the Skraelings?" Axis shouted, not caring if his voice carried back to the Skraeling camp. "What about recompense to this land, this one here and now that we stand on, for the misery inflicted on it? What about recompense for—"

"Axis—"

"—all the Isembaardians who died. Godsdamn it, Isaiah! You abandoned Isembaard to its fate, too! This is a most unbecoming character trait of yours."

Isaiah had paled, and now took a step back. "I don't expect you to understand, but—"

"You are right. I *don't* understand."

With that, Axis turned on his heel and stalked away into the night.

After a moment, Isaiah walked on into his camp.

Inardle stood a long time in the darkness between the two camps, feeling keenly her isolation.

Stuck between two camps, as her entire life had been.

What Isaiah had revealed to her had shocked her to her very (*River Angel*) core. She had spent her entire life reviling her Skraeling heritage.

Now . . . did she have to admire it? Yearn for it? Or should she loathe it all the more for the foulness it had come from?

And were the Skraelings to decide her fate as well?

She did not know how to react, or what thoughts to muster. So she did the only thing she could actually think of doing.

She walked after Axis.

* * *

Inardle thought Axis might lash out at her in his anger, but he didn't. He was sitting in the dark some twenty paces out from the border of Isaiah's camp, and said nothing as Inardle came up and sat down beside him.

"I don't know what to do, Axis," she said.

He didn't respond, and Inardle hadn't really expected him to. She just needed to talk and it kept her that one step further from madness if she talked to an actual person rather than muttered away to herself.

"I cannot believe Isaiah acted as he did," Axis said, and Inardle blinked in a little surprise.

"He bears a heavy burden of guilt, I think," she said. "Not so much for the Skraelings, but for what they have done. If he had realised sooner . . . or thought to discover what had become of the River Angels once he had cursed them . . ."

"Is it going to ease his guilt by handing them the power to destroy even more? I can see no sense in the man!"

Inardle thought somewhat wryly that the only reason Axis talked to her so freely now was because he had (if perhaps only momentarily) found someone else to hate more than her.

"I don't really hate you so much," he said, and Inardle jumped, making Axis grin slightly.

"That thought was written all over your face," he said. "I didn't need to shuffle through your mind to realise it. I wouldn't have tried to save you from the Lealfast if I had really hated you."

"And I thank you for that," she said. "If you hadn't warned me, they would have killed me with their first volley of arrows. I was unaware and they had a clear shot. But . . . how did you know?"

Axis explained to her how he had used the vision of the eagle. "It was a trick from long ago in my past, using a friend from my past."

He paused, listening. The Skraeling horde was close enough that they could hear the whisperings and mutterings coming from within their mass. It sounded like a hissing sea, undulating this way and that.

"They are surely having a fine time considering what Isaiah has shown and offered them," Axis said.

"It would have come as a huge shock to them," Inardle said. "What Isaiah showed them of their past, certainly, but also his unexpected offer, no conditions attached, to do whatever they choose. I don't think anyone has offered the Skraelings that kind of option before. Everyone has used hate or fear or force to control them. Now a god has walked up to them and said, 'Here is unlimited beauty and power and it is yours if you want it. No strings.'" She gave a chuckle. "They'll be sitting there trying to find the trap."

"Is there one, do you think?"

"I don't know," Inardle said. "I think Isaiah's offer is genuine . . . but maybe there is a twist in its tail."

"Which way will the Skraelings choose? Not the first option, surely. Not death."

"Actually, they will yearn for that," Inardle said. "Instant destruction, yes, but it also means instant peace. I think the Skraelings yearn for that."

Axis wondered if Inardle also yearned for the blessed peace of death. "Is there a chance they will choose it?"

"No. They might yearn for it, but they will also be dazzled by the idea of beauty, of which they have never had any, and of power, which they have always craved. Axis, they are hateful creatures, given to treachery and slaughter, but they also know that. They hate themselves as much as does everyone else. Now they are being offered a way out."

"So which of the other two options?"

"I think they will take the third. To restore themselves if they want. It is the most dangerous one for us, for you, for the Isembaardians, for Isaiah, for everyone save themselves. They will see power in that choice, and so they will take it." She gave a small shrug. "Of course, then they will fight incessantly about whether or not they should take that step. Maybe Isaiah has outwitted them, after all."

"Not the second option?" Axis said. "Isaiah immediately restoring them to River Angels?"

"No. I think they might see a trap there, or suspect a trap."

"They are suspicious creatures."

"As are you." Inardle wished immediately she hadn't said that, but Axis gave a small smile and a tilt of his head, merely acknowledging the remark.

"How do you feel, Inardle? About your River Angel heritage?"

She drew in a deep breath. "How do I feel? More confused than ever. I have always hated my Skraeling blood . . . but now I discover they were once magical, beautiful creatures. But . . . oh, what despicable creatures. Should I loathe my River Angel heritage even more than my Skraeling heritage?"

"It explains your mystery," said Axis. "Your abilities. How you . . . frost."

That was leading the conversation onto metaphorical ice and Inardle shifted nervously. "I hadn't expected flattery from you back there," she said, referring to Axis' comments on the Lealfast's beauties.

"I surprised myself." Now he turned his head and smiled at her. "Perhaps, sitting there in front of that horde of hideous creatures, you didn't seem so vile after all."

Inardle felt even more uncomfortable. "More flattery."

"Perhaps," Axis said. He stretched away some of the stiffness and tiredness in his back. "Tomorrow will be interesting."

"So it shall," Inardle said.

They sat for a while in silence, then Inardle rose, said goodnight, and walked back to her assigned tent.

CHAPTER TWENTY-FOUR

The Outlands

I nardle walked into the tent, stopping in surprise when she saw the woman sitting on one of the two camp beds.

She hadn't realised she would be sharing.

The woman was looking at her with some discomfort, which Inardle realised was probably because the woman was unfamiliar with winged creatures and didn't quite know how to converse with one.

Or perhaps that she, too, was surprised at suddenly finding herself sharing.

"I am Inardle," Inardle said.

"Hereward," the woman said. "I am sorry . . . you are here because . . . ?"

"Isaiah told me I could use this tent."

"Oh."

"He didn't say anything?"

Hereward's face twisted with bitterness. "He loathes me and suspects me of foulness."

Inardle, who was still standing just inside the tent, not sure if she should progress further, just raised her eyebrows.

"He suspects I harbour the One," Hereward said. "He cannot make up his mind whether to kill me or not."

"Oh," said Inardle, not knowing what to say. *Why had Isaiah put her in here?* Stars, she'd rather sleep outside in the cold.

"I suppose you want to go, now," Hereward said.

"I think perhaps—"

"I don't harbour the One!" Hereward said. "Why does he believe it?"

"Why *does* he believe it?"

"Because the Skraelings insinuated it."

Inardle risked a small smile. "Then perhaps he is a fool for believing the Skraelings before you. Look, Hereward, I am tired and I need to sleep. Do you mind if I rest on the spare bed?"

Hereward shook her head. "The guards let you in?"

Guards? Then Inardle remembered there had been a group of soldiers around a campfire close to the tent. Maybe they were, indeed, guarding it.

That thought made Inardle wonder anew at why Isaiah had put her in here.

"Yes," she said.

"Have you been sent to interrogate me?"

Oh stars, Inardle thought. "No. How do you know Isaiah? What are you doing here?"

Briefly Hereward told Inardle of how she'd escaped Aqhat with her comrades, how she'd watched them being murdered by the Skraelings (which made Inardle wince), met with Isaiah on the banks of the River Lhyl, and their subsequent history.

"You are not an Icarii, are you?" Hereward said as she concluded.

"No," Inardle said, by this time sitting on the spare bed and wishing beyond anything she had never entered this tent. She wasn't surprised Isaiah had put guards on this woman. "I am a Lealfast. A race from the north." She couldn't be bothered with the long explanation. "I am tired," she said, lifting her legs onto the bed and lying down on her side, wrapping her wings over her body like a blanket. "I think I will sleep now."

And get up before dawn and beg Isaiah for a different berth for the next night. Or just drift the air in invisible form. Anything but another meeting with Hereward.

"If you see Isaiah tomorrow," Hereward said, "can you please ask if . . . if . . ."

Her eyes suddenly filled with tears, and Inardle was irritated to feel some sympathy for her.

"Of course," Inardle said, and closed her eyes.

She heard Hereward sigh, then the sound of her lying down

as well, and Inardle relaxed. Praise the gods, the woman was going to go to sleep.

Inardle breathed in deeply and regularly, calming herself, putting the day's events behind her. She drifted into sleep and broken dreams of drowning in poisonous waters, until she woke abruptly at the sound of Hereward drawing in a shocked, terrified breath, then of scrabbling about on her bed as if she were trying to back away from something.

Gods . . .

Inardle opened her eyes reluctantly, then jerked into full wakefulness.

Ozll was standing just inside the tent flap.

"How did you get past the guards?" Inardle said, sitting up warily. She glanced at Hereward.

The woman was now out of bed and crouched terrified in the back corner of the tent. Given what Hereward had told her earlier of her experiences with Skraelings, Inardle wasn't surprised.

"I drifted," Ozll said enigmatically, and Inardle didn't push any further on the issue.

Ozll stood there, his large clawed hands clasped before him, looking uncomfortable.

"What do you want?" Inardle said.

"To talk."

"To *me*?"

"Of course," said Ozll, looking surprised. "Who else?"

"Not Hereward?"

Ozll's face creased even deeper in confusion, and Inardle nodded to Hereward crouched and trembling at the back of the tent.

"No," said Ozll. "Why her? I want to talk to you."

Well, thought Inardle, he hasn't come to chat to the One, then. "What do you want?"

"We are torn," Ozll said. "We thought to ask your advice."

"You must really be torn," Inardle said, "if you have come to *me*."

"You are not as hateful as Eleanon or Bingaleal," Ozll said.

"Bingaleal is dead."

Ozll's face creased in a huge smile. "Really?"

"Really." Inardle thought there was something odd, different, about Ozll's face—besides the smile. She narrowed her eyes, trying to work it out.

Ah . . . his eyes were now slightly less perpendicular than they had once been. The top one appeared to have shifted slightly toward the centre of his face.

"Is Isaiah trying to trick us?" Ozll said.

"No," Inardle said, "I don't think so. I think he feels enormous guilt at leaving you for so long. Leaving you to create the havoc you have. He feels for all those you murdered."

"Is that the only reason he feels guilt?"

Inardle shook her head slowly. "He feels it for you, too. That he forgot you. I don't think he meant to. He just . . . got caught up in other things."

"What do you think of the River Angels?" Ozll said, and Inardle wondered where all this was going.

"That they were very beautiful and very powerful," Inardle said, "and incredibly vile for what they did."

Ozll nodded, deep in thought. Then he sighed. "Thank you," he said to Inardle. His eyes slipped over to Hereward and he snarled, exposing all his terrifying teeth.

Hereward shrieked, Ozll grinned, and then he was gone.

"Go back to sleep," Inardle said to Hereward. "He won't come back."

"What was he doing here?" Hereward said, still not rising from her defensive crouch.

"He wanted to ask advice on a deal Isaiah had offered the Skraelings earlier this evening."

"But why ask *you*?" Hereward said, finally starting to unwind herself.

"Because I am half Skraeling," Inardle said and, not able to resist, bared her teeth at Hereward herself.

CHAPTER TWENTY-FIVE

The Outlands

They met at noon the next day. Isaiah, Axis and Inardle walked out once more to meet the Skraelings. Again they walked into a cleared circle in the heart of the Skraeling mass where, as before, Ozll, Mallx, and Pannh awaited them.

No one sat this time.

Ozll stepped forward from his two companions, and Inardle noticed that now the more regular alignment of his eyes was far more noticeable. She looked at Mallx and Pannh.

The same thing was happening to them.

"Have you made your decision?" Isaiah asked Ozll.

"Yes," the Skraeling replied. "We choose the third option. Give us the power so that we may return to River Angels as we wish."

Isaiah's mouth curved in a very small smile. "There is no magical enchantment or spell, Ozll. No giving of 'power'. It is just a piece of advice, but it does come with one or two cautions."

Ozll frowned. "Advice? Traps?"

"Pieces of advice only, my friend. When you want to return to River Angels, then you must seek a large body of inland water. Not the ocean, but a large body of water bounded by land."

The Skraelings hissed.

"You are creatures of water," Isaiah said. "You will need to confront your fear of it one day."

"Well, then," Ozll said. "What do we do once we find our large body of water?"

"Then, as one—you must not do this individually—step into the water, as *one*, mind you . . . and you drown yourselves."

The Skraelings erupted. The entire mass seethed forward, clawed hands grabbing, jaws salivating, throats shrieking.

Axis caught hold of Inardle, pulling her against him, reaching for the sword at his hip, but Isaiah stood his ground.

"It is no trick," he said. "In order to return to River Angels you must drown yourselves. You must pass through death, via water, then you will return in your true form. It was why I made you loathe water, so that you would not return to your true form by accident."

The circle had now contracted about Isaiah, Axis and Inardle until its inner edge was no more than an arm's length from them.

"Isaiah!" Axis hissed.

Be still, Isaiah said to him. *We will be safe.*

"It is no trick," Isaiah said, slowly and deliberately, holding Ozll's furious stare.

"He just wants to murder us *en masse*!" Pannh said. "We are not that stupid!"

"If I wanted to destroy you I would only need to lift this finger," Isaiah held up the middle finger of his right hand, "and it would be done. I wouldn't bother trying to persuade you to drown. I don't have the time to waste on such entertainment."

Ozll stared at Isaiah. "I don't believe you," he said, but his voice was unsure and he shuffled his feet.

"You wanted control, yourself," Isaiah said. "Now you have it. It isn't easy, but then you chose the least easy of all the options."

"Maybe we'd prefer option two, after all," Mallx said. "You change us, here and now."

"Too late," Isaiah said. "You have made your choice."

He paused, looking about the close circle of still hissing and muttering Skraelings, catching every silvery-orbed eye he could. "I *am* telling you the truth. You now have the knowledge to return yourselves to River Angel form if you so desire. But it will be your choice on the where and the when, and I am going to emphasise again what I said—you need to do this *en masse*. As a group you must step into the water. Otherwise it will fail and you will all just die."

"We will all just die anyway," a Skraeling muttered behind them.

Axis stepped forward. "Look at *me*," he said. "I have been through death and back again. You can do it, too. It takes courage and resolve, but you *can* do it. And think what will happen if you do," he said. He dropped his voice a little, emphasising each of his following words carefully. "And if you do discover courage and resolve within you, then look at what you might become."

Axis lifted a hand, indicating Inardle. "But you will become *more* than her. Far more. More beautiful, more powerful. Nothing that splendid comes easy. I had to fight for everything I became. So will you. Have the courage to accept the future you have always wanted. You will need no power to lust after, for you will have power. You will need no lord to cower before, for you will be lords yourselves. No one will ever again regard you with revulsion."

He paused. "Not even me. Not even the Icarii. You will be princes within the circle of princes."

The Skraeling were quite silent, staring entranced at Axis.

"Go and take your future," Axis said. "Go."

"We can be princes?" one of the Skraelings asked.

"Every last one of you," Axis said. "Envied, by all creation." He hoped he wasn't overdoing it. Flattery was going to be the only thing that would get the three of them out alive.

"Princes . . ." Ozll murmured, and suddenly his right eye shot all the way over to the right side of his face so that, once more, his two eyes sat evenly settled in his face.

Ozll nodded. "We will take it, Isaiah." He waved a clawed hand, and the horde of Skraelings began to shuffle back, opening up the circle and the avenue back to safety.

Isaiah nodded at the Skraeling, then he turned and walked away, Axis and Inardle following.

None among the three dared breathe in case the Skraelings changed their minds.

When they were halfway down the avenue, Ozll called to them.

"Wait!"

They stopped, turning about slowly.

Ozll hurried up to them. "I will give you something in return," he said, "for the choice you gave us."

Isaiah raised an eyebrow.

"The One resides now in someone else," Ozll said.

"Who?" Isaiah said.

"We are not certain," said Ozll. "It was why we did not attack you instantly. We were scared the One might be within your number and we might eat him by mistake. But that woman you brought before us. He is not in her, and we doubt he resides anywhere within your army, for we should have felt him by now."

"And yet, knowing this, you did not attack," Isaiah said.

Ozll shrugged.

Isaiah smiled, happy with the choices that had been made here today. "Do you know where the One might be?"

"No true idea," said Ozll, "but we suspect Elcho Falling. If not with you, then where else?"

"Then I shall hurry to Elcho Falling and discover for myself," Isaiah said. He turned to go, but Ozll again called to him.

"Isaiah!" Ozll held out one of his great misshapen hands pleadingly. "Where is the nearest large body of water?"

By the gods, Axis thought, *they're actually going to do it!*

Isaiah held Ozll's gaze a moment. "Elcho Falling," he said. "The lake that surrounds Elcho Falling."

Then he, Axis and Inardle turned once more and walked back to the Isembaardian camp.

The next day, when Isaiah rose and instructed the soldiers to break camp to ride once more for Elcho Falling, it was to discover that the entire horde of Skraelings had vanished.

Every last one of them.

CHAPTER TWENTY-SIX

Isembaard

Maximilian and his small party made good time in their journey east. The horses were a true boon, indeed, and everyone gave silent thanks for their appearance.

One day, when Maximilian estimated they were two or three days away from Hairekeep, the horse carrying Doyle, who was riding out front, shied so badly it almost threw the man.

Doyle brought the horse under control quickly, then shouted back to the others to keep their mounts under tight rein.

"Look!" he cried, pointing to the patch of sandy ground just to the north of the road.

"Merciful heavens," Maximilian murmured as he drew in his horse behind Doyle's.

The soil to the northern side of the road was very sandy, with little vegetation. Now, as they all sat their nervous horses and looked, the sand rose up in the shape of a series of hands, all stretching eastward. The hands alternately beckoned to the group of watchers, then pointed eastward.

"They are telling us to hurry," Ishbel said.

"Aye," Maximilian said, then he gave a small jump and pointed to a different patch of ground. "Look there!"

Just in front of the hands, and a little further along the road, a series of footsteps appeared in the soil, rushing eastward.

"Hurry, hurry," Maximilian said.

"They must be tormented, indeed," Serge said, "to have managed this."

Maximilian looked at Avaldamon. "Avaldamon? You look worried."

"I don't know," Avaldamon said. "I don't like it."

"You think it is the One?" Ishbel said.

"I don't know," Avaldamon said once more. "It . . . it reminds me of something Boaz told me about the land when the creature called Nzame ruled over the glass pyramid. Nzame turned the land to stone with countless tiny pyramids, all with a single eye in each face, dotted about. This is different, but it just made me recall that."

"We shall be careful, then," Maximilian said.

Avaldamon hesitated, but then spoke the thought that had been worrying him for many days . . . ever since Ishbel and Maximilian had told him about Josia's plan to save the people trapped inside Hairekeep. "How much do you trust Josia, Maxel? Ishbel?"

"With our lives," Ishbel answered for them both. "He has been through a nightmare of an existence, Avaldamon. He is for us. He has no reason to harm us."

Maybe no, maybe yes, Avaldamon thought, but he nodded to Ishbel and Maximilian. "We shall be careful," he said, and with that they resumed their journey east, the hands and running footsteps urging them to hurry.

[Part Three]

CHAPTER ONE

Elcho Falling

Kezial stomped his feet as he marched through his encampment. Eleanon had insisted Kezial's army camp on the north side of the lake which surrounded Elcho Falling.

Eleanon said it would be better. Give the Isembaardians more space.

Kezial knew differently. What it meant was that the Lealfast Nation encampment—that which had once been Armat's encampment—sat between Kezial's group and any possible route that Isaiah and his army, approaching from the south, might take. There was little chance Kezial could renege on his alliance with Eleanon and, in the middle of the night, decamp to join with Isaiah. The route to the west was blocked by the turbulent open channel to the sea and the citadel of Elcho Falling itself; the route south was blocked by the lake; the route to the east by the Lealfast themselves.

So Kezial and his men idled in their camp, doing little but keeping themselves fit through weapons practice and spending the rest of their days and half their nights staring at the citadel in the middle of the lake and wondering when, or if, they were ever going to see the inside of it.

Kezial had had enough. He'd been demanding to see Eleanon these past few days and only now had the summons come.

Kezial was thinking very seriously that Isaiah would perhaps have been the better option.

Even Maximilian.

But extricating himself from this alliance was going to be . . . tricky. In fact, it was likely to be quite murderous. The

Lealfast outnumbered Kezial's men, had the not inconsiderable advantages of magic, invisibility and flight, and were hot-tempered and unpredictable to boot.

Kezial felt trapped and he didn't like it.

Eleanon had a tent in the middle of the Lealfast encampment and that was where Kezial expected to meet him. Instead, however, one of Eleanon's sub-commanders directed Kezial to a relatively isolated spot on the shore of the turquoise lake.

There Kezial found Eleanon, sitting on a barrel of wine, contemplating Elcho Falling rising in the centre of the lake.

Eleanon looked up at Kezial's approach, smiled, and indicated another barrel set to one side. "Sit yourself down, Kezial."

Kezial sat, cleared his throat, and opened his mouth to speak.

"You are feeling restless," Eleanon said, forestalling Kezial. "You feel yourself trapped, you're thinking that Isaiah might be the better option, but you are unsure of how to ally yourself with him without being slaughtered by my command." His smile broadened into the false and insincere. "Am I right?"

Kezial wondered what to say.

"Yes, I am right," Eleanon said. "I do not blame you, for I doubt I would be thinking any differently were I in your position. Your options are, after all, fairly limited. Kezial, my friend, we have not had much chance to talk since your arrival. Since intuiting your concerns and restlessness, I have decided to share with you some of my plans."

How magnanimous of him, Kezial thought.

"What do you know of Elcho Falling?" Eleanon said.

Kezial blinked, a little surprised by the question. "Little save that it is a powerful citadel, magical, that many lust after it. You, Maximilian, Isaiah, this One of whom I've heard spoken, the girl Ravenna who aided us against Maximilian. Doubtless many others."

"Aye," Eleanon said. "Many lust after Elcho Falling, and we do so because of its power, which we might want to control. Or, equally, because of its power of which we might be afraid and which therefore we seek to destroy. Maximilian thinks to control it, Isaiah likewise. The One wishes to destroy it, because Elcho Falling threatens his own power."

"And in which camp do you fall?" Kezial said.

"I want both," Eleanon said. "I want to destroy it and rebuild it to my own needs; to rebuild it in a manner in which it will recognise me and only me as its master."

"Oh, so you've taken the easy option, then."

Eleanon laughed. "I am going to like you, Kezial."

"Why do you need me?"

"To aid me in my quest, naturally. I am set against everyone else: Maximilian and his allies, Isaiah, and the One."

"I thought you were allied with the One."

"Now not so much," Eleanon said.

Kezial thought about that, and it made him nervous. Eleanon was thinking to betray the One? "You forgot Ravenna."

"No, I have not, but I will return to her later."

"So, you want me to help you destroy and then rebuild to your own needs this great citadel—which currently appears to have you locked out—and in reward you will now proceed to promise me the very earth. Yes?"

"No," Eleanon said quietly. "I am going to offer you your lives, Kezial. I am going to offer you the chance to return to Isembaard, or wherever it is you wish to go, once I have Elcho Falling. That is all. Just a chance to live."

Kezial regarded Eleanon stonily.

"I could slaughter you now," Eleanon said quietly, and such menace came over his face then that Kezial believed him absolutely. "You try to attack me and you are dead. Every last one of you, within the hour. You try to escape now and you are dead. Every last one of you, within the hour. Agree to aid me, and you live. It is a simple choice."

"But as you yourself said, you have set yourself against everyone else: the One, who I have heard is a great and powerful god; Maximilian; Axis; Isaiah . . . and whoever else decides to come riding over the horizon claiming a part of Elcho Falling. How can you possibly win?"

"By doing what I am absolutely best at," Eleanon said. "Dark deception. Help me, Kezial."

Kezial didn't know what to think. He really wanted to know what had become of Armat's army. It had been hundreds of thousands strong. Had Eleanon destroyed it? Or was it, as Armat had said, sitting inside Elcho Falling waiting to sally forth and—

"There is only one entrance and exit from Elcho Falling," Eleanon said. He indicated the archway set in the western wall of the citadel. "Anyone entering or exiting has to cross over a narrow causeway through the lake. How vulnerable are they at that point, Kezial?"

Very vulnerable, Kezial thought, as am I, if you have this little trouble reading my thoughts.

Eleanon's mouth curved in a small, cold smile. "Precisely, my friend. Very vulnerable. Of any force issuing forth, we only have to concentrate on a tiny proportion of it as it leaves the citadel."

"The Icarii . . ." Kezial said.

"Mostly dead, now," Eleanon said. "I made sure of that." He paused. "As for any force trying to enter . . . same problem. It is forced to congregate at a single, vulnerable point. Trapped, in essence. There are many soldiers within Elcho Falling—Outlanders, Maximilian's own men, others, but they stay there for that very reason. They'd be slaughtered."

He shifted, reaching across the space between them and resting a hand on Kezial's shoulder.

Kezial tensed, and Eleanon gave his best impression of a reassuring smile. "I need to touch you, Kezial. I want to show you something, and for that you need to see with my eyes, not with your useless, human ones."

Eleanon tilted his head back toward Elcho Falling. "See."

For a heartbeat nothing happened, then Kezial gasped. It was if the substance of Elcho Falling had vanished. There remained the faint outline of walls, but essentially the entire structure had become completely transparent. Eleanon's vision was looking right through Elcho Falling.

Kezial could see no people, but what he did see shocked him to his core.

There was something dark and vile in the heart of Elcho Falling. It looked like a cone-shaped, twisted mountain of sinister evilness, rising from the very base of the citadel. It had roots that stretched through most of the lower levels and walls of the citadel, and right under the lake itself. It looked like a cancerous growth, as yet small, but with deadly potential.

"You are going to use that to destroy Elcho Falling?" Kezial said.

"Partly," Eleanon said. He lifted his hand from Kezial's shoulder, and the vision faded. "Partly, also, I am going to use her."

Now Eleanon nodded to one side, and Kezial looked.

A woman in mid-term pregnancy stood there. Kezial thought he'd never seen a more miserable nor more bedraggled woman, and felt a shiver of shock go through him when he realised it was Ravenna.

Where was the beautiful marsh witch who had captivated the Isembaardian generals with her power and glamour?

"Ravenna has come to a sad fate," Eleanon said. "Ishbel got the better of her, I am afraid. See those dark bloodied bands about her?"

Kezial nodded, unable to speak. He actually felt sorry for the woman.

"They are the physical manifestations of the curse Ishbel laid upon her. The curse cut Ravenna off from all her power and disinherited her unborn son from Elcho Falling and isolated her from society." Eleanon paused. "Of course, I have altered the curse a little now. To suit my purpose."

Ravenna flinched, and Kezial's sympathy increased. He had thought himself trapped, but he realised that it was as nothing compared to Ravenna's entrapment. If Kezial was lucky, he and his men might escape with some semblance of life. He doubted very much Ravenna would manage that much.

"I will be sending Ravenna inside shortly," Eleanon continued, "in order to further my cause—and yours, too, Kezial—and to seed that disaster which shall fell Elcho Falling."

"Then you'll need to do it soon," Kezial said, "before either Maximilian or Axis or even Isaiah return."

"No," said Eleanon. "That is not my plan at all. In fact, I am sitting here idling, and allowing you to idle, Kezial, because I very much want everyone who wants to get back inside Elcho Falling to actually *get* back inside. You see, Kezial, I have devised the most malevolent and devious of plans. Would you like to hear it?"

Kezial looked at Ravenna again. Tears were trickling slowly down her cheeks.

"Yes," he said, returning his eyes to Eleanon. "Yes, I would."

CHAPTER TWO

Hairekeep

Maximilian and his party sat their horses and looked at Hairekeep in the distance.

None of them spoke.

Gone was the lovely rose and cream sandstone fort that Maximilian, Ishbel, Serge and Doyle remembered. In its place rose a vile twisted pyramid of darkness. It extended another five times higher into the sky as the former fort.

On either side of the roadway the sand hands still waved and pointed forward, but their movements were slower now, and the watchers could see that as the hands neared Hairekeep they tended to cringe rather than wave or point.

"Are you certain you trust Josia?" Avaldamon said quietly.

"He is a Persimius," said Maximilian. "And *you* have met and trusted him."

"I never said that I trusted him."

"Avaldamon," Ishbel said, "we need to do this. There are tens of thousands trapped in there. Can any of us just ride by?"

"I could," Serge and Doyle said together, and Ishbel shot them an irritated glance.

"Well, neither Maxel nor I can," she said. "There are families in there, *people*. I can't just—"

"Oh, for the gods' sakes," Avaldamon said, "what would happen if you and Maxel don't come out? What would happen if—"

"We will come out," Ishbel said. "What could defeat the power of Maxel and I combined?"

"The One," Avaldamon said. "Don't overreach yourself, Ishbel."

"We're going in," Ishbel said, and in such a manner that there was nothing more to be said.

They rode closer, stopping some fifty paces out from the black, twisting pyramid. This close it was apparent that the entire structure was moving slightly as it corkscrewed its way to its pinnacle high in the sky.

"I am going to say this again," Avaldamon said, "no matter how much it annoys you, Ishbel. This structure is seething with the power of the One. He is alive and more powerful than ever. Don't go in there."

"I am not—" Ishbel began, but Maximilian reached over and put a hand on her arm.

"Avaldamon, trust us," he said. "We know what we are doing."

"And how many fools have spoken those words as their last," Avaldamon muttered. Then, louder, "Maxel, there is a far greater and far more important battle awaiting you. You can't—"

"Oh, leave it, Avaldamon," Serge said, not unkindly. "We'll settle ourselves down for a game of dice and watch the horses while the heroes go and do their thing."

Thus saying, he and Doyle swung off their horses and settled themselves cross-legged on the roadway, Serge pulling out a bag of dice.

Avaldamon sighed, and dismounted as well. "I wish you well," he said to Maximilian and Ishbel. "But please, think of yourselves before those people. If it *is* a trap, then get out. Leave them."

"I promise," Maximilian said.

He and Ishbel dismounted, handed the reins of their horses to Serge, nodded at Avaldamon, then walked toward Hairekeep.

There was a single door in the base of what had once been the sandstone fort. Maximilian took one of Ishbel's hands, pausing them both at the door. It was cold here, unnaturally cold, and they both shivered.

"Are you sure, Ishbel?" he asked quietly.

She nodded.

"You know what to do?"

"Yes, the foundation stone is easily accessible. I should be able to unwind it, and," she squeezed his hand, "with you with me I shall not have the same troubles and concerns which beset me in DarkGlass Mountain. It will be all right, Maxel. Not pleasant, but all right."

Maximilian glanced up at the darkness extending so far above his head. He could see hands and faces pressing against the blackness, as if the tormented people inside were pressing their flesh against the walls.

"It is like the inside of the Infinity Chamber," Ishbel said, looking also. "Then, the hands aided me. Perhaps they will here, too."

Maximilian smiled at her, then leaned forward and kissed her softly. "Are you ready?"

"Ready."

"Then let the Lord and Lady of Elcho Falling go forth and do battle," he said. He took a deep breath, took the final step toward the door, opened it, and both entered.

"You really don't like this, do you," Serge said to Avaldamon, who was sitting looking toward the fort anxiously.

Avaldamon shook his head. "There is something wrong, wrong, wrong about this. There is the stink of trap, but I cannot see what it is. I don't like it that Josia has involved himself in this. There is no reason why he should . . ."

"He is a bodiless spirit locked in a memory palace," Doyle said. "If it was me, I'd be trying to get my fun wherever I could."

"Still . . ." Avaldamon said. "Still . . ."

"Do you want us to . . . ?" Serge said, raising his eyebrows at Hairekeep.

"No, no. Stay here. There will be nothing you can do. This is power beyond you."

"I'll try not to take that personally," Doyle said, his voice humorous. Then suddenly he started. "By the gods! Is that Ishbel's rat?"

Serge and Avaldamon turned to look where Doyle pointed.

Ishbel's rat sat perched on a rock a little distance away, staring intently at Hairekeep.

Ishbel and Maximilian stood a few paces inside Hairekeep, still hand in hand.

The atrium of the structure stretched up as far as they could see, probably right up to the pinnacle itself. Around the walls wound balconies and stairs.

They were all empty.

There was no sign of any people.

Ishbel frowned. "It isn't like what Josia told us would—"

Then she and Maximilian jumped as a low moan reverberated through the interior of Hairekeep. It tore at their nerves and the deepening physical chill which accompanied it sent further shivers down their spines.

"I don't like this," Maximilian murmured. He looked over his shoulder, reassuring himself the door was still there.

"Ishbel!"

She spun about.

The door had vanished. There was no sign of it, or where it may once have been. Behind them wound staircases and balconies as well, everything twisting up and up and up.

The moan sounded again, then suddenly morphed into a sibilant hiss that lifted the hair on both Ishbel's and Maximilian's heads.

Before either could react, something screamed. It was so harsh that both of them cried out and crouched low, hands over ears.

The next moment came a grinding crash, and everything about them changed.

"Shit! Shit! Shit!" Avaldamon sprang to his feet, staring in total horror at what Hairekeep had become.

"What is it?" Serge shouted, as the fort changed shape and, at the same time, extended even further into the sky so that it almost blocked out the sun.

A vast shadow stretched over the land, falling across the

three men standing with the horses and stretching for thousands of paces beyond them.

"Hairekeep has turned into the physical manifestation of the Twisted Tower," Avaldamon said. "Maxel and Ishbel's memory palace." He stared at the door, then looked up and up the ninety levels of corkscrewed tower to the single window at the very top. "Oh my gods . . ." he whispered.

They rose in horror, staring about. They were standing in an exact replica of the interior of the Twisted Tower, save that everything—the walls, the stairs, the tables, all the objects on the tables and flat surfaces—was made of bone.

Human bone. The small bones made up the objects, while the furniture and walls were made of tens of thousands of femurs and scapulas and skulls.

Her hand trembling, Ishbel lifted one of the objects, the pedestal belonging to a table lamp, and looked carefully at it. Each of the bones in its construction had writing inscribed into it.

I was once Ursula, mother of Claudat, wife of Imeldam. Now I belong to the One.

I was once Killony, daughter of Houral. Now I belong to the One.

I was once Mersiny, wife of Insharah, mother of Eleany, Faran and Jaillon. Now I belong to the One.

"Maxel," Ishbel whispered, and dropped the object.

It shattered into dusty fragments at her feet.

"We need to get out of here," Maximilian said, and, taking Ishbel's hand once more, turned for where the door had been.

It was actually there. But in the instant after they'd taken their first step toward it, bones began to appear as if from nowhere and piled up at fantastic speed to cover the door completely . . . and continued to spill rapidly toward Ishbel and Maximilian.

The door vanished within a heartbeat, and the entire ground floor chamber of the Twisted Tower began to fill with bones.

Maximilian pulled Ishbel toward the stairs that led upward. They raced up them just in time, as the bones filled the entire first chamber.

Then the second chamber began to fill.

Avaldamon felt as though he had turned to stone in his horror. All he could do for the moment was stare; he could not move nor think. The massive structure of the Twisted Tower looked as if a gigantic fist was squeezing it from the very bottom. The tower was contracting, ever upward, as though that fist were trying to squeeze Ishbel and Maximilian toward the . . .

Avaldamon's eyes drifted up to the window at the very top of the tower.

That window was death, whichever way he looked at it. Maximilian and Ishbel would die if they so much as looked through it, and they would also die if they were literally squeezed through it.

Everything here had been a trap set by the One.

By Josia.

Avaldamon could not think. He tried so hard to order his thoughts, but such was his state of shock—at what was happening before his very eyes and at the realisation of who Josia now was—that his thoughts felt as though they'd been buried in deep thick sludge—

A movement to his right caught his eyes.

Serge and Doyle, drawing their swords.

"No!" Avaldamon managed. "No."

Thank the gods, his mouth and thoughts finally seemed to be working again.

"We have to—" Doyle began.

"No," Avaldamon said yet again. "Touch that tower and you both die. Leave it to me. I am a Persimius and I was trained in the Twisted Tower. I know what to do. The thing is . . ."

He turned to look directly at Serge and Doyle. "The thing is, it will kill me, but at least in the doing I can stop this nightmare and hopefully free Ishbel and Maximilian."

He stopped, expecting to have to field protests from both men.

Neither of them spoke. They just looked at him expectantly.

Avaldamon repressed a sigh. They were former assassins, after all. What was the value of human life to them?

"I will die," Avaldamon said, "but I hope that Ishbel or Maxel, pray to the gods both of them, will live. Serge, Doyle, if they don't, then you need to do something very, very important for me."

"Name it," Serge said.

"Get to Elcho Falling as fast as you can and tell whoever commands that citadel that Josia is now the One. The One has inhabited Josia. Do you understand?"

"It is a simple enough concept to grasp, Avaldamon," Serge snapped. "Josia—the One—set this trap?"

Avaldamon nodded.

"Then go aid Ishbel and Maximilian," said Serge, "and Doyle and I shall say prayers each day hereafter for the peace of your soul."

Avaldamon grinned slightly. "I have died before, my friends. This won't be as bad as the giant river lizard. And I have been to the Otherworld before, and I know who waits for me there. My royal Princess, my wife. I have little to lose in this action, my friends, and much to gain."

He gave a nod at the two men, then Avaldamon turned and ran for Hairekeep.

"Maxel, what can we do?" Ishbel managed between gasps as Maximilian hauled her up one more flight of stairs. They could no longer afford to stop and rest—the bones were cascading upward as fast as they could run.

Soon, Maximilian feared, they'd not be able to outrun them any more.

"I don't know," he said, and pulled her onward.

Avaldamon ran to within ninety paces of the parody of the Twisted Tower, then stopped. He steadied his breathing, took another ten or fifteen paces toward the tower. Stopped again.

He rubbed sweaty palms down his clothes. He was

nervous, not at the thought of death, but because he did not want to get this wrong.

Avaldamon would get one chance only.

He closed his eyes, took a deep breath, and turned his mind, just slightly, enough to put himself into that peculiar mentality that all Persimians cultivated for their dealings with the Twisted Tower.

Then he began to walk toward the tower, very deliberately, with slightly longer than normal strides.

As he walked, Avaldamon counted out each step.

"Now look to the pathway," Maximilian had said to Ishbel when first he took her to the Twisted Tower. "There are eighty-six steps to reach the door. You always need to take eighty-six steps, and you must learn to count them as you approach. Soon the eighty-six will become second nature."

"Why eighty-six?" Ishbel had said.

"The tower is a thing of order. It is also a thing of immense memory . . . ordered memory. If you approach it in a disordered manner, then that disorder will reverberate throughout the entire tower."

Avaldamon was now taking increasingly long strides. He was very close to the tower, and as he neared it he shouted out the numbers of the final three steps. "Seventy-seven! Seventy-eight! Seventy-nine!"

Then he grasped the door handle, turned it, and wrenched the door open.

Something screamed. Avaldamon was not sure if it was himself or if it was something within the tower, but the instant he'd opened the door he had felt the entire fabric of his body starting to wrench apart.

The tower was a thing of order, and he had approached it in a most disordered manner.

About him the entire tower vibrated, at first gently, then so violently that Avaldamon felt his body flail about.

He decided it *was* himself who was screaming.

He stopped screaming at that very instant his body disintegrated completely.

* * *

Maximilian and Ishbel tumbled to the floor of the eighty-first level, losing their footing as the tower began to reverberate.

"What is happening?" Ishbel screamed.

"Disorder," Maximilian whispered, and his blue eyes suddenly turned emerald as he wrapped his arms about his wife.

Avaldamon sighed, stretched slightly (more than glad to feel his limbs all in good order), then blinked in amazement.

He had come directly into the Otherworld.

He had thought the journey might take him a while, as it had the first time he had died. Then he saw the reason he had come so directly.

Josia was hurrying toward him. Avaldamon felt a moment of fear, then realised this was the real Josia.

"What has happened?" Josia said.

"Well, surely you know what has happened to you," Avaldamon said wryly.

"Yes, yes, the One ambushed me," Josia said. "But Maxel? Ishbel?"

"Was it you trying to call Maxel?"

"Yes, but I could never reach him. Avaldamon, what has happened to them?"

Avaldamon looked about. "Well, they're not here, which is the best thing I can say."

Even the One was not totally sure what had happened. By Infinity, it had all been going so well, and then Avaldamon . . .

The One was trying to keep his rage in check. Perhaps Maximilian and Ishbel *were* dead, crushed in the rubble of Hairekeep. He managed a grin as he stood at the window at the summit of the Twisted Tower and surveyed the carnage below.

He'd had them so fooled.

Ishbel had almost murdered him with the destruction of DarkGlass Mountain. The One had escaped only at the last moment and only by using the full extent of his ability to manipulate the power of Infinity. He'd been forced to sacrifice life in the flesh to take possession of the bodiless Josia. But, oh, what a hiding place! Bodiless or not, the One could still exert his power over events, still use the power of Infinity.

Still . . . the One missed the feel of wind against flesh, and the warmth of the sun.

CHAPTER THREE

Hairekeep

Serge and Doyle literally did not know what had hit them. They'd watched in horror as Avaldamon tore apart, then saw the entire tower reverberate and collapse.

Before they could say anything, or move, or even blink, something hit them with such resounding force it threw them to the ground and knocked them unconscious.

Doyle was the first to regain his senses. Before he opened his eyes, Doyle was aware of the most appalling stink.

It was the stench of rotting flesh, and it was so bad, so overpowering, that Doyle found it almost impossible to breathe. Coughing and gagging, he pushed a weight away from his chest, opening his eyes only slowly. He'd thought the weight had been Serge, but when he blinked and finally managed to focus his eyes, Serge saw that he'd been covered in the bones and rotting flesh of one of their horses.

"Serge? Serge?" Doyle could barely get the words out, the stench in his throat was so overwhelming. He struggled to his feet, slipping in the slime of the flesh and bones about him, and moaned in revulsion as he surveyed the scene about him.

For as far as Doyle could see, lay rotten flesh and bones. There was a pile of it, perhaps fifty paces high, where Hairekeep had once stood, but the entire landscape was covered in a carpet of rotting, dismembered corpses.

Above the malodorous layer, the buzzing of millions of tiny black flies.

"Gods . . . gods . . ." Doyle muttered, unable to comprehend the enormity or the disgusting nature of the disaster.

These must be the remains of the people the One had trapped in Hairekeep.

He wondered for a moment why he and Serge were still in one piece when their horses had disintegrated, then realised that the horses, which they had so "miraculously" discovered to aid their journey, had likely been constructs of the One, too.

"Serge? *Serge*?" Doyle yelled, struggling about, trying to find his friend.

"Serge?" He slipped and slid, once or twice falling to his knees, always scrambling back to his feet with a cry of disgust, twice stopping to retch up bile. Eventually, he saw a movement to one side and he waded over, tearing away a pile of rotten-fleshed bones and skulls to reveal Serge, coughing and gagging as he regained consciousness.

Doyle helped him up and for long minutes they stood, rooted in horror, trying to get their gag reflexes under control and trying to come to terms with what had happened.

"Fuck," Serge eventually muttered, which, so far as Doyle was concerned, summed up the matter succinctly.

"Maxel and Ishbel?" Serge continued.

Doyle indicated the huge pile of bones and flesh on the site Hairekeep had once occupied. "If they're anywhere, they're in that pile."

Serge muttered an obscenity again, then the two men started to move through the sludge of body parts and bones toward the larger pile.

"How in the gods' names are we going to find them in that?" Doyle said as they neared.

"Perhaps we won't," said Serge. "Perhaps we just need to keep on walking through this obscene sea of flesh and try to get to the coast as fast as we may. We need to get word to Elcho Falling."

"Or perhaps we just need to sail south as fast as we are able to get away from this whole disaster," Doyle said under his breath. Then, a little louder: "Who needs to fight an enemy who can do *this*?"

"Let's just see if we can find what happened to Maxel and Ishbel first," Serge said mildly, knowing Doyle was just venting his disgust and despair.

They reached the pile and stared at it, not knowing where to start. Then Doyle jumped, and pointed. "Look!"

Serge moved his eyes to where Doyle indicated, expecting to see either Maxel or Ishbel, but instead he saw a rat jumping up and down on a spot about a third of the way up the pile.

"Is that . . ." he said.

"If it is Ishbel's rat," Doyle said, "then perhaps it is showing us where they are."

"Or perhaps it is a trick of the One, luring us to our deaths."

"If the One had wanted us dead he would have killed us when the tower disintegrated."

"Maybe he is just toying with us," Serge said.

"Then stay here," said Doyle, "while I go look."

He began slipping and sliding up the mass of bodies, and after a moment Serge followed him.

By the time they got to the place where the rat had been, it had vanished, but there was a tremble of movement in the bones and flesh covering the spot and Doyle and Serge began to dig furiously.

It was foul work, but perhaps half a man's height down they saw a hand waggling at them.

It was Maximilian's hand, and the two men dug all the faster, eventually pulling Maximilian free and Ishbel a moment after him.

Both were in a terrible state, covered in rotting slime and almost unrecognisable, gasping and heaving for breath, but they were alive.

The One stood staring out of the Twisted Tower, leaning on one hand as it rested against the side of the window.

Before him he could just make out Maximilian and Ishbel scrambling from the filth that had once been Hairekeep.

He was cold with fury and frustration.

He had come *so* close.

His hand trembled and he had to stand, clenching his fists to stop himself shaking.

So close . . .

The One should have attacked them while he had them

both in the Twisted Tower, but he had been too wary of their combined power, and he did not know if the Twisted Tower was capable of aiding them as Elcho Falling had.

Three hours later the four had reached land free of human flesh and bone, but they didn't camp until they had put some distance between themselves and the last remains of horror.

Doyle set a fire and the four sat in silence cleaning themselves as best they could with cloth strips from a shirt out of the packs Serge and Doyle had retrieved before they'd begun their wade eastward through the tides of death.

On the walk out of the nightmare each pair had told the other what they'd seen and heard, sharing information. Now they were content to just sit, rest, and come to terms with what they'd all experienced.

"What now, boss?" Serge said after a time.

Maximilian didn't know what to say. He was exhausted, almost too fatigued to think. He felt deep guilt at what had happened at Hairekeep . . . surely he could have foreseen that disaster?

Avaldamon had needed to die in order to save Maximilian and Ishbel from their pride and stupidity.

"I think we need sleep," Ishbel said, knowing how Maximilian felt. She, too, couldn't believe they'd managed to be fooled so easily and that Avaldamon had given his life for them. "We're all tired and overwrought."

"No," Maximilian said, "we need to *think*. We just can't pick up our bags and continue on as if nothing has happened." He looked back to where he could just see, faintly, the end of the area covered in bones and flesh. Even at this distance, if the breeze gusted the right way, he could smell the stink of putrefaction.

"Josia," he continued. "Josia . . ."

"We couldn't have known—" Ishbel began.

"I should have *thought*!" Maximilian snapped.

Ishbel wet her lips, not knowing quite what to say. "Maxel, we need to get to Elcho Falling and warn—"

"We can't leave it that long!" Maximilian said, then apologised to Ishbel for his tone. "I'm sorry. I just . . ."

"I know," she said, as gently as she could.

Maximilian sighed, bringing his emotions under control. "We can't leave it that long. The One is not going to rest in his Josia existence and just wait for us to arrive at Elcho Falling. I gave Axis and through him, Georgdi and Insharah, and gods alone know who else at Elcho Falling, the means to communicate with Josia. Except it isn't Josia they are communicating with, is it? It is the One, and the possibilities for deception are boundless."

"He's going to be even more pissed now he failed to kill you and Ishbel in Hairekeep," Serge remarked.

"Thank you for that observation, Serge," Maximilian said. He rubbed his face with a hand, trying to dredge up the energy he needed to think.

"I have heard a little of Josia and the Twisted Tower," Doyle said. "Maximilian, he can't leave the Twisted Tower, can he?"

"No," Maximilian said, "not if he has inhabited Josia's fleshless existence. He is as trapped in the Twisted Tower as was Josia."

"He needs flesh?" Doyle said.

Maximilian nodded. "In order to leave the Twisted Tower, yes, although I have no idea where the One might find it. He had to wait until Kanubai took corporeal form before he could make the jump into it. Taking 'flesh' is not an easy thing to accomplish if you are not born into it."

"What real damage can he do from the Twisted Tower, then?" Serge said.

Ishbel winced.

"*That* much fucking damage!" Maximilian hissed, waving a hand at the slaughter they'd just taken three hours to walk out of.

No one said anything for a long minute.

"Is it possible to block off the Twisted Tower?" Ishbel said eventually. "Block it off completely from the world of the living?"

"Yes," Maximilian said, "I've been sitting here thinking about it. It can be done, but . . ."

"It is dangerous," Ishbel said.

Maximilian gave her a small, bleak smile.

"What do you need to do?" Ishbel said.

"The actual process is simplicity itself," Maximilian said, "and it reflects somewhat the action Avaldamon took in order to save us."

"The path . . ." Ishbel said.

"Aye, the path that connects this world to that of the Twisted Tower. The path is important . . . it must be negotiated exactly each time—which is the weakness Avaldamon exploited to save us. And if it is not whole, if it is not complete, then no one can enter or leave. The One's connection to this world would be lost."

"He couldn't use the window?" Ishbel said. "He, as Josia, used it to communicate with Elcho Falling."

"No," said Maximilian, "The important connection is that path. When that is disrupted, even the window will be useless."

"Are you certain?" Serge said.

"I am *really* reconsidering the wisdom of travelling with you," Maximilian said, but this time there was no rancour in his voice.

Serge gave a small tip of his head in apology.

"You said it was dangerous," Ishbel broke in, "and yet you also said it was simplicity itself."

"All I need do is lift the initial stepping stone on the path," Maximilian said. "Take away that first stone, that first step, and that will break the connection completely. But . . . while bending down and lifting a slab of stone is not too difficult, if the One knows I am there, and I can't imagine he won't feel it at all, then . . . all he need do is open the door to the Twisted Tower and, while he can't actually walk out, he can unleash his power down the path. He could kill me right then and there. I don't think he'd miss an opportunity like that, Ishbel."

"So . . ." Ishbel said. "He needs to be distracted. At the window."

"Yes," Maximilian said. "If he is distracted at the window, and if he is not made suspicious by that distraction, then I might have a chance."

"How can we distract him?" Ishbel said.

" 'We' can't do it," Maximilian said. "It needs to be whoever he usually talks to within Elcho Falling. Hopefully, that will not arouse his suspicion."

"How do we contact Elcho Falling to arrange that?" Ishbel said.

Maximilian gave her a weak and melancholy smile. "That's what I have been worrying about. It will take us weeks to reach Elcho Falling, at best. I can't leave it that long."

"Maxel?" Ishbel said.

"I can't leave it that long, Ishbel, it wouldn't be—"

"Maxel, it is the rat."

Everyone turned and looked to where she pointed.

There, trundling along as if nothing worrisome had perturbed its day, was Ishbel's rat. It wandered to and fro at the edge of the circle for a bit then, having accepted a scratch of his whiskers from Ishbel's fingers, he settled down on the pack which contained the *Book of the Soulenai*.

"If it wasn't for him," Doyle said, "we wouldn't have found you."

"Then he is welcome enough to the warmth of the fire," said Maximilian.

CHAPTER FOUR

Isembaard, and the Outlands

Maximilian slept that night, so deeply he might almost have been dead, and while he slept, he visited with the dead.

Once again he travelled into the Otherworld, feeling someone's desperate need to meet with him.

This time, however, Maximilian met up with the person who had summoned him hither.

Josia.

Maximilian stopped dead, narrowing his eyes in suspicion.

"It *is* I," Josia said.

Maximilian said nothing.

"*Really*," Josia said.

"I have come to vouch for him," said another voice, and Maxel looked.

There stood Boaz.

"Your father?" Maximilian said.

"He has moved further into the Otherworld to see his wife, my mother," Boaz said. "Do not fret for him, Maxel. He is content."

"This *is* Josia?" Maximilian said.

Boaz grinned. "Yes. This *is* Josia. Thank the gods you escaped, Maxel, although we had to cancel the welcome party we'd arranged for you and Ishbel."

Maximilian allowed himself to relax a little. "Josia, forgive me for—"

Josia raised his hands. "I cannot fault you for your doubt. I tried to warn you, Maxel, but I couldn't get through. I am sorry about what has happened. I had no idea I was so vulnerable to the One. I feel ill at the thought of him within the Twisted Tower."

"Yes," said Maximilian, "I need to talk to you about this." He outlined to Josia and Boaz what he thought to do— isolate the One within the Twisted Tower. "Is this possible? Can the One then reconstruct some connection to the mortal world from the window?"

"Taking that first stepping stone will cut him off effectively," said Josia. "Can he rebuild a connection from the window?" Josia blew out his cheeks, thinking. "I don't know. Maybe. But for now . . . if you can take that stone and isolate him it would help. You need someone to distract him from the upper window, don't you?"

"Indeed," said Maximilian. "Even if *just* for a moment. He will need to physically race down ninety levels to get to the front door and open it before he can do me any harm, and that should give me enough time to upend that stone."

"Ha!" Josia said. "Given that the Lords of Elcho Falling have been trampling on it for thousands of years, that may be harder than you think. But yes . . . you need someone to lure him to that window. Someone he won't suspect. Someone from Elcho Falling. Georgdi is the one he currently speaks to from time to time, I believe."

"Georgdi. Yes. Can you reach him? Can you co-ordinate the timing?"

"No," said Josia, "I can't reach Georgdi. He will not be receptive either to me or the Otherworld. It was hard enough to drag you here. The only person I can contact effectively will be someone who already has intimate knowledge of the Otherworld."

Maximilian grinned. "Axis."

Axis tossed, drifting in and out of sleep. Isaiah was pushing his army hard as they travelled north, and they no longer even took the time to establish their tents at night. Instead, everyone rolled up in blankets on the ground, and this night Axis seemed to have found himself a particularly stony patch.

It made sleeping uncomfortable, but that didn't stop Axis, just before dawn, from drifting into a deep slumber.

In the morning, Axis sought out Isaiah and took him to one side so they could converse privately. In as few words as possible, Axis outlined what Josia had told him.

Isaiah stared at Axis, appalled. "*Josia* is the One?"

"Well, not the Josia now in the Otherworld, no, but the Josia in the Twisted Tower—"

"Yes, yes, I understand." Isaiah took a moment to rub his forehead, momentarily closing his eyes. "Thank the heavens Maxel and Ishbel survived. Now Maxel wants us . . . someone . . . to distract the One while Maximilian attempts to isolate him within the Tower. I don't like that, Axis. It is hugely dangerous, both for whoever tries to distract the One, and for Maxel."

"It has to be done, Isaiah."

Isaiah sighed, and nodded. "When can you contact the Enchanters within Elcho Falling, Axis?"

"Not this far out. It is too risky. We need to be closer."

"And I actually want to be *in* Elcho Falling when this happens, Axis."

"No," Axis said. "That will be too risky as well. If the One knows you are in Elcho Falling he is unlikely to come to the window. He will fear that you will recognise him. Currently he doesn't realise we—you and I—know who he is. He wouldn't have been able to overhear the conversations that took place in the Otherworld. Besides, we'd have a better chance at achieving what we need at Elcho Falling if the One is confined useless within the Twisted Tower. It needs to happen before we enter, Isaiah."

"So you will need to converse with one of the Enchanters outside Elcho Falling. The One might not hear that?"

"He might," said Axis, "but, remember, he doesn't know that *I* know who he is. All I need do is to ask StarHeaven—I have an easy communication with her—to ask Georgdi to speak to Josia at a specified time before we engage in battle with Eleanon and the Lealfast. He should ask Josia if he has any information . . . whether about Maxel or the Lealfast, I don't care. It would be a natural thing for me to do. Georgdi won't know the real reason I am asking him to call to Josia."

"It is risky. Georgdi might not do it—it would be close to battle, he could be distracted . . ."

"Than I will need to impress on him the importance of asking and of asking at the precise time."

"It could all fall apart so easily . . ." Isaiah said.

"I know," Axis said, "but what choice do we have?"

CHAPTER FIVE

The Outlands

They rode north-westward until Isaiah and Axis estimated they were no more than two or three days from Elcho Falling.

The Skraelings had not returned, and none of Isaiah's scouts could find them. Axis fretted about it, as he suspected Isaiah did also, but little was said.

Whatever happened with the Skraelings, happened, and there was little they could do save prepare as best they could for any eventuality.

They did not see a Lealfast, either, although Inardle said they were above, flying invisible.

That worried Axis as much as the continued absence of the Skraelings.

Two days from Elcho Falling Isaiah ordered the army to camp. He wasn't riding any closer until he had a clearer idea of what he faced.

Isaiah and Axis stood apart from the camp, staring into the distance where they could see Elcho Falling.

"Do you have news from the Enchanters inside Elcho Falling?" Isaiah asked.

"The Lealfast Nation continues to stay in Armat's former camp." Axis briefly described the layout for Isaiah. "Kezial and his army are camped about the northern part of the lake."

Isaiah grunted. "Eleanon is keeping them as distant from us as he can, lest Kezial change his mind."

"*Is* Kezial likely to do that? Lamiah did, after all."

Isaiah chewed his cheek, thinking. "I'd always had great hopes for Kezial. I was disappointed when he'd decided to join with Armat, although I can understand why. Eleanon obviously does not trust him."

"It is something to keep in mind."

"Yes. Axis, what of those inside Elcho Falling?"

"They are well. StarHeaven said Georgdi and Insharah are mightily relieved to see us and are preparing the welcome party for our arrival."

"And, um, have they heard from Josia?"

"Indeed. Georgdi told me happily enough that Josia told them Maxel and Ishbel are still deep inside Isembaard, travelling slowly."

Isaiah grunted. "When does Maxel need us to—"

"Tempt the One to the window of his tall, tall tower?" Axis took a deep breath. "Dawn tomorrow. I do not think I will sleep tonight for worry."

"Neither will I." Isaiah stood a little while in silence, thinking of what Maximilian would attempt in the morning, and trying *not* to think of what would happen if he failed. Eventually, he forced his mind to other matters. "Has Georgdi any news of the ship he sent south?"

"Yes," Axis replied. "Georgdi said he has received a signal that the ship is waiting for Maxel and Ishbel on the east coast. Maxel and Ishbel cannot be too far from it now. Josia, the *true* Josia, told me that they are moving fast for the coast."

Isaiah gave a nod and steered the conversation away from Maximilian and Ishbel. At the moment he simply did not want the worry to distract him. "I wish I could *see* what is happening . . . how Eleanon and his forces have arrayed themselves. They are above us. Why haven't they attacked? *I* would have probed at an approaching army's defences, to discover their mettle. But he hasn't."

"Who knows the maddened ways of Eleanon?" Axis said, then he smiled. "But a bird's-eye view I can give you, my friend."

"The eagle is here?" Isaiah cast his gaze upward as Axis nodded toward a speck in the sky.

"My friend eagle," Axis said softly.

* * *

They looked through the eyes of the eagle as it soared high into the thermals. Below they could see themselves, the tiniest of specks on the ground, while between them and the eagle's position they could see the distorted air left by the invisible Lealfast fighters.

"Shetzah!" Isaiah muttered to Axis. "There are thousands of them above us. Axis, can you ask the eagle to fly closer to Elcho Falling?"

Axis nodded, and spoke to the eagle. *Friend eagle, can you approach Elcho Falling safely?*

From the south and east, said the eagle, *yes. But I do not want to fly above the Lealfast encampment, nor above Elcho Falling itself.*

It will do nicely, friend eagle, I thank you. Go as close as you dare, but do not endanger yourself.

Isaiah and Axis waited as the eagle soared closer to the citadel. He approached from the easterly route, up the canal which connected the citadel's lake with the Infinity Sea. Axis studied the thick reed banks to either side of the canal with interest, the germ of an idea forming.

From the eastern canal the eagle tipped his wings and veered northerly, over Kezial's encampment, giving Isaiah and Axis a clear view of the Lealfast Nation's camp to the west.

We thank you, friend eagle, Axis said to him. *Fly away now, linger no longer lest the Lealfast attack.*

That evening Axis and Isaiah sat alone at a campfire, talking. Axis had asked that none of the others join them. What he wanted to say he wanted only Isaiah to hear.

"I wonder if we ride into a trap," Axis said.

Isaiah nodded. "But of what kind?"

"I don't know. But I do not like the fact that Eleanon allows us to approach so unharried. Why? He has the strength and the advantage. If I commanded a winged force of the magnitude of his I would have attacked many days before this. They have no reason to allow us so close to Elcho Falling, or to allow us to continue toward Elcho Falling."

"Aye. I agree. What are you thinking?"

CHAPTER SIX

Elcho Falling and Isembaard

Axis hardly slept for worrying. Everything could go wrong far too easily. He wondered if Maximilian, somewhere on the northern plains of Isembaard, was also lying awake, perhaps staring at the stars, wondering if Josia's message had got through to Axis, and if Axis and Georgdi could coordinate enough to accomplish what Maximilian needed.

If only he could tell Georgdi the reason behind what was about to happen. It would make everything so certain. But Axis couldn't tell him. He didn't know if the One could intercept his mental speech or not, and he didn't know if Eleanon could. Too many uncertainties.

Too many things to go wrong.

Axis sighed, turning over restlessly in his blankets to stare at the stars.

Maximilian was so anxious he could not even lie down. He spent the night pacing about the camp, sometimes standing for almost an hour at a time, staring northward.

He loathed the fact he had so little control. He depended on Axis and Georgdi coming through for him: the plans had to be ferried from Maximilian to the land of the dead, and from there back to the land of the living where so many other factors could warp the original message.

Axis had only to sleep in and everything would fail.

Eleanon could attack precipitately and neither Axis nor Georgdi would be able to follow through.

Georgdi, not knowing what was at stake, could prefer to have his breakfast than to contact "Josia" so early.

"I am thinking he *wants* us in Elcho Falling, or at least very, very close to it. I have no idea why, or what he has planned . . ."

"Again, I agree," Isaiah said. "And again I can see that you want to say more, so speak it."

Axis sighed, playing for time as he ordered his thoughts. "I don't think we should give Eleanon what he wants."

"Explain."

"I don't think we should allow *all* of us to be herded into Elcho Falling."

Isaiah nodded slowly, smiling. "I was going to suggest the very same thing."

Now it was Axis who grinned. "Of course you were! You just wanted me to have the honour of suggesting it first!"

They both laughed, spending a moment pouring ale into mugs and sipping it.

"You want to remain outside?" Isaiah said to Axis.

"Yes. I had thought to keep a small force of men with me, but I think the Lealfast would spot us too easily. One man stands a chance of remaining hidden."

"You'll be spotted anyway," said Isaiah. "The Lealfast have the advantage of flight."

"Not necessarily," Axis said. "I have an idea about that . . . but just imagine, Isaiah, how useful I could be outside Elcho Falling. I can sound out Kezial. Keep an eye on Eleanon. Be *watchful*. And we can keep in contact easily."

Indeed, said Isaiah in Axis' mind, *so long as you don't wander more than a day's walk away*.

One of Axis' fingers tapped at the rim of his ale mug as he thought. "Isaiah . . . how helpful can those juit birds be?"

Isaiah chuckled. "Depends what you have in mind."

"Can we speak to them?"

"In the morning, my friend. Now, tell me what it is you have planned."

As Axis and Isaiah sat at their campfire, so Kezial and Eleanon stood at the edge of the Lealfast encampment, staring south.

"Isaiah isn't far away," Kezial said.

"Two days," said Eleanon. "But I doubt he will march straight into our maws. Kezial . . ."

"Yes?"

"The Skraelings have vanished."

"What?"

"Many days ago."

"You made no mention of this."

Eleanon shrugged, dismissing Kezial's anger. "They were herding Isaiah and his army northward . . . and then one dawn my scouts reported the entire horde had vanished."

"How could they just 'vanish'?"

Another shrug, and Kezial bit down a bitter retort. What else was Eleanon keeping from him?

Likely an entire "horde" of secrets.

"Can Skraelings just vanish?" he asked Eleanon.

"It is possible. Who knows what the One has done to them." Eleanon paused, and Kezial sensed that Eleanon was now getting to the reason he had summoned Kezial.

"Isaiah is also travelling with a few million, give or take five or six, pink birds."

Kezial gaped at him, unable for the moment to speak.

Eleanon turned his cold eyes on Kezial. "Do you know what these pink birds are?"

"Are they tall gangly things, long necks and legs, over-sized beaks?"

"Yes. They apparently squabble a great deal. They arrived at Isaiah's force just ahead of the Skraelings."

Kezial's mouth curved in a small smile. "Then they are most likely juit birds. They come from a lake to the south of Aqhat."

Eleanon's gaze grew more intense. "And what significance are the juit birds? For what reason do they attach themselves to Isaiah?"

"As for reason, I am guessing they escaped the Skraelings who—"

"But the Skraelings had left Isembaard, massing north." Kezial shrugged.

"What significance, then?" Eleanon said, his tone now growing as sharp as his eyes.

Kezial held his gaze steadily. "No signi water birds, they squabble a great deal as yo they are truly terrible eating. I have no idea attached themselves to Isaiah's army, but if I w truly irritated about it."

"They're trouble," Eleanon said. "I can smell trouble about them."

Kezial shrugged. "They are silly pink birds," "They have no significance at all beyond that, Elean

Later, when Kezial was alone in his tent, he spent lon sitting at his camp table, staring at the moths flutterin the bowl of the lamp.

Isaiah has the juit birds?

Kezial had been down to Lake Juit several times. F been there when Isaiah had pulled Axis from the world.

The juit birds were not just "silly pink birds" at all. were one of the great mysteries of Isembaard.

Kezial began to think carefully about his next move

No one else in Maximilian's camp slept, either. They sat around the campfire, eyes following Maximilian as he paced, and no one, not even Ishbel, dared say a word to him.

Axis rose well before dawn. He tried to keep his activities routine—*perhaps the Lealfast were watching him from above, relaying his movements to the One*—but he was too restless to do much other than dress, fidget, ignore the food one of the soldiers brought him, and wander around the campfire, turning to watch the eastern sky for the first intimation of dawn every minute or so.

If he were being watched, Axis knew he could be making either Eleanon or the One, or both, very anxious. They would wonder what he planned.

He waited as long as he could, then he called to Star-Heaven.

StarHeaven! StarHeaven!

It took her a moment or two to wake from her sleep, moments that Axis spent pacing back and forth cursing under his breath. *StarHeaven!*

Yes?

I need you to wake Georgdi. Now. Ask him to call Josia to his window from his magical Twisted Tower. Tell Georgdi that Isaiah and myself consider a dawn attack and we wonder if Josia can tell us the disposition of the Lealfast and Kezial's armies. Can you do that?

Axis—

StarHeaven . . . do . . . it . . . now! I need Josia to advise us!

Then, risking everything, Axis sent her a bolt of pure emotion—a combination of anxiety and urgency and desperation. Icarii rarely used pure emotion to communicate. It was unsettling and physically disturbing to the recipient, but Axis hoped that it would impress on StarHeaven, like nothing else, the sheer urgency and importance of his request.

He felt a stunned silence from her. Then . . .

Immediately, StarMan. I understand.

Thank you, StarHeaven. Please let me know immediately you have spoken to Georgdi. And please impress on him the—

I understand, *StarMan*.

Axis shut up. He wanted to shout at StarHeaven all the way along the corridors of Elcho Falling into Georgdi's quarters, but he literally bit his tongue and kept his mind quiet.

Maximilian stopped suddenly, then turned to the campfire. "It will soon be time," he said.

Ishbel and the two Emerald Guardsmen rose.

"Do you have the tools?" Serge said. Last night he and Doyle had taken two sturdy knives and fashioned them into digging tools.

Who knew how tough that simple stepping stone would be to raise.

"Yes," Maximilian said. He looked at Ishbel and she came over to him.

"Ishbel . . ."

"What is it?"

Maximilian hesitated. "I don't know what might happen. I don't know what might go wrong."

"Maxel—"

"Listen to me a moment, Ishbel. *If* it goes badly wrong either you or I, or both of us, are going to have to untether ourselves from the Twisted Tower."

"What? I don't understand."

"The Persimius kings and princes," Maximilian said, "kept open the pathways to the Twisted Tower so that, should they ever need the knowledge, there it sat. Every young prince learned the pathways to the Twisted Tower. I had to teach you. Remember?"

She nodded.

"For thousands of years," Maximilian continued, "in a direct unbroken line, all the princes and kings of the Persimius name kept open the pathway. Each of them travelled there and back. Each kept the mental skills needed to reach the Twisted Tower. *That is the real connection.* At the moment, Ishbel, you and I are the only two remaining alive who have the skills needed to reach the Twisted Tower and that is enough to keep the Twisted Tower tethered to this world. It is needed, it is used. Our minds, Ishbel, are the machinery that connect the Twisted Tower to this world."

"I still don't understand what you are trying to tell me."

"If we forget those skills, Ishbel, if we lose them, *then there is no connection left between this world and the Twisted Tower*. It will simply drift off, perhaps even evaporate completely, I don't know, but there will no longer be any connection between this world and it. We are the bridge, Ishbel."

He took a deep breath. "Losing the Twisted Tower and all its knowledge is the last thing I want to do. I would prefer that I disconnect the pathway so that, if needed at a later date, I can put the stone back and reconnect ourselves to the tower. But if I cannot do what I intend this day, then we may have to untether our minds from the tower. If I fail, and the One takes me, then *you* will have to do it. Untether the Twisted Tower from this world."

"And lose you with it?" Ishbel said.

"If need be, yes. Ishbel, we have to be prepared for this."

She gave an unhappy nod. "How do we lose the skill?"

"It is actually fairly simple. You remember how I put my hands about your head? How I cradled it?"

"It felt as if your fingers dug into my mind, shifting it slightly, twisting it."

"And thus we can 'untwist' our minds. It is easier if we do it simultaneously, if we take each other's heads in our hands and twist away the other's mind, but we can also do it to ourselves. Ishbel, if I am trapped, will you do this?"

"I would prefer it if you came back."

That raised a slight smile from Maximilian. "I would prefer it, too. I would prefer it if we do not lose the Twisted Tower completely. But . . . if what I try does not succeed . . ."

She nodded. "Come back, Maxel."

He kissed her. "Be prepared. Do what you need to."

They held each other a moment, then Maximilian moved away.

"Bloody Axis," Georgdi grumbled, hauling himself out of his bed.

"It *is* urgent," StarHeaven said, watching restlessly as Georgdi fumbled with his breeches and boots.

"I don't see why he couldn't have waited until—"

"Do it *now*, Georgdi," StarHeaven said, and something in her tone made Georgdi pause and look at her with sudden understanding in his eyes.

"Very well," Georgdi said, rising and grabbing a shirt and jerkin as he walked over to the window. He slipped his arms into the shirt, pulled it over his head, then called for Josia as he slid the jerkin on.

"Josia? Josia? There is a matter of urgency. May I speak with you?"

Maximilian hovered at the very edge of the Twisted Tower's strange immaterial world for as long as he dared, then stepped forth to the beginning of the path.

He stood there, not daring to breathe, certain that the One would any moment fling open the door and destroy him . . . then he looked upward.

It was a long, long way to the top of the tower, but he could see a tiny figure there, balanced easily on the window-sill, one leg swinging in the air.

Maximilian felt a rush of gratitude for everyone who had come through for him at this moment, then he bent down to the ground, drawing the digging tools from his belt.

"Path, I break thee," he murmured, then jemmied one of the tools under the thick stone of the first step.

"Axis would like to know how the Lealfast and Isembaard-ians are disposed," Georgdi said.

"Now?" Josia said.

Georgdi spread his hands in a gesture of innocent help-lessness. "Who can know the ways of the StarMan," he said. "I'm sorry to raise you at such an unearthly hour, Josia . . . or do you not sleep at all? I've often wondered how you—"

Josia made a noise of irritation. "The Lealfast are arrayed as they were last night when Axis had his damned eagle out flying. The Isembaardians the same. I don't know why Axis has to ask me. *Now.*"

"Maybe he doesn't trust the eagle," Georgdi said and, as the words fell from his mouth, he had an extraordinary revelation.

Axis didn't trust Josia.

And as he thought so, Josia caught his thought, and everything changed.

The stone was thick and settled firmly into the soil by thousands of years of the booted feet of the Lords of Elcho Falling passing over it.

Maximilian dug around it frantically, earth flying everywhere scratching and grazing his fingers. Every now and then he'd glance upward, his heart racing.

And then he would bend to his work, beads of sweat on his forehead, and he cursed the damned, damned stone.

"Maximilian!" Josia hissed, and Georgdi took several paces backward as Josia suddenly turned into something dark and loathsome.

Georgdi heard StarHeaven cry out and scramble for the door and Georgdi took a moment to hate her for being closer to the door than he.

By all the gods in heaven, what was it that now writhed in the window?

"Go!" Georgdi managed to wrench from his fear-tightened throat, and he wasn't sure if he meant it for the thing in the Twisted Tower's window, or for himself, or for StarHeaven.

All three he decided.

"I am going to kill you," the malevolent mass in the window said, and Georgdi hoped he meant it for someone other than himself.

Maximilian knew the instant the One realised. It hit as if all the force of one of these cursed stepping stones was thrown from the window of the Twisted Tower and he cried out in horror.

His fingers scrabbled frantically, but the stone still wouldn't move, it still wouldn't move, the cursed bloody thing still wouldn't move . . .

* * *

The One flew down the stairwell of the Twisted Tower. He
had morphed into a mass that was not human or animal or
anything even remotely recognisable as one of the creatures
of this world. He was sheer anger and hatred and fear, pure
emotion and power, a whirlwind of Infinity gathering to
himself ever more dark energy and force as he rounded each
bend in the stairwell.

When he reached the bottom of this tower and opened
that door, nothing was going to save Maximilian.

Not this time.

Maximilian could sense the One flying down the stairwell,
feel him coming closer and closer with every heartbeat.

"*Move,* you sod!" he hissed at the stone, thinking that if
he couldn't get it in the next moment or so he would give up
and flee.

*But he'd never have another chance. The One wouldn't
allow him near the Twisted Tower again.*

Now he could hear the One roaring, screaming out what
he intended to do to Maximilian once he flung open that
door . . . and the stone moved under Maximilian's fingers. He
thought for an instant that his fingers, now wet with sweat,
had slipped on the stone, but, no, it had moved.

He scrabbled even more frantically, trying to get his fingers under the stone, and then, suddenly, appallingly, the
One flung open the door of the Twisted Tower and rage and
power seethed down the path toward Maximilian.

CHAPTER SEVEN

Isembaard

Ishbel had been pacing back and forth just beyond the warmth of the fire, her eyes constantly on Maximilian's form where it reclined to one side.

Serge and Doyle sat by the fire, their eyes tracking Ishbel.

"Ishbel—" Serge began, unable to bear the tension any longer, when Maximilian twitched, his eyes flew open and he rolled to one side before scrabbling to his feet.

"Ishbel!" he cried. "We have to—"

She knew, instantly. Before Maximilian had finished speaking, she was with him, grabbing his head in her hands.

"We have to—" he began again, taking her head in his hands.

"I know," she muttered. "Do it *now*, Maxel!"

Serge and Doyle had sprung to their feet. They didn't know the specifics of what was happening, but they reacted instinctively to Maximilian's obvious fear and urgency by unsheathing their swords.

"Shetzah!" Doyle cried, turning in a tight circle.

They had walked far from that ring of disintegrating bodies around Hairekeep, but now, as Serge and Doyle watched in horror, those dismembered bits of bodies—in a state of ghastly putrefaction—began bursting from the earth all about them. The body parts writhed on the surface of the ground for several heartbeats then, to the guardsmen's horror, the bodies began to reassemble themselves.

Already the lower half of a man's torso was staggering toward Maximilian's camp, its arms, shoulders and chest scrabbling furiously after it before they caught up and the arms began hauling the chest and shoulders up their companion legs.

Behind it, thousands of bodies were, in fits and starts, sorting themselves out for an attack on Maximilian.

A black mist rose over the entire field of the reassembling dead.

The One's power.

Doyle glanced at Ishbel and Maximilian.

They were standing close, holding each other's heads in their hands and apparently unaware of the rising death about them.

Eleanon was sitting on a stool in the middle of the Lealfast camp, shaving his chin, when he felt the influence and power of the One surge into the land.

His hand halted, then dropped the razor as Eleanon rose, looking frantically about.

By the stars, what was happening! Was he under attack from the One?

All he could feel was death rising in a great tidal surge about him.

Eleanon began to panic.

They took a long moment to reorientate and concentrate, to shut out what was happening about them, to forget, as much as they were able, the sense that the One's power roared toward them.

They had to forget, somehow, that they were within moments of death and concentrate only on each other.

"Do you feel?" Maximilian murmured.

"Yes," Ishbel whispered, and then they slid fingers of power into each other's mind, and gently twisted.

"I don't like these odds," Serge muttered, standing shoulder to shoulder with Doyle, facing the advancing horde of half-reconstituted bodies lurching toward them. They were within fifteen or sixteen paces and both men could hear the peculiar squelchy sound of the bodies' movements.

Very few of them had found their heads.

"You don't say," Doyle said, squaring his legs as he adjusted his balance.

To one side, the rat scrambled over to where Ishbel had left the *Book of the Soulenai*, and tucked its front paws inside the front cover of the book.

The first of the bodies reached the campsite, and Serge and Doyle stepped forward, fighting with the skills of former assassins and current Emerald Guardsmen.

Their swords flashed in the firelight, slicing through bodies on both forward and backward swings.

Bodies, dismembered, fell to the ground and began once more to reassemble themselves, their movements frantic.

More and more of the dead lurched into the camp, and Serge and Doyle began to sweat, then, horrifically, Doyle slipped in a pool of rotten blood and fell over, one shoulder and arm slamming into the fire and sending up a shower of sparks and flames.

Now, Maximilian said, and something simultaneously clicked in both of their minds.

Emptiness, where once had rested the knowledge to walk the paths to the Twisted Tower.

For the first time in thousands of years, there was no Persimius left alive who could remember the pathways to the Twisted Tower.

For the first time in thousands of years, there was no connection left between the Twisted Tower and this world.

All the bodies shambling toward the camp suddenly stopped, then fell apart.

Serge stared for one single heartbeat, then he spun around and helped Doyle roll away from the fire, and to beat back the flames that licked at his jerkin.

No! the One screamed as he realised what had just happened, what they had done. He still stood at the open doorway of the Twisted Tower, staring down the path.

But now, instead of looking at Maximilian and Ishbel's camp, he looked into a featureless void.

No.

Untethered, the Twisted Tower gently spun away into eternity.

Eleanon had just been about to scream for the Lealfast to rise into the air and to escape, escape the One's wrath, when he froze on the spot, his mind trying to grasp what had just happened. First, the One's full power surging into this world from the Twisted Tower, raging at . . . *someone*.

Then, nothing. It stopped, like a gushing faucet dammed in an instant.

There was *no* sense of the One.

Eleanon's mouth opened, then closed, his mind churning. How . . . what . . . had Maximilian somehow cut off the Twisted Tower? It was the only thing that made sense.

Eleanon stood there, all his senses scrying.

The One was gone.

Truly gone. Not relocated, not dismembered, not hiding.

Gone.

Completely.

But . . . and again his senses scried forth . . . Eleanon's ability to touch Infinity had not been affected. It still throbbed through him, nowhere near the same power as that the One had commanded, but still there.

Coming through the Dark Spire.

There was no one to stop him now.

Exultation filled Eleanon, and he sprang into the air. He went up and up and up, high into the sky, almost vertically, his powerful wings driving him upward at an extraordinary speed.

Then, when he was a mere speck in the sky, Eleanon flipped over and plunged for the earth, wings left limp to stream behind him, rippling in the force of the downward plunge, feathers ripping out now and again, leaving a haze of soft white to drift down in the wake of his crazy plunge.

He pulled himself up just before he hit the ground, landing breathless before the Lealfast elder, Falayal.

"The One is gone!" Eleanon hissed, his face jubilant. "*Nothing* stands in our way now!"

Falayal gaped, trying to find something to say.

"But I can still feel the power of Infinity," he said finally.

"It is still here. We can still touch Infinity through the Dark Spire. Maximilian must have cut the One off. Ha! The Lord of Elcho Falling may have thought to have done himself a favour, but he has done us an even bigger act of kindness! The pathways to the power of Infinity remain open, yet the One himself has been isolated. Nothing can prevent us taking what we want now, Falayal."

Falayal looked at Eleanon, then finally, slowly, he smiled.

Maximilian and Ishbel let go of each other's heads, then fell into a tight embrace.

"Thank the gods," Ishbel murmured, hugging her husband to her as hard as she dared.

He laughed, kissing her forehead and cheek and mouth. "What can stop us now?" he said. "It is home to Elcho Falling for you and me, my darling."

To one side, Doyle—his garments a little singed—and Serge sheathed their swords, grinning at the couple. Then Doyle looked to the left of Maximilian and Ishbel, and frowned.

"The rat and the *Book of the Soulenai* have vanished," he said.

The One could not believe it. He was utterly stunned in disbelief.

Tricked.

By something so simple a child should have thought of it.

He stood at the open doorway of the Twisted Tower, one hand resting on the doorframe, staring down what had once been a path but which was now black, empty nothingness. All the One's rage had gone. Emptiness had replaced that, too.

Think. He had to think.

Maximilian and Ishbel had cut the ties from their world to the Twisted Tower. They had destroyed their knowledge of how to tread the path between their world and this tower, and thus cast it adrift.

Where was he? *Where was he?*

Anxiety now replacing his initial disbelief, the One looked about, sensing empty wilderness. Had *his* connection to Maximilian's world been lost, too?

Nothing . . . there was nothing?

Now the One had to fight down panic. Surely there must be something . . . *some* connection remaining?

Nothing. He could sense nothing.

Suddenly the One moved. He took a single step back inside the Twisted Tower, slammed shut the door, and with huge, hungry strides raced up the stairs toward the top chamber.

CHAPTER EIGHT

The Central Outlands

The Skraelings had not actually left the site where they had camped just outside Isaiah's encampment.

They had just slewed slightly through reality. Just as they vanished from the sight of Isaiah and Axis and all who accompanied them, so also Isaiah and his companions and army vanished from the Skraelings' sight. The entire Isembaardian army could have marched through the Skraeling mass and felt nothing more than the brush of air against their legs, while the Skraelings themselves would not have been aware of them.

They had sequestered themselves from reality in order to debate their future.

The Skraelings were consumed by a welter of emotions. Foremost was anger—aimed, initially, entirely at Isaiah. Isaiah had turned them from their enchanted, powerful form into these repulsive creatures who had no beauty and no dignity and no power. He had then forgotten them, leaving them to drift for aeons as creatures hated by all other races. Then, having suddenly remembered his oversight, Isaiah had returned to the Skraelings the power to choose their own destiny, the power to return to their form of River Angels, but only via the medium of *water*, of *drowning*.

That was, for the Skraelings, the ultimate cruelty. The ultimate spitefulness. Isaiah *knew* they hated and feared water. He *knew* it, yet he'd made it a precondition that they embrace this terror if they wanted once again to be River Angels.

And who really knew if this wasn't simply some plan to just slaughter them? Tell them some fabulous tale about long lost mystery forms, convince them that all they had to do to regain this form and mystery was to drown themselves.

Maybe Axis had planned the entire thing.

This stank of the StarMan.

Probably backed up by Inardle. She was a Lealfast. She hated them as much as Axis did.

From their anger at Isaiah the Skraelings morphed seamlessly into hatred of Axis. He was the BattleAxe, the Star-Man, he the one who had slaughtered so many of their cousins in Tencendor. He was their implacable enemy.

Why had they not killed him when they had the chance? When he sat among them? Why had they not also killed Isaiah and Inardle when they, too, sat among—

"Stop," Ozll said into the maelstrom of rising, black emotion. "Stop. Isn't this what condemned us in the first instance? Isn't this what we want to discard and leave forever behind us? Or is this what we want to remain, forever? Brothers and sisters, cousins and friends, *look* at us. *Look* at us. Then remember what Isaiah showed us. That was not a lie. It was memory. Truth. It was from whence our memories of Veldmr came. Stop. Think. We've allowed our emotions to overcome our intellect."

He paused, looking at the doubt in all the faces surrounding him. "Yes," Ozll said, "we do have intellect, and we could have pride in ourselves again. But we need to discuss this rationally and we need to come to a decision about what to do from a place of calmness. Not from a state of fear or anger or suspicion. Now, who will speak?"

The mass was quiet a long time. The Skraelings found it difficult to damp into quiescence their habitual suspicion and fear and anger. All three states were by now so natural to them it was difficult to let go of them.

Finally, a young female Skraeling by the name of Graq spoke. "What are we now?" she said. "Do we want to stay this way?"

That was rare straight speaking, and the Skraeling mass responded by moaning, their bodies weaving to and fro in distress.

"We are hateful," one among them hissed.

"Ugly," said another.

"Far uglier *now* than before," another said. "We grow uglier with each day. And more hateful."

"But don't we *like* being ugly and hateful?" someone asked. "All run in fear of us. Don't we like that? Don't we feed from their terror?"

Many among the Skraelings began to weep, great painful sobs that left their silvery orbs quivering in distress.

"No," Ozll said for them all, "we don't like that. And perhaps we'd like to change, now we have been given the opportunity."

He hesitated a moment. "And perhaps we have been too consumed by emotion these past days and hours to have noticed something. Something important. Who knows what it is?"

No one spoke for a long time, although many brows creased and mouths mumbled.

"The One is gone," Graq said, eventually. "The One is gone very, very far away."

"Yes," Ozll said. "We are now masterless. Again. And maybe that is a good thing, for maybe we might like to consider the opportunity to be our own masters, for a change."

CHAPTER NINE

Elcho Falling

Isaiah stood motionless in the dim pre-dawn light. It was a week since Maximilian had succeeded in trapping the One inside the Twisted Tower. Over the past two days Isaiah had moved his army north to the very boundaries of Elcho Falling. He was directly south of it now, within fifty paces of the lake, the citadel looming high above him, his army arrayed in battle gear in formation behind him, Kezial's force and the Lealfast similarly arrayed some five hundred paces further up the lakeside.

Everyone had deployed yesterday.

The night had been spent waiting.

"You have not slept," Axis said quietly to one side. The general Lamiah stood to Isaiah's other side. All three had stood here in lengthy silence, watching, waiting, thinking. "Are you all right? You look exhausted."

"I have been preparing a treat for Eleanon," Isaiah said. "I will explain once it is fully light."

He looked a little anxiously to the east as he said this, and Axis had to bite down a further query.

"What is going to happen today, Isaiah?" Lamiah said.

"You know I think that Eleanon is going to play at keeping us out of Elcho Falling," Isaiah said.

"Yes," Lamiah said, "you have told me what you and Axis think. But are you certain?"

Isaiah gave a hollow laugh. "No. I am not. But why else has he allowed us to get this close?"

"Perhaps because he has a trap waiting," Lamiah said.

Isaiah and Axis said nothing. They also worried about this. It was all very well to theorise that Eleanon had not attacked them because he wanted them to enter Elcho Falling . . . but why would he do that? And what if he actually wanted them to get this far in one piece so that he could catch them in some as yet unsuspected trap? Too many what ifs.

"Too many unknowns," Lamiah said, echoing the thoughts of the three men. "Eleanon holds all the cards. We are going to be forced onto a tiny exposed causeway to enter Elcho Falling, and he has a massive winged force."

"Plus Kezial's force," said Isaiah.

"Isaiah?" Axis said, nervous and jumpy and wishing Isaiah would tell them what he'd been doing all night.

"Are the men prepared, Lamiah?" Isaiah said.

"Yes," the general answered, "they know what to do and say if they get into hand-to-hand fighting with Kezial's men."

"Are you ready, Axis?" Isaiah said.

"Yes," Axis replied. "Isaiah, what were you doing last—"

"I see the juit birds are in position," Isaiah said.

Axis bit back a hiss of frustration. It was growing lighter and he looked toward the lake.

There bobbed the millions of juit birds, apparently oblivious to the extraordinary citadel rising at their backs or the opposing armies gathered on the shore.

Axis and Isaiah had conversed with the birds a week ago. It had been the most amazing conversation; Axis had understood most of it, but it had been difficult. It was similar to communicating with the eagle (Axis glanced up, searching for that speck in the sky, but as yet it was too dark to see him), but more . . . garbled.

The juit birds were not easy about it, but they had agreed to Axis and Isaiah's request.

Stars alone knew if they would go through with it, and stars knew what the Lealfast had made of the birds' appearance.

"Have any of the scouts spotted the Skraelings?" Isaiah said.

Everyone remained worried about the Skraelings. They could appear at any time to create mayhem and destruction, and none knew which side they'd attack, or even if they would discriminate.

"And Georgdi and the other commanders in Elcho Falling?" Isaiah asked Axis.

"They are prepared," Axis said, "for just about anything—they have as little idea as we as to what to expect from this day. But whatever eventuates, they have manned the entrance into Elcho Falling. They are prepared to help if they think we might need them, but they know that to assay forth will create even more problems if we need to get into Elcho Falling."

"There are tens of thousands who may need to get into Elcho Falling in a hurry," Isaiah said, "and the only entrance they have is that narrow causeway. We can't afford to—"

"They won't come out of Elcho Falling unless it is absolutely necessary," Axis said. "Isaiah, for all the gods' sakes, what were you doing all night?"

"Creating mayhem," Isaiah said, "and I fear what I have done very much."

Axis shared a look with Lamiah.

"*What have you done, Isaiah*?" Axis said.

"It is light enough now," Isaiah said, and he nodded to the east, over the Infinity Sea.

Axis and Lamiah looked.

"Stars . . ." Axis murmured. Then, louder, "Isaiah, what *is* that?"

"It is a mayhem," Isaiah said.

All three stared east. In the far distance, over the Infinity Sea, gigantic black clouds roiled and lightning flashed. Axis, with his powerful Icarii vision, could see the waves beneath the storm clouds churning, the waters punctuated with what appeared to be thousands upon thousands of strikes by hailstones, or . . .

"Ice spears," Isaiah said, very softly. He sighed, raising his voice a little. "I am Water. I am a god. I have more powers at my fingertips than most mortals could even begin to imagine. The ability to create a mayhem is one of the most powerful of them."

"It is a storm," Lamiah said.

"No," said Isaiah. "It is not a storm. At the moment it looks like one, but there is a reason this is called a mayhem.

I can create it . . . but I cannot control it. It will be a storm such as none of you have ever witnessed or endured, and it will be desperate."

"Why create it if it is that dangerous?" Axis said. "What will happen? How long will it last?"

"I made it because I do not trust this day ahead," Isaiah said. "I wanted some insurance and this is it. It will truly turn this battle into mayhem, and you two will need to prepare the soldiers as best you are able. It *will* strike the Lealfast from the sky, though. No one will be able to fly in this. Axis, make sure the Icarii within Elcho Falling know to stay *inside*."

"Will it damage Elcho Falling?" Axis said.

"No," Isaiah said, but his worried glance at the citadel belied his denial.

"When will it arrive?" Lamiah said.

Again Isaiah looked toward the mayhem. "It is moving faster than I'd thought," he said. "We have perhaps two hours, maybe less."

"Shetzah!" Lamiah muttered, then he was off, striding for his horse.

"Stars, Isaiah," Axis said. "Should we retreat?" *This was such a fucking bad idea, Isaiah*, he thought, not caring if Isaiah picked up the thought. "If we get caught out in the open in this then—"

"We're going to get caught out in the open no matter what we do now, Axis. There is no shelter anywhere save within Elcho Falling. We don't have a choice any more. I'm sorry. Mayhems are always difficult to manage. But if nothing else it will protect us against the Lealfast, and last night I could not sleep for worry that Eleanon has something deadly to throw at us."

Axis muttered something uncomplimentary, but he supposed he could understand Isaiah's reasoning. "What should I do?"

"As we have planned," Isaiah said. "Both the lake and the juit birds will protect you. The mayhem will last—" he glanced its way again "—maybe three or four hours. We will just have to survive it."

Axis looked at the approaching massive tempest. "Well . . . if it keeps the Lealfast off our backs . . . when do we move, Isaiah?"

"Now."

Eleanon wheeled far above them, cloaked in invisibility. He, too, watched the mayhem.

He had a good idea what it was.

Eleanon smiled. It would work even better for him than for Isaiah. Then his smile died as he once more looked at the lake, now densely covered with bobbing pink-feathered bodies.

They were far too quiet.

He could control virtually everything . . . save those damned inscrutable birds.

CHAPTER TEN

Elcho Falling

"W hen?" Kezial said, curtly. He sat his horse on a small rise to the west of the battle. Eleanon was standing to one side, his gaze fixed on the fighting. Wind from the approaching mayhem whipped about them, making the horse skittish and raising goosebumps on Kezial's flesh.

"Soon," Eleanon said, the feathers on his wings rippling in wild patterns in the wind.

Kezial bit back his frustration. He wanted to order his men in—if not for quite the same reason Eleanon might want to order them in.

He took a deep breath, concentrating on the battle.

Isaiah's army had marched forward just after dawn, to be instantly attacked by the Lealfast. They'd been at it for half an hour now . . . and mostly the tide was turning in the Lealfast's favour. While not many of Isaiah's soldiers had fallen, they were pinned to the ground, shields in defensive array over their heads as the Lealfast attacked from above.

"That storm looks vicious," Kezial observed.

Eleanon shot him an amused glance. "Attack, then," he said.

Kezial hesitated a moment, staring at Eleanon, then he kicked his horse forward, signalling to his army. It began moving immediately.

Eleanon watched for a while, until Kezial's men were almost ready to join in the battle, then he sent a pre-arranged signal to the Lealfast.

They would keep attacking Isaiah's army for another ten minutes or so, then they had the freedom to attack anything and anyone they wanted.

Including Kezial and his men.

Eleanon smiled to himself, then his form frosted, iced over, and vanished completely.

All that was left on that windy hilltop was Eleanon's final whisper.

Ravenna.

Axis was crouched down, buffeted by bodies, under a cover of shields raised over the unit of men he was with. A constant rain of arrows drummed down on the shield cover; no one underneath could do much save crouch and wait. But the Lealfast were doing nothing more than keeping everyone pinned underneath the shields. Axis knew that Eleanon had other abilities and strategies . . . if this was all the Lealfast were going to do then maybe this was just going to be a play-acting battle, after all.

And if it were play-acting, then why? Why?

It was dim underneath the cover of shields, the light cut by the close-pressed bodies, the shields, and the approaching mayhem. Axis relied on vision sent by the eagle circling high overhead to learn what happened in the vicinity.

The mayhem was now very, very close, and the eagle was concerned. Axis knew he would stay only a few more minutes before wheeling off to seek shelter. Axis took the opportunity to have a quick look over the scene far below the eagle—Kezial was now pushing his army toward this!—then broke off the vision.

Go friend eagle, he said. *Save yourself from Isaiah's mayhem.*

I wish you well, the eagle said, and then he was gone.

Isaiah, Axis said.

He felt Isaiah twist his consciousness toward Axis, but he did not respond in words.

When will you use the juit birds? Axis said.

It is time now, Isaiah said, *the mayhem is almost upon us. I will delay no longer. Be ready.*

Kezial is on his way.

I know. Be ready, Axis.

Then contact with Isaiah was broken and Axis looked about him at the men of his unit.

"Be ready," he said. "This infernal drumming of arrows will shortly, I pray to all gods, be replaced with the drumming of bodies."

Now, whispered Isaiah.

Axis heard it, felt it, even over the sound of the arrows thudding into the shield cover. A sudden pressure in the air, literally making everyone in his unit sway and stumble slightly, then the beat of millions upon millions of wings.

He waited, counting under his breath for no other reason than it gave him something to do, then, shockingly, even though he'd been expecting it, the sound of bodies falling from the air.

The shield cover broke under their weight, but the need for the shield cover was now gone.

"Attack!" Axis cried. "Attack!"

He twisted about, drawing his sword, and plunged it into the Lealfast who lay stunned and injured on the ground.

Another hit behind him, and he swivelled about, and his sword flashed again.

All about Axis the Isembaardians were taking out the birdmen who fell stunned to the ground, and Axis halted a moment, waiting for the next Lealfast to drop from the sky.

He looked up and saw a sky covered with pink. The birds had done nothing but risen straight through the overhead Lealfast fighters. There were so many millions of the juit birds that they had filled the sky, creating such havoc and turmoil they had pushed the Lealfast out of the air.

Axis heard a sound, and it took him a moment to realise what it was.

He was laughing.

Far back, toward the rear guard, Inardle and Hereward sat their horses, watching fearfully. Isaiah had left the entire encampment behind, all the tents, the equipment, the storage wagons, and the two women had taken to horseback and hovered within the rear units, awaiting their chance to dash into Elcho Falling.

Inardle glanced at Hereward. The woman was scared, but courageous with it. The two women exchanged a glance, then Inardle looked toward the approaching storm. She did not know what it was, but knew it was a created magic.

Isaiah, most likely, although Inardle would not have put it past Eleanon, either.

Whoever, they had conjured up a monster. Inardle had no idea how anyone was going to survive if it hit before they had reached shelter.

She didn't know what to do. She had wanted to take to the air and flee, but any one among the Lealfast would have shot her down. She wasn't sure why they hadn't already, to be honest. Stars alone knew she must stick out like a sore thumb sitting in the back lines on this skittery horse.

The Lealfast had pinned down most of Isaiah's army under shield cover. As she didn't know why the Lealfast hadn't attacked her yet, Inardle also didn't know why Eleanon hadn't ordered his fighters to do more than just pummel the army with arrows. Eleanon, as the entire Lealfast, commanded so much magic after their union with the power of Infinity . . . surely they could have broken apart that pitiful shield cover . . .

She gasped aloud when the juit birds rose into the air. It was beautiful, magical and horrifying all at once. No one in the air above them had a chance of avoiding their inexorable rise.

The juit birds were such a solid mass, rising directly upward . . .

Inardle winced when they hit the Lealfast.

Then Hereward cried out. "Inardle! Kezial's men!"

Inardle looked.

Kezial's army had joined with Isaiah's on its western flank.

The two Isembaardian armies clashed in a spark and ring of swords . . . and almost no deaths, let alone injuries.

At that line where the two armies met, Isembaardians who owed their allegiance to Kezial leaned in to their countrymen who owed their loyalty to Isaiah and whispered in harsh, breathless tones, "We wish to join with you, not fight you!"

To be met with the inevitable chuckle and response,

"And we have been told to welcome you, and invite you into Elcho Falling. Here now, wave that sword about a bit. You don't want that Lealfast lord to think you're deserting, do you?"

And so, up and down that western line of fighting, men grunted and groaned and clashed swords in desperate battle, and every so often one would fall and roll under the feet of his neighbours.

But, strangely, there was no blood.

Eleanon strode back and forth on the shores of the lake, well back from the fighting. He had just called the Lealfast back—those that were still capable—and now the air overhead was thick with Lealfast streaming toward the mountains where the rest of the Nation waited.

Eleanon was furious, almost incandescent. He should have foreseen this and he hadn't. Just the simple fact of all those birds rising at the same time . . .

"Fuck you, Isaiah," Eleanon muttered. "You may smile today, but tomorrow you will pay."

Or perhaps even sooner. Eleanon glanced once more at the mayhem. It was very close now, only minutes away. Already the wind was whipping the waters of the lake and the feathers of Eleanon's wings into violent whorls and eddies. Lightning forked through the roiling clouds.

"You have overplayed your hand there, my friend," Eleanon muttered. "The birds were enough. No Lealfast was ever going to hang around long enough to be buffeted by that. But you . . . oh, you my friend . . ."

Eleanon grinned, then it died. He still had one or two things to take care of here, before he, too, could escape.

Axis looked up. The mayhem was now virtually upon them, and all about juit birds were settling back onto the lake water, tucking their heads under their tightly folded wings and curling their bodies into tight pink balls, huddled close together on the water, their long, long legs dangling deep into the lake, acting as stabilisers.

If Axis didn't move now, he would lose his chance.

Again he risked a look about him. The fighting had all but stopped, and he could see Isaiah in the distance, rousing the men, urging them to flee to the gates.

Axis glanced that way.

They were open, and Axis could see someone gesturing wildly: Georgdi, possibly, although now that the rain was starting to drive down it was difficult to tell.

"Good luck!" Axis shouted at those men about him close enough to hear, then he ran as hard as he could for the lake and dived in.

Isaiah's army, now merged with that of Kezial's, surged toward the gates of Elcho Falling. Tens of thousands of men milled about on the shoreline leading to the causeway, thick with fleeing men.

Then, in an almighty and terrifying clap of thunder, the mayhem hit. Men, horses, anything not tied down were bowled over in the tempest. Rain drove down, and intermingled with it were tiny spears of ice that, if they struck a body at the wrong angle, drove deep inside the flesh. Wind shrieked, rendering hearing and voice useless.

Anyone still on their feet could only crouch down and stumble forward, hand on the shoulder or back of whoever it was in front of him.

No one could see a thing.

It suited Eleanon perfectly.

He, like everyone else, was buffeted and pummelled. But, unlike most others, he also had considerable power and resources at his disposal and it was enough to keep him on his feet and still capable of independent movement and action.

He moved toward the gigantic mass of men struggling frantically to get inside Elcho Falling.

It was bleak, darkest night now, hail and ice raining about, yet still Eleanon laughed. He reached the outer edge of the great struggling mass, steadied himself, then reached about behind him and grabbed the woman he'd been dragging all this way.

Ravenna.

Go now, Eleanon whispered in her mind, his voice as cruel as the ice splintering down from the sky. *Go now and work my will within Elcho Falling. Go!*

Then, without waiting for any answer, he unceremoniously pushed her into the mass of men fighting for entrance into the citadel.

At the same time he activated the enchantment he'd worked on her earlier, making her invisible.

Just until she'd done her task.

Axis had sunk deep into the waters of the lake. He'd risen quickly, but had then to fight his way through the tightly packed bodies of the juit birds in order to get his head above water.

He'd thought he wasn't going to make it and it was only at the very last moment, when his lungs were on fire, that he'd managed to wedge his head between two juit birds and gasp desperately for air.

He couldn't see much, but what he could appalled him.

Rain and ice and forks of lightning speared down from the sky. All about, wind howled in great vortexes of destruction. Axis realised that he was actually in one of the most sheltered spots he could possibly be: the bodies of the juit birds protected his head from the worst of the tempest, while the fact that their heavy and tightly packed bodies covered the entire surface of the lake kept it reasonably still.

Axis could see shapes that he assumed were men huddling for shelter on the shoreline, but apart from that . . . nothing.

"Good work, Isaiah," Axis muttered sarcastically, then apologised to the birds on either side of him as he grabbed a leg in each hand to stabilise himself further.

The birds took no notice of him.

Inardle and Hereward had borne the full force of the mayhem. They'd both been blown off their horses, and by sheer luck Inardle had managed to grab Hereward's ankle before she was blown away completely.

Inardle had the strength of the Icarii and the blizzard

endurance of the Skraelings. With one hand she gripped Hereward's ankle, and with the other she pulled herself up the woman's body until she was able to shelter her with her own body and wings.

"Just stay low!" Inardle hissed into Hereward's ear. "We can't move from this spot until after the storm has—"

Inardle stopped suddenly.

Something icy and agonising had just sliced into her lower spine.

She let out a low moan that was instantly whipped away in the wind.

"Inardle?" she heard Hereward say, and she felt the woman's body twist under hers so Hereward could look Inardle in the face.

Inardle didn't care. She was aware of little save the splintering fingers digging into her spine.

Hello, sister, Eleanon's voice said in her mind. *Did you think I'd ever forget you?*

Inardle screamed. Eleanon's fingers had somehow managed to dig themselves into her back, then wrap themselves tightly about her spine, crushing it.

"Inardle?" Hereward shouted, unable to understand what was happening.

"Oh, shut up," Eleanon said, and materialised long enough to dig his other hand into Hereward's throat, bursting apart the scar the One had left.

Blood spurted forth again. Hereward, her arms and hands trapped under Inardle's body, could do nothing.

I have a little spot prepared for you, sister, Eleanon said into Inardle's mind, and then she was screaming helplessly as Eleanon lifted her by her spine into the heart of the mayhem.

Below, Hereward reached for her throat, but before she could wrap her hands about the spurting wound, the wind caught her and she was rolled over and over along the ground, leaving it soaked in her blood as she went.

By the time her body rolled to a stop, she was dead.

CHAPTER ELEVEN

Elcho Falling

The One was completely unaware of the battle and weather raging about Elcho Falling. He stood at the window in the top chamber of the Twisted Tower, his form once more that of a glass man, which form he had constructed from the glass objects within the tower. One hand rested on the window frame, one foot on the low sill, and his other hand extended very slightly in front of his body.

The One's eyes were closed and his body relaxed despite its somewhat awkward pose.

He was seeking the one being he thought he might still have a chance of contacting within Maximilian's world.

The Dark Spire.

The One was Infinity; it was the very fabric of his being. The Dark Spire, too, had been woven from strands of Infinity.

There must still be connection between him and it, somewhere.

But, oh, the One had to be careful. Doubtless, Maximilian and Ishbel, and probably even Eleanon, were all congratulating themselves on their sudden freedom from the One. If he did manage to contact the Dark Spire, the One did not want any of them to know of it.

No one.

Not this time.

This time the One was going to take no risk at all.

Every particle of his being was concentrated on this task, although a watcher would not know it from his easy stance. His senses wandered through Infinity, looking for that single strand that would connect him to the Dark Spire. It would be here, somewhere. He just had to find it.

Patience. Patience.

Within the confines of the Twisted Tower, lost in those dark spaces between eternity and Infinity, a millennium passed, and still the One did not move.

Then, he found it. A single gossamer strand, a filament so thin and nebulous it almost did not exist, but nevertheless it was *there*.

The hand the One held slightly extended from his body twitched then grasped, and the One's eyes flew open.

They were black, wide, staring, and stars revolved within their depths.

Slowly the One drew his hand toward his belly until it connected with the slight depression that passed for a navel in his glassy flesh.

A moment passed, then the One laughed, soft and triumphant, as the strand connecting him to the Dark Spire materialised as a silvery umbilical cord stretching from the One's belly and out the window of the Twisted Tower until it vanished in the vast emptiness of space and Infinity beyond.

The One felt the soft touch of the existence of the Dark Spire within his flesh. Oh, it was so far away, so far, but the gossamer thread was real enough, and the connection strong enough, for what he needed.

A smile suddenly appearing on his face, the One grasped the gossamer thread between his hands and, without hesitation, stepped through the window of the Twisted Tower into the void.

StarDancer slept peacefully in his mother's bed. His parents, StarDrifter and Salome, had kept him largely shielded from the events and worries of the rest of Elcho Falling and Star-Dancer spent his nights and days in gentle contemplation of the intricacies of the Star Dance, and little else. It might have seemed strange that the baby could sleep so solidly through the battle and tempest that raged outside, but, despite his extraordinary Enchanter abilities, StarDancer did sleep solidly for he was still a baby and sleep could conquer most babies, even under extreme circumstances.

StarDancer rarely dreamed in his sleep or, if he did, it was of pleasant things, such as his father's enchanted singing or the soft comfort of his mother's breast.

But in this sleep, something reached out and grazed StarDancer's mind . . . as though something had brushed past him in the midst of his unconsciousness.

He stirred in his sleep, unnoticed by Salome, who stood at the window of the chamber, staring at the events unfolding below.

He dreamed of a man, climbing up a rope arm over arm, body twisting beneath him as he climbed.

Below the man, darkness bulged and bubbled as if it were reaching for the man, or perhaps as if it was angry the man had escaped.

StarDancer felt unceasing threat from this man and, worse, he thought the man had realised his presence. He fought to free himself from the dream, but for long moments could not and in those long moments felt the man's eyes move about and settle slowly on him.

He awoke, suddenly, as someone who has had cold water dashed in their face. For a long moment he lay still, shaken by his dream vision and the threat that had emanated from the man, then he moved his head and saw his mother turn about in awareness of his wakefulness.

Salome came over, picked him up and cuddled him close, and in his delight at her love, StarDancer pushed to one side the fading memory of the dream. He was safe, now.

CHAPTER TWELVE

Elcho Falling

Isaiah thought that if there was one thing he'd change in his long existence, it would have been not to have made that foolhardy decision to create the mayhem. Maybe it had worked some good, but mostly it drew havoc down on the people he had least intended—his own army.

About three-quarters of the army finally made their way inside Elcho Falling after hours of tempest. The other quarter were dead or blown away. Isaiah was the last to enter the citadel, clinging to one side of the entrance arch, peering back into the catastrophic storm, trying to see if there was anyone left alive still to come in.

He couldn't see a thing apart from the blanket of pink juit birds swelling up and down on the lake's surface. They, at least, looked intact, and Isaiah hoped that Axis, too, was safe in their midst. For a moment he thought about calling out for Axis, suggesting that he abandon his plan and head inside Elcho Falling for safety, but Isaiah doubted he could make either his physical voice or his mental one strong enough to penetrate the mayhem.

He felt something tug on the sleeve of his jerkin and he turned his head.

Georgdi was there, gesturing frantically.

Isaiah sighed and stepped inside Elcho Falling.

Georgdi had the gates shut the instant Isaiah was in.

The sudden silence was astonishing. Isaiah had to stand, blinking, trying to make sense of the absence of the screaming of the wind or the driving of the rain. The initial chamber of Elcho Falling, the columned ground floor, was full of men wet to the bone, dripping both blood and water, and sitting slumped against columns or standing about in dispirited groups.

"We are taking them to their quarters as fast as we are able," Georgdi said to one side, "and feeding them once they are there. Elcho Falling has provided clothes and warmth for them."

Isaiah nodded, unable for the moment to speak.

"What happened to those who didn't make it?" Georgdi said, and Isaiah gave the man a bleak look.

Stupid question.

"Isaiah," Georgdi said quietly, "what happened with Josia the other day? What was going on?"

"Josia was the One," Isaiah said. "Maximilian needed him distracted while he isolated him within the Twisted Tower. Maximilian—"

"Axis?" a voice called. "Axis?"

"Oh gods," Isaiah murmured as StarDrifter came striding over.

"Where is my son?" StarDrifter said, glaring at Isaiah as if Isaiah had left him outside intentionally.

"Did no one tell you?" Isaiah said. "Oh, well, Axis decided to stay outside. He thought it better that—"

"Outside in *that*?" StarDrifter said.

"Yes, outside in *that*," Isaiah responded, trying to remember if he had ever liked Axis' father or not. It was all so long ago, and far too wearying to stretch his mind back. "He is safe enough, StarDrifter."

"I'll take you to your chamber," Georgdi said to Isaiah. "Rest a while, eat. Then we can talk."

"I—" Isaiah began.

"And I suppose that witch woman has stayed out there with him," StarDrifter said.

It took a long moment for Isaiah to work out what StarDrifter meant. "Inardle? She isn't in Elcho Falling?"

"No one has seen her," Georgdi said. "Only men have come in."

"There was another woman," Isaiah said. "Hereward. Thin, dark hair . . ."

Georgdi shook his head.

"Shetzah," Isaiah muttered. *Had they both been lost?*

"Come," Georgdi said, and Isaiah allowed the man to lead him away, leaving StarDrifter standing glaring at the closed gates.

Outside, the mayhem finally began to abate.

Ravenna stood among the crowd of sodden, exhausted men within the ground floor chamber. She remembered coming here with a thousand or so of Armat's men, surprising Maximilian, and she looked to the curving staircase almost expecting to see Maximilian in that spot again.

But of course he wasn't here, now.

Men moved about her, but none acknowledged her. She tried speaking, she even shouted, but none paid her any attention. Their eyes slid over her, their consciousnesses refusing to acknowledge her.

Eleanon had reworked Ishbel's curse well.

Ravenna wrapped her arms about herself, shivering. She was cold and hungry and every joint ached.

As for her belly . . .

She didn't cry. Ravenna had cried so much over the past days and weeks that she didn't think she could ever cry again. She hated herself that she had trapped her son in this nightmare, too. All she wanted for him was life, and a happy one at that, but what had she managed? To trap him in this dismal existence . . . Gods knew what would become of him, or if he would survive what was to come.

All her fault . . .

How had she come to this?

"Reckless ambition," she murmured. "And stupidity. And of the two, the stupidity has been my worst enemy."

She wished for a moment that her mother were here. But she had killed Venetia, hadn't she? Killed her own mother.

Ravenna turned away, leaned into one of the beautiful columns, and wept yet again.

Outside, Axis wiped his eyes of water. The mayhem had vanished almost as abruptly as it had seemingly arrived. Around him the juit birds were slowly untangling their legs, pulling their heads out from under wings and blinking their pale eyes.

"I thank you for your shelter," Axis said, and those birds closest to him nodded in acknowledgement—graceful, grave bobbings of their head.

Very slowly, Axis began to swim through the birds, apologising as he went.

He had a long way to go before the Lealfast made their reappearance.

Inardle woke slowly, aware of little else save the terrible pain in her back and shoulders where Eleanon had gripped her. She tried to move grateful that at least her legs responded (*stars, she had been sure Eleanon had severed her spine*), but discovered she was restrained by something binding her tight.

She felt about with her hands—it was too dark to see—and her breath caught as she realised she'd been imprisoned in an ice ball. She was lying on her side, curled up, her wings wrapped about her, her legs drawn tight to her body, and she could extend none of her limbs save for the tiniest amount.

Inardle went cold, due not so much to the nature of her prison but to her utter shock.

Eleanon had imprisoned her within an ice hex.

There was no way to escape.

Ever.

The ice hex was unbreakable.

She would die here. Slowly. Of starvation and despair.

Isaiah had only had time to strip off his wet clothing and sink down to the bed of his chamber, when there was a knock at the door.

It opened. Insharah stood there and behind him, almost unbelievably to Isaiah, stood Kezial.

"Well met again, Insharah," Isaiah said. "You have been having adventures since last I saw you."

Insharah had the grace to flush slightly as Isaiah obliquely referred to Insharah's betrayal of Maximilian and Axis by deserting to Armat.

"And you, Kezial," Isaiah said.

"The time for apologies has long passed," Kezial said. "Besides, you wanted me in here."

Isaiah tipped his head in acknowledgement.

"I bring news of Eleanon," Kezial said.

"Perhaps we need to call Georgdi and—" Isaiah said.

"It can't wait," said Insharah. "Kezial, tell him."

"Eleanon's plan was to allow everyone into Elcho Falling anyway," Kezial said. "He plans on destroying Elcho Falling."

"How?" Isaiah said, now standing and pulling on fresh clothes.

"He has a dark spire deep within the citadel—" Kezial began.

"We know of that," Insharah interrupted, explaining to Isaiah.

"And he has inserted Ravenna into Elcho Falling in order to—" Kezial continued.

"How?" Isaiah said, ignoring Kezial's wince of irritation at being interrupted yet again.

"How did he insert her?" Kezial said. "Undoubtedly during the chaos and confusion when your delightful little storm hit. She is in Elcho Falling now, Isaiah. Somewhere. Disguised. She will destroy this citadel and all within it."

"Call the other commanders," Isaiah snapped to Insharah, "and show me to whatever command chamber you have here while you're at it."

CHAPTER THIRTEEN

Elcho Falling

"I thought Ishbel had cursed Ravenna," Georgdi said. They were once more grouped around the central table in the command chamber, this time with the addition of Isaiah and Kezial to StarDrifter, Insharah, Ezekiel, and Egalion. Garth Baxtor was also here, sitting to one side, looking worried and uncomfortable.

Isaiah, on the other hand, had automatically taken the commander's position at the table and everyone from Georgdi down deferred to him instinctively.

"I know nothing of this," Isaiah said. "Tell me."

Georgdi, aided by StarDrifter butting in every few sentences, told Isaiah briefly of what had happened when Ravenna had lured Maximilian to his murder, and then how Ishbel had murdered Lister — at which Isaiah remarked that he'd known of Lister's death, but not the details—and had cursed Armat and Ravenna.

"Armat is now dead, too," Georgdi said, "killed by Elcanon, but Ishbel cursed Ravenna threefold. She disinherited the son Ravenna carried to Maximilian from Elcho Falling—"

"I would have done far worse," StarDrifter muttered.

"She cut Ravenna off from the Land of Dreams, the source of Ravenna's power, and she cursed her to forever be an outcast, rejected by all communities."

"But," Kezial put in, "Eleanon has somehow altered these curses. I don't know how. He referred to it only obliquely and I am certain now that he knew I'd defect, so anything he told me needs to be treated cautiously. But I do know that Ravenna was able to ghost about the outskirts of the Lealfast camp without any problems."

"So you may be wrong about Eleanon wanting to destroy Elcho Falling," Isaiah said.

Kezial shook his head. "No, I think that is true enough. Eleanon wanted you to know that. He wants you to be afraid. And I think he also wanted to boast a little."

"Ravenna," Isaiah said. "What was she sent inside to do, Kezial?"

Kezial shrugged his shoulders. "I don't really know. She has a clear mission, but . . ."

"It could be anything," StarDrifter said. "Perhaps an assassination. She is a dab hand at assassination."

"It is something to do with that Dark Spire," Kezial said. "But what . . ." He shrugged again.

"I am going to need to see this Dark Spire," Isaiah said to Georgdi, and Georgdi nodded.

"It is a grim thing," he said. "None of us can understand it, nor stop its inexorable growth. I'll take you down, once we're done here."

"Garth knows Ravenna well," Insharah said. "It is why we asked him here to this meeting, Isaiah."

Isaiah turned his attention to the man sitting uncomfortably at the end of the table. "Garth?" Isaiah said.

"Garth Baxtor," Garth said. "I knew Ravenna when we were youths."

"They were largely responsible for releasing Maximilian from his imprisonment within the Veins some years ago," StarDrifter said, and Isaiah nodded.

"Ah, yes, I have heard of you. Garth, tell me about Ravenna."

Garth looked unhappy, and Isaiah didn't wonder at it. He would be torn between his friendship with the woman and the knowledge of what she had become and how she had betrayed Maximilian.

"I can't believe that she is totally lost to either ambition or horror, Isaiah," Garth said. "Or maybe I just don't *want* to believe that. But . . . I don't know what I can say that may help."

"We need to find her," Isaiah said. "How would we do that? Would she come if you called her?"

"Do you want to use me to set a trap?" Garth said. "I don't know if I—"

"She has already murdered Maximilian once," Isaiah said, then he sighed. "We need to find her, Garth. But why do I suspect it is not going to be easy?"

Axis swam his way around Elcho Falling to the reed banks that lined the channel leading eastward to the sea. He hauled himself out of the water and onto a floating patch of thick, dry reeds. He took off his clothes and wrung them out as much as possible, spreading them among the reeds to dry, then sat revelling in the sunny afternoon that the mayhem had left behind.

He could see no Lealfast anywhere. He looked upward, glad to see the black speck of the eagle circling high overhead.

Friend eagle. You are well?

I am, StarMan. I am glad to hear your voice. That was an evil storm.

Ha! Axis thought. It was an evil storm, indeed. Wait until I speak to Isaiah. *Are there any Lealfast in the area, friend eagle?*

No. They have flown to the mountains to the north-west. They will be wary of the juit birds.

Axis could hear deep amusement in the eagle's voice and he grinned. He said goodbye to the eagle, wishing him well, and asking only that the eagle warn him if he saw any Lealfast approaching.

Then he lay back on the reeds, fingers laced underneath his head, and stared into the blue sky.

Isaiah?

Isaiah took a few minutes to answer and when he did it was to remark somewhat sharply that he didn't want Axis berating him for the ferocity of the mayhem.

How many lost? Axis asked.

Isaiah hesitated. *Too many. Axis, Inardle and Hereward are missing, they did not make it inside. If they remained outside, the mayhem would have killed them.*

Axis did not know how to react, even within himself.

Hereward he had hardly known, and he had little emotional response to her loss.

But Inardle?

Maybe she has rejoined with—he said.

No, Isaiah said. *She was terrified of the Lealfast, Axis.*

She can look after herself, Axis said.

Isaiah replied with a mental shrug and changed the subject. *Ravenna is inside. We are looking for her.*

Have you had a chance to examine the Dark Spire? Axis said.

I am on my way to it now. Otherwise, all within are well. StarDrifter is annoyed that you are outside, though.

Axis laughed, imagining his father's biting comments to Isaiah about leaving Axis outside.

Axis, I do have some interesting news.

Yes?

Georgdi says there is a back entrance to Elcho Falling. He asked about it some time ago. It is of little use militarily as it can only be used by a few people at a time, but, knowing of it, there's no reason for you not to rejoin us. If you still feel you need to be ranging outside Elcho Falling, then you can leave again.

Really? Where is it?

How good a swimmer are you? Isaiah asked.

Ravenna stood before the Dark Spire. It was a horrid thing, reaching up through three of the lowest levels of Elcho Falling and pushing at the fourth level. It twisted and twined, with great pulsing veins and thick roots that vanished into the stonework of the citadel.

It breathed, very slowly, in and out.

Ravenna had wrapped her arms about herself. *She was so cold.* She had a series of tasks to accomplish and Eleanon's spite, left deep inside her, niggled and bit at her, pressuring her to begin them.

But for the moment, Ravenna just stood and stared.

There were others in the chamber with her. Icarii Enchanters and a few Isembaardian soldiers. None of them saw her or in any way realised her presence. Eleanon's and Ishbel's curses, entwined together now, hid her from their perception. One or two of them had actually bumped into her, but still they did not realise, cursing their lack of coordination as they stumbled, moving on.

The Dark Spire . . . Ravenna stepped forward, reaching out one trembling hand to touch the foul thing.

And then she stopped, staring upward, sending her senses straining through all the levels of Elcho Falling above her.

She had heard a baby gurgle in delight.

Salome sat in the chamber she shared with her husband, StarDrifter, Talon of the Icarii, and bounced their son on her knee. StarDancer had grown well since his birth, and had developed his powers quickly, as did all Icarii Enchanter children (Salome could barely remember her life in Coroleas, when she had fought to live as the human Duchess of Sidon, and not as she lived now, an Icarii Enchantress). She had once delighted in intrigue and despair, but now she delighted in nothing but the love of her husband and their glorious son.

He was an Enchanter, like his parents, and a powerful one. Now, as he bounced up and down on her knee, Star-Dancer shared his joy in life with his mother and he burbled with laughter.

StarDancer was but a baby, after all, delighting in his mother's love, and he had yet to tell his mother about his dream.

Ravenna's hand dropped away from the Dark Spire and fell back to her belly. She stared upward, her eyes filling with tears.

There was a baby above, burbling in delight.

Ravenna was struck deep with guilt again, guilt that she had condemned her own son to gods knew what. He might never have the chance that the baby above obviously did . . . he might never be able to sit on her knee and burble in delight.

Ravenna took a step away from the Dark Spire, wanting nothing more than to fade away into the shadows and weep, when she froze.

A group of men had entered the chamber, and among them was Garth Baxtor.

One of the men was Isaiah. He stepped forward to the Dark Spire, examining it closely.

He moved close to Ravenna, and she shrank back, distrusting his acute senses and power.

But he did not acknowledge Ravenna or give any indication that he knew of her presence. He was close enough to reach out a hand and grab her if he had wanted, so Ravenna assumed that Eleanon's and Ishbel's twisted curses were so powerful they could dupe even a god.

What hope for her or her son, then?

Isaiah was concentrating fully on the Dark Spire, his face twisted into an expression of distaste, and Ravenna took the opportunity of his preoccupation to move away from both Isaiah and the spire.

Perhaps the stairs, and the baby . . .

But Garth stood on the stairs, blocking her path, and he looked about.

"Ravenna?" he called, softly. "Ravenna? I am sure you are here."

Ravenna froze, unable to take her eyes from Garth. Could he see her? Could his Touch, and the fact that he had known her so well and for so long, circumvent the curses that bound her?

"Ravenna? Please, if you are here, speak to me. I will not harm you."

He could not see her. He was only casting out in hope. Yet, even so, Ravenna was sorely tempted to step forward and take his hand.

Of everyone in this fortress, Garth was the only one Ravenna could be sure would not judge her. He would remember all the times they had shared, the laughter, the adventures.

"Ravenna?" Garth called out now, so softly and yet with such warmth and comfort, that Ravenna barely restrained another sob.

Surely it would be all right if she touched him, just for one moment—

And then riveting pain grasped her mind, making her stumble backward, hands clutching at her head.

Eleanon.

Ravenna, are you ready to commence your duty?

Isaiah looked away from the Dark Spire toward Garth Baxtor. "Garth?" he called. "What is it?"

Garth hesitated, then sighed. "Nothing. I was just hoping that maybe Ravenna was here, and might respond to me. Just a forlorn hope, Isaiah."

He walked closer to Isaiah. "What do you think of it?" Garth said. "It is a foul thing indeed."

"Have you tried with your Touch, Garth? Can you make anything of it?"

"Aye, I have tried. All I can say, Isaiah, is that it is foulness incarnate. It feels to me like a cancer, but one with direction and purpose. It is growing into something, but I cant tell what? You?"

Isaiah turned his eyes back to the spire, studying it. "It is a nightmare from another time and place. It is Infinity itself stepped into this world. It is coldness and darkness and hatefulness, and, as you say, Garth, all with a purpose and direction. I do not know if anyone can truly control what this is, or will become. I think this, right here, is Maximilian's worst enemy."

Axis sat on his reed bed, disconsolately pulling on his clothes and wishing he'd just braved the mayhem and got into Elcho Falling via the front door. The back door didn't sound like any fun at all. He was just about to slip into the water when one of the juit birds swam up to him and looked him in the eyes in that uncomfortably direct manner of the juit.

StarMan.

My friend juit. What may I do for you?

We have discovered something, StarMan. We think you need to see it.

Axis repressed a sigh. *What manner of thing?*

Something left by the Lealfast.

His interest pricked, Axis nodded for the juit bird to lead on as he entered the water.

Damn, it was cold!

The bird led him part way round the northern shores of the lake which surrounded Elcho Falling, and nodded at the reed banks there.

Axis, who had decided he was thoroughly sick of swimming and of pushing through juit birds while he was doing so, as also of being constantly wet and cold, heaved himself into the squelchy reed banks and began poking amongst them. For a few minutes he found nothing and was thinking longingly of hot food and a warm dry bed nestled within Elcho Falling, when suddenly he bent back a tangle of reeds and stilled.

It took Axis a moment to realise what it was . . . a dome of ice bobbing among the reeds that looked like it extended into the water, forming a ball.

He pushed away the reeds that clung to the top curve of the ball like wet, bedraggled hair.

Axis froze as his hand parted the final few strands.

Inardle's face, warped by the ice, stared back at him.

CHAPTER FOURTEEN

The Central Outlands

The Skraelings remained lost in their reflections and choices, completely unaware of what happened in the world. They had the ability to turn themselves back into River Angels if they so chose, and they could do this freely now they found themselves masterless with the mysterious disappearance of the One.

Would they like to change? Did they want to take this opportunity?

They could become creatures of beauty and of astounding power. Fairy-like creatures of water. Consideration of water gave the Skraelings pause, particularly as attaining their River Angel form meant drowning themselves in its vileness, but for the moment they passed over it and thought only of the beauty and power of the River Angels as Isaiah had showed them.

"But of course," Ozll said into the Skraelings' reflection, "the River Angels were not just beauty and power, were they?"

The Skraelings considered this also, and took pause to resent Ozll a little, for he'd begun to sound as if he were their conscience, and that they did not like.

"They were quite murderous," said the female, Graq. "They were vile, too. Isaiah showed us that. Do we want to be that?"

One of the nearby Skraelings opened his mouth to say "Yes!" then shut it again without speaking. A puzzled look came into his eyes.

"We don't want to think of that," said another Skraeling. "We want to be River Angels. They were beautiful and powerful and . . . we would have no lords other than ourselves!"

"But do we want to be lords like those?" Graq said, earning herself many resentful looks, although none spoke against her.

"These reflections are truly painful," Ozll said, "and they make me want to curl up and cry."

At that almost childish admission, all the Skraelings relaxed. He remained one of them, after all.

"If we return to the form of River Angels," said Ozll, "then we would return to being beautiful and powerful, but infinitely murderous because of that. We were once murderous as River Angels, we remained murderous as Skraelings. Do we want to return to that? Do we want to *remain* that?"

His voice was genuinely bewildered and emotional, and all the Skraelings listening curled their toes and dropped their eyes.

"Would a touch of beauty and a bit more magic really change us that much?" Ozll said. "Wouldn't we be just as foul as River Angels, if more beautifully so? Wouldn't we *really* prefer to be something other than foul, and murderous?"

Now thoroughly discomforted, many of the Skraelings wondered if they might murder Ozll, just to shut him up.

"Can't we just make a decision one way or the other?" one of them muttered.

"We need to make the right one," Ozll said, and everyone sighed, a great gust of regret and self-loathing that whispered over the plains of the central Outlands.

CHAPTER FIFTEEN

Elcho Falling

For a long, long moment Axis did not know what to think or how to react. Then it struck him through his fugue of shock that Inardle's face did not exhibit terror so much as resigned desperation.

"Inardle?" Axis said. He still could not think correctly. What was she doing curled up so tight in this ball of ice? His hands slipped a little on the ice and, as they did so, the ball turned over in the water. Axis continued to roll it over.

Inardle was wound so tight Axis wondered if she could move at all. She was curled almost into a foetal position, her wings wrapped about the front of her body. He turned the ball a little further, his breath hissing out softly between his teeth as he saw that Inardle's spine was streaked with blood. The blood had melted a little into the ice, imparting a rosy hue to most of Inardle's back.

Axis wondered if this was yet another of Inardle's tricks.

He was so sick of her tricks.

Surely she wouldn't try this one again. *Poor Inardle. Trapped and in pain, needing Axis to rescue her.*

"Inardle?" he said again. Then, *Inardle?*

Nothing. He'd rolled the ball of ice completely around and again he looked into Inardle's ice-warped face. Axis ran his fingers over the ice, sensing it not only with his physical senses, but with his Enchanter powers as well.

This was a powerful hex.

Well, Axis hadn't expected much else. It wasn't as if Inardle had somehow got herself melted accidentally into a giant hailstone during the mayhem, was it?

It was a Lealfast hex. Axis could feel that much. And

more . . . there was more than the power of the Star Dance here. Magi power perhaps, or threads woven from Infinity.

Axis still didn't know what to do. Inardle was alive, he could see her blink occasionally. He supposed he couldn't leave her here.

He also didn't know how he felt. Anger, mostly, he decided after some reflection. *What was she up to now? Why was she always such a bother?*

Buried very, very deeply was a little fright on her behalf and that made Axis even angrier. He didn't want to feel frightened for her.

Axis sat back on his haunches on the unsteady reed bed, thinking. He *couldn't* leave her here, but he was certain he couldn't do much about the ice hex, either. Could Isaiah break it? Isaiah had healed Inardle from the poison, using the water element so strong in her body . . . he might be able to fix this, too.

Isaiah? Axis called.

Eleanon had moved a little closer to Elcho Falling from the mountain retreat where waited the rest of the Lealfast Nation, but not so close he would be noticed by Axis' eagle which circled high over the citadel.

He'd have to do something about that eagle, sooner or later.

But the eagle was not Eleanon's immediate concern. The juit birds were.

They were a terrible, crucifying nuisance.

Eleanon suspected them of some magical power, but they didn't even have to use that against the Lealfast. All they ever need do was to repeat their manoeuvre during the battle the day past—rise up in their millions into the air—and they'd batter any Lealfast out of the sky who happened to be above them.

The juit birds would have to go. And, in the going, Eleanon was going to teach Isaiah and everyone else within Elcho Falling a terrible lesson.

They were not in control.

Eleanon was.

He was already invisible. Now he settled himself on the

ground an hour's flight from Elcho Falling, staring with his bright, power-enhanced eyes toward the citadel.

Ice crept up his spine and frost encased his entire being outlining him to any curious eyes nearby.

Eleanon was talking to the Dark Spire.

Axis pushed the ice ball through the water with one hand while trying to paddle with the other.

He was in a foul temper. The ice ball kept bobbing back at him and pushing him under the water; the juit birds were reluctant to move out of the way and kept pecking at both the ice ball (it refused to crack under the onslaught) *and* Axis; and Axis knew that this journey, as irritating as it was, was going to be nothing compared to the hell of trying to get this thing into Elcho Falling.

Isaiah thought he might be able to do something about the hex.

Axis thought that if, after all this effort, Isaiah couldn't do anything, then Axis was personally going to break the ice ball over Isaiah's head.

He kept grimly paddling and pushing and cursing every pink-feathered bird that pecked at him, as well as Isaiah simply for existing, and Inardle for getting herself into this mess. Damn it! Why couldn't she have managed to walk into Elcho Falling along with everyone else? Why couldn't she have simply died in the mayhem, as Hereward undoubtedly did? Why, always, was she in such a state of crisis?

Axis was within twenty paces of Elcho Falling's eastern wall when a juit bird to his right suddenly gave a squawk and disappeared under water, as if something had grabbed at it.

Axis stoped paddling, frowning a little at the vacant space where the bird had been, then, suddenly, to his right another bird squawked and then vanished underwater.

The great mass of juit birds began to fluff themselves out nervously.

Another one vanished, sucked underwater.

Suddenly the lake was alive with the sound of juit birds screaming and lifting into the air. Axis could do little but to cover his face with his arms and hope the ice ball didn't drift away too far as he was buffeted by birds rising out of the water. He thought the noise and movement would abate after a moment or two, but it kept getting worse, and Axis risked a look.

What he saw froze him momentarily in horror.

Black tentacles—*roots! They were roots from the Dark Spire!*—were rising out of the water and grabbing juit birds out of the air. The great mass of birds was in such panic that they were blundering into each other in the air, sometimes knocking each other out of the air without any help from the roots, of which there appeared to be thousands, waving about in the air, grabbing birds and dragging them back underwater.

Something pushed past Axis' face and reared into the sky.

It was another root.

Axis almost panicked, then realised the roots were after the birds and likely didn't realise his presence. Eleanon, who Axis was certain lay behind this, probably did not know such a tasty prize floated about with the juit birds, otherwise Axis was certain he, too, would have been grabbed and sucked under.

He rolled over in the water, looking for the ice ball.

It floated close by, and Axis kicked over to it, giving it an almighty push toward the rising water wall that comprised the lower third of Elcho Falling. At least now he didn't have a mass of birds bobbing about the water to hinder his progress. He put all his strength into swimming and pushing the ball ever forward. Now and again another root would rear up beside him, grabbing a juit bird from the air and pulling it back down again.

But the tentacles were grabbing fewer and fewer birds as they were, finally, untangling themselves from their panic and rising higher and higher into the sky, out of the reach of the roots.

Axis hoped the roots wouldn't try to find a new target once the birds had all vanished.

The ice ball hit the solid water wall of Elcho Falling, bouncing back against Axis' face and making his nose bleed. As much as he wanted to take the time out to curse the damned thing, he simply reared up out of the water, taking a deep breath as he did so. Then he fell down hard on the ball, pushing it under water.

Stars, this was hard! The ice ball was buoyant, and it kept trying to push Axis back toward the surface. But Axis pushed down with all his strength, driving the ball down three paces until the gaping mouth of an underwater tunnel appeared.

Thank the stars it was large enough to push the ice ball into!

Axis almost didn't manage it. The ice ball wanted to bounce its way back to the surface, and Axis had to exert all his strength, using both hands and feet, to push it into the tunnel opening.

Then, mercifully, once it was in it bobbed straight up the tunnel, seeking the surface within Elcho Falling.

Axis swum in after it, relaxing in relief.

Prematurely, as it happened.

Just before he got his legs inside the tunnel, something grabbed one of his ankles.

The root wrapped itself tightly about his ankle, tightening like a vice.

Axis fought back both the pain and the panic. He tried to kick at the root with his free foot, but his lungs were by now screaming for air, and his strength was rapidly waning. As much as he tried to cling to the sides of the underwater passage, the root was dragging him inexorably back out into the lake.

There was no more air in his lungs. Now panic did threaten to overwhelm him but, just as he felt his fingers lose their grip on the rocks of the tunnel, he felt someone swim past him.

A moment passed, then suddenly, thankfully, his ankle was free and strong arms had wrapped themselves about Axis.

Isaiah.

A few heartbeats later Axis' head broke water inside Elcho Falling, and he heaved in great lungfuls of air as Georgdi and Insharah between them hauled him out of the water, Isaiah lifting himself out a moment later.

* * *

Outside, all the juit birds who had escaped the roots formed a massive pink cloud high in the sky. They circled Elcho Falling once, then, affronted and frightened, they began the long flight home to Lake Juit.

Eleanon watched them go. He squatted on the ground with his arms wrapped about his knees, his chin resting on his arms, and he watched the birds lift in panic into the sky, sort themselves out, then head south.

They would not return to Elcho Falling.

He sighed, standing. He wished Maximilian and Ishbel would hurry back to Elcho Falling. He wanted them inside for his final attack on the citadel. In the meantime, however, he could consolidate his power and prepare the Lealfast Nation for what lay ahead.

Just before Eleanon lifted off he paused, sending his senses scrying out for the ice hex.

It was no longer floating tangled in the reed banks.

It was inside Elcho Falling.

Eleanon stilled, then he burst out laughing, punching the sky in triumph.

"Welcome to hell, Axis," he said.

Then he rose into the air, flying back to the Lealfast Nation.

Axis was dead.

CHAPTER SIXTEEN

Elcho Falling

Isaiah looked at the ice ball bobbing about in the small pool of water that led to the underwater tunnel, then looked at Axis. The StarMan was sitting on the edge of the pool, coughing water out of his lungs and waving off the concerns of Georgdi and Insharah.

Isaiah's attention turned back to the ice hex. He nodded at a guardsman standing by and together they hauled it out of the water, cursing as it almost slipped from their grasp on several occasions.

Then Isaiah squatted down to run his hands lightly over its surface. He could just make out Inardle inside, curled into a tight ball. He rolled the ball over a little so he could see her face.

Her eyes were closed.

Isaiah glanced at Axis, now standing and stripping off his sodden clothes for dry attire, then grasped the ice hex a little tighter, sending his senses scrying inside.

Axis tossed aside the towel he'd been using to dry his hair, and walked over to Isaiah. "Can you help?" he said.

"No," Isaiah said, standing. "She's too far gone, Axis."

Axis stared at Isaiah. "No, surely . . . there must be something you can do."

"She's too far gone, Axis," Isaiah said, "and the hex is too tightly wound." He began to walk toward the door leading from the chamber.

"No," Axis said.

Isaiah turned back to him. "Leave it, Axis." He nodded at the guardsman who had helped him haul the hex from the water. "Push it back into—"

"No!" Axis said, taking a step forward to block the guardsman's approach.

"She is well on the path to her Otherworld, Axis," Isaiah said. *"Let her go.* Isn't this what you have always wanted?"

Axis opened his mouth, then closed it again. *What did he want?*

"There must be a chance," he said. "She's not gone completely yet. What is it you are not telling me, Isaiah?"

Isaiah walked back to him. "That ice hex has been constructed with great and malevolent care, Axis. You want honesty from me? There is a small—a *tiny*—chance that Inardle might be dissuaded from the path she takes now and led back to this life. Who knows if she wants that? Eleanon—"

"Let me take that chance, Isaiah," Axis said.

Isaiah took a deep breath as if controlling anger. "Listen to me, Axis, and listen to me well. That ice hex was not designed to trap Inardle. It was designed to trap you. Inardle is the bait. Eleanon constructed a hex that will trap you into a journey from which you likely will never emerge. It is a hex designed to isolate you completely—from this world *and* from the Otherworld. It is a hex designed to trap you in some horror that I cannot understand." Isaiah frowned. "I don't understand it . . . it involves someone . . . a name I don't know . . ."

"What?" said Axis. "Who?"

Isaiah looked at Axis steadily. "The hex involves someone named Borneheld. Inardle has been sent to be his wife."

Borneheld.

Axis thought his heart would stop. *Borneheld? Inardle had been sent to be his* wife?

"Who is Borneheld, Axis?" Isaiah said. "And why would Inardle be sent to be his wife?"

"He . . ." Axis had to clear his throat. "Borneheld was my brother. Half-brother. We shared the same mother. We were bitter, hateful rivals in life. We loved the same woman—Faraday. She left me to be his wife. I killed him, eventually, after great wars that cost tens of thousands of lives. I, ah . . ."

I battled him to the death in the Chamber of the Moons in a duel that dragged on for an entire night.

"I killed him, eventually," Axis finished.

"Be sure that Eleanon knows this history," Isaiah said. "He has constructed a hex that he is certain will both tempt you and destroy you."

Axis was so shocked by the revelation of what the hex contained that his mind could not grasp what Isaiah was saying, let alone the implications of it.

"Walk away from it, Axis," Isaiah said. "That hex is truly evil. We can destroy it and farewell Inardle's soul. There is no reason for you to enter it."

If Axis "walked away from it", would Inardle be trapped forever as Borneheld's wife?

Faraday had suffered terribly as Borneheld's wife. Terribly. Axis had been her only hope of escaping him.

Axis' mind filled with memories of that terrible night when he had battled Borneheld. They'd met in the Chamber of the Moons in Carlon. Two hundred people had filed into the circular, columned chamber to stand silently in the inadequate torchlight watching the duel between the brothers. Axis had fought only with his powers as a soldier and swordsman. He'd tossed aside his Enchanter's ring to Faraday's dismay (oh stars, Faraday had been there, watching!) and had faced Borneheld only with his sword. Borneheld had fought with muscle and tactics honed by countless battles, Axis with the grace and fluidity of the Icarii and the skill of a Battle-Axe. They had been evenly matched.

It had been a terrible battle. The chamber was filled with the sound of swords clashing, the heavy breathing of the combatants and the scuffing of their boots across the green marbled floor. StarDrifter had told Axis later that the combination of these sounds had made a strange, dark music—an echo of the Dance of Death, the Dark Music of the stars.

All Axis could recall of the battle was the hatred he'd felt for Borneheld, his exhaustion, and the growing terror that he might be the first one to slip and offer his throat to Borneheld's sword. By the end of that bleak night both had been drenched in sweat, their limbs trembling with fatigue.

There was something about that night Axis had forgotten? What was it? What was it?

There had been some ally . . . someone who had given him that single moment, that sliver of an edge against Borneheld that had, in the end, enabled Axis to defeat his brother.

The heart, the heart torn and bloody in his hand, lifted up and tossed to . . .

Axis' head snapped up and he looked Isaiah directly in the eye.

This was no longer about Inardle.

It was about Borneheld and about a brotherly feud that, even after almost fifty years, still smouldered red hot.

And it was about the eagle.

"I'm going in," Axis said, "and I'm taking along a friend."

CHAPTER SEVENTEEN

The Twisted Tower

The One climbed along the gossamer connection between himself and the Dark Spire, passing unhindered through the wastes of Infinity. Gossamer-like it may have been, but the umbilical cord that connected him with the Dark Spire was of Infinity itself, strong enough to support him.

As he drew closer, the One became more aware, through his increasing contact with the Dark Spire, of what was happening at Elcho Falling.

There had been a battle and much bad weather. Eleanon was concentrating, not on Elcho Falling, but on Axis, which for the moment suited the One well . . . may they both keep themselves occupied and unaware of what the One was doing. Maxel and Ishbel were still far, far away in Isembaard.

Good, that was very, very good. Either or both of them might have a chance of realising what the One was up to if they had been at Elcho Falling, but they were not. They were far away and by the time they returned it would be too late.

There were two things that concerned the One as he drew closer to the Dark Spire.

One, the fleeting impression that, momentarily, someone had seen him: a passing contact within the echoes of Infinity.

A child, perhaps, for the One sensed the presence was still somehow unformed, not yet solidified into the rigidity of adulthood.

For the moment the One ignored this. The impression had been but fleeting, and it had been but a child. He would come back to it.

The second problem was Ravenna. The marsh witch was inside Elcho Falling. The One could sense her strongly from the Dark Spire. She was somehow closely connected to the spire . . . had Eleanon employed Ravenna for his purposes? The One could think of no other reason Ravenna would be at Elcho Falling, let alone fiddling about with the spire.

The One crawled closer to the Dark Spire, hand over hand, its presence growing stronger each time one of his fists closed a little closer along the umbilical cord.

Ravenna. Maybe she could be useful.

CHAPTER EIGHTEEN

The Ice Hex

Axis walked through snowdrifts heavy with ice, each step an effort as his legs pushed through the snow.

He was freezing, despite the heavy cape he'd bought with him, and his arm ached from the weight of the eagle where it perched hunched and unhappy.

About him the sky hung heavy and leaden, merging with the thick fog that made the landscape to either side of the path indiscernible. Sometimes the fog shifted slightly and Axis thought he could see frozen trees, stripped bare of any life and hung only with icicles; sometimes the fog shifted slightly and he saw shapes, massive creatures almost indistinguishable from the moisture-laden air in which they lurked.

Axis moved through his own little world, pushing ever deeper into the hex. Occasionally he glanced upward, as if to see the sky.

But that was useless. The fog encased him, the snow entrapped him. There was nothing but to battle ever onward.

Isaiah had not wanted Axis to go. He had shouted and begged, arguing that this was nothing but a construct of Eleanon's, designed to trap Axis completely within the hex, but none of it made any difference. If it was a trap, then Axis admitted himself trapped.

Borneheld was too appalling a fate to leave anyone to suffer.

Eventually Isaiah had stopped shouting and begging and had admitted Axis to the hex. Axis had taken one last long look at Isaiah's face, seeing the sadness there, then he had turned and walked forward into the snow and ice.

It reminded Axis a little of that journey he'd made so long ago to Gorgrael's Ice Fortress. Gorgrael had been a half-brother, too.

They had battled, too.

Faraday had been present for that, too. Well, only in spirit for the last little bit of it. Gorgrael had killed her in an effort to distract Axis.

Brothers, thought Axis. *What a trial they always were.*

He kept pushing through the snow and ice, heading inexorably for whatever confrontation awaited him.

This really did remind him of the journey he'd taken toward Gorgrael's Ice Fortress.

Which brother was he destined to meet, then? One—or both?

As he kept pushing through the snowdrifts, stumbling now and again, Axis found himself remembering that journey. Faraday had been with him for much of it, sad and beautiful, concerned with her son who, at that time, Axis had not known about. She had been concerned also by what she perceived as her fate—her death at the hands of Gorgrael.

Faraday had always been so damned fatalistic.

Axis kept on striding, his eyes fixed ahead. Lost in memories of Faraday and that long ago journey.

Faraday had not completed the journey—at least, not with Axis. She had been taken by Timozel before they'd reached the Ice Fortress.

Timozel's hand had emerged from out of the snow and ice and fog, snatching at Faraday's ankle.

"Gotcha!" he had crowed.

"So fatalistic," Axis murmured to himself, wiping away the frost that formed about his eyebrows and eyelashes. He pulled the hood of the cloak closer, pushing his feet and legs through the knee-high snowdrifts, remembering, remembering, remembering . . .

After a long, long while, Axis became aware a figure drifted along the road ahead of him.

Tall, willowy, beautiful, ethereal.

Fatalistic.

Axis looked at the eagle. *You know what I require of you, my friend?*

The only response Axis received was a glare from the bird.

Even if I am trapped, you will not be, Axis said to the bird.

It is the only reason I agreed to aid you, StarMan, the bird said, and Axis nodded.

Be safe, he said, and launched the bird into the air.

He waited until the eagle had vanished into the fog, then Axis set off after Inardle, lengthening his pace and pushing more forcefully through the snowdrifts.

"Inardle?" he called, as he neared.

She stopped, but did not turn to look at him, not even raising her head when finally he stood before her. Her arms were wrapped about her shoulders, her head hung low, her wings dragged in the snow behind her.

The feathers were thick with ice and Axis wondered at Inardle's strength to be able to drag such a weight behind her.

Faint trails of old blood marred her lower back.

Axis looked at Inardle's downcast face and his heart cracked open. He'd never seen her look like this. Never.

Inardle had given up entirely. She was lost in despair so intense and so deep that Axis did not think there could be a way out for her.

"Inardle?"

Finally, Inardle raised her face to him, gave him a long look, then she brushed past him and walked on.

"Inardle," Axis said, catching up to her and taking one of her elbows in his hand to try and slow her down. *Stars, why was she in such a hurry?* "Inardle, stop, I pray you. Where are you going?"

She pulled her elbow from his grasp and took a step forward.

"Inardle!" Axis grabbed both her shoulders and wrenched her about to face him. "Where are you going? It is I, Axis."

Finally, Inardle spoke. "It does not matter who you are," she said. "Let me go, please. I have a marriage I am cursed to make."

"Inardle, this is not your battle, nor your history. Eleanon has—"

"Cursed and hexed me, Axis. He has bound me with powers from which I cannot escape. Where I go now is the fate he determined for me. I am to be Borneheld's wife."

"You do not have to . . . Inardle, turn from this fate and come back with me."

"I can't," she said. "I am lost now. I go where the lost go."

Axis felt her move against his hands, trying to break free to continue her journey, and he tightened his grip.

"There is no need to be lost or frightened or despairing, Inardle," he said. "You can come back with me. I remember the way."

Even as he said it, Axis wondered if he did remember or not.

Inardle shook her head. "No. I cannot go back, nor can you now. We're both trapped. You should not have come after me, Axis."

"I couldn't leave you to—"

"Why did you come, Axis?" Her voice broke on that. "For what purpose? You are dead and lost now, too. It was such a stupid thing to do."

Then she pulled herself out of Axis' hands and continued her sad march forward.

Axis stood in the snow, tugging his cloak tighter in the bone-numbing cold, watching Inardle draw slowly away from him, thinking about what she had said and why he was here. For what purpose *was* he here? To chase some long gone dream? Recreate some glorious moment so that he could . . . do what? Live again? Be purposeful again?

What did he want?

A purpose? A love? Glory?

Or was it just to save Inardle?

No, there was more to it than that. Eleanon had set the trap well. The moment Axis had known Borneheld waited inside the ice hex, he could no more have resisted the urge to enter than he could have willed himself to stop breathing.

Axis sighed, then walked after Inardle, struggling through the snow until he finally caught up with her.

She didn't look at him.

"I'll walk with you," he said, and together they trudged through the snow and ice, half frozen within this strange hexed world, toward whatever awaited them.

CHAPTER NINETEEN

The Sky Peaks

The Lealfast Nation had congregated on the lower slopes of the Sky Peaks to the north-west of Elcho Falling. Here they waited for Eleanon and, as he approached, the elder, Falayal, moved forward to greet him.

"You have been keeping your plans too close to your chest, Eleanon," Falayal said, in no mood for the courteous. "The Nation wonders, *I* wonder, if perhaps we should return to the frozen northern wastes. We have had enough of traipsing about after power. It appears that we will never—"

"You know that the One has been trapped within Infinity," Eleanon said. "There is now no barrier to our taking Elcho Falling and—"

"No barrier save Isaiah, and Axis, and Maximilian."

"And they are no barrier at all," Eleanon said, his voice now several levels lower, his eyes sharp as he looked at the elder.

Falayal regarded Eleanon with ill-disguised cynicism.

"I am thinking of the *Nation*," Falayal said, "not your personal ambitions."

"And *I* am thinking of the Nation!" Eleanon said. "By the stars and Infinity, did we not agree to merge with the One? To march together into a future unbounded by either our Skraeling or Icarii blood? We are all changed by the power of Infinity! And now the One is useless, we can take Elcho Falling and—"

"*How* can we take Elcho Falling?" Falayal said.

"It is what I have come to discuss with you, my friend," Eleanon said. "The time is almost here when we can step forth and claim our new heritage. It is time for the Lealfast to march toward their future."

"How?" Falayal said again.

"With some song and dance and music!" Eleanon said. "As well as a little help from the Dark Spire." He put his arms about the shoulders of the other Lealfast man and led him away slowly, talking softly.

When, finally, he halted and ceased speaking, Falayal's face was white with astonishment, his eyes glittering with ambition.

There was a frisson of excitement running between the two men that was almost palpable.

"It is too easy," Falayal said, in a tone which suggested he felt he ought to voice some token concern but didn't believe that concern in the slightest.

Brilliance is oft easy, Eleanon thought. "You agree?" he said.

Falayal hesitated, then nodded.

"It will need to be taken to the Nation," he said.

"Of course," Eleanon said. "It would be impossible without their agreement and compliance. I can address them this evening, as the first stars rise in the dusk sky."

"When?" Falayal said, and Eleanon knew he didn't refer to the assembly this evening.

"As soon as Maximilian and Ishbel return," Eleanon said. "Then we can move. But we need them inside Elcho Falling."

"Naturally," Falayal said. "You will address the Lealfast Nation this dusk, and they will agree. They will *shout* for you, Eleanon. Then . . . we begin training?"

"Then we begin training," Eleanon said. "This will be a great dance. One that will be remembered throughout eternity."

CHAPTER TWENTY

The Ice Hex

A xis glanced upward once or twice, wondering if he would see the eagle, but the surrounding fog was so thick and so closeting that the effort was useless. Axis gave up wondering about the eagle and instead tried to think through the hex that Eleanon had created.

Or recreated. Once more he was to meet Borneheld in battle. Axis and Borneheld had been rivals in many areas: parental affection, power at the Acharite court, success on the battlefield, but all of these rivalries had coalesced into the war over Faraday. Faraday and Axis had loved each other, but Borneheld had won Faraday as his wife—and that was always Borneheld's greatest triumph over Axis.

Faraday may have loved Axis, but she had left him to marry Borneheld.

How Borneheld had laughed in Axis' face and taunted him with his sexual conquest of the woman Axis loved.

Now Eleanon wanted Axis to relive this all over again, save with Inardle now playing the role of Faraday. What did Eleanon expect Axis to do . . . battle and kill Borneheld once again, and then free Inardle—and himself—from this hex?

No, no, there must be something else . . .

There was a trap here somewhere.

This wasn't a hex to trap Inardle. It was a hex to trap Axis.

They struggled on through the snow and ice. Inardle kept her head down, not looking at Axis, trapped in her own misery. She kept her hands wrapped about her shoulders, and her wings, still dragging behind her, were now so heavy with ice that Axis was amazed she could still move. Axis wished he could do something for her, but she rejected any overture.

They struggled through the snow.

After what felt like many hours something rose out of the snow before them. Axis was so astounded, almost frightened, that he stopped, staring ahead.

Inardle kept on walking, her head bowed, and Axis did not even know if she realised what lay in front of her.

It was a perfect representation of Carlon—the beautiful lakeside city that had once been Achar's capital—save it was now constructed entirely from ice. Walls, streets, gates, turrets, the great palace at its highest point, even all the pennants and flags . . . all ice.

Inardle trudged forward.

Axis stared at the city, stared at Inardle—incredulous that she should just ignore this—then forced himself after her.

They walked on.

The gates of Carlon lay open before them. Axis felt as if he walked through a dream—or was it a nightmare? Everything was as he remembered and everything brought back so many memories. They walked through the gates—Inardle still not showing any indication she realised they'd stopped walking through snowdrifts and now trod ice cobbles—and climbed the road that wound upward through the city toward the palace. Axis kept glancing to the side and behind him, wondering what ghosts lurked down side alleys and behind buildings.

But there were none. Just Axis and Inardle, climbing ever upward to the palace.

The gates to the palace lay open.

Inardle kept walking, a little faster now that some of the ice on her wings had grated off on the cobbles.

Axis hung back for a moment, remembering everything that had happened in this palace.

Now Borneheld waited.

Axis glanced upward again. The fog had lifted and he saw a black speck high in the sky.

Thank the stars. Axis hurried after Inardle. He turned the cloak back over his shoulders, giving his hand free access to the heavy sword at his hip.

And the dagger in his boot.

They worked their way through the palace, moving ever upward. They walked through wide corridors, hung with vast tapestries depicting scenes from Achar's glorious past and lit with ice lamps that emitted a cold, hard light.

There was no one in the palace, save he who waited in the Chamber of the Moons.

"Inardle," Axis said, "wait."

Unexpectedly, Inardle stopped, raising her face to look at Axis.

Axis reached out a hand, wanting to touch her, but not daring. He let his hand drop. "Inardle, whatever happens in that chamber, I *am* going to free us from this hex."

Her mouth curved very slightly in a sad smile. "You do not know Eleanon. He wants neither of us to leave. You should not have come after me."

"I could not let you go to Borneheld, Inardle."

"Would he be any worse than you?" Inardle said, and she turned and walked forward.

This *was* a nightmare, Axis decided.

They walked on.

Eventually they turned a corner in the main corridor and, there before them, lay open the doors to the Chamber of the Moons.

Axis could hear a faint murmur coming from it, as if hundreds of people waited inside. "Inardle—" he began.

"Too late, now," she said, and walked inside.

Axis hesitated a moment, then he, too, stepped inside.

And back into nightmare.

It was almost precisely as he remembered from that long ago night.

The Chamber of the Moons was the main audience chamber of the royal palace of Carlon. It was a huge circular room with an outer rim of alabaster columns supporting a soaring domed roof enamelled in a gorgeous deep blue. Gold and silver representations of the moon in the various phases of its monthly cycle floated amid myriad bejewelled stars across the enamelled dome. The floor was an equally spectacular affair of a deep emerald-green marble shot through with veins of gold. Even here, even in this construction of ice, the colours shone pure and unadulterated.

It was a spectacular chamber.

Axis lowered his eyes from the dome to the hundreds of shadowy people lurking behind the columns. They were not real, just shapes drifting and whispering among themselves.

Then he looked to the dais. When Axis had been a young man, BattleAxe of the Seneschal, this had been the domain of King Priam, Axis' uncle. Then, after Priam's murder, Borneheld had taken it as his own.

Now Borneheld sat the throne in the centre of the dais again, staring at Axis.

Inardle stood slightly to one side of the dais, facing Borneheld, but for the moment Axis barely noticed her.

His entire attention was centred on Borneheld.

Who could have imagined that Eleanon's power could have constructed such a remarkable likeness?

Borneheld grunted, lifting a leg over one arm of the throne and slouching comfortably. "Likeness? Not at all, brother. It is I in truth and actuality and flesh. Borneheld. You thought you'd killed me, but here I am again. Aren't you glad to see me?"

Axis just stared.

"You could come back from the Otherworld, brother," Borneheld said. "Why not I?"

He stood, then, a hulking muscular man, dark to Axis' fairness, bulky to Axis' leanness. They had shared a mother, but it had been their different fathers who had contributed most to each man's being.

There was a flutter at the door and both men looked.

The eagle sat atop one of the doors and as they watched it flew high into the dome, settling on a rafter close to one wall.

There it began to preen at its feathers, disinterested in the reunion below.

"Ah," said Borneheld, "the eagle. How I remember *that*." He took a step forward, all menace and triumph. "But what use shall it be for you tonight, Axis? I have no heart left!"

Borneheld took hold of his gem-laden jerkin, ripping it apart, and Axis took a half step back in horror.

Borneheld had no chest—only an empty cavity that showed his spine and ribs.

And no heart.

Borneheld began to laugh. "I have no heart left, Axis. How do you think to murder me this time?"

Axis went cold. *This* was Eleanon's trap.

Borneheld, unintentionally giving Axis time to think, had turned to Inardle. "Oh," he said, "she's so beautiful. Far more so than Faraday, don't you think, Axis? Special. Magical. I am going to enjoy her . . . although I'll need to beat the magical out of her."

He looked back at Axis, sly and vicious. "I used to try and beat the magical out of Faraday. Did you know that Axis? It didn't work, of course, but it kept her quiet, and that was all I needed from her. Silence. And compliance."

Axis knew Borneheld was trying to goad him, so he ignored his brother and instead walked a little closer to Inardle, holding out his hand. "Inardle, come away with me. Don't stay here with—"

"Don't touch her," Borneheld said, stepping between Inardle and Axis. "If you want her, you'll have to fight for her." Again that sly, vicious smile. "Just as we did half a century ago. Old times, eh?"

He laughed, and Axis gazed at Inardle.

She avoided his eyes, looking miserable and trapped.

Just as Faraday had so often looked.

"Prophecy binds her, Axis," Borneheld said, "just as it did Faraday. Prophecy is a terrible thing to try and break."

Now Axis stared at Borneheld, aghast. For some unknown reason what Borneheld had said struck a chord deep inside Axis, and in a blinding moment of revelation he knew how he could break the hex, what Eleanon's trickery demanded he do, but . . . oh stars . . . oh stars . . . no wonder Eleanon thought he had Axis trapped.

And thank each and every last one of the gods he'd brought the eagle.

"Then let Prophecy work itself out once more," Axis said, and he drew his sword with a harsh rasp of steel.

* * *

Time passed, and its passage was marked only by the ringing of steel through the Chamber of the Moons. Axis and Borneheld fought as they had fifty years earlier, evenly matched with skill and strength. Occasionally one would misstep and slip, and the other would lunge for the kill, only to have the one who had misstepped rebalance at the last moment and counter the assault. They moved about the central floor space of the Chamber of the Moons in a slow, measured dance of steel and hatred, boots sliding across the green marble, swords arcing and flashing in the light of the ice lamps, the shadowy watchers swaying to and fro as the combatants swayed to and fro, the murmur of their voices rising and falling as a distant surf in the background.

Every so often Borneheld's jerkin would gape open, and his empty chest cavity yawned mockingly before Axis.

Hours passed, and the lamps burned low. Both men fought with weariness now. They dripped with sweat, their movements, once so lithe, now leaden and fatigued. Both had been nicked numerous times, and blood glistened jewel-like among their clothes and the droplets of sweat glistening on their faces and arms.

At no point did either man drop his eyes from the other. They had waited through death for this chance to yet again work out their resentments and hatreds. The woman and the hex were mere excuses. In reality, each hated the other so much they would willingly have fought this duel over the rights to a blade of grass.

After hours of fighting Axis could barely stand, and knew he'd have to finish this soon. He'd managed to drive Borneheld back toward the dais, where Inardle sat on its lower step, dispirited and uninterested in the battle waged before her.

Then, just before they reached the dais, the eagle, far above and still intent in its preening, discovered a particularly disarranged bundle of feathers on its chest and it attacked them in a bout of irritated housekeeping. It tore out a small, downy feather, spitting it from its beak, then bent back to the task at hand.

The feather fell softly through the air. It floated this way and that, now rising, now falling, now wafting this way, now that. But always it drifted lower and lower until it began to jerk and sway as it was caught by the laboured breathing of the combatants just below it.

It almost lodged in Axis' hair and Axis flicked his head, irritated by the feathery touch along his forehead, distracted enough that he only just managed to parry a blow close to his chest.

The feather, dislodged from Axis' hair, spiralled upward a hand's-breadth or two, then, caught in a downward movement of air, sank toward the floor. Borneheld had not noticed it and Axis had forgotten it as the brothers began a particularly bitter exchange, fighting so close that they traded blows virtually on the hilts of their swords, taking the strain on their wrists, both their faces reddened and damp from effort and weariness and determination and hate.

The feather settled on the marble floor.

Axis suddenly lunged forward. Momentarily surprised, and caught slightly off-guard, Borneheld took a single step backward and . . . lost his balance as his boot heel slipped on the feather.

It was all Axis needed. As Borneheld swayed, a look of almost comical surprise on his face, Axis hooked his own foot about the inside of Borneheld's knee and pulled his leg out from under him.

Borneheld crashed to the floor, the sword slipping from his grasp and Axis kicked it across the Chamber. Fear twisting his face, Borneheld scrabbled backward, seeking space in which to rise. He risked a glance behind him—

There Faraday had once struggled, held firm in the grip of Jorge.

Now Inardle sat, not two paces away, staring at Axis as if with a horrid fascination.

They always looked at Axis before they looked at him.

Borneheld tried to shuffle away as Axis placed his booted foot squarely in the centre of Borneheld's empty chest, raising his sword. But, instead of bringing the blade down to sever the arteries of Borneheld's neck, Axis twisted the sword in his hand and struck Borneheld a stunning blow to his skull with its haft, leaving the man writhing weakly, semi-conscious. Then Axis threw the sword away.

Inardle looked at Axis, bewildered. Why did he not finish Borneheld off with a quick, clean blow?

Axis raised his face and stared at her, and it was the most devastating look Inardle could ever remember seeing in anyone's face.

"I'm so sorry, Inardle," Axis whispered, then he stepped forward, taking the knife from where it had rested all this time in his boot, and dealt her a sharp blow to the side of her head.

Inardle slumped to the floor, semi-conscious and writhing very slightly as Borneheld did a few paces away.

Axis felt sick, but he knew he had to do this, as quickly as possible, before his courage failed him. He sank to his knees, straddling Inardle, and hauling her roughly so she lay on her back under him.

She raised one hand weakly in protest but, still struggling for consciousness, let it drop back to the marble floor.

I'm sorry, Axis said to her, over and over. *I'm sorry . . . I'm sorry . . .*

He ripped open her robe, exposing her breasts, then, crying out in horror, he plunged the knife into the skin and flesh atop Inardle's sternum and hauled it downward, opening up her chest.

Blood spurted everywhere.

Oh stars, oh stars . . .

Then Axis took the haft of the knife in both hands and, before he could even think about what he was doing, slammed the blade into Inardle's sternum, twisting it so the bone cracked in two.

Axis tossed away the knife and then, before going any further, made the mistake of looking into Inardle's face.

It would haunt him the rest of his life. She stared at him in pain and horror, which was what he had expected, but also with the dismay of someone who has been betrayed so deeply that their minds simply cannot encompass the depth of that betrayal. She looked at him in question and pain and love and supplication, as if hoping that somehow he could explain away with a smile and a joke what he was doing.

Axis? Her lips formed the word, but could not speak it, and Axis sobbed, dragging his eyes away from hers. He looked back to the nightmarish mess of her chest, at the blood pumping forth so that his lower body, and almost her entire torso and much of her wings, were soaked in it, then he dug his fingers between the cracked sternum and with one huge effort tore her ribcage apart.

The sound of the splintering bones in the chamber was shocking, and Axis gagged, so sickened and horrified at what he was doing that he thought he could not bear to continue.

But he had to . . . he had to . . . he could not stop now.

His arms bloodied to the elbow, his shirt soaked in Inardle's blood, Axis dug both hands into her chest and wrapped them about her frantically beating heart . . .

Then he tore it out, spraying blood over an area five paces in diameter.

"Take it!" he screamed to the eagle. *"Take the damned thing now!"*

And with all his strength, Axis tossed Inardle's beating heart high into the air.

The eagle launched itself from its perch, its scream merging with Axis' now wordless shrieking, and plummeted downward, seizing the heart in its talons.

Axis screamed again. *Go! Go!*

There was a blinding flash of light and suddenly both eagle and heart had vanished.

Axis forced himself to look downward.

Inardle, unbelievably, still had a single breath of life left in her. She stared at Axis, managed to half raise a hand.

I wish . . . she mouthed, and then she was gone.

Axis stared, his breath heaving in and out of his chest, his mind barely working.

Oh gods . . . what had he done? What had he done?

There was a slight scuffle of noise behind him, and Borneheld grabbed at one of Axis' ankles.

"Gotcha!" he crowed.

Axis reacted instinctively and with all the hatred for his brother and his grief for Inardle combined. He whipped about and struck Borneheld a massive blow across his face.

Borneheld's grip on his ankle loosened and Axis rose to his feet and kicked his brother in the face, maddened with grief and despair, and loosing all of that grief and despair on Borneheld.

He paused, his breath heaving in and out of his chest, then Axis kicked Borneheld again, and then again, and then yet again, until all sound in that death chamber was only the sound of a boot thudding into splintered bone and flesh, over and over, and the sound of a man's heartbroken sobbing.

CHAPTER TWENTY-ONE

Elcho Falling

An infinity of time had passed, and yet almost none at all. The One felt as if he had spent millennia crawling, hand over hand, along the cord which connected him to the Dark Spire, but he was aware also that very little time had passed in Elcho Falling's world.

No matter. Just so long as he achieved his goal.

As the One drew near to the Dark Spire he became more cautious. He wrapped his presence in subterfuge and mystery, that none might detect him, and at the same time sent his presence and power crawling ahead along the cord into the Dark Spire to prepare the way . . . to prepare his hidey hole. It wouldn't last long, not beyond the return of the Lord of Elcho Falling who could surely sense his presence, but until then the One thought he could remain undetected.

Unless that baby realised his presence.

The One put hand over hand, pulling himself ever closer to the Dark Spire.

Ravenna was aware that somehow the Dark Spire was changing. Each time she went back to it for another egg she could feel something different about the spire, something darker, something more secretive. She felt a growing power within the spire, but assumed that was because it was gathering itself for the moment it had birthed its last egg and could grow into its full potential.

One afternoon, when she trudged down the stairs to the basement chambers of Elcho Falling to attend the spire, her mind was everywhere but on her task. Despite the fact she found it distasteful—and she hated the fact she had no choice in the matter—Ravenna had become so used to her chore of removing the eggs from the spire and placing them about Elcho Falling she now conducted the business in a mild daze, her thoughts elsewhere.

Today she was thinking about the baby that lived higher in the citadel. She had managed a few hours the previous day to creep about Elcho Falling and discover who it was.

StarDrifter and Salome's son. He was a powerful boy, and handsome, but Ravenna envied Salome simply for being able to love her son without the burden of curses. Star-Dancer, the baby, would grow happy and healthy into his full heritage.

Not so Ravenna's son.

Ravenna had not entered StarDrifter and Salome's chamber. She remained in the corridor, leaning against the wall of the chamber, sensing the presence of the child within. She would have stayed there for hours, save that StarDancer had realised *her* presence and Ravenna had hurried away, fearing he would say something to his parents.

Apparently he hadn't, for she remained undiscovered.

That brief time spent huddled against the wall whetted Ravenna's curiosity about StarDancer. *So powerful, so keen. What must it be like to have a child of so much ability and potential? Could her son be as powerful if he had the chance to grow into* his *full potential?*

StarDancer consumed her mind as she approached the spire. She was concentrating entirely on him and paying her routine business with the spire no mind at all. Ravenna wandered about the spire, her mind alerting her to the moment of arrival at the source of another egg and she leaned down to the spire without thought of what she was doing.

As her two hands came close to the side wall of the spire, two green glass hands reached out and grabbed her wrists, and before she had time to draw a shocked breath Ravenna found herself in the ground floor of Elcho Falling only to realise an instant later that it was a corrupted version.

Elcho Falling's ground floor columned chamber was full of colour and majesty, but this chamber was grey and black hued and its columns were stunted and askew. There was no sense of magic here, either, only an emptiness and a sense of waiting.

And something else.

Another presence.

At first Ravenna thought it was Eleanon, but she quickly realised that this presence was vastly more powerful. She turned about, staring, her heart thudding in her chest as she saw that in the distance, beyond five or six rows of columns, the chamber disintegrated into black nothingness.

"Infinity."

The word whispered out to her, and Ravenna spun around, trying to locate the person who had spoken.

"Who's there?" she managed, her voice dry with fear.

"Do you not recognise this place?" the voice said.

Ravenna swallowed, still turning, if more slowly, her eyes darting everywhere.

This unknown stranger was so powerful . . . so dangerous.

"Who are you?" she said, glad her voice was a little stronger now.

"An old friend," said the voice, and from behind one of the columns stepped a man made entirely of green glass. In the centre of his chest revolved a golden pyramid.

Ravenna froze. *The One.* She had never seen him before, but this could be nobody else.

"Hello, Ravenna," the One said softly. He came to a halt a few paces away from her, smiling a little as she tensed. "You are being very brave. Tell me, do you not recognise this place?"

"It is the interior of the Dark Spire," Ravenna said, guessing.

"Very good! I knew you were going to be useful. I was, for instance, greatly inquisitive regarding that baby which so consumed your mind as you pattered about the Dark Spire on your business."

Ravenna instantly tried to empty her mind of all thought.

"Too late," the One whispered. Then, in a louder voice: "You are Eleanon's plaything, yes?"

"Yes," Ravenna grated.

"Not any more," the One said.

* * *

StarDancer lay in his cot and screamed. He rarely cried, let alone screamed, but right now he wanted his parents as fast as they could possibly reach him. The Icarii woman who had been watching him stood by his cot, not knowing what to do. Her first instinct had been to hold StarDancer, but the boy had only screamed the louder when she'd tried to pick him up.

StarDrifter and Salome rushed into the chamber, convinced their son was being murdered, or was caught in a fatal brainstorm. But the instant they entered the chamber StarDancer quietened, the only sign of his recent distress the trail of tears on his downy cheeks.

"What happened?" StarDrifter said to the Icarii woman, FlightMeadow.

"I don't know!" FlightMeadow said. "StarDancer was sleeping peacefully, then he just began to scream. I tried to pick him up. But . . ."

By now Salome had her son in her arms and both she and her husband regarded FlightMeadow with cool, accusing eyes.

"I didn't . . ." FlightMeadow said, drifting to a halt at their regard. *Damn it, why did StarDancer have to do this when* she *was minding him?*

"Perhaps you could leave us alone with our son," StarDrifter said, and FlightMeadow gave a curt nod and left, vowing not to volunteer for babysitting again.

"StarDancer?" StarDrifter said.

I had a dream, StarDancer spoke into his parents' minds.

"Everyone dreams, sweetheart," Salome said, stroking her son's cheek. "They are but dreams, releases of our nervous energy, nothing more. You must not be afraid."

This was more than a dream, StarDancer said.

"Tell us," StarDrifter said, sitting down on the bed, slowly rocking StarDancer to and fro.

I dreamed of the mighty universe, StarDancer said. *I dreamed of its vast emptiness.*

"The voids between the stars," his father said, "nothing more."

I dreamed of a threatening presence moving through the void as a man would climb a rope.

"Just a dream," Salome said.

It was real. .

Salome and StarDrifter shared an indulgent smile.

He was coming here. A frightening man. I dreamed of him before.

"Just a dr—" Salome started to say again.

It was real! StarDancer cried. *Not a dream!*

"Perhaps you dreamed of WolfStar," StarDrifter said. "WolfStar was an ancient ancestor of ours. He jumped into the Star Gate—you remember me telling you of this—and wandered through the spaces of the stars for millennia. Eventually he returned, evil creature that he was, and created havoc within our family and Tencendor."

StarDancer was silent as he considered this. *Whoever it was*, he said eventually, *he is here now. Within Elcho Falling.*

"Don't worry, my sweetheart," Salome said, taking her son from StarDrifter and rocking him gently in her arms. "We have you safe."

Just a dream, she mouthed over StarDancer's head to StarDrifter, and again they shared an indulgent smile.

CHAPTER TWENTY-TWO

Isembaard

Maximilian and his party had been pushing hard for the Isembaardian east coast. They'd travelled all day and well into each night, stopping only for a brief meal from their dwindling supplies and a few hours' sleep before rising before dawn the next day. All of them were close to exhaustion, crabby, hungry and a little anxious about what might await them on the coast. What if no one from Elcho Falling had managed to send a vessel south? What if there was a vessel, but it was under the control of someone antagonistic? Maximilian had heard nothing from the north for a long time and no way of knowing what had played out at Elcho Falling. Were former allies now enemies? And where were the Skraelings? Had some of them come back, hoping for a quick seaside snack?

The disappearance of the rat and the *Book of the Soulenai* had not worried them overmuch. The book had clearly nothing more for them, as also the rat, and Maximilian and Ishbel decided both had vanished until they were needed again.

But everything else . . . Hairekeep had taught everyone to be careful. The One was finally gone; or so they thought. Maximilian, while optimistic the Twisted Tower was now drifting further and further from their world, was not prepared to depend on that belief totally.

The One had surprised them before.

Maximilian held up his hand, stopping his companions.

They had entered Isembaard's only eastern port earlier. The small town—little more than a village—was completely deserted. No people, no dogs, no rats.

The Skraelings had been active here.

They had been walking through the abandoned town, looking down every side street and alley, keeping alert for any danger. Now, as they reached the single pier and the crescent of fine sand that defined the beach, Maximilian stopped them, nodding to the middle of the pier.

There sat a man before a metal circular bowl in which smouldered a small fire. He appeared to be toasting a fish over the coals.

"I'll go ahead," Maximilian murmured.

"We'll come with you," Ishbel and Serge said at the same time, while Doyle nodded his general agreeance with the statement.

"I should—" Maximilian said.

"We'll come with you," Ishbel said, "and don't argue the point, Maxel. We're all too tired for it."

Maximilian thought about sighing, but he was too fatigued even to do that, let alone fight with Ishbel. "We'll need to be careful," he said.

"Do you sense anything wrong?" Serge said.

"Apart from the fact I can't see a bloody ship anywhere?" Maximilian said. "No, I sense nothing wrong. Come on, then. Let's get this over and done with."

They walked forward, and as their boots struck the timber decking of the pier, the man half turned and saw them.

He did not appear worried, or even particularly surprised, to see the four people walking up the pier toward him. He carefully balanced the stick holding the fish on the side of the brazier, then rose, wiping his hands down his leather trousers.

He was a tall, lean man, dark haired and with the weather-beaten, stubbled face of an experienced seaman. His eyes were bright brown specks almost completely lost behind wrinkles and wreaths of skin, and his teeth were startlingly white and strong when he smiled as the four neared.

"You're the ride, then," he said.

"The ride?" Maximilian said, feeling stupid in his weariness.

"The passengers I was sent to pick up," the man said.

"We were expecting a ship," Ishbel said.

The man looked at her. "And I was expecting a little courtesy, perhaps."

"I apologise," Ishbel said. "My name is Ishbel Persimius, and this is my husband, Maximilian. Our two companions are Doyle and Serge."

The man nodded at each in turn. "I am Abe Wayward," he said. "Who do you think sent me to wait for you?"

For a moment Maximilian could make no sense of the question, then he realised Abe was testing them. Maximilian managed a moment of inner humour, thinking that here he'd been, scrying out everything he could about this man, and yet here Abe was, testing *them*.

"It would have been either Axis SunSoar," said Maximilian, "or Georgdi, the Outlander general. The message would have originated from Elcho Falling, what you would have known as Serpent's Nest before . . ."

"Before everything went awry," Abe said, and nodded. "Good enough. Georgdi it was. Sit down and we can have a meal of carawait fish before we go. Tide won't be right for sailing until this evening, anyway."

"You have a boat?" Ishbel said, hoping her question didn't sound as desperate as she felt, or that Abe once more decided she was being impolite.

Abe nodded over the side of the pier. "Right there."

As one the four stepped up to the side of the pier and looked down. Far below, tied to the carbuncled piles of the structure, was a small sailing vessel little bigger than a rowing boat.

None of them knew what to say.

Abe chuckled at the looks on their faces. "The Outlanders are not known for their great fleet, my friends. We have a few fishing boats, but that's it. For everything else seaworthy, we depend on what the Vilanders supply us. They're the sailing nation, not us. Georgdi should have asked the Vilanders to send one of their cargo cobs to fetch you, eh? You could all have had individual cabins with velvet curtains, then."

"It looks an honest boat," Maximilian said, not knowing what to say.

Now Abe's chuckle turned into a hearty laugh. "And to think you're going to have to sit in it all the way north toward Margalit . . . or is it Elcho Falling you want to reach?"

"Elcho Falling," Maximilian said.

"Elcho Falling, then," Abe said. "Well, she's surely an honest boat, and keeled and rigged for speed. If the weather gets rough, then there'll be enough hands on deck to bail her out. Difficult when I'm on my own. And look on the bright side . . . it's not too far to lean over the side when you decide you're going to lose your breakfast."

"We are grateful for any ride," Maximilian said, "for we are heartily sick of using our feet. Sitting down on the journey sounds like heaven to me. Thank you, Abe Wayward. We shall be glad and grateful to accept your aid."

Maximilian stepped forward and offered Abe his hand.

Ishbel, Serge and Doyle all watched, their eyes sharp.

Abe didn't miss their scrutiny. He smiled once again, and grasped Maximilian's hand. "Do I pass?" he said.

Maximilian gripped the seaman's hand, holding it for a long moment, staring the man in the eyes.

Then he nodded. "You pass, my friend. I apologise for my suspicion. We have had trials on our journey to meet you."

"Then we shall have much conversation on the way north," Abe said, "between bouts of bailing."

CHAPTER TWENTY-THREE

The Ice Hex

Axis dragged Inardle's bloodied corpse through the snow of Eleanon's ice hex. He had his arms wrapped under hers, clutched across her ruined chest, her body held awkwardly to one side as he tried to avoid her dragging wings.

She was almost rock solid both with rigor mortis and with the ice which had formed about her body. Only his Icarii strength meant Axis could keep dragging her like this—even the strongest human would have collapsed many hours ago.

Axis stared straight ahead, thinking of nothing more than placing one foot before the other, and thus dragging his burden just that bit further forward. He thought he was retracing the same path he'd taken to reach the icy recreation of Carlon, but he wasn't sure. He didn't really care if he wasn't. If he was wrong it meant that he would die cursed inside this hex, but Axis felt that his own heart had gone, along with Inardle's, and right now death felt like a perfectly viable, even preferable, option.

Axis had decided he was very tired of life and of all the horrors it put in his path.

He struggled onward, every muscle in his body screaming in agony, his breath frosting out of his mouth and rasping in his throat, icicles forming in his hair and hanging from his eyebrows and in his re-growing beard.

Inardle was icy cold in his arms. The blood from the wound in her chest had frozen all over her body . . . save in that small area where her body touched Axis' hip. There the constant friction of living flesh against corpse had melted the blood, and Axis could feel it squishing underneath his clothes and trickling slowly down his leg into his boot where it froze all over again, sending splinters of ice into his flesh with every step.

He badly wanted this nightmare to be over.

Axis stopped, eventually, worn almost to complete exhaustion. He stood, his chest heaving, staring ahead, his arms slipping on Inardle's body. He sobbed, fighting to keep hold of her, knowing that if he allowed her to slip into the snow he'd never find the strength to lift her and continue on his way.

It was so silent in this hex. The fog clung to him; he could barely see three paces ahead. If he held his breath, if only for the brief moment he was able, there was utter silence all about him, mocking him.

What if he couldn't find his way out? What if Eleanon was somewhere, right now, laughing at Axis' pain?

It was that thought that galvanised Axis back into movement.

By the stars, Eleanon was going to die for the pain he had caused. Axis felt the beginnings of a deep, cold anger, the kind that never faded, just grew and grew until eventually it needed to be assuaged in the only way possible—a death. Either Axis', or the one on which the anger focussed.

"I'll kill him for you," Axis whispered, managing to heft Inardle's corpse a little more securely in his arms, and taking a step forward.

"I'll kill him for you."

Another step forward.

"I'll kill him for you."

Another step.

Time passed.

Inardle was now a solid block of ice, and Axis' own arms had been so frozen into that ice that he no longer had to spend any strength holding her, just in dragging himself along, and therefore her. Axis had not rested. There was no way he could sit or lie, for to do so would be to kill himself. He had to keep taking step after step, and feeling muscles tear in his chest and shoulders and back every time he did so.

Even his mantra of "I'll kill him for you," had disintegrated into a harsh gargle with each step.

Axis now existed on pure anger and some vague memory of what it meant to cling to life.

And so he took one step, and then another, and then, by some miracle, yet another.

Time passed.

Axis was now barely alive himself. His head and shoulders were almost covered in ice, and his upper body had now been completely absorbed into the ice that encased Inardle.

He could barely breathe.

He knew that he would die within the next few minutes.

Three more steps.

Maybe four.

Then he would allow death to claim him, too.

On the third step Axis and Inardle fell right through the icy path and into deep water.

The water was, in fact, very cold, but to Axis it felt like it boiled against his skin, scalding his flesh. He tried to drag in a breath to scream, but the ice constricting his chest wouldn't allow him to do it.

He tried to struggle, but his arms were caught in ice, and he couldn't do that, either.

Oh stars! Stars! He was going to drown!

Still bound to the ice-encased Inardle, Axis began to sink deeper and deeper, dragged ever lower by her weight, water filling his mouth and throat, and he choked, the movement in his chest causing him agonising pain.

He fought desperately, and suddenly he felt the ice about his chest and arms loosen and then crack, and then the ice gave way entirely and he flailed about as the burden of Inardle sank into the depths beneath him and he fought for the surface.

His head broke the surface and he heaved in lungfuls of air. His entire body screamed in pain, but he didn't care, he could breathe, he could breathe . . .

Axis blinked, his vision blurring and then clearing.

He was floating near the reed banks in the channel that connected Elcho Falling's lake with the sea. Axis turned in the water.

Yes, there was Elcho Falling, glorious in the sunlight.

Axis turned on his back and floated, glorying in the pain as both sun and water massaged away the ice and stiffness from his limbs and body.

There was a sudden rush of bubbles to one side, and the water erupted as Inardle's corpse broke the surface.

It had defrosted and the water about her was stained with blood and clots from the gaping cavity in her chest.

Inardle.

Axis paddled over to her, once more grasping her under the arms and rolling over on his back so that he supported her body and exposed it to the sky and sunlight, her wings limp and heavy and trailing to either side of Axis' body.

He shook his head, clearing his vision of the final few droplets of water, then he looked up into the blue, empty sky.

"*Do it!*" Axis screamed. "*Do it now!*"

For a moment, nothing.

There was a flash high in the sky, and then a black spot, plummeting downward.

Do it! Axis screamed in his mind. *Do it!*

The black spot fell closer and closer, moving so fast that its form blurred.

It was only just before it hit that Axis could clearly see what it was.

The eagle, bearing Inardle's heart in its talons.

The next instant Axis' world erupted into a cascade of bubbles and boiling water as the eagle's impact, carrying almost more magic than Axis could bear, drove himself and Inardle deep into the water.

CHAPTER TWENTY-FOUR

Elcho Falling

Ravenna drifted to and from the Dark Spire, midwiving the last of the horrible thing's eggs, and trying very hard not to think about what the One demanded she do for him. She had thought Eleanon a vile taskmaster, but the One . . . Ravenna spent her time wishing she were anywhere but here.

The Land of Dreams, back in the arms of the Lord of Dreams, Drava.

Back in the marshes, in her mother's house.

Ravenna wondered if Drava ever thought of her, or if he remembered her.

She wondered if her mother's house in the marshes had fallen into disrepair and disappeared into the marsh.

But why wonder now, when all this was denied her forever? She had chosen a bad path in life, and it had led her to the very gates of Hell itself.

Elcho Falling was crowded with soldiers and with many different races. Icarii, Isembaardian, Escatorian, Outlander. All of them hurried and scurried everywhere and their leaders spent much of their time studying, and worrying over, the Dark Spire.

They did not see what Ravenna knew it contained. The One had hidden his presence very well.

He did not need to show his hand. He had Ravenna to do his work for him. Ravenna's only hope lay in wondering if Eleanon would notice that she had slipped beyond his control to that of a new master. But she did not hold out much hope. Eleanon had shown no interest in her once he'd managed to secrete her into Elcho Falling. He would be thinking that the curse he had added to Ishbel's curses would be enough to keep her to her duties.

Even if Eleanon did realise the One's presence (which Ravenna doubted very much) he was highly unlikely to mount a rescue of Ravenna from the One's clutches.

Eleanon did not have the power to confront the One.

So Ravenna went about her task of shifting the eggs, because for the moment this was what the One required of her, no longer doing it for Eleanon's benefit. As she moved within the citadel she noticed its inhabitants also worried and studied a ball of ice in the bowels of the citadel. Ravenna didn't know what it was, but Isaiah and Georgdi, as well as Axis' body servant Yysell, often spent hours in silent vigil, as if waiting for something. Yesterday the thing had blackened, and cracked in half, revealing nothing inside save a little melting ice. There was much consternation.

When it happened, Ravenna had been there placing one of the Dark Spire's eggs in its hiding spot within the walls. She had watched for a moment as Isaiah and Georgdi shouted and then fell into a grave silence. Ravenna had drifted away, uncaring, lost in her own problems.

They had not seen her—no one ever saw her—and Ravenna did not care what it was that so concerned them.

They would not have much longer to worry about the broken ice ball as the Dark Spire was now perilously close to breaking into the chamber where, from what Ravenna understood, an underwater tunnel led back into the lake.

On this day Ravenna was, as usual, engaged in her work. She had spent the night huddled in a never-used doorway, dozing off and on, often waking with a jerk thinking she could hear the baby somewhere in the levels far above her and feeling sick to the stomach as she thought about what she had to do for the One.

Now, early in the morning, she took herself down to one of the lower levels from where the Dark Spire twisted its way higher into the citadel.

As usual, there were guards and one or two Enchanters there, but Ravenna took no notice of them. She walked slowly about the base of the spire, looking for any small lumps or protuberances.

Ah! There! Ravenna glanced about to make sure no one was looking directly at her—they might not see her, but they would see the change in the surface of the spire—then bent over, her hands working away to release the egg.

It felt loathsome, cool and clammy, and she could feel the One within, watching her, but Ravenna forced herself to ignore it. Her fingers burrowed deeper and deeper until . . . pop! The small jet-black egg popped into her hands.

Ravenna quickly backed away from the spire, her eyes darting to look at the other people in the room, but none had noticed anything. Sighing in relief, she allowed the egg to dictate where it wanted to go.

Up!

Ravenna climbed the main stairwell of Elcho Falling. She shared the stairwell with many others, but none saw her and did not notice even when they occasionally brushed past her. She climbed many levels until the egg urged her toward a chamber on the eastern side of Elcho Falling.

There, at the egg's prompting, she laid it against the stone wall where it met the floor. The egg burrowed its way into the outer wall of Elcho Falling and vanished.

Ravenna had set hundreds of these eggs over the past weeks.

She knew that, one day, they would hatch and create havoc within Elcho Falling.

She didn't care. Very soon she would be unleashing her own havoc.

Ravenna turned and walked back to the Dark Spire.

Once there she began searching for the next egg. She walked around and around the spire, concentrating.

Nothing.

Ravenna felt sick. Were there no more? If there were no more eggs, then she would need to move onto the task the One had set her.

The eggs, initially easy to find, had, in the past few days, become ever scarcer. Instead of placing ten or fifteen a day, there had been only eight, and then five, and yesterday merely three.

Perhaps her time working as the Dark Spire's midwife was almost at an end.

Her feeling of nausea grew as she continued to walk about the spire for another two hours.

Nothing.

Eventually she stopped. There were no more eggs. The Dark Spire had finished with her.

Now you must do what I need, the One whispered in her mind.

Ravenna swallowed. Oh gods . . .

Now, the One said. *The eggs are set. Now you do what I need, before it is too late.*

Ravenna took a step away from the spire toward the stairs leading upward.

Another step, then she turned for the stairs and walked up, one leaden foot in front of the other.

CHAPTER TWENTY-FIVE

Elcho Falling and Surrounds

She opened her eyes. It was so warm! Where was she? The sky was blue above her, enormous, infinitely blue. There were some birds nearby—she could hear their soft chattering—but none in the sky.

It was so warm. She was bathed in sunlight. She could feel it playing along her flesh.

Rivers ran wild in her blood, and for a while she lost herself within their rhythm.

Gradually she became aware that she lay on something soft.

Inardle turned her head. Reeds. There were reeds everywhere, and the surface she lay on was undulating, very slightly. She lay in the reed beds. She watched the reeds moving in a gentle breeze.

Their movements mirrored the running of the rivers in her blood.

There were insects crawling up and down the shafts of the reeds, dragonflies here and there among their bushy heads.

It was so pleasant here. She didn't have to think. She could just lie still.

After a long while, Inardle turned her head in the other direction.

Axis sat, a few paces away, leaning back against a thick stand of reeds. He was naked, his clothes spread out as if drying.

Behind him, in the distance, Elcho Falling.

She looked once more to the sky.

There were several Lealfast above, invisible to most eyes, circling and watching.

Inardle wondered what they made of her lying here so exposed.

Then she thought of Eleanon, and the river within her turned bleak.

Inardle looked back to Axis. He was watching her and gave a small smile at her regard.

Inardle rolled her head again to look at the sky. She lifted a hand, laying it on her sternum between her breasts.

The skin was soft, unbroken, not even by a scar.

"I am sorry," Axis said, very softly. "It was the only way to escape the hex."

Inardle gave a nod. "I have been dreaming," she said.

Axis said nothing, waiting.

"I dreamed I ran with the Skraelings," she continued.

"Was it reality?" Axis asked.

Inardle gave another nod. "We ran in a strange, strange place. Axis, the Skraelings are in a strange place, both physically and mentally."

"In what manner?"

"They are going to return to the water, Axis."

"Here?"

She gave yet another nod.

"When?" Axis said.

She shrugged. "When they wish."

They fell into silence, and Inardle slept once more.

Isaiah stood with Georgdi on one of the balconies on the eastern wall of Elcho Falling.

"What are they *doing*?" Georgdi said.

Isaiah didn't reply immediately. He, as everyone else, had been convinced that Axis and Inardle were lost when the ice hex turned black and crumpled apart, but a few hours ago one of the guards had reported that the pair lay in a small circle of trampled reeds to the east of Elcho Falling.

Isaiah and Georgdi had rushed to see. At first they'd thought one or both might be injured, but now it was apparent both were well enough.

"Gods alone know what they are doing," Isaiah said. "But Axis is aware of the way into the citadel, and if he chooses not to take it . . . well . . ." He paused. "I'll place a lookout here to keep an eye on them, but for the moment, my friend, we have worse things to worry about than when Axis and Inardle might rouse from their stupor long enough to let us know what happened."

"You can't contact them?" Georgdi said, knowing of Isaiah's ability to speak with Axis over considerable distance.

Isaiah gave a little shake of his head. "He's actually cut himself off. Whatever happened to them has changed both somewhat. I think they are both readjusting to the land of the living. They're doing it in a bloody dangerous spot, but that's what I think is happening. They were in there for many, many days, Georgdi."

Georgdi heaved a theatrical sigh. "These winged races . . ." he said, then he and Isaiah turned and walked back into Elcho Falling.

When she woke, Axis was still sitting, watching over her.

"It is pleasant here," Inardle said.

Axis gave a small smile. "Yes. It is. I worry about being so exposed, though. When you feel able, we should move to a place more concealed."

"There are Lealfast overhead," she said.

Axis glanced upward, his eyes creasing in worry.

"Don't worry about them, Axis," Inardle said.

He looked back to her, his expression still concerned.

"Don't worry about it," she said again. "How long have we been here?"

"We returned from the hex yesterday. You have slept through the night and through half of this day."

Time must have passed, she thought, for Axis was clothed now. His clothes must have dried. "It was a terrible journey out of the hex, Axis."

"I thought you were dead."

"I dreamed. I ran with the Skraelings. But I also dreamed of you."

He shifted slightly. "Inardle, I am sorry for what I did. I—"

"Eleanon made that hex and made those circumstances

which meant you needed to kill me. It was the only way out for you. It was the only way for you to survive the hex. But . . . why am *I* here? I should not be here. I was to have died, no matter what."

I have changed, she thought. *The river runs murderous in me, now.*

"Ah." Axis smiled so broadly his entire face was wreathed in laughter lines. "Eleanon created a hex that was to recreate for me my battle with Borneheld. It was perfect, Inardle, his trap was perfect. Either both you and I died trapped in the hex, or I lived, but at your expense. Eleanon thought of everything. Save for one thing."

Save for two things. "Which was?"

"Eleanon had heard of the story of my battle with Borneheld in the Chamber of the Moons. He'd assumed that the battle was about one thing—our bitter, hateful rivalry. The Chamber of the Moons was where it was to be settled. But a battle to the death to end a rivalry wasn't the ultimate purpose of that night. The ultimate purpose was a rebirth—in the original situation, the rebirth of an Icarii prince named FreeFall. *That* was the magic that encased that night. Eleanon didn't realise it. That magic was there again . . . I could sacrifice you, but I could also bring you back."

"You dragged me through the ice and the snow. You risked everything. Ice encased your chest and you could not breathe. You dragged me back through the ice and the snow."

Axis didn't say anything for a moment, remembering that terrible journey. "Yes," he said, finally.

"I know of it," Inardle said. "I know how bad it was. Thank you." The rivers ran gentle now, and Inardle understood they would never harm Axis.

"Do you know what I swore to do, during that journey?" Axis said.

Now Inardle regarded him with very bright eyes. "Kill Eleanon."

"Yes. I will do that for you."

Inardle rolled her head so she stared at the sky. The Lealfast had long gone—to report her life to Eleanon, no doubt.

Axis wanted to kill Eleanon.

A small smile curved Inardle's mouth. *Only if he got to her brother before she did.*

Whatever ties had bound her to the Lealfast had now broken completely.

"Don't worry about the Lealfast," she told Axis. "I will know if they return, and I know they will not be able to harm us."

"Are you sure?"

"Yes."

She could see that Axis didn't understand, but she saw also that he decided to trust her.

"Very well," he said. "Sleep for a while longer, Inardle. I will build a fire for the evening and we can talk some more then."

"I would like to talk about Azhure," she said, and Axis nodded.

"We can talk about Azhure."

She slept, and the rivers raged.

"They are alive?" Eleanon stared at the scouts. *"They are alive?"*

"Yes, brother," replied one of the Lealfast who had circled high above the reed bank where Inardle and Axis rested. "They have a little camp in the reed banks just east of Elcho Falling. They . . ."

Eleanon didn't hear much else the scout said. *How could they still be alive?* Axis, perhaps, if he'd had the wit and the balls to murder Inardle (and Eleanon had gambled on him having neither). But the *pair* of them should not have survived.

There was no way Inardle should ever have emerged from that hex save as a brutalised corpse.

"Brother?" the scout said. "What should we do? We could attack and—"

"No," Eleanon said. "This is *my* battle." It had always been going to come down to just him and Axis, hadn't it?

Eleanon looked at the sky. Night was not far away. Did he want to attack at night?

Something made him hesitant about a night attack.

Best to wait until morning.

"Dawn tomorrow," Eleanon said, naming five other Leal-fast he wanted to accompany him. "We will attack at dawn tomorrow."

The scouts left and Eleanon walked a little way from the Lealfast encampment in the mountains to the north-west of Elcho Falling, and stared into the distance where his eyes could just pick out the citadel glimmering in its turquoise lake.

Axis and Inardle's survival was irritating, *frustrating*, but it could be reversed easily enough. Just another day.

Everything else, though, had fallen neatly and swiftly into place. The Lealfast Nation was set to descend on Elcho Falling the moment Maximilian and his wife were inside. And they were on their way—Eleanon's scouts reported the pair close to Elcho Falling in their pathetic little boat. Another few days at the most.

As for Ravenna . . . well, Ravenna had done her duty and Eleanon didn't care what happened to her. If she were discovered, and if she told all, there was nothing that could be done by those in Elcho Falling.

She had fulfilled her purpose and for the moment Eleanon forgot her.

As he did so, the additional enchantment he had wrapped about Ishbel's curse began, very slowly, to disintegrate.

Ravenna slowly ascended the great staircase of Elcho Falling. She took her time, using her senses to scry out the location of the baby.

He was here, somewhere.

StarDancer.

She ascended floor after floor, until she reached a level where the sense of the baby was so strong her eyes filmed with tears.

Oh gods, how had she come to this?

She wandered along a hallway, then entered a spacious chamber lit by the light from a large arched window in the citadel's northern wall.

A winged woman sat by that window and in her arms she held a small baby.

She was nursing him.

Ravenna felt a dark stabbing pain of jealousy. Would she ever get that chance? Would Fate, the One, and all the others who hated her leave her alone to enjoy her son?

But at least his meal bought the boy some time. His last time with his mother.

Ravenna settled back into the shadows to wait.

When Inardle woke again, she saw that Axis had somehow found a large bronze curved bowl and in it glowed a small fire.

She sat up, feeling more awake, more *connected*, than she had on the two previous occasions when she had spoken to Axis.

Yet still the river flowed within her, deep and comforting.

"Where did you get that?" she said, nodding at the bronze dish and fire.

"I was once StarMan and Star God," Axis said. "Are you saying a small dish and fire is now beyond me?"

She smiled at him. "You have your clothes, and yet I have none. What happened to my robe?"

"It was too badly torn and stained, Inardle. I discarded it."

She nodded, understanding. "I shall need another."

"Perhaps we could—" Axis began, but she lifted a hand, waving him to silence.

"Do you remember that time when I lay injured in the column escorted by the Emerald Guard? You left us to meet up with Maximilian, and then you and he rode out to meet us as we rejoined with you."

"Yes," Axis said, "I remember that time."

"You remarked that I looked very well . . . I was wearing a rather lovely silvery robe, I believe, and you asked where it had come from."

He smiled. "You said that not all your command of the Star Dance was as fragile as I seemed to think."

"I did. I was, of course, at that time trying to hide from you that my command of the Star Dance was actually very powerful, but I could not resist a little boast. Shall I now show you from where my clothes came?"

"Please do."

Axis' eyes were twinkling, and Inardle returned his smile. "Do you like green on a woman?"

"I could get used to it," he said.

"Then I shall wear green," Inardle said. She rose, moving about the perimeter of the circle of trampled reeds, moving slowly and seductively, every so often glancing over her shoulder to make sure Axis was watching.

He was, an amused look on his face.

As she moved, Inardle collected a dozen straight reeds.

She came back to the centre of the circle and sat down to one side of the fire. She glanced at Axis, then laid the reeds out before her in an interlocking grid pattern.

"So," she said.

"So," Axis echoed. "So . . . ?"

"So," she said and, taking the lowest reed in the loose grid, she lifted it up high.

Axis had expected all the other reeds to fall asunder, but to his amazement, as Inardle swept that lower reed into the air, so all the reeds glimmered and, suddenly, what Inardle billowed in the air was not a reed, nor a collection of loosely interwoven reeds, but a length of lovely gossamer green material.

Inardle laughed at the expression on Axis' face. She rose, shook out the material, wrapped it around herself, and stood before Axis clothed in a lovely form-fitting green gown that swept down to her ankles.

"Could Azhure do that?" she asked.

"Azhure could do many things," Axis said, "but not that."

Inardle sat down. "Talk to me of Azhure. We never spoke of her before."

No, thought Axis, *we never spoke of her before*. He had not wanted to discuss Azhure with Inardle, because he would have felt uncomfortable doing so. Now, however, he felt no qualms and instead felt a great ease in talking of her to this woman.

"It was strange for me," he said, "when first Isaiah pulled me back into life. Azhure was in the Otherworld, but here I was, with a brand new life. We'd been lovers and companions for, what? Fifty or so years. To suddenly be without her . . . it was strange and unsettling.

"But even more unsettling and strange was how quickly I readjusted to the lack of her company. I still loved her, I still *do* love her, but . . . I don't miss her. Life caught me up in its embrace. There were more adventures to be had." His eyes twinkled. "More women to meet."

"Ah, so there was a stream of women before me."

"No. None before you. I'd met Ishbel and was attracted to her, but the idea of seducing her was merely an intellectual exercise. I never for a moment thought I'd actually carry it out."

"Besides, you'd need to have competed with Isaiah and Maximilian and you must have feared failure."

Axis laughed. "You have a sharp tongue on you, Inardle." She gave a little shrug.

"So," Axis went on, "there was no one before you."

"And what I did to you," she said, "how I betrayed you, must therefore have stung doubly."

"Yes," he said. "I'd wanted to love again, but didn't know how. And then there you were, and I was losing myself in you, and then . . ."

They sat in silence, looking at the flames of the fire rather than at each other.

"I also understand," Axis eventually said, softly, "how difficult it must have been for you. How torn you must have been. How difficult it might have been to have approached me. I did not allow you an easy path to confidence."

"But here we are now," she said.

"Yes," Axis said, looking at her fully, "here we are now."

She raised her face and looked him in the eye. "I have changed, Axis. If I'd been brought back to life anywhere other than the water I would have been who I once was . . . but that didn't happen. I regained life in the water. I have changed."

"I know," he said. "The River Angel runs deeper in you than previously."

Ravenna waited until Salome lay down to sleep, her husband beside her.

Neither of them—nor the child this time—realised her presence.

She waited until they were asleep and the baby asleep in the cot beside their bed.

She walked calmly forward and picked up StarDancer.

He looked at her, blinking in confusion as he woke, then his eyes widened.

I am sorry, StarDancer, Ravenna said to him. *I have come to kill you.*

Then before StarDancer could react, Ravenna clutched him close and ran from the chamber as fast as she dared.

Elcho Falling erupted into pandemonium.

CHAPTER TWENTY-SIX

The Central Outlands

The Skraelings knew that Inardle had changed. The knowledge rippled through the entire congregation in a painful shockwave of realisation.

While they had been sitting here debating and complaining and remaining utterly, utterly indecisive, Inardle, a Lealfast, had changed.

Inardle was now a River Angel.

"How could she have done that!" a Skraeling cried. "How?"

"What if all the other Lealfast choose to change?" another said.

"What if we miss out?" said yet another, getting right to the crux of the matter.

"We have not yet made a decision!" Ozll shouted into the confusion. "We have not decided whether or not we want to—"

"We think we do!" came back a roar of tens of thousands of Skraeling voices.

"Why," Ozll shouted, far louder this time, trying to get control of the situation, "don't we talk to Inardle and see what she has made of herself. Then we can decide if we, too, want to go the same way. She can be our guide. If we like what she is, then we, too, shall . . . take the plunge."

It was an unfortunate metaphor, reminding the Skraelings that the only way to return to their River Angel forms was to drown themselves.

"At least we know Isaiah wasn't lying," Ozll said, his voice milder now the hubbub had died down. "At least we know the return to River Angel form is possible."

This statement reassured the Skraelings and they nodded their heads, prepared to listen once more to Ozll's guidance.

"I suggest," Ozll said, "that we find Inardle. We examine her and we make our decision on what she has become."

"Good idea," Graq said, and Ozll smiled at her and thought it strange he'd never truly noticed her before.

As the Skraeling herd rose and began drifting northward, Ozll gravitated to Graq's side.

She risked a small smile at him, although with her great jaws and fangs it displayed more as a snarl than anything else.

"Do you think," she said, "drowning would hurt?"

CHAPTER TWENTY-SEVEN

Elcho Falling and Surrounds

E leanon and the five Lealfast with him circled high above the reed beds. It was just on dawn, and they could easily make out Axis and Inardle lying together by the dish of coals in the midst of the reed bed.

Eleanon thought they must have come back from the dead minus their wits.

"He is the StarMan," one of the Lealfast said. "We should be careful."

"We will be careful," Eleanon said, "but remember also that we are at one with Infinity as well as controlling the Star Dance. He has nothing—look, a mere dagger. He may try and hide . . . but he cannot harm us."

"And Inardle?"

Eleanon made a dismissive gesture. "She has always been weak. Come, it is time."

Axis woke slowly, using these early waking moments to remember the night and to smile as he stretched along Inardle's body.

Then he opened his eyes, and saw Eleanon and five other Lealfast standing on the other side of the fire, and adrenalin rushed through his system. He gave Inardle a shake, then rose to his feet, glancing at the pile of his and Inardle's jumbled clothes lying a few paces away.

Eleanon gave a cold smile, moved his hand, and the clothing burst into flames.

"How did you get Inardle out?" Eleanon said.

She was on her feet, too, standing close to Axis.

"He dragged me out through sheer force of love," she said. "You wouldn't understand it."

"Oh, what trite words you spout these days, Inardle!" Eleanon said. "I was always wary of sending you to Axis' side, but, oh no, you said you were strong enough. Well, you weren't, Inardle. You were weak. So tell me, and this time I demand it, how did you get her out alive, Axis?"

"I didn't," Axis said. "I got her out dead. It was what happened after that was the interesting bit."

Eleanon frowned. Neither of them appeared particularly worried. Both stood, relaxed, confident. "And that was . . . ?"

Axis waggled a hand. "A little bit of water, a little bit of heart, a little bit of eagle, and a little bit of—"

"Take them," Eleanon snapped, gesturing to his five companions as he lost patience.

The five fanned out, moving around the fire on both sides toward Axis and Inardle.

"Stand back," she murmured, and Axis felt a frisson of excitement in his belly as he took two steps back.

The moment he moved, so the five rushed them, but Inardle was faster.

She changed in an instant, losing her form of a winged woman to become what Axis could only describe later as a column of water with a vague humanoid shape.

I could see a head, he was later to say to Isaiah, *and I could see shoulders and two appendages that must have been arms, but there were no other features. Just a thick winding column of blue-white water the height of a woman.*

Axis took a moment to glance at Eleanon's face. The Lealfast man was astounded.

As well he might be, for he would have no idea of his own River Angel heritage.

The five Lealfast had been very close when Inardle changed. Before they could stand back, or lift into the air, she leaned forward and the two arm-like appendages swept out before her, lengthening until they were three or four times their original length.

First one, then two, then all five were swept up. Axis, watching, didn't know quite what happened, but one moment they were taken and the next moment they were lying dismembered in the nearby water.

Inardle took a step toward Eleanon, but he was already gone, lifting high into the sky.

"Later," Inardle said, returning to her fleshed form. Then she looked at their pile of smouldering clothes. "I can see I need to make us both some new attire."

Axis just stood, looking at her. He almost could not believe what he had just witnessed.

Inardle smiled, her eyes cold.

The guard assigned to keep an eye on Axis and Inardle was standing, staring open-mouthed at the scene.

He, too, could not believe his eyes.

He turned to the balcony doorway which led to a short corridor off a main passageway, trying to catch the attention of one of the soldiers hurrying to and fro.

Isaiah needed to know about what he'd just seen!

It took the guard long minutes to attract anyone's attention with his calls—unable to desert his post lest anything else noteworthy occurred on the reed bank—and when someone finally did appear, it was a flustered sergeant-at-arms who was none too pleased that a more lowly ranked guard wanted him to take a message to Isaiah.

"I have better things to do than run messages to the damned Tyrant," the sergeant said.

"It is important!" the balcony guard said.

"You want me to tell him that the woman Inardle turned into a murderous column of water and slaughtered five Lealfast?"

The guard nodded.

"For the love of the gods!" the sergeant said. "We have a full-blown crisis happening inside and you want me to tell the Tyrant that—"

He stopped, looking at the guard's face. "Oh, *very* well. But I am going to have your balls if the Tyrant snaps at me for wasting his time."

The guard thanked him, then turned to look at the reed bank.

Axis and Inardle had vanished.

CHAPTER TWENTY-EIGHT

Elcho Falling

Elcho Falling was in total panic. StarDrifter, Salome and every other Icarii within the citadel were searching high and low for StarDancer. No one knew what had happened— the baby had been there one moment and gone the next. The Icarii Enchanters, and most particularly his two powerful parents, could sense him, and occasionally hear his cries, but they could not locate him.

A powerful enchantment, dark and sinister, concealed him.

Isaiah was at his wits' end. Quite frankly, he could have done without this latest drama. He was sick with worry about the Dark Spire, with wondering where Maximilian was, with what Eleanon and the Lealfast might be planning, and with what Axis and Inardle might be up to as they lounged in the reed beds.

The last thing he needed to fret about was a baby. StarDrifter and Salome were turning the citadel upside down. Isaiah had organised search parties, but most of all he wanted StarDrifter and Salome to *calm down* and let the the rest of them carry out a systematic and organised exploration of the citadel.

Isaiah hoped this was just a case of baby-snatching and not something more sinister.

"Isaiah?"

Isaiah turned from talking to Georgdi, almost snarling at the interruption.

Damn it, the last thing he needed was a rampant Star-Drifter riling up the entire citadel!

It was Garth Baxtor, and Isaiah subsided, apologising for his black look.

"It's about the baby, StarDancer," Garth said.

"Yes?" Isaiah said, all his bad temper returning.

"I think it might have something to do with Ravenna," Garth said.

Ravenna! Isaiah had forgotten all about her, and he realised that had been a stupid thing to do. "Ravenna?" he said.

Garth made a helpless gesture. "It is just a feeling, Isaiah, and I am sorry to trouble you with it. But if she had taken the baby . . . no one can see her . . ."

"Why would she take the baby?" Isaiah said.

"Maybe it is part of Eleanon's plan. If he could see this amount of disruption . . ."

Isaiah took a moment to think it through. Maybe Garth had a good point. "So, if Ravenna did have the child, how would we find it?"

"I don't know. No one can see Ravenna, and if StarDrifter and Salome can't scry out their own son with their powers . . ."

Then what good is any of this? Isaiah thought, but discarded the thought. Garth was only trying to help and none of this current consternation, or the lost baby, was his fault.

Isaiah rested a hand on Garth's shoulder. "Thank you, Garth. I'll—"

He was interrupted by the approach of a sergeant-at-arms from the Isembaardian forces.

"Yes?" Isaiah snapped, not liking the look on the man's face. *More bad news.*

"Excellency," the man said, "I have news from the guard on the balcony."

"Yes?"

"He said, um . . ."

"Oh, spit it out, man!"

The sergeant major took a deep breath. "He said that Axis and Inardle were attacked by six Lealfast. He said that Inardle turned herself into a column of murderous water and slaughtered five of the Lealfast. The sixth escaped."

Isaiah stared at the sergeant, and then burst into laughter. He clapped the man on the shoulder. "Thank the gods for some good news!" he said. "Tell the guard he is due some goodwill on my part, and you, too, for relaying this news."

The sergeant-at-arms bowed and retreated, the fact that his head remained on his shoulders goodwill enough for him.

Axis' head broke the surface and he blinked the water out of his eyes, taking several deep breaths. *That journey had been far better than the last.*

Beside him Inardle emerged, not in the least out of breath.

There were several soldiers standing in the small chamber which held the entrance pool, and two of them held out their hands to help Axis and Inardle out of the water.

"I hope you didn't want a welcome home party, Star-Man," one of them said. "There's a bit of a fuss happening right now."

Ravenna sat behind a tall stack of boxes in a storage chamber. She held StarDancer in her arms, but loosely, and the baby was calm now, regarding her with curious violet eyes.

Who are you? he asked her.

"My name is Ravenna," she said.

I have heard of you. You were once a marsh witch, yes? Very powerful.

"Once."

Now many have wrapped you in their curses.

Tears slipped down Ravenna's cheeks. She knew she had to kill the baby, the One demanded it of her, but she couldn't . . . she couldn't . . .

Why do you want to kill me?

"I do not wish to, but I am obliged to by one of the curses placed upon me."

Cursed by whom?

"By the One."

Now StarDancer wriggled a little in his excitement. Of course! Now it was all making sense! He must have dreamed of the One! *The One is here, in the citadel?*

"Yes, he has hidden himself in the Dark Spire."

He has only just moved here, from a place very far away.

"Yes."

Ah, StarDancer said, understanding.

"He thinks you will expose him. Tell others where he is."

StarDancer's small mouth curved in a smile. That was likely not the reason the One wanted him dead.

"Axis!" Isaiah embraced Axis, then turned to look at Inardle. He took her face in his hands, looking deeply into her eyes.

"So," he said, smiling a little now.

"So," she said.

"How does it feel?" Isaiah said.

Inardle shrugged a little.

Isaiah sobered. "I heard what happened with the Leal-fast, Inardle. Be careful of what you now control."

"Of course," she said, and Isaiah let her face go.

"Your brother has been stolen, Axis," he said. "The citadel is in an uproar. Inardle, is this something Eleanon would have engineered?"

"How should I know?" she said. "But . . . no, I would have thought not. I have never heard him express any interest in Salome's baby."

"Garth thinks it may be Ravenna," Isaiah said, and explained to Axis and Inardle how she'd come to be in Elcho Falling. "None of us can spot her, not even Garth. Inardle . . . is it possible . . . ?"

"You want me to look for the baby?" Inardle said.

"If you could," Isaiah said. "You may be able to see through Eleanon's magics where none of us can."

"You want *me* to look for *StarDrifter's* baby?" Inardle said. "How would he feel about that?"

"Profoundly grateful, if you found his son," Axis said.

Inardle shot Axis a cynical look, but inclined her head. "Very well. Can you show me the chamber from which he was taken?"

The One has cursed you and you shall be forced to kill me? StarDancer said to Ravenna.

"Aye. I can delay," Ravenna said, "but eventually I will kill you. I cannot help it. I will dash you from one of the high windows. I am sorry. I do not really wish to do it."

Ravenna, who else has cursed you? I can sense that Ishbel

*has placed three tight and binding curses about you, but
there is one other besides that of the One . . .*

"Eleanon, the Lealfast who has besieged Elcho Falling,
placed a curse on me as well, warped in with Ishbel's. It
conceals me from the regard of others in Elcho Falling, and
it forced me to do his bidding."

Which was . . . ?

"Which was to midwive the Dark Spire's terrible eggs and
place them within the walls of Elcho Falling. I do not know
what they do there. StarDancer, I am sorry." Ravenna rose,
not understanding why she was telling StarDancer this much.
Perhaps she owed him some kind of explanation. "The urge
to kill you now is overwhelming. I can delay no longer."

*I can remove the One's curse from you, as well as Elea-
non's.*

"*What?*" Ravenna, who had taken several paces already,
now stopped dead. "How is that possible?"

*I am very powerful. I can do this. I could also remove
Ishbel's curses, but I do not dare that far. I like and respect
Ishbel and would not undo her work without permission. I
can remove both the One's and Eleanon's curses and then it
will be your own decision whether or not you kill me.*

"You can remove the One's and Eleanon's curses?"

Yes.

"But you are just a mere baby!"

No mere baby. Again StarDancer's mouth curved in a tiny
smile. *I am the most powerful Enchanter the Icarii have ever
known. More powerful even than the great WolfStar, whom
my father has told me about. More powerful than my brother
and able to manipulate the Star Dance as easily as he. I am
no "mere baby". I can sing an enchantment, Ravenna, that
will rid you of two of your three curses. Would you like me to
do that?*

"Yes," Ravenna whispered. "Yes."

Imagine, StarDancer said, *what I will be like as a full
adult, if I can do this much as a baby.*

StarDrifter was unhappy about involving Inardle in the
search. He paced the chamber he shared with Salome and,

until so very recently, his son, and sent dark looks shooting between Axis and Inardle.

Salome stood to one side, her face pale with anxiety, her eyes reddened from weeping.

She did not look at Inardle.

Inardle did not appear to notice either of them. She walked over to the cot where StarDancer had been sleeping and traced her fingers over its contours.

"Who here has worried about their child recently?" she said.

Everyone in the room—Isaiah, Axis, Garth, StarDrifter and Salome—looked between themselves.

"*I* have worried about a child recently!" StarDrifter grated.

"Not you," Inardle said. "Someone else has been here, desperately worried about a child."

"You can feel that from the cot?" Garth said.

"Yes," Inardle said. "You might, too, if you lay your fingers on it. Could your Touch feel it?"

Garth walked over and lay his hand on the cot. He was quiet, then he looked up. "Yes," he said. "Ravenna."

"Ravenna is worried about StarDancer?" StarDrifter said.

"She was pregnant with Maximilian's child," Garth said, "and Ishbel cursed it . . . perhaps Ravenna worries about its health. Whatever, Ravenna has been here, and there is deep worry associated with her presence. Regret. Sorrow. Fear for the future. So much bad feeling."

"So now we must find Ravenna," Inardle said, all practicality.

"Can you see her?" Salome said, speaking for the first time since Isaiah had brought Axis and Inardle to the chamber.

Inardle gave a slight shrug and StarDrifter lost his temper completely.

"You don't give a damn, do you? This is my *son*, and he has been stolen from me, and you don't give a single damn where he is. I—"

"StarDrifter," Axis said, trying to reach out to his father.

"You have every reason to hate me and the Icarii," StarDrifter snarled at Inardle, "and you see this as your chance to gloat that—"

"StarDrifter," Isaiah said, "shut up now or by the gods I will stand down every one of the search parties and send them off for a well-earned meal and a rest. Yes, you have lost your son, but, damn it, StarDrifter, everyone is trying to help you!"

StarDrifter glared at Isaiah and sent another simmering look of ill will toward Inardle. He folded his arms and turned away.

Axis closed his eyes briefly, then looked at Inardle. "Inardle?"

She was still affecting cool indifference. "This way, perhaps," she said, indicating the door to the external corridor.

"Oh, *brilliant* deduction," StarDrifter muttered.

"If you want," Inardle said, "I *will* stop right now."

"No," Axis said, literally stepping to stand between the two of them. "Inardle, please, do it for me."

She looked at him, and Axis could see a glint of humour in her eyes.

She was enjoying herself.

Inardle, he said. *Please.*

Her mouth curved, then she turned and walked for the door. "Ravenna has left a clear enough trail," she said. "For *my* powers to pick up, at least."

There, StarDancer said. *Does that feel better?*

Ravenna could not answer immediately. She sat, cradling StarDancer in her arms, tears running down her cheeks.

Ishbel's curse remained, but to be freed of the two hateful and dark-fingered powers of Eleanon and the One. Oh gods . . . oh gods . . .

No doubt the One will be raging within the Dark Spire.

Ravenna managed a smile through her tears. "Good." Her smile slipped a little: "He cannot reach me now?"

No.

Ravenna relaxed. Freed of the One's power, and of Eleanon's. This child was remarkable and, even more remarkable, what he had done had not even hurt her. Ravenna had forgotten what it was like not to be hurt and humiliated by another.

I have a favour to ask of you.

Now Ravenna tensed. So there *was* to be a price paid, after all.

I am not going to plead for my life—that is your decision truly. But before you decide, can you tell me about the powers you had as a marsh witch? And of this Land of Nightmares which exists beyond the Land of Dreams? Can you explain to me its parameters and meanings?

"Why?" Ravenna said.

To sate my curiosity.

Ravenna shrugged. So far as prices went, this was but a mild one. "As you wish."

Inardle led them through Elcho Falling, down the main staircase, along a corridor some eight or nine levels above ground level, then up a smaller service stairwell for another five or six levels. Here, on a small landing where small hallways led deeper into Elcho Falling, she called everyone to a halt.

"I will go on alone from here," she said. "Ravenna is close."

"I should come with you," Garth said.

Inardle considered him, then nodded. "Very well."

They walked along one of the hallways, leaving behind a group of restless and variously suspicious people.

"Do you know where we are?" Inardle asked Garth.

"This place is too huge for me to have been through it completely," Garth said, "but these levels are generally storage levels. Dormitories, command chambers, living quarters and so forth are much higher in the citadel."

"There is something bleak ahead."

Garth caught at Inardle's elbow, stopping her. "Inardle . . . Ravenna has done much damage, and she is a changed woman since I first met her . . . but she has also done good and came originally from a good place. I've heard a little of what you are now. Please . . ." He stopped, not knowing how to continue.

To his surprise Inardle gave a small smile and squeezed

his hand reassuringly. "I have more sympathy for her than you might believe," she said, and with that they walked on.

Inardle led them eventually to a chamber stacked to its ceiling with what looked like boxes of blankets and pillows. There was a small space between the boxes, and Inardle, Garth directly behind her, threaded her way through.

Inardle stopped, holding up a hand to silence Garth. She looked back at him, then pointed ahead and moved her finger, indicating something about the curve in the narrow passageway.

Garth nodded his understanding.

They moved forward, slowly and carefully.

Inardle hesitated just at the curve of the passageway between the piled-high boxes, then she stepped around it.

"Hello, Ravenna," she said.

Garth was directly behind Inardle, and he looked over her shoulder.

His first thought was that he was surprised that he could actually see Ravenna, the second was horror at her appearance. She was skeletally thin, her skin almost grey, her general appearance unkempt and ill.

He looked at her belly. She still appeared to be pregnant, but she was in such a poor condition, he wouldn't gamble on the health of the baby.

Ravenna held a baby in her arms: StarDancer.

"Ravenna?" Garth said softly.

Ravenna looked up, her eyes filled with tears. "I was to kill him," she said. "I couldn't do it."

Much later, when Isaiah had caused Ravenna to be locked in a comfortable yet secure room, he met with StarDrifter, Salome, Axis and Garth in the Talon's chamber. StarDrifter sat with his son held tight in his arms and Isaiah did not think he was going to let him go any time soon.

"StarDancer is well?" he asked the boy's parents, relieved that Inardle was not present.

"Yes, thank the Stars," StarDrifter said, his face still drawn and tense.

"And Ravenna?" Isaiah asked Garth, knowing the physician had been to see her.

"She has been very unwell," Garth said, "but should grow better with rest and good food." He paused. "The child she carries is not doing well, though, and there is a danger Ravenna will miscarry it. Hopefully as Ravenna improves, so will her child."

"She is a great danger to us," said Salome, "and should be murdered herself."

She has come to regret her actions, StarDancer said, his words clear in the minds of all in the room. *She did not kill me.*

He paused, and when he spoke again his mind-voice was heavy with power and concern.

The One is here.

"What?" everyone else said simultaneously.

In the Dark Spire.

"But none of us—" Isaiah began.

He has concealed himself well. None of you could spot him. I could not even discern his presence. But he is here, have no doubt.

"So that is he of whom you dreamed," StarDrifter said. "We should have listened to you."

Yes.

"Shetzah!" Isaiah cursed. "We must—"

Nothing you can do shall repel him, StarDancer said. *He is too powerful. Not even Maximilian can match him now.*

Axis looked at his brother, wondering that none of them questioned what StarDancer said.

Stars, the child commanded everyone in this room!

Axis felt a stab of resentment, both at StarDancer's power and at the unquestioning acceptance of it by everyone, including himself.

But there is something that can be done.

"What?" Isaiah said.

It needs to wait until the Lord of Elcho Falling has returned, StarDancer said. *But until then, Ravenna needs to be kept well and safe. She must not be murdered.*

[Part Four]

CHAPTER ONE

The Twisted Tower, and the Coast of the Outlands

Inardle's attack on himself and his companions had shocked Eleanon. Not just the attack, but her chilling murderousness with it.

That hadn't been the Inardle Eleanon had known.

What had happened to her? Had the ice hex somehow changed her? Eleanon didn't know how Axis had managed to get her out, or how he had managed to restore her life (for Axis would have needed to kill Inardle to escape Borneheld).

But most of all, Eleanon could not comprehend what Inardle had become and he feared that it was somehow his ice hex that had caused the transformation. If so, that hex had been a critical mistake.

The thought that he may have made a critical mistake unsettled and frightened Eleanon.

In order to distract himself, Eleanon concentrated on fine-tuning the training the Lealfast Nation needed for the final confrontation that would see Axis and Inardle and all others within Elcho Falling dead, and the citadel his.

The Lealfast Nation had settled on the gentle slopes and meadows just below the Sky Peaks, far to the north-west of Elcho Falling. Here Eleanon could train the Lealfast with no one watching . . . although had they seen, Eleanon did not think they could have made any sense of what happened.

Today, as in the many days before, Eleanon stood in the centre of a large meadow.

About him the Lealfast Nation had arrayed themselves in ten gigantic circles that rotated about Eleanon. Each alternate circle moved either sunwise or anti-sunwise, and they moved slowly and deliberately to the beat that Eleanon clapped out with his hands. Occasionally Eleanon shouted instruction to this circle or that, keeping them in step with all the other Lealfast.

When Eleanon was satisfied, he quickened the beat of his hands. The circles began to move faster, although still deliberately, a stunningly choreographed dance with every single one of the Lealfast keeping place and pace perfect. And they *were* perfectly in step. Every one put their right foot down with everyone else's right foot, and thus with their left foot.

Eleanon himself, in the centre of the circles, began to move, looking this way and that, his body trembling with the vibrations caused by the hundreds of thousands of feet placed perfectly in time to the beat of the dance.

He staggered slightly, losing his footing as the earth shook beneath him, and then Eleanon lifted into the sky, still clapping. As he lifted, he shouted, and so all the Lealfast, a quarter million of them arranged in concentric circles, raised their faces to the sky and shouted and clapped their hands.

The earth in the centre of the circle shuddered violently, then lifted, dirt spraying everywhere within a radius of fifty paces.

Eleanon, hovering in the sky, gave a small smile of satisfaction.

It would be good.

"Maxel?" Ishbel said, half rising from where she'd been dozing in the belly of Abe Wayward's boat. Abe was forward, checking the rigging, Doyle was still fast sleep in the prow and Serge was manning the tiller, apparently sent into a catatonic state by the gentle rhythmic lull of the waves.

But Maximilian . . . Maximilian was sitting bolt upright just down from the tiller.

"Maxel?"

Maximilian smiled. "Look, sweetheart, you have dozed away all this time and missed the view to the north."

Ishbel frowned at him, then swivelled so she could look forward.

"Oh!" she gasped.

Elcho Falling rose on the horizon, the three rings of its crowns turning lazily in the brilliant sun, sending glints of gold scattering over the sea.

CHAPTER TWO

Elcho Falling

They were tacking slowly up the channel that ran from the Infinity Sea to the lake that surrounded the citadel.

Everything was very quiet.

The citadel appeared to be intact, but there were no Icarii in the sky, no Lealfast, and no armies in the surrounding landscape. Maximilian was not sure what he'd expected, but somehow it was not this.

"Perhaps they're all still abed," Doyle remarked.

Maximilian exchanged an anxious glance with Ishbel, then touched Abe on the arm.

"Slower, if you can," he said.

"I'm tacking as slow as possible," Abe replied. "To go slower I'd need to take down the sail and allow us to drift. But that would leave us without any options should danger threaten."

Did danger threaten? Maximilian wondered. *What in the gods' names was going on?*

"Have you tried to contact anyone in—" Ishbel began to say, then gave a shriek of surprise as a column of water reared up from the channel behind her and crashed into the boat.

They all jumped a little and Serge and Doyle reached for their swords. Before anyone could take any further action the column of water resolved itself into a dripping wet and very naked Inardle.

She grinned at the startled expressions on everyone's faces. "Did I surprise you? I do apologise. Put those swords away. I am of no harm to you."

Neither Serge nor Doyle sheathed their swords, but Inardle took no notice. She reached over the side of the small boat, scooping up a handful of water and tossing it into the air in a spray of emerald and silver droplets. At the height of their arc, the droplets shimmered and transformed into a length of blue-green material which Inardle snatched out of the air then wrapped about her body, clothing herself in a matter of moments.

Her smile widened. "I have been learning new tricks," she said. "Maximilian, all inside Elcho Falling will be more than pleased to see you. Look . . ."

She pointed at a balcony about halfway up the citadel.

Black dots stood there waving.

"Isaiah," Inardle said, "and Axis and Georgdi. Happy to see you home and to hand over all their unsolvable problems."

Maximilian gave a half-hearted wave to the distant balcony, but quickly centred all his attention on Inardle.

"What did you just do? The water . . ." he said.

"Ah, who and what I am now is a matter for discussion over a glass of wine," she said. "You are all well?"

"Yes," Maximilian said. "But—"

"Isaiah and Axis asked me to come greet you and see you inside Elcho Falling," Inardle said. "Most of the news can wait until then, Maxel, both yours and ours."

Maximilian regarded her keenly. There was something wrong—he could recognise it in the shadows of her eyes.

"Where are the Lealfast?" Ishbel said. "And Isaiah . . . he managed to get inside Elcho Falling? With his army?"

"The Lealfast Nation rest in the Sky Peaks," Inardle said, "but they maintain patrols over Elcho Falling. There are a score of them invisible above us now, but they are unlikely to attack while I am here. I can explain all this later. Who is your captain, Maxel?"

Maximilian took a moment to realise what Inardle meant. "Abe," he said, nodding to the man. "Abe Wayward."

"Abe," Inardle said, smiling at him. "Set full sail for the lake and travel about the southern aspect of the citadel. On the western side you will find a causeway, and if you could manoeuvre us close to where that causeway meets the entrance to Elcho Falling then I would be most grateful."

"And Isaiah's army?" Ishbel said, a little tightly, irked that she had to press for a response to her question.

"Mostly safe inside Elcho Falling," Inardle said. "Isaiah can tell you the tale. It wasn't his finest moment."

Before Ishbel could pepper her with more questions, Inardle indicated the lake into which they had just sailed. "This could be dangerous," she said. "The Dark Spire, which Eleanon had placed within the citadel, has grown . . . much more so than when you last saw it, Maximilian. We had the juit birds here . . . did you know that? Well, that is a tale also that can wait for later, but we had millions of juit birds here and they were chased away by hundreds of . . . roots, I suppose you could call them, or fingers, from the Dark Spire, that rose from the water and snatched the birds from the lake and the air. So, this journey may become a little more adventurous than anticipated . . . and thus I am here. I may be of some use against them."

"Inardle," Maximilian said, "what has happened to you?" *And what is so wrong inside Elcho Falling?* he wondered.

She gave a little shrug of her shoulders. "There is much to share, on both our sides, I imagine. Wait until we get inside Elcho Falling, Maximilian. It can all wait until then."

Despite Inardle's warnings about the danger from the Dark Spire, they sailed around the southern walls of Elcho Falling without incident, and Maximilian felt his spirits rise as they approached the causeway. As they came alongside it, Abe held the boat steady while everyone climbed out, the great doors to Elcho Falling opened, and there stood Axis and Isaiah, wide grins on their faces, and suddenly the Lord of Elcho Falling was home.

Maximilian sat slouched in his chair, long legs stretched out before him, rubbing away slowly at his forehead with one hand, unable to sort his thoughts.

"The One is in the Dark Spire?" he finally said. He and Ishbel had shared news with Axis, Isaiah, Georgdi and StarDrifter, and it wasn't until the last few minutes that the others had told Maximilian and Ishbel the terrible news about Ravenna, the Dark Spire and the One.

Maximilian finally dropped his hand and managed to look Ishbel in the eye.

She looked as stricken as he felt.

They had been so sure he was gone . . . so sure.

"Are you *certain*?" Maximilian added.

"My son has said so," StarDrifter said.

"That would be StarDancer," Axis said, annoyed that he had to clarify the situation . . . StarDrifter obviously felt he only had one son.

"Ravenna has confirmed it," Isaiah added. "We can find no fault with what StarDancer has said. The One hauled himself through Infinity and into the Dark Spire, using some kind of gossamer umbilical cord."

Maximilian felt like mumbling an obscenity, but he contented himself with sharing another look with his wife.

They had been so sure.

"What will it take to best this beast from Infinity?" Ishbel said, and Maximilian felt a stab of dark resentment toward her for mouthing the question.

"I will need to think—" he began, but StarDrifter halted him.

"StarDancer says he has a solution."

Maximilian raised unbelieving eyebrows. A *baby?* "And the solution would be . . . ?"

"He has not said," StarDrifter said. "He wanted to wait until you and Ishbel had returned."

"I should speak with Ravenna first," Maximilian said.

"No," StarDrifter said, "speak with StarDancer, then Ravenna, if you wish. StarDancer said he would need to speak with you first . . . with all of us," he added.

They moved to StarDrifter and Salome's chamber. Salome held StarDancer in her arms, the others sat grouped about, the baby the centre of attention.

"You asked to talk with myself and Ravenna," Maximilian said, feeling uncomfortable being thus summoned to a baby's presence.

I am grateful you agreed, StarDancer said, the words clear in everyone's mind.

"The One is back," Maximilian said.

In the Dark Spire, StarDancer said. *He hauled himself back through Infinity and—*

"You are certain?" Ishbel said, her voice hard.

I am certain. You can ask Ravenna to confirm it.

Maximilian gave a nod, not wanting to think about Ravenna. She, and whatever mischief she'd done within Elcho Falling, was a problem that would need to wait until after this. "Your father said you had a solution."

The One is very powerful, StarDancer said. *I doubt there is any in the chamber who can best him, including you, Maximilian.*

Maximilian's mouth tightened. "Elcho Falling and I have managed before."

You only deferred the problem. You have tried, Elcho Falling has tried, Ishbel has tried. None of you bested the One; you have merely postponed the problem. Every time the One has bounced back, stronger than previously. Now he is back yet again, freshly infused with the power of Infinity, and wrapped in the protection and sorcery of the Dark Spire, which I think is intended to destroy Elcho Falling. Do you have a plan, Maximilian?

"I have not inspected the Dark Spire yet." Maximilian was growing more irritated by the moment.

Then do that, StarDancer said, *after I have spoken.*

"And you advise?" Ishbel said, her voice laced with a little sarcasm.

I do not blame you for distrusting me, StarDancer said, *but hear me out, please. The One draws his power from Infinity. What can any of us in this room do against him? There is only one person who can successfully contain the One.*

"And that person is?" Maximilian said.

Ravenna.

"No!" Ishbel said, shifting as if she meant to rise before deciding to perch stiff-backed on the edge of her chair. "*Ravenna?* She has done nothing but betray Maximilian and Elcho Falling. You think . . . what? That *she* can some-how destroy the One? She does not have the power, and even if she did then she would use it to destroy *us*, not the One!" Ishbel looked to Maximilian. "Maxel?"

"I agree," Maximilian said. "I cannot see how Ravenna has either the power or the goodwill to destroy the One for me and Ishbel. She is more likely to betray us."

The One sent her to kill me, and she did not. Ravenna regrets what she has done to you.

Ishbel gave a soft snort.

"Please listen to what my son has to say," StarDrifter said. "If *I* had listened to him earlier then we would have been warned about the approach of the One. As it was, I laughed away his concerns. Please do not laugh away what he has to say now."

Maximilian gave a small wave of his hand. "Then speak, StarDancer. How is it that Ravenna shall save us and Elcho Falling from the One?"

Hear me through before you object, StarDancer said. *Ishbel must remove the three curses she placed on Ravenna: restoring Ravenna to her power as a marsh witch, allowing her once more to touch the Lands of Dreams and of Night-mares, removing the curse that makes it almost impossible for Ravenna to remain within any community, and, finally, removing that curse that stripped Ravenna's son of his rights as heir to Elcho Falling.*

Ishbel sent a shocked and disbelieving look to Maximil-ian, but he raised a hand to ask her to remain silent.

"And then?" Maximilian said.

Then Ishbel needs to divest you of your power as Lord of Elcho Falling, and—

He got no further. The chamber erupted in uproar. Maxi-milian, Ishbel, Axis and Isaiah all leapt to their feet, protest-ing loudly.

Listen to me! StarDancer's voice cut through all of their protests. *Listen to me!*

They quietened, but remained standing.

If Ishbel removes from Maximilian his power as Lord of Elcho Falling, then Ravenna's baby, as heir—remember

*that Ishbel will have restored him to that status once she
removes all her curses from Ravenna—becomes the Lord of
Elcho Falling.* StarDancer could feel the protests building
within his listeners, but he ploughed on regardless. *Once the
One emerges from the Dark Spire, which he will have to do,
he will be after one thing—the Lord of Elcho Falling. In
order to take the citadel and all its power, he will need to
destroy its Lord. He will home in on Ravenna and her
baby—and then Ravenna, now restored to her full power as
a marsh witch and she was once very, very powerful, will
drag the One through into the Land of Nightmares. The
Land of Nightmares can do what nothing else can—contain
the One. It will not destroy him, but he will not be able to
escape it.*

"And Ravenna and her child?" Axis said before either
Maximilian or Ishbel could speak.

*They too will be trapped within the Land of Nightmares,
with the One*, StarDancer said. *For eternity.*

"No," Ishbel said. "This is not possible. You can't expect
any of us to trust Ravenna, or to remove from Maximilian
his power and authority as Lord of Elcho Falling!"

"If the Lord of Elcho Falling will be trapped inside the
Land of Nightmares for an eternity," Isaiah said, "what will
happen to the citadel? And to Maxel?"

Both will continue, said StarDancer. *Maximilian as a
mortal man, as a king if he wishes, and Elcho Falling as
a mere citadel, no longer a portal into any other realm. It is
the price both Maximilian and Elcho Falling will need to
pay if they wish to rid themselves of the One.*

"And how can you be certain that the Land of Nightmares will hold the One?" Axis said.

"It can," Maximilian said softly. "It can. Drava once told
me of its properties."

It can, echoed StarDancer. *Ravenna told me of its properties.*

"No one can trust whatever Ravenna says!" Ishbel all but
shouted. "How many times has she betrayed Elcho Falling
and Maximilian? *How many times?*"

All I have done is to tell you what can be done, Star-

Dancer said. *Whether or not you choose to follow this route is entirely your decision.*

Ishbel made a sound of disgust, turning to Maximilian. "Maxel, this is nonsense. We can't trust Ravenna. I will not remove my curses. And never, *never* will I consent to strip you of your powers!"

"Can Ishbel do this?" Axis asked.

"Yes," Maximilian said quietly.

"I will not do it, *any* of it!" Ishbel said.

"I—" Maximilian began.

"No!" Ishbel shouted.

Maximilian stepped forward and took Ishbel by the shoulders, pulling her stiff body into a brief embrace. "I will talk with Ravenna," he said, "then again with you. Then we will decide."

He walked from the room, and Axis looked to Isaiah. "There has to be another way," he said.

CHAPTER THREE

Elcho Falling

Maximilian did not go straight to Ravenna. Instead he went first to the Dark Spire.

It was far worse than he could have imagined. The Dark Spire had grown physically since he'd last seen it (it now had grown through six levels, by the gods!), but, far more, Maximilian could sense the damage it had done to Elcho Falling. Somehow, the spire had grown *into* Elcho Falling.

He paused, gathering his courage, then crouched down at the base of the horrid thing, feeling it gently with his fingers.

It felt like cool living flesh.

Living, indeed.

Maximilian withdrew his hand, feeling cold to the very core of his being. He could feel the One inside, and feel also the layers of protection wrapped about him.

Hello, Maximilian, Lord of Elcho Falling.

Maximilian did not respond. He rose, and left the chamber.

Maximilian paused outside the guarded chamber which held Ravenna and looked at the man who had risen from a chair placed by the door.

Garth Baxtor.

"Have you spoken with her?" Maximilian said.

Garth inclined his head. "Welcome home, Maxel."

Maximilian grunted. "It is not a particularly warm welcome . . . have you heard about the One?"

Garth nodded.

Maximilian's eyes drifted to the locked door. "How is she?"

"She is not well, for she has been badly treated by both

Eleanon and the One, but she is not dying. If she were restored to her power she—"

"I do not yet wish to speak of 'ifs'. Just of the here and now."

"Then she is grey and tired and underweight, but all of these conditions can be remedied with time and care."

"And the baby?" Maximilian said softly, his eyes still on the door.

"Underweight as well, and not particularly strong."

Now Maximilian shifted his eyes back to Garth. "Your prognosis, if you please?"

"As Ravenna's health improves, then so shall his."

Maximilian drew in a deep breath. "I am faced with a terrible decision."

"If you need to talk, then I am here."

Maximilian nodded, and rested his hand briefly on Garth's shoulder. "How is Ravenna," he said. "Not her health, her . . ."

"She is more the girl we once knew," Garth said. "She does regret what has happened, Maxel, and now she will help if she can. Her ambitions are long lost."

"But do I trust her?" Maximilian murmured, then he stepped past Garth and nodded at the guards to unlock the door.

He paused inside the door as the guards closed it behind him, his eyes adjusting to the lower light in the chamber.

He caught her movement first, shifting as she swung her legs over the side of her bed so that she sat on its edge.

"Maximilian." Ravenna's voice caught, as if she were nervous, but Maximilian didn't allow himself to trust whatever emotion she chose to show him.

He walked over to a chair that sat a couple of paces from the bed, and sat down. "What have you done to Elcho Falling?" he said.

"I removed eggs from the Dark Spire and have placed them in the walls of Elcho Falling."

"What is their purpose?"

"I don't know. I *don't*, Maximilian," Ravenna added at the

expression on his face. "Eleanon told me to do it. *Made* me do it. I was not allowed a choice."

Maximilian forbore to ask what her choice may have been, had she been able to make it.

"Ishbel's curses left me vulnerable—"

"Don't make excuses," Maximilian said. "I don't want to hear them."

"But if I had not been so cursed then I—"

"Could have done what? Destroyed Elcho Falling of your own volition, rather than Eleanon's?"

Ravenna dropped her eyes.

"Will you tell me where these 'eggs' are?"

"They are scattered evenly about the outer walls of the citadel. Start at the second level, the outer eastern corner, and from there you should be able to sense them out easily yourself."

"And can I do anything about them?"

"I doubt it."

A muscle worked in the corner of Maximilian's jaw. "What are the Lealfast doing? What are their plans?"

"I do not know this, either, Maximilian, truly. Maximilian—"

"Now you work for the One."

"No. StarDancer broke his hold over me."

"StarDancer is truly powerful."

"Perhaps he can aid you against the One."

Maximilian allowed a small silence to develop. "Did StarDancer tell you of his plan?"

"That I should trap the One in the Land of Nightmares? Yes?"

"Dare I ask if you think it has any merit?"

Ravenna gave a small, sad smile. "It will work, Maximilian, but only if you trust me completely and I cannot see the day you could do that."

"That is the first piece of truth you have spoken since I came in that door, I think."

"It has all been truth."

Maximilian grunted. "It is the perfect plan for you, isn't

it. You get the power of the Lord of Elcho Falling for your son after all this."

For *our* son, Ravenna thought. "And yet be trapped inside the Land of Nightmares. I do not think that is power for him. Our son will never enjoy the privileges of Elcho Falling."

"Are you trying to tell me that you are willing to trap yourself *and* your son in the Land of Nightmares for an eternity?"

"Yes, to make amends for all I have—"

Maximilian cut her off with a harsh bark of laughter. "How long would that selfless resolution last, then? A year? A hundred? A thousand? Eventually you would grow tired of your promise and your repentance, and you would escape the Land of Nightmares and haul the One with you."

"Speak to Drava, Maximilian. Speak to the Lord of Dreams. Once I am trapped with our son and the One inside the Land of Nightmares, Drava can cut it off entirely from your world and his. He has been longing to do that for aeons, I think."

"I have had enough of casting the One in various prisons," Maximilian said. "I cannot believe that this would work."

"Speak to Drava. I am sure you would trust him."

Maximilian rose from his chair. "I do not trust you, Ravenna, nor this apparent repentance of yours."

"Nonetheless, it is genuine, Maximilian."

He studied her a moment, then banged on the door for the guards to let him out.

"I'm sorry, Maxel," Ravenna said. "For everything."

But Maximilian had gone, and did not hear her.

He paused in the corridor outside, shaking with anger and such deep regret that he did not think he could bear it.

He heard Garth walk up beside him.

"How did it end like this?" Maximilian said, his voice breaking down. "How could it *possibly* have ended like this?"

Garth didn't know what to say. How *could* it have ended like this? The bond the three of them had shared, the adventures, the laughter.

The journey beyond the hanging wall.

How could it have ended like this?

Garth felt tears well in his own eyes, and he put a hand on Maximilian's shoulder and stood close while they both wept.

While Maximilian was with Ravenna, Insharah sought out Ishbel.

"My Lady?" he said, as he entered the chamber where she sat.

"Insharah," Ishbel said, rising. She had much to do and consider, but she knew why Insharah had come, and Ishbel knew she owed him this and did not begrudge the interruption. She took Insharah's hands and kissed his cheek in greeting. "It is good to see you, and once more allied with my friends. Come, sit."

"My Lady," Insharah said, "I, as all my countrymen at Elcho Falling, need to know what you and Maximilian found in Isembaard."

Ishbel felt her tears welling, and wished she had the power to stop it. Insharah had not yet heard the story of Hairekeep, unless Axis or Georgdi had told him in the meantime . . . and he wouldn't be sitting here with such hope in his eyes if he'd heard that dreadful tale.

"There is little good news, Insharah. I am so sorry. We were at Aqhat and travelled north then east through Sakkuth and past Hairekeep. There . . . well, all those who had sheltered at Hairekeep had died."

Insharah sat back, withdrawing both physically and emotionally from Ishbel.

Ishbel remembered the piece of bone she had read with the name of Insharah's wife on it. She wanted to tell him, but couldn't.

He knew, anyway.

"Thank you," Insharah said in a flat voice, and he rose and left the chamber.

Ishbel sat for a long time, staring at the closed door, tears running silently down her face, wishing there had been something else she could have told him. Then she stood and walked to the chambers she shared with Maximilian.

CHAPTER FOUR

Elcho Falling

Ishbel waited for Maximilian in their chamber at the very top of Elcho Falling. Above her the stars reeled, and the rings of the golden crown swung lazily around the citadel. The luxuriously appointed chamber glowed with soft light.

She glanced upward, knowing that there were Lealfast almost certainly hovering above. Ishbel wanted to close the roof, but didn't want to give the Lealfast the satisfaction of knowing their presence had made her nervous.

So she wandered the chamber, waiting for Maximilian, her mind unable to stop worrying about what StarDancer had said.

Ishbel wondered if it would have made much difference to their current predicament if she had killed Ravenna when she'd had the chance, rather than bind her with curses. Even cursed, Ravenna had managed to create havoc.

StarDancer's solution was unthinkable. There must be another way of dealing once and for all with the One. They couldn't trust Ravenna. And Ishbel *knew* she couldn't divest Maximilian of his power. If she struggled, Ishbel thought she might, just *might* be able to think of some circumstance where she removed the curses about Ravenna (but that was, indeed, close to impossible), but to divest Maximilian of his power . . . unthinkable! Further, to allow Ravenna's child to assume the rights and privileges and power of the Lord of Elcho Falling, and then to have those rights and privileges and powers trapped in the Land of Nightmares?

Impossible. Impossible. Not only would it mean the end of Maximilian as Lord of Elcho Falling, but it would mean the end of the line of Lords of Elcho Falling, for the current Lord would be trapped in the Land of Nightmare.

Everything Maxel and she had fought so hard for would be as naught.

StarDancer's "solution" was no solution at all. It demanded too high a price. It was just another trap, yet another nightmare. It would destroy as much as the One would destroy.

Perhaps more.

Gods, they may as well just hand everything to the One now! Would that not be better than seeing the line of the Lords of Elcho Falling die within the Land of Nightmares?

"We can't possibly allow it," Ishbel muttered, her loathing of Ravenna and everything she represented now consuming her.

If it wasn't for Ravenna . . .

"Ishbel."

She spun about, her face lighting up as Maximilian walked into the chamber.

Ishbel's smile died as she saw his face. Maximilian looked exhausted and emotionally drained. She started toward him and, as she did so, Maximilian waved a hand, almost without thought, and closed the roof over their heads.

Whatever was the matter, he didn't want to share it with the Lealfast.

"Maxel?"

He took her hand and tried a small smile for her, which faded the moment it appeared. "Come sit with me, Ishbel. I need to rest and we need to talk."

Ishbel waited until they were seated on a couch near a small brazier she'd lit earlier, then she wrapped his hand in both of hers. "What happened, Maxel? Did you examine the Dark Spire, talk to Ravenna? What do you think. Should we—"

He gave her a small smile. "Too many questions, my love. But yes, I examined the Dark Spire and I talked to Ravenna. Neither was a particularly pleasant experience."

"The Dark Spire?" Ishbel asked, not wanting to hear of Ravenna just yet.

"It is terrible, Ishbel. It has grown through many levels

now, and has formed itself into a representation of Elcho Falling itself. It has birthed eggs . . . Ravenna has taken these and planted them about the outer walls of Elcho Falling. She told me where to look . . . Ishbel, I can't do anything about them. They are like little cancers. They have grown deep into the fabric of Elcho Falling itself, in scores of different locations. I can't get them out without destroying Elcho Falling in the process."

Ishbel didn't know what to say, or what to ask next. The very thought terrified her.

Oh, why hadn't she killed Ravenna when she had the chance?

"How bad *is* it, Maxel?"

"I don't know. I will investigate more tomorrow. But it is bad. I have no idea how to remove them, or even how to stop them growing."

"Can Garth help with his Touch?"

"No. Garth has tried. Nothing."

"Did you feel the One within the spire?"

Maximilian gave a terse nod. "I can feel him, but can do little against him. I cannot penetrate the spire, and even if I could . . . gods, Ishbel, I remember the power that the One sent seething down the path from the Twisted Tower toward me. He is so much stronger now than when the citadel expelled him. I fear that neither I nor Elcho Falling can touch him."

"Oh Maxel . . . there must be something we can do."

"I went to see Ravenna."

"I wish I had *killed*—"

"Ishbel, don't say it." Maximilian paused, his tongue running about his lips. "I talked to her, Ishbel. She confirmed what StarDancer said."

"You can't possibly be thinking—"

"I can't bear to think it, Ishbel! How can I trust her? How? To give her back her power and then to leave the fate of Elcho Falling in her hands? I cannot countenance it!"

Ishbel relaxed a little. She had not dared to admit it even to herself, but a tiny part of her had been terrified that Ravenna would somehow dupe Maximilian into agreeing to StarDancer's plan.

"Then what can we do, Maxel?"

"I knew there would come a time when I would regret the loss of the Twisted Tower," Maximilian said, "and this is it. While none of the knowledge in the Twisted Tower pertained specifically to the Dark Spire—who could have foretold it?—or to the One, there might have been something amid all those objects and memories that might aid us."

"Like what?"

"Something, perhaps, on how to repel disease within Elcho Falling's walls. On how to repel weakness. On how to repel invaders. I don't know, Ishbel. Both of us have been through every single object in that tower, but how many hundreds of memories and knowledges did we set to one side, thinking we would not need them in the raising of Elcho Falling?"

Ishbel nodded. When they had gone through the Twisted Tower with Josia they had specifically concentrated only on the knowledge needed to raise Elcho Falling. Everything else they had glimpsed was enough to remember objects, but they had not remembered specific details.

After all, they could always go back to the Twisted Tower whenever they needed to retrieve further information.

"I know on the forty-seventh level," Ishbel said slowly, her brow creased as she thought, "there was something about the walls, something to do with . . . construction . . . or the enchantment that went into them . . ."

"I thought I could remember a group of objects on the nightstand on the eighteenth level," Maximilian said. "They were to do with the integrity of the structure. I think."

"I . . . I don't think I can remember those."

"Damn it!" Maximilian said.

"We can't go back, Maxel. We'll just have to live with it."

"Or die by it," he said.

They sat in silence a little, then Maximilian spoke again.

"Ishbel, what if we reconstruct every level of the Twisted Tower on paper? Remember every object we can. Rebuild the Twisted Tower in plans and drawings. Plot every object. Then . . . maybe . . . maybe we might remember something."

She kissed his cheek. "You are tired, I am tired, and we

are both too weary to think. Come to bed. We haven't slept in a real bed for a very, very long time."

."We are going to need to do this, Ishbel."

"I know. But for now come to bed."

Then her eyes focussed on something a few paces behind Maximilian's chair.

It was one of Elcho Falling's servants.

She closed her mouth, wet her lips, still staring beyond Maximilian, then said, softly, "Maxel . . ."

"Hallelujah!" Eleanon cried as the scout reported back to him. "Maxel and Ishbel are home!"

He turned to Falayal, standing nearby. "We move in the morning," he said. "Get the word out. We rise before dawn and leave so we arrive at Elcho Falling as the sun rises. Falayal . . . it won't be long, now. From tomorrow, Elcho Falling will be isolated from the outside world."

"And then . . ." Falayal said. "Are we ready?"

Elcanon grinned. "Yes," he said. "We are ready."

CHAPTER FIVE

Elcho Falling

Axis tipped his chair back, rested one of his booted feet against the edge of the table in the command chamber, and looked at Isaiah standing by the empty fireplace.

Isaiah returned his regard with one of his inscrutable expressions.

Axis shifted his eyes to Inardle, also sitting at the table. She merely looked bored.

"Well," said Axis, "where is Maxel? He calls us from our beds before dawn, then leaves us sitting here while he, no doubt, breakfasts in luxury while we—"

The door opened and Maximilian and Ishbel came in. Both looked exhausted, their eyes dark shadowed and their faces pale.

Obviously not such a good breakfast, Inardle said privately to Axis, and he flicked a look her way, but did not respond.

"What is wrong?" Isaiah said, waiting until Maximilian and Ishbel sat down before he, too, took a place at the table.

"We're sorry to have kept you waiting," Maximilian said. "Ishbel and I have had little sleep, what with this and that. Elcho Falling's servant came to speak with us last night. Now we need to talk to you."

"No one else?" Axis said. "Not Georgdi, nor Insharah, nor StarDrifter, nor Kezial, or—"

"No one else," Maximilian said. "You are my core commanders."

"Not even StarDrifter?" Axis said.

"I wanted to keep it to the bare minimum," Maximilian snapped, "so that I might avoid as much unnecessary talk and query and questioning and damned arguments as I could. Trust me when I say I am now reconsidering *you*!"

From the corner of his eye Axis could see Inardle bite the corner of her lip, and he shifted his gaze so that he could not see her at all. He hoped Maximilian had not caught her amusement.

"I apologise," Axis said to Maximilian. "You've had a bad night. What's wrong?"

"We face danger on several fronts," Maximilian said, "and that does not include Elcho Falling itself, which will be the battlefield." He looked about. "Is there no tea here? I would have thought that—"

"It is coming," Inardle said. "Just talk, Maxel. Don't worry about the tea."

Maximilian sighed. "We face danger on several fronts. From the One, from the Dark Spire, and from Eleanon and the Lealfast."

He was going to say more, but just then there was a tap at the door, and a servant came in bearing a tray with tea and some breakfast biscuits on it.

Maximilian made an impatient gesture, despite his irritated query for tea a moment earlier, but Axis waved him into silence, rose, took the tray from the servant and placed it on the table as the servant left, closing the door behind him.

Axis poured everyone a mug of tea, then handed the mugs around, giving everyone a thick warm biscuit as well.

"And there ends my menial duties for the day," he said. "Maxel, speak, if you will."

Maximilian took the time to sip his tea. He crumbled his biscuit into pieces, but did not attempt to eat it.

"For the moment I will leave the problem of the One," he said, "and discuss the Lealfast and the Dark Spire. Eleanon and the Lealfast are closely connected to the Dark Spire. In the absence of the One—or at least in the supposed absence of the One, for I do not doubt the One has kept his return hidden from Eleanon—Eleanon has been the driving force behind the continued growth of the Dark Spire. He was the one who planted it in Elcho Falling, and he has been the one who has continued to nurture it, sending Ravenna to midwive its mischief. Eleanon no doubt thinks that the Dark Spire will prove his main weapon against Elcho Falling. Ishbel?"

She continued. "Last night Elcho Falling's servant came to us to talk about the Dark Spire."

"Not the One?" Isaiah said.

"Elcho Falling can do little against the One," Ishbel said, "certainly not while he hides within the spire, and likely not once he emerges if he carries with him the full power of Infinity. Elcho Falling does not believe it can expel the One again, as it did on his earlier visit. It thinks the One's power has strengthened enormously during his journey through Infinity into the Dark Spire."

"But Elcho Falling has spoken of the Dark Spire," Axis said.

"Yes," Ishbel said. "I think the citadel fears the Dark Spire almost as much as the One. Essentially, the Dark Spire is a creation of both the power of Infinity and of the Lealfast. Eleanon *thinks* he controls it, but in reality the Dark Spire will likely prove far too powerful for him. Infinity will rope out of it once it has reached its full potential, and Eleanon, or any mortal who thinks to manipulate it, will be destroyed."

"But the Lealfast *made* the Dark Spire," Inardle said. "Hundreds of generations ago."

"They did," said Ishbel, "but not alone. They used the help of the Magi who had escaped Ashdod. The Dark Spire connects directly into the power of Infinity, particularly now the One inhabits it. The Dark Spire has also worked its way into the very fabric of Elcho Falling. It eats of Elcho Falling's nature. It imbibes Elcho Falling. It plans to *become* Elcho Falling."

Maximilian took over the speaking. "But first it must destroy Elcho Falling as it currently exists. Or at least partly destroy it, enough that the Dark Spire can then recreate Elcho Falling in its own image, or to its own purpose. To be brief, the One and Eleanon intended to use the Dark Spire to destroy Elcho Falling, then to rebuild it to their own needs, and to control the power of Infinity that would flood out of it."

"The Dark Spire is intended to be the ultimate gateway

into Infinity," Ishbel said. "It will channel the complete, dark power of Infinity into this world."

"Power the One will then control," Isaiah said.

"Aye," Maximilian said. "Currently Eleanon may think he is going to be the Dark Spire's master, but in reality it will be the One who will control all this power. Elcho Falling tells me that the One is the only creature capable of controlling it, for once the Dark Spire takes Elcho Falling's place, once it *becomes* Elcho Falling, then the dark power of Infinity will ripple out from this place and will, eventually, consume the entire world. Nothing will survive. Nothing. The Dark Spire shall be the ultimate Infinity Gate, and the power it will channel into this world will destroy it. The One will become master of death and destruction, and glory in it."

There was silence for a moment.

"Cheery news," Axis said, finally. "What can we do?"

"For the moment I do not believe Eleanon knows of the One's return," Maximilian said. "The One will want Eleanon and the Lealfast to continue on their path—previously agreed between them before Eleanon believed the One had gone and that he could become the spire's only master—which will be to nurture the spire, and to give it what aid it needs to grow to maturity when, so I believe, it will destroy Elcho Falling and take its place. Of course the One has other plans for that moment, but for the time being I believe Eleanon and the Lealfast remain critical to the spire's continued development.

"Axis, I am going to place you and Isaiah in complete control of the Eleanon and Lealfast problem. If you can stop them, then perhaps we can stop the Dark Spire before it becomes too powerful,"

"And you and Ishbel?" Axis said.

"We need to be elsewhere," Maximilian said. "You and Isaiah will take on this task. You are willing?"

Axis and Isaiah looked at each other, and both smiled.

"Aye, we can do it," Isaiah said, "and be glad of the duty."

"Good," Maximilian said, "you have my authority for anything that is needed. Everyone in Elcho Falling is under your command."

"Well, that's this morning taken care of," Axis said with
a grin. "What do you want us to do this afternoon?"

Everyone chuckled.

"And I?" Inardle said as the amusement died.

"You," said Maximilian, "I need to trace the Skraelings.
I think they are going to be critical to Axis and Isaiah's success. We need to know where they are, Inardle. And what
they plan. You are now a River Angel. You should have the
skills needed to track them down."

She smiled, pleased with her task.

"You and Ishbel said you would be concerned elsewhere,"
Isaiah said.

"We need to find a way to negate the One and stop the
Dark Spire becoming a gateway into Infinity," Maximilian
said. He glanced at Ishbel. "When we untethered the Twisted
Tower from this world, we lost all the information within it.
However, we think that if we redraw plans of each level of
the tower and place within those drawings all the objects we
can remember, then we may recall some vital information
that can aid us against the One and the Dark Spire."

"Elcho Falling itself was no help?" Axis said.

Maximilian gave a shake of his head. "No. Elcho Falling
is as flummoxed by the Dark Spire as any of us. Some things
it controls itself, others it depends on its lord. I need to find
the solution to the Dark Spire and to the One. *I* need to find a
means to remove both the spire and the One. Axis, Isaiah, I
am sorry to leave you with the burden of Eleanon, but Ishbel
and myself need to do this and we need the time to do it—
which you need to give us. We have to spend however long
it takes to remember every single object within the Twisted
Tower, and its purpose."

"I notice that none of us have discussed StarDancer's
plan," Axis said quietly.

"His plan is impossible," Ishbel said. "None of us can
trust Ravenna."

Axis looked down to his hands, loosely folded in his lap.

"*You* think StarDancer has the right idea?" Ishbel said.

Axis looked up again. "I think it is a terrible idea," he

said, "but we need to consider it. Ishbel, we may *need* to consider it."

"Not unless you and Isaiah intend to fail in stopping Eleanon and the Lealfast," Ishbel snapped.

Axis was about to reply, but Inardle's head jerked toward the window where the day had just dawned.

"Speaking of the devil," she said, "the Lealfast have arrived."

CHAPTER SIX

Elcho Falling

They stood on the balcony, looking westward over the lake. Tens of thousands of Lealfast were landing, standing about in groups as they settled on the ground. They were chatting, relaxed and confident and seemingly oblivious to the regard they knew must be emanating from Elcho Falling.

There were footsteps from behind them—Georgdi.

"They're settling all about the lake," he said to Maximilian. "Surrounding us."

Maximilian gave a weary smile. "It is Axis' and Isaiah's problem, now," he said, then he turned to the two men. "Ishbel and I will be in our eyrie at the very top of Elcho Falling. If you need us, climb upward through stairwell after stairwell. Eventually you will come to a blank sandstone wall. Place your palm upon it, so, and the door will open for you. I have instructed Elcho Falling to allow the two of you to enter."

Maximilian turned for one final look at the Lealfast, then back at Axis and Isaiah. "I wish you good hunting," he said, then he took Ishbel's hand and left the balcony.

Georgdi looked at Axis, raising an eyebrow.

"Maxel and Ishbel are otherwise occupied," Axis said. He briefly outlined to Georgdi what Maximilian had told them earlier. Then he leaned on the balcony railing, looking over the view before them. "Eleanon has brought the Lealfast back to destroy Elcho Falling, thinking he can recreate it using the Dark Spire."

"How will he do that?" Georgdi said. "How would *any-one* think to tear this citadel apart? It is a veritable mountain.

The Dark Spire is growing up through the citadel, yes, but at such a relatively slow rate that months will pass before the structure of Elcho Falling can be seriously compromised."

"The 'eggs'," Axis said quietly. "They are scattered throughout the walls. Somehow they will hasten the process. But how? For the moment they simply sit there. How will Eleanon activate them? A word? An enchantment? A clap of his hands? How can we stop him if we don't know what he plans?" He watched as wave after wave of Lealfast landed on the shores of the lake, then straightened and looked to Inardle. "Any idea?"

"No," she said. "I had no idea the Dark Spire could do what it does now, let alone what else it, or its eggs, *might* do or how Eleanon may use them. Axis, Isaiah, I need to leave Elcho Falling to go in search of the Skraelings. I will need to do this soon because, even though that Dark Spire grows only slowly, it currently threatens the chamber where the entrance to the back tunnel is. Another day or so and I might not be able to leave that way. I had thought to leave today, before the Lealfast returned, but now . . ."

"You can't slip by them?" Axis said.

"Not in my Lealfast form," Inardle said. "There are too many of them. They'd spot me instantly. I am sure now they saw us leave Elcho Falling previously, and let us pass, to toy with us."

"And in your River Angel form?" Axis said.

"I would still be spotted," Inardle said. "I can slide about as water, but . . . I fear they'd still spot me. If there was a rainstorm, however . . ."

Inardle stopped, looking significantly at Isaiah.

"Oh no . . ." Georgdi and Axis said together.

"Just a rainstorm," Inardle said. "Not a mayhem. Isaiah, can you do this?"

"I have little finesse when summoning wind and rain," Isaiah said. "The mayhem I summoned on the day we entered Elcho Falling was far more than I'd wanted. I can start the process. I cannot control it."

"But all would be safe within Elcho Falling," Inardle said. "Only the Lealfast would be exposed to its full force."

"Now there's a thought," Axis said. "Inardle, even with a mayhem as strong as the one we endured on the day of battle . . . could you still escape without harm?"

"Yes," she said.

Axis looked at Isaiah.

Isaiah sighed. "I can summon one overnight for you, if you wish. It will require the night air to form."

"Then I will leave tomorrow morning," Inardle said. "And even if the back tunnel is unusable by then, I could slip out the front gates."

"And for this day," Axis said, "we watch the Lealfast."

The Lealfast arrived in wave after wave, finally congregating in full force by mid-morning. They did not set up one large camp as they had previously, instead making twelve smaller camps at equal distances about the lake.

Their older camp, Armat's original camp, still stood in some tatters near the far end of the causeway. Once the full might of the Lealfast had arrived, a large group of them—perhaps twenty thousand—began to systematically clean away any trace of it.

Isaiah and Axis stood on the balcony of the command chamber, both leaning on the railing, watching in some puzzlement.

"They are being very tidy," Isaiah said, as he watched two of the Lealfast rise into the air with a folded tent between them. They flew westward for perhaps three hundred paces, then they dropped back to the ground, placing their folded tent on a growing (but very orderly) pile of the remains of Armat's camp.

"They are shifting it back from the shores of the lake," Axis said.

"But why?" Isaiah said. "Why do they need that space? None of their new camps need that area . . ."

"And why twelve separate camps?" Axis said. "Does Eleanon fear attack? Is he separating his people for safety? It would be harder for us to attack twelve separate encampments than one large one."

"It would be impossible for us to attack one large one in

the first instance," Isaiah said. "We'd be massacred trying to leave Elcho Falling. What is he doing?"

Axis gave a little shake of his head. "Isaiah, we really need to be thinking about what we can do to, first, defend Elcho Falling, and then, second, destroy what Eleanon is going to . . . stars, Isaiah! What is *that*?"

Isaiah was already shading his eyes from the bright sun, looking westward. There was a line of Lealfast flying in, but oh, so slowly. They were flying in pairs, holding between them slings that carried . . . that carried . . .

"Can you see, Axis?" Isaiah said. "Your Icarii eyes are better than mine."

"I love it when gods confess a weakness," Axis muttered, shading his eyes and peered intently into the distance.

"Rocks," he muttered. "They're carrying boulders in those slings. Stars, Isaiah, they must be strong!"

"Boulders? What for?" Isaiah strode back into the command chamber, shouting to Insharah and Georgdi who stood there inspecting plans of Elcho Falling with some of their captains.

As the men moved, Isaiah turned to step out onto the balcony, only to be stopped by Axis jogging into the chamber.

"They're flying around the other side of Elcho Falling," Axis said, and together the two men ran through the corridors of Elcho Falling, reaching a balcony on the eastern side of the citadel in ten minutes.

They were both slightly out of breath as they stared in bewilderment as the pairs of Lealfast flew the boulders in slings over the channel that connected Elcho Falling's lake with the Infinity Sea. There the birdmen positioned themselves carefully, before letting go of one end of their slings.

Boulder after boulder crashed into the channel.

"What is he doing?" Axis said.

Isaiah did not immediately answer. They continued watching as scores of pairs of Lealfast flew in to dump boulders in the channel.

"He wants to block it off," Isaiah said, eventually. "He's closing the channel to the ocean beyond."

Inardle had joined them, and she shook her head at their unspoken query. "I'm sorry," she said. "I don't know why."

"Does the channel have any significance to the lake or Elcho Falling?" Axis asked Isaiah.

"And I would know that because . . . ?" Isaiah said.

"Because you and Lister worked your damndest to get Maxel to the point of raising Elcho Falling so I thought you might know something about the structure!" Axis snapped.

Axis took a deep breath, muttering an apology. "I'll have to ask Maxel. He won't like being disturbed this quickly."

Isaiah gave a shrug.

Axis reached the very top of the stairs, out of breath and cursing Maximilian's choice of location for his private apartment. There appeared to be a solid sandstone wall before him, but Axis placed his palm on it as Maximilian had instructed, and within a moment the entire wall dissolved, revealing yet another set of stairs.

Sighing, Axis began the climb.

Fortunately, in only twenty or so steps Axis found himself in a wondrous circular chamber. It seemed to be open to the sky, although, as the air within the chamber was still, Axis assumed there was some kind of barrier between the room and the outside.

Maximilian and Ishbel were sitting on a couch by a table completely covered with pieces of paper.

They were looking at Axis patiently.

Axis apologised for disturbing them as he walked over, then told them what the Lealfast were doing.

"That channel is not particularly deep," Axis concluded. "It will be filled within a day or two if the Lealfast keep this up. Maxel, what significance does the channel have? Does Elcho Falling *need* to be connected to the Infinity Sea?"

As he spoke Axis looked down at the papers scattered across the low table. They were diagrams of rooms, carefully filled in with shapes of objects, each of those labelled.

"No." Maximilian leaned back in the couch, looking even more exhausted than when Axis had seen him earlier. "The channel was formed when the sea rushed in during the raising of the citadel—waters from the sea formed the lake, although the lake is now fresh water rather than sea water."

"Will the lake dry out if it isn't replenished?" Axis asked.

Maximilian thought, then shook his head. "I doubt it. The waters of the lake are as magical as Elcho Falling itself. Even if they were not, the lake is deep and extensive. Natural rainfall would be enough to keep it filled. It would take decades to dry out."

"Then why is Eleanon filling the channel in?" Axis said.

"I have no idea, Axis. If you would excuse us . . . Ishbel and I would like to get another level drawn and its objects identified before we have a rest."

Axis murmured a goodbye, turning to walk away.

But just as he reached the stairs leading downward, he stopped, and turned about.

He'd just had an idea.

Maximilian and Ishbel regarded him with ill-disguised impatience.

"I beg your patience," Axis said, walking quickly back to them. "Maxel, when you, Ishbel, Serge and Doyle left for Isembaard, how did you do it? When Elcho Falling expelled the Lealfast and the One, how did it manage it?"

Maximilian leaned back in his chair, folding his arms and regarding Axis with narrowed, thoughtful eyes.

"Elcho Falling assisted Ishbel and our two companions by transferring us directly into Aqhat," Maximilian said. "It was a strange mechanism . . . it required the transference of matter the other way—"

"The juit birds," Axis said.

Maximilian nodded. "And as for the Lealfast and the One, Elcho Falling expelled them as my murderers—Ishbel had spattered them with my murdered blood, and thus Elcho Falling rejected them." He glanced briefly at Ishbel, who was frowning, then returned his regard to Axis. "What are you thinking?"

"I'm thinking that we have two ways at least to get men out of Elcho Falling."

Maximilian continued to look at Axis, not speaking, thinking.

"Well?" Axis said after a lengthy pause.

"You want to get soldiers out to attack the Lealfast," Ishbel said, "without exposing them to the difficulties of being penned up on the causeway."

"Yes," Axis said.

Ishbel and Maximilian exchanged a glance.

"The first method," Maxel said, "expelling them as traitors, can not be used. No one here is a traitor—"

"At least we pray not," Ishbel muttered.

"And even if so," Maximilian said, "not in the numbers that could be of any use to you. I hope."

"And the second method?" Axis said. "Using the same kind of transference that got you down to Aqhat?"

Ishbel and Maximilian exchanged another glance.

"Can it be done?" Axis said.

"It is *possible*," Maximilian said, "but this is a powerful piece of magic you are asking me—even Ishbel and myself combined—to work, Axis. How many men would you want to attack the Lealfast? A hundred thousand? Two? Neither or us could manage that many."

"How many could you manage?" Axis said.

"Maybe nine or ten thousand," Maximilian said, "so long as they didn't go too far. And this method of transference demands that something be transferred back *inside* Elcho Falling. And the only thing nearby are the Lealfast. Ah, Axis. No. Ten thousand men won't be of any use. You'd be slaughtered by the Lealfast."

"How many Lealfast would need to be transferred inside?" Axis said, and Maximilian grunted impatiently.

"A thousand maybe."

"Why so few?" Axis said.

"It is a complicated calculation of power," Ishbel said. "The Lealfast, with their command of both Infinity and the Star Dance, command much power, so fewer of them would be needed to counterbalance ten thousand fighting men."

Axis tried a smile. "Even if I were with them?"

"Even if you were with them," Maximilian said. "Axis, I do not like this and won't agree to it. It is a desperate measure for a desperate moment. You'd have almost no chance out there . . . ten thousand against a quarter of a million? No. Never."

"Maxel—"

"No, Axis. Now, if you would leave us to our work . . ."

They spent the afternoon watching the Lealfast drop boulder after boulder into the channel. They also continued eradicating Armat's camp, and consolidating the twelve Lealfast camps, which were set well back from the shore of the lake.

Axis had told Isaiah about his discussion with Maximilian, hoping for some support from him, but Isaiah had only shrugged and said he could understand Maximilian's reluctance.

It was close to dusk when Axis realised at least one part of the mystery.

"They're keeping clear a ribbon of land about the shores of the lake," he said to Isaiah as they stood on the eastern balcony, watching the boulders drop. "They're keeping their own camps at a distance, and they're clearing away Armat's camp which, for whatever purpose they have, was obviously in the way."

"Then . . ." Isaiah said slowly, his eyes narrowing as he thought, "they are not closing off the channel so much as completing the land circle about Elcho Falling? They are encircling us with clear land."

But why? Axis wanted to scream, knowing it would do no good.

Inardle was with them, and now she touched Isaiah on his arm to gain his attention. "I need to go tomorrow to find the Skraelings," she said. "I can't get out of here unless you make your mayhem. The sky is clear for hundreds of leagues, and Georgdi tells me that summer in the Outlands is inevitably dry."

Isaiah nodded. "Very well, then. I will build it overnight," he said. "If nothing else it will put a stop to whatever the Lealfast do."

CHAPTER SEVEN

Elcho Falling

The mayhem rolled in from the sea, spitting fire and ice, drenching Elcho Falling and the surrounding landscape in pelting rain. The wind was not as bad this time, but it was still a terrible storm.

Eleanon and Falayal watched it approach. Both wore irritated expressions, but neither looked particularly worried or angry.

"Well, it surprised me Isaiah left it this long," Falayal said. "I'd expected it yesterday."

"Perhaps Isaiah is growing old," Eleanon said, "and mayhap grows weak. This doesn't look as terrifying as that one he summoned during the battle."

"But bad enough. We'll need to leave soon."

Eleanon nodded. "Do it now," he said. "There is no need to linger. Fly an hour to the north. You shall be safe there. This storm is only very local. Return once it is calm."

"You *will* be safe?" Falayal said.

"You wouldn't be pleased to see me gone?" Eleanon replied.

"Don't be foolish, Eleanon," Falayal snapped. "We'd be lost without you."

And pray you don't forget that, Eleanon thought.

"Keep well," he said, "and so shall I. And by the time this is done, you can be assured that Isaiah will never, never summon a mayhem again."

Falayal grinned at Eleanon, then he was gone. A few minutes later the Lealfast Nation rose into the approaching winds, veering northward.

* * *

Axis watched the Lealfast leave, feeling some deep satisfaction that the storm forced them to flee.

He wondered how often Isaiah could summon these mayhems.

But for now he stood in the chamber which held the pool leading to the underwater escape from Elcho Falling. Apart from Inardle, who stood before him, the chamber was empty.

There were cracks in some of the walls, though. It would not be many more days before the Dark Spire broke through to this level, likely destroying this chamber in the process.

"Be safe," he said to her. They were standing close but not touching, and Axis was feeling awkward. He hated goodbyes, and he had a terrible feeling that Inardle might not come back—or at least not as someone who would want to be his companion.

She smiled. "I will be safe. I do not fear the Skraelings."

"Still . . ."

She leaned into him, their bodies touching in myriad places, and they kissed, softly.

"You are a different person, now," Axis murmured as she leaned back.

"Which do you prefer, Axis? This, or the other?"

"Come home," he said.

"This is not your home," she replied, the waters shifting behind her eyes, and with that ambiguous reply she turned away from him and disrobed. She gave him one last, long look over her shoulder, then, before Axis could say anything else, turned into a column of water, which then crashed into the pool.

This is not your home, she had said, and Axis stood there for a long time, staring at the blank pool, feeling terribly lonely and dislocated.

Eleanon had escaped into invisibility as the Lealfast Nation left, and secreted himself within the reed banks surrounding the eastern shores of the lake. He would get wet, violently wet, but the thick, tall reeds would give him protection against the ferocious winds.

The mayhem hit suddenly, forcing Eleanon to grab onto

thick bunches of reeds to keep himself from being blown away and sucking the air from his lungs. For long minutes it was all Eleanon could do to breathe and keep himself within the shelter of the reeds, but gradually he became used to the wind and the driving rain and managed to settle himself in among the reeds in such a manner that he no longer needed to fear being blown away.

He was drenched, and the sheer force of the storm had stripped away his cloak of invisibility, but that no longer perturbed Eleanon. No one in Elcho Falling could possibly see him through the thick, sheeting rain.

He relaxed, communing with the mayhem, seeking to understand it amid all its twists and secrets.

It was not, for one as skilled as Eleanon, all that difficult. The mayhem was a very basic enchantment, although one wrought with a vast power that Eleanon could not match.

Matching that power did not worry Eleanon.

All he wanted to do was reflect it.

Eventually, even as the storm worsened about him, Eleanon began to grin.

Then, he began to commune with the Dark Spire.

Deep within the Dark Spire, the One concealed himself from Eleanon's power. It was easy enough to do and he did not want Eleanon realising his presence.

If Eleanon knew the One had returned, he'd not do what the One wanted, which was to continue to aid the Dark Spire.

The One lurked in the shadows of his power and listened to what Eleanon whispered to the Dark Spire.

He grinned. It was a shame Eleanon would eventually have to die, for he was gifted with a fine sense of humour.

There were several Enchanters, as always, hovering about the Dark Spire deep within Elcho Falling. They were there to watch it and, in the most hopeful of universes, to glean some understanding of it.

They were also here maintaining a watch lest the One's presence grow closer.

But for today, as for the past few months, there was nothing they could learn.

One, an Icarii named StarSlider, had just decided he would return to one of the higher levels in the citadel when he paused, frowning at the Dark Spire. There was something odd . . . StarSlider couldn't quite place it and he was about to call out to the other two Enchanters present when he stopped, mouth agape.

Storm clouds had gathered about the spire's peak.

"Spring—" StarSlider began to call to one of his companions, SpringStar, but suddenly lightning forked out of one of the clouds and struck close by him.

StarSlider jumped out of the way, then cried out in horror as torrential rain swept him off his feet and toward the Dark Spire.

The mayhem had come to visit within Elcho Falling.

Completely unaware of what was happening behind her, Inardle merged with the water as she entered the underwater tunnel, moving with it and through it until she entered the lake. Here she paused, looking around.

Above her, the surface of the water was pockmarked by the driving rain—Inardle could see each individual droplet of rain drive into the water, briefly creating a long foaming tunnel before it lost its energy and merged with the waters of the lake.

Far beneath her Inardle could see the 'roots' of the Dark Spire lying along the bottom of the lake. They were longer and thicker than she remembered and she wasted a moment wondering for what purpose they were intended, and for what purpose they might be used.

What would a River Angel do with those long, black, tapered fingers?

Finally, Inardle looked toward the entrance of the channel to the sea.

The water was still murky from the settling boulders, but Inardle could see that the channel was now well over halfway blocked.

Another day, once this mayhem was done, and the Lealfast would have completed their task.

A sigh ran through her being and Inardle turned for the lake's edge. She could not afford to waste any more time for Isaiah had told her the mayhem would be sharp and furious, but not lengthy.

At the edge of the lake, Inardle flowed onto the gravelled edge of the land. She moved fast, a writhing stream of water that, in this storm of raindrops battering into the ground, was virtually invisible.

She slithered as fast as she could, working her way over the dips and cracks in the earths surface, following the natural contours of the land.

Axis had been climbing the main staircase toward the command chamber, needing to speak with Isaiah, but within the space of a breath he was pummelled to his knees, gasping for breath as howling winds and driving rain filled the interior of the citadel.

He couldn't understand what was going on—had the walls of Elcho Falling been breached? Water began pouring down the stairs and Axis was swept to one side. He grabbed at a newel post and wrapped his arms around it for support. Several soldiers, less fortunate than he, tumbled past him in the torrent of water.

What was happening?

Eleanon has reflected the mayhem inside, Isaiah said in his mind.

Stars! Axis tried to think, shaking water off his face in a useless attempt to stop the rain-blindness. *Isaiah*, he said. *What can you do? Can you stop the mayhem?*

No, came the response, and Axis cursed. He began to inch his way up, grabbing at the newel posts, pushing with his feet, slipping every so often but hanging on grimly as the water raged past him. Above the noise of the storm he could vaguely hear shouts and thumps—people doing whatever they could to escape the mayhem.

At the next landing a hand reached down to grab him.

It was Georgdi, with a rope about his waist which extended back into one of the chambers running off the central staircase.

Georgdi was shouting something, but Axis could not make it out. He just gripped Georgdi's hand and slowly the two men, aided by someone unknown keeping a firm pull on the rope, worked their way into a chamber off the stairwell.

Here it was a little calmer—the wind and rain still bore down on them, but at least they were out of the raging torrent of the central staircase.

Georgdi shouted something almost unintelligible at Axis, which Axis interpreted as *What the fuck is happening?*

Axis gestured uselessly, then, pulling Georgdi as close as a lover, shouted in his ear, "We'll have to ride it out!"

Georgdi nodded understanding, and then the two men and their companions huddled in the shelter of the door and a large table as the mayhem screamed about them.

Throughout Elcho Falling men and women sheltered from the storm as best they could. Water from the torrential rain swept down corridors and tumbled down stairs in rushing waterfalls, semi-filling lower chambers before slowly draining out into the lake via sewers and pipes in the citadel's walls. Someone had the foresight to open the doorway in the great entrance arch and water cascaded out the opening as if from the bursting of a great dam.

In their top chamber, Ishbel and Maximilian were no luckier than anyone else. They sheltered in the lee of a closet, watching in disbelief as all the charts and diagrams and notes that they had made about the contents of the Twisted Tower were swept away.

The One? Ishbel said in Maximilian's mind.

No, he replied. *Eleanon.*

Privately, he wondered if Axis and Isaiah could manage the Lealfast, and, as the storm swept on and on, drenching and ruining every piece of furniture in their once-lovely chamber, Maximilian had to fight to believe that something postive could be done, and that there really wasn't any merit in the idea of just abandoning Elcho Falling to whatever Eleanon wanted of it so he and Ishbel could live out what remaining months they might have in some distant, sunnier and *drier* land.

At storm's end, almost two hours later, Inardle was very far away, still unknowing of what had happened behind her.

Eleanon sat among the reeds, revelling in the sun as it peeked its way through the dissipating clouds, staring at Elcho Falling and imagining the chaos within.

He shook out his wings slowly, spreading them to dry in the sun, confident that that was the last mayhem Isaiah would summon in a very, very long time.

CHAPTER EIGHT

The Outlands

Inardle found the Skraelings far, far sooner than she had thought. She'd returned to her Lealfast form once she was well away from Elcho Falling, flying south high and fast, putting as much distance as possible between her and the citadel before the Lealfast returned to it after the mayhem. She'd thought to have needed to have travelled many scores of leagues, but in fact she discovered the Skraelings not four hours south of Elcho Falling. She was flying over the gently rolling grassy hills, enjoying the sun, when, quite abruptly, the entire herd of Skraelings had materialised below her.

Inardle actually gave a small cry of surprise. She slowly, carefully, spiralled down toward them, landing on the grass some ten or twelve paces distant from their forward edge.

She looked them over—they were very, very different to what she had last seen. Most had reverted to their usual Skraeling form from the gross monstrosities their association with the One had warped them into, but a few . . . a few seemed to have altered further yet. Their huge silver orbs had become much smaller and more elongated and were grey rather than silver, while both their clawed hands and their once-terrible fangs seemed almost mild in comparison to what once they had been.

One of their number, one who had undergone such change as to appear almost handsome, rather than repulsively ugly, stepped forward.

"Inardle," he said, "we have come to meet you."

Inardle stared, recognising the voice before she recognised the form. "Ozll," she responded. After an awkward silence, she said, "You've changed."

He frowned. "How so?"

"You are becoming beautiful."

He stared, then seemed to dismiss the comment. "We have been coming to meet with you, Inardle."

"So you said. Why did you want to—"

"You have been changed."

Inardle stilled. She did not know how to respond, or how Ozll, or any other of the millions of Skraelings present, might feel about her now.

"We need to talk with you," Ozll said, and Inardle nodded.

"Shall we sit?" she said, folding herself cross-legged to the ground.

Ozll stepped forward, sitting down before her, and the mass of Skraelings swarmed about them, surrounding them completely, before settling to the ground themselves.

"You have been changed," Ozll said once again. "We want to know what happened. How it felt. What it has done to you. We are curious."

"First," Inardle said, "let me show you." She stood, stretched her arms up above her head, looking skyward . . . from the tips of her fingers and progressively down her body she turned into a beautiful column of green water. She had a basic form of arms, head and body, but the only clear, visible facial features were her eyes. Everything else was . . . liquid, virtually formless.

The Skraelings gasped and hissed, then murmured in a swell of sound as Inardle returned to her Lealfast form and sat once more.

"You are River Angel," Ozll said, his voice soft.

"When I wish," Inardle said.

"Tell us how you drowned," Ozll said. "Did it hurt? Were you scared of the water?"

"I was not killed by water," Inardle said, "but rather by Axis' blade when he tore my living heart from my breast."

The Skraelings had been fascinated by Inardle before this statement. Now they were spellbound.

Inardle explained how she and Axis had been trapped in the ice hex constructed by Eleanon, and how the only way for him to get her out was to murder her, then drag her back to the waters surrounding Elcho Falling.

"He bathed my torn, cold corpse in the lake of Elcho Falling," she said, "knowing the properties it contained for one with blood such as mine, and from the sky he commanded down an eagle who bore my heart back into my breast. It was . . ." she paused, remembering, "such power as you cannot imagine. Terrible. Painful. Beyond any words of mine to describe. But, in coming back to life, I was reborn with my River Angel potential awoken within me."

"So," Ozll said, "this is not something the mass of Lealfast could do? Jump into the waters of Elcho Falling and . . . transform?"

"No," said Inardle. "I don't think so. It was a combination of Axis' magic and my blood that worked my transformation."

All the Skraelings relaxed, many smiling, and Inardle realised they'd been worried that the Lealfast, too, might transform into River Angels. "You knew I'd changed," she said.

"Yes," Ozll replied. "Thus we came to find you. Inardle, we need to know, what have you become now you are a River Angel?"

Inardle frowned, puzzled. "What do you mean?"

"Inardle, have you murdered since you were reborn?"

Inardle didn't know what to say. "Um . . . yes . . . several Lealfast. They attacked myself and Axis, and so I was forced to—"

She stopped, shocked by the look in the Skraelings' eyes.

They looked sad, almost as if they were disappointed in her, and it was such a strange expression for them to assume that Inardle simply didn't know what to think.

"You have killed," Ozll said. "Did you assume the form of a River Angel to kill?"

"Yes," Inardle whispered.

"Thank you, Inardle," Ozll said, rising, and bringing to their feet the assembled millions of Skraelings with him. "That was what we needed to know."

He began to turn, and Inardle called out to him, holding

out a hand. "Wait! Ozll, I—all at Elcho Falling—need to know what you intend to do! Will you—"

"Goodbye, River Angel," Ozll said, and before Inardle could answer, the congregation of Skraelings vanished, millions upon millions of them, and she was left standing alone in the vast plains of the Outlands, holding out her hand imploringly to a people who no longer wanted to know her.

CHAPTER NINE

Elcho Falling

Elcho Falling was a nightmare to clean up. Everything inside had been water damaged, and close to half of the furniture and bedding had been rendered unusable.

Worse, scores of people had died, drowned or battered to death in the torrents of water that swept down staircases or filled lower chambers.

Among those who had died were the three Enchanters who'd been in the lower basement chamber with the Dark Spire. No one knew if the Dark Spire had killed them, or if they had drowned when the lower chambers had filled with water, but any knowledge they may have had about the cause of the mayhem moving inside had died with them.

Maximilian was furious at the intrusion of the mayhem into Elcho Falling. He knew he shouldn't be. He knew that neither Isaiah nor Axis could possibly have predicted this, but still he was angry. He knew this was likely a product of his frustration more than anything else, but it didn't stop him spending a good few long minutes shouting at both Axis and Isaiah before he finally quietened, and apologised.

"The mayhem destroyed all the work Ishbel and I had done on cataloguing the items in the Twisted Tower," he said. "We'll need to start all over again."

"I'm sorry, Maxel," Isaiah said.

Maximilian gave a little shrug of his shoulders, accepting the apology. They were standing on the largest landing of the main staircase, backs against a wall as scores of people hurried past carting bedding and clothes to windows and balconies to be draped out in the open air. Ropes had been strung between many of the balconies to hang sheets and blankets. Maximilian thought that from a distance Elcho Falling must look like a laundress' tower.

"Can it happen again?" Axis said. "I mean, can Eleanon now direct anything we do *outside* of Elcho Falling, *inside* Elcho Falling. If I direct a soldier to shoot an arrow at a passing Lealfast, will Elcho Falling then be filled with thousands of arrows bouncing about?"

Maximilian gave a small shake of his head. "I talked to Elcho Falling before I came down here, worried about the same thing. Apparently what Eleanon did was take the enchantment of the mayhem and reflect it inside via the Dark Spire. Neither Elcho Falling nor myself believe that an ordinary occurrence—a non-magical occurrence—can be reflected the same way. But it does dampen your use of the Star Dance, Axis, as it does whatever you can summon, Isaiah. Be careful."

Georgdi approached them, climbing the stairs. "The lower chambers have been drained of their water," he said. "The Dark Spire . . . you need to see the Dark Spire, Maximilian."

Maximilian began the walk down the stairs.

Axis could barely believe it. Maximilian had told them that eventually the Dark Spire would recreate Elcho Falling within itself, but this . . .

Since the mayhem the spire had grown, pushing through three more levels (and into the chamber that had held the pool leading to the tunnel to the lake); detritus from the broken floors lay scattered about the chambers the spire had grown through, making walking difficult. But, more than its growth, it was the change in the spire's appearance that shocked everyone.

It was developing balconies and windows.

As yet these were mere bumps and depressions in the outer skin of the spire, but their overall pattern clearly revealed what one day they would become.

"Worse news," said StarDrifter, coming down the stairs behind them. "The Lealfast have returned."

* * *

Axis and Isaiah stood on one of the eastern balconies, looking out to where the Lealfast had recommenced their slow flying in of boulders to dam off the lake about Elcho Falling. Maximilian had returned to his eyrie, to Ishbel and their task of finding a way to remember all the objects in the Twisted Tower, and StarDrifter and Georgdi were occupied inside, supervising repairs. Axis had warned StarDrifter about using the Star Dance, and asked him to spread the word among the remaining Enchanters.

Stars . . . 'remaining Enchanters'. At this rate StarDrifter would be Talon of nothing but memories.

"Have you heard any word from Inardle?" Isaiah said.

"No."

"I wish I knew what was happening with those damn Skraelings," Isaiah said. "They have the power to completely destroy us if they decide to combine with their old allies the Lealfast and attack."

"She will contact us as soon as she can," Axis said.

"We don't even know if she escaped," Isaiah said.

Axis repressed a sigh. "*If* she escaped, and once she has news, then she will contact us as soon as she can."

They watched for a few more minutes as two more pairs of Lealfast flew in and dropped their boulders into the channel. Axis and Isaiah could make out the shadows of the submerged boulders now—they were only just under the surface. In only a few hours the lake would be dammed completely.

"*Why* do they want that ribbon of land surrounding Elcho Falling's lake?" Axis muttered. "For what purpose are they going to use it?"

"Well, I, for one, have had enough of this standing about uselessly," Isaiah said. He stepped to the door leading inside Elcho Falling and shouted for a couple of bowmen.

"Stars, Isaiah," Axis said as two Isembaardian bowmen hurried out onto the balcony. "Be careful."

"Maximilian said this would not harm us," Isaiah said, and Axis wondered if Maximilian had any idea, really. He wanted to ask Isaiah to wait a few minutes just to warn the people inside Elcho Falling, but Isaiah was not in any mood to wait.

"Shoot those two Lealfast," Isaiah said to the bowmen, indicating a pair of Lealfast flying in with a boulder in a sling between them. "Can your arrows reach that distance?"

"Easily, Excellency," said one of the men, and without further hesitation they raised their bows, fitted their arrows, and let fly.

The arrows flew straight and true, arching high over the lake before beginning their descent toward the Lealfast.

"They are flying true!" Isaiah said, but, no sooner were the words out of his mouth than the waters of the lake erupted and twin black tendrils reached into the sky, snatching the arrows as they fell and bearing them back underwater.

The four men on the balcony stood in silence, shocked.

"A volley," Isaiah snapped. "Shoot a volley."

The bowmen again raised their bows and, their movements honed by years of practice, shot a volley of arrows into the air toward the Lealfast. These—because of the speed at which they were delivered, as many as six per breath between the two men—were not so accurately aimed, yet nonetheless they flew toward the Lealfast.

A score of black tendrils erupted from the lake, snatching the arrows from the sky.

"*Shetzah!*" Isaiah cursed.

The Lealfast continued to drop the boulders. They had not once glanced toward the arrows.

CHAPTER TEN

The Outlands

The Skraelings hovered, partway between full reality and their dream state.

Their meeting with Inardle had confused and upset them. They had almost agreed among themselves that they would become River Angels, that they did have the courage to step into the water and drown, but Inardle's news . . . that she had killed . . . had deeply upset the Skraelings.

At some point in both their physical and mental journey from who they *had* been toward who they *might* be, the Skraelings had developed a deep antipathy to killing. They had spent their entire lives killing; their culture and very sense of self worth had been largely based on slaughter, yet now . . . now the idea that they might lay hand to another and tear them apart, caused the Skraelings to feel deep abhorrence.

As they sat, considering, they were unaware that their talons were receding, and their over-sized jaws finally shrinking to normal size, and their teeth turning from fangs to grinding molars.

Isaiah the Water God had set them on a course that, whether or not it ended in their becoming River Angels, would change their lives forever.

Knowledge of their beginnings and contemplation of their own nature had done within a few short weeks what no army had ever been able to do in decades of trying: destroyed forever the threat of the Skraeling.

"What do we want to do?" Ozll asked into this grey sea of contemplation. "Who do we want to be?"

"Not a River Angel if the first thing Inardle did in her new form was to embark on murder," said Mallx.

"But the life of the River Angel is so compelling," the female Graq said. "It calls to me. It runs in my blood."

Ozll nodded, and there was a murmur of assent among the great herd.

"But—" Mallx said.

"I know," Ozll interrupted. "We all sway toward the life of the River Angel, but we wonder if it might be viler than our current incarnation."

He paused. "I have an idea, strange as it may be to you."

"I think I know what it might be," Graq murmured, and Ozll looked at her, and nodded.

CHAPTER ELEVEN

Elcho Falling

Eleanon stood in the pre-dawn, looking at Elcho Falling glimmer in the last light of the full moon.

A week, no more, and it would be his.

Seven days.

"The magic is all worked?" Falayal said quietly at Eleanon's side.

Eleanon gave a terse nod.

"And the One? He absolutely *is* vanished? You are certain?"

"The Twisted Tower now drifts many lifetimes away from this world," Eleanon said. "The One is," his mouth lifted slightly at the pun, "quite out of the equation now, Falayal. Is everyone ready?"

"Yes," Falayal said, "and anxious and excited all at the same time. You are sure this will—"

"It *will* work!" Eleanon said fiercely. He took a calming breath. "Everyone knows what to do?"

"Yes. When will we start?"

"In an hour. When the light is good. If anyone trips over a shadowed pebble then the day's work is lost. Falayal . . . I need a little peace and quiet. I need to touch the Dark Spire."

Falayal bent his head in respect, moving away into the dim light. Eleanon stood a few minutes longer, staring at Elcho Falling, waiting for Falayal to make his way back to the nearest Lealfast camp, then he took a deep breath, then another, then closed his eyes.

Friend, he called, and the Dark Spire responded.

* * *

An hour after dawn the Lealfast moved. They gathered first in massive groups in a clear space just beyond each of their twelve encampments. Everyone save the infirm, the youngest children, and the disabled. They did not speak; they kept their eyes downcast; they seemed unaware of each other.

Eleanon stood on a small rise to the north, perhaps fifty paces away. Once all the Lealfast had gathered into twelve huge groups, and were still, Eleanon raised his hands, paused, then gave a resounding clap.

The Lealfast began to move, very slowly, but with precision and purpose. Long lines of Lealfast wound out of the twelve groups, some moving in lines westward about the lake, some in lines going eastward. As they moved, Eleanon kept up a slow, rhythmic clapping, and all the Lealfast moved in time to his beat.

As they marched, they kept their eyes turned downward.

Line after line emerged from the twelve camps until, well over an hour later, the lake was encircled by twelve concentric lines of Lealfast, alternate lines moving in different directions.

As soon as the lines had formed, Eleanon stopped his clapping, and the lines fell still.

"What are they doing?" Axis said, keeping his voice muted for no reason that he knew of, save that this was, at the very least, an awe-inspiring sight. Now he could see why the Lealfast had needed the shoreline kept clear, and why they'd needed to dam the channel.

Eleanon had wanted to complete the circle.

The dam had been finished off with soil and trampled reeds, and the reed beds to either side had been beaten down to create a solid surface.

Isaiah didn't answer. He took a step forward on the balcony (they watched from the north face of Elcho Falling this morning), put his hands on the railings and narrowed his eyes.

"Isaiah?" Axis said.

One of Isaiah's hands came up briefly. *Wait.*

Axis looked back to the circles of stationary Lealfast, then past them to where Eleanon stood on his rise.

As if he knew Axis had shifted his regard to him, Eleanon raised his hands again, and recommenced his clapping.

Now it was a slow, powerful beat. On the fifth clap, the rings of Lealfast moved, instantaneously, and all in step. Each circle moved forward, each alternate circle moving in a different direction. They marched, not as an army, but with a slight spring in each step, so their feet slapped down absolutely in time with Eleanon's clapping.

"Shetzah," Isaiah murmured.

Axis thought that Isaiah spent way too much time muttering curses these days and little enough time on explanations.

"Isaiah?" he said, his voice edged with frustration.

All the circles were moving, springing up and down in perfect time with Eleanon's slow, heavy clapping.

"Look at the lake!" Isaiah said.

Axis looked. The surface of the lake rippled with thousands of tiny wavelets, emanating in perfect circles from the shoreline and running toward Elcho Falling.

Then Isaiah grabbed Axis' hand and rammed it down on the balcony railing. "Feel!"

The railing vibrated under Axis' hand with tremors perfectly attuned to the marching dance of the Lealfast and Eleanon's hands.

Axis raised his eyes and stared at Isaiah.

"When I led an army," Isaiah said, his voice low and intent, "my army never marched over a bridge. They walked, all discordant. They did not march, on my orders. Did you ever march a large cohort of men over a bridge, Axis Star-Man?"

"No," Axis said, feeling sick to his stomach.

"No," Isaiah echoed. "No. Never. Army commanders know how dangerous it is to march men in rhythm over a bridge because of the risk the rhythm will set up a fatal reverberation through the bridge and bring it down."

Axis pulled his hand away from under Isaiah's. "What can we do?"

"We meet in the command chamber, with Georgdi and Insharah and StarDrifter, and we stay there until we have a solution!"

* * *

Ishbel and Maximilian stood at the edge of their eyrie, looking down.

Like Isaiah, they well understood the significance of what Eleanon attempted.

"We're going to have to leave Isaiah and Axis to try and do what they can," Maximilian said. "We still have so many levels to work through."

Ishbel laid a hand on his arm. "Then we'd best get to work," she said.

Maximilian gave her a faint smile. They'd worked through the night redrawing designs and diagrams, remembering the levels they'd already been through. It had been easier and quicker this time and currently there were diagrams for fully one-third of the Twisted Tower, but there was a long way to go.

"Indeed," he said, and together they turned away from the view and went back to their work.

The Lealfast continued their slow marching dance about Elcho Falling. Everyone in the citadel could feel it—a slight tremor under their feet or hands. It was only the slightest of tremors, yet still it unnerved everyone in the building.

Isaiah and Axis met with StarDrifter, Georgdi and Insharah in the command chamber. None of them sat. None wanted to sit and feel the floor and chairs vibrate. Instead, they all remained on their feet, moving restlessly about the chamber, trying, uselessly, to escape the sensation felt through their feet.

"We need to do something!" StarDrifter said.

"What?" Axis said. "Send out the army? They'd be slaughtered as they issued down the causeway, and Maximilian does not want to risk a transference. Should we rain arrows down on the Lealfast? We tried that, and look what happened. Send in the Strike Force? Oh wait, the Strike Force is useless."

"Axis . . ." Georgdi murmured.

"Well, *you* tell me what we can do!" Axis shouted, frustrated beyond measure. Oh stars, to be on horseback and riding the plains, not stuck in this tower of death!

"How long will it take?" Insharah said to Isaiah, and it took Isaiah a moment to realise what he meant.

"To destroy Elcho Falling?" he said. "Not in a day, nor in several days. But a week or more of this . . . and, I wager, with an escalation as that week progresses? Any building will have cracked and fallen to its destruction by then. With Elcho Falling, I just don't know."

"We need to inform Maximilian about this," StarDrifter said.

"Maxel will be well enough aware of it," Axis said. "He knows. He and Ishbel have their own concerns. *We* need to deal with this."

He turned to Isaiah. "Isaiah . . . we can discuss trying to physically stop the Lealfast. Would a counter-rhythm help? The danger is that a regular, rhythmic beat will shudder Elcho Falling apart . . . but what if it was arrhythmic? Can we turn it from a regular beat to a discordant one?"

Isaiah stared at Axis. "By the gods, Axis, you may have some—"

He was interrupted by StarHeaven, who was in such a rush she almost stumbled in the door.

"Isaiah, Axis," she said. "Come see. Now . . . please."

They hurried out of the chamber after StarHeaven. She led them down two flights of stairs, then into a chamber that backed onto the external wall of Elcho Falling.

"Look," StarHeaven said, pointing at a spot on a wall clear of any furniture.

There was a dark splotch on the wall from where lines of fracture radiated outward.

With every succeeding tremor, so the fracture lines spread a little further.

Axis stared, then hurried to a nearby window, hanging out to inspect the exterior wall.

"They've gone right through," he said. The outer wall was sheer water here, but the fracture lines manifested themselves as bloodied lines in the water.

"It is one of Ravenna's 'eggs'," Isaiah said. "Georgdi,

Insharah—organise your men. I want an inspection of every wall in this citadel."

As they hurried away, Isaiah turned to Axis. "Are you certain Maximilian wants Ravenna kept alive?" Isaiah said. "Because if I had the option of laying my hands on her right now, I would tear the traitorous bitch from limb to limb."

Three hours later Isaiah and Axis had the results of Georgdi's and Insharah's search.

There were almost one hundred and fifty "eggs" embedded in the walls, all in the lower third of the citadel where the walls of water merged into the walls of crystal, and all were breeding fracture lines.

The Lealfast continued their slow, rhythmic circling of Elcho Falling until dusk when, the moment Eleanon stopped beating his hands, they too stopped, broke out of their lines, and walked wearily back to their camps for a good evening meal and a night's rest.

CHAPTER TWELVE

Elcho Falling

Maximilian and Ishbel sat sifting through the floor by floor plans of the Twisted Tower. They had stayed up all night, save for two brief rests, and were now exhausted, but they had only five more levels to go.

Maximilian reached down a hand to lift up one of the diagrams, then swore softly as a vibration sent it skittering just beyond finger reach.

The Lealfast had started the second day of their encircling rhythmic march not an hour ago.

Ishbel looked at him. Her eyes were hollow and ringed with fatigue, her skin drawn and grey. Maximilian lifted the hand he'd tried to use to pick up a diagram and cupped her face.

"We are almost done," he said.

"Maxel . . . the Lealfast are going to dismember Elcho Falling if we don't find a way to break the power of the Dark Spire."

"I know. Ishbel, be still. We will finish these last five levels and then we will rest."

"But—"

"We will rest, Ishbel. Elcho Falling will not fall today."

Ishbel pressed her cheek against his hand briefly. "We have reconstructed the objects in eighty-five levels of the Twisted Tower, Maxel. There is nothing yet to help us against the Dark Spire *or* the One. What hope we find something on the final five levels?"

"Ishbel—"

"The Dark Spire is nothing our forebears could have anticipated, Maxel. We are going to find nothing. We have spent useless days here making lists, and for what? For what?"

"Ishbel . . ."

She rose, walking away. "There is nothing we can do. Nothing at all."

Maximilian watched her walk away. There *was* one last thing they could do before they had to turn their minds to what StarDancer suggested. "Ishbel?"

She had halted by a chest. Now she turned slowly to look back at Maximilian.

"There is one person who has successfully countered the power of Infinity," Maximilian said.

Ishbel frowned briefly, then her face cleared. "Boaz," she said, naming her ancestor. "But he encountered nothing like the power of the One."

"Nonetheless . . ."

"Nonetheless, it is worth a try."

CHAPTER THIRTEEN

Elcho Falling

"Starprifter and I have spent half the night talking," Axis said to Isaiah as they hurried down the stairs toward the chambers that contained the Dark Spire.

"We are sure," StarDrifter said, two steps behind Axis and Isaiah, "that we can create discord with music. And bells."

"Bells?" Isaiah said, turning just enough to shoot a quizzical look StarDrifter's way.

"Bells," said StarDrifter. "I sent out the Icarii early this morning, to the storerooms. We found a case of brass bells, all different sizes. Perfect."

Isaiah gave a grunt. "Elcho Falling always provides. So . . . you think you can sing our way out of this?"

"It is a possibility," Axis said. "All Enchanters have perfect pitch, StarDrifter the best among all of us. And we think we've figured out the tune and the rhythm that will counteract what the Lealfast do. You'll need your earmuffs, though. It won't sound good."

"Eleanon won't be able to reflect it back at us?" Isaiah said. They had reached the first of the chambers where the Dark Spire had broken through, and they stopped to talk.

"We don't think so," Axis said. "This is not something we're sending 'outside' of Elcho Falling."

"Besides," said StarDrifter, "what could be the worse thing to happen? A cacophony of discordant noise reverberating through Elcho Falling?"

Isaiah wondered that, if combined with the vibrations the Lealfast were sending throughout Elcho Falling, such a cacophony just might be the death knell for the citadel. The previous day's fracture lines had remained open, although masons had worked frantically overnight to close them with mortar. It had made no difference as the cement remained in place only an hour or two before crumbling and falling out of the cracks.

"There is the One to consider, too," Isaiah said. "Do you really want to initiate a possible confrontation with him?"

"We need to risk it," StarDrifter said. "Come, we have all the Enchanters in Elcho Falling waiting in the chamber below. The sooner we start . . ."

He was gone, Axis after him, and Isaiah stood a moment longer, thinking, frowning.

Isaiah hesitated another heartbeat, before he ran lightly down the stairs after them. "Axis," he said, taking the man by the elbow just as he was sinking into the group of thirty or so enchanters gathered to one side of the Dark spire. "Axis, I'm not risking you here. Go further up into the citadel, I—"

"Why?" Axis said.

"Because every single damned Enchanter left in existence is now gathered in this chamber. If anything goes wrong . . . even if Eleanon does nothing, the One may act . . ."

StarDrifter nodded. "Go, Axis." Then he looked at Isaiah. "You are wrong, in that Salome and StarDancer are not here. But I take your point. It is better we do not risk Axis as well."

"Thank you, StarDrifter," Isaiah said. "Axis . . . go." He waited until Axis had, reluctantly, climbed the stairs, then Isaiah looked about the group of Enchanters. "Good luck be with you."

Then Isaiah, too, was gone.

StarDrifter looked about the group. "Remember what we discussed."

Everyone nodded back to him.

"*Feel* the rhythm of the vibrations," StarDrifter said.

Many of the Enchanters closed their eyes, merging with the beat of the Lealfast feet.

"Now take that beat," StarDrifter said, very softly, "and destroy it."

As one they drew in a deep breath, held it, and began to sing. At first their voices were beautiful, merging perfectly

with the vibrations sent through Elcho Falling by the encircling marching Lealfast. Some voices were soft, others
strong, but together they merged to form a beautiful melody
that soared from the lower chamber up the stairs and far up
into Elcho Falling.

High above, Isaiah and Axis paused, listening.

Then the song changed, becoming ever more discordant.
It was as if the Enchanters had captured the Lealfast rhythm
and then warped it to their own wants. As they changed the
song, so now some among the Enchanters took up their bells,
and began to ring out terrible, discordant chords.

"It sounds," Axis murmured to Isaiah, "a little like the
Dark Music of the stars."

"What—" Isaiah began, then groaned, bending over
slightly as he put his hands to his ears.

Axis ignored the discordant noise as best he could, bending down and putting his hand to the floor.

The vibrations were now out of time, moving all over the
place.

Soldiers walking over a bridge, not marching.

Eleanon stood on his rise as he had the day before, his
hands clapping slowly, relentlessly, as the Lealfast Nation
marched to his beat about Elcho Falling's lake in concentric circles.

He looked toward Elcho Falling, and his eyes glittered as
he realised what the Enchanters were trying to do.

"Don't," he whispered as if the Enchanters could hear
him, and as he whispered, every Lealfast lifted his or her
head and screamed, a high-pitched terrible sound that shot
across the lake.

The Dark Spire shrieked, taking the screams of the Lealfast
and magnifying them a hundredfold. Virtually imprisoned
within the chamber, the frightful sound had the force of an
explosion, lifting the Icarii Enchanters from where they sat
and dashing them against the walls.

The Dark Spire held that shriek for thirty long, terrible
heartbeats.

When it stopped, nothing within the chamber moved.
Save the faint, rhythmic vibrations across every surface.

The One chuckled deep within the Dark Spire. He had only
to wait for his opportunity; Eleanon was doing all the work
for him.

Given the Lord of Elcho Falling's ineptitude thus far, and
that of all his commanders, the One knew he would find the
final challenge laughably easy.

There was nothing anyone could do to stop him now.

Axis almost fell down the stairs in the rush to reach the
chamber. His ears rang with the terrible shriek, almost as if
it still sounded, and he stumbled over and over, his muscles
trembling both with the after-effects of the shriek and with
fear.

When he reached the chamber, Isaiah and a dozen others
behind him, Axis stopped, appalled.

Enchanters lay scattered and broken in piles of blood and
feathers.

Axis forced himself to step into the carnage. He bent
time and time again, only to find that the Enchanter whose
name he called softly was dead.

Then he rolled one over, and found him still breathing.

"Get Garth and Zeboath!" Axis yelled. "Quick!"

"Axis," Isaiah said, rising from the body of one of the
Enchanters and Axis' heart almost stopped at the expression
in Isaiah's face.

Axis forced himself over to the Enchanter Isaiah stood
over.

It was his father, StarDrifter.

"He still breathes, Axis," Isaiah said. "Just."

CHAPTER FOURTEEN

Elcho Falling

Inardle sat in the grass about a half day's walk from Elcho Falling. She could clearly see it in the distance and could just pick out the circles of the Lealfast Nation around the lake.

She had no idea what Eleanon was doing, but she did know he was making it extremely difficult for her to return to the citadel.

Any one of those Lealfast would spot her, even in her River Angel form, if she tried to access the lake.

Inardle could have tried to reach Axis with her mind voice, but she was afraid Eleanon would pick up the communication.

Eleanon was too attuned to Inardle for Inardle's own safety.

So Inardle sat there, chin resting on her arms wrapped about her knees. Chewing her lip, wondering.

Just after noon, she saw a shepherd and his flock of sheep passing in the near distance.

Nine of the Enchanters had died. The others were injured to some extent, but Garth expected them all to survive.

He drew Axis back from StarDrifter's bed, where an anxious Salome hovered, and spoke with Axis quietly.

"His eardrums have been damaged and also his eyes. Not permanent in either case, but your father is going to need rest and quiet for some time. As do the other Enchanters."

Axis nodded his thanks, appreciating Garth's aid and words. Then he turned away, leaving the chamber. He was furiously angry. Partly at circumstance, but mostly at himself for having suggested this catastrophic plan.

Damn it! Was there no action they could take against Eleanon? Everything he or Isaiah tried was thrown back in their faces with deadly, contemptuous ease.

Axis paused outside his father's door, then slowly climbed the stairs toward the command chamber.

All about him Elcho Falling vibrated and cracked.

Axis thought about asking Maximilian one more time about the transference idea.

Eleanon stopped the beating of his hands before dusk and, as they had the previous day, the Lealfast filed back to their individual camps for the night. Eleanon was himself about to return to his tent when he saw, to the west, a shepherd driving his small flock of sheep toward the lake.

Eleanon frowned, for there were few passers-by at Elcho Falling, and he moved to intercept the man.

He was clearly frightened and fell to his knees before Eleanon.

"Please, my lord," the man said, "my sheep need to water and I saw this lake . . ."

Eleanon regarded him, trying to scry out any deception, but all he felt was sheer fright from the man.

Ah, he was but a common shepherd, and when Eleanon was Lord of Elcho Falling, he would be a generous lord.

"You may water your flock," Eleanon said, "but be quick about the business." As soon as he had finished speaking Eleanon turned away as another Lealfast called him urgently.

The shepherd stammered his thanks, immensely grateful that Eleanon was distracted and moving off. He rose to his feet, clicking his tongue at the sheep who followed him obediently.

The shepherd moved his flock to a spot halfway between two of the Lealfast camps, and the sheep lined the shore, some falling to their knees in order to drink. The shepherd unclipped the drinking flask he had at his belt, unstoppered it, and leaned down to the water.

Inardle flowed out of the flask and into the water, silently thanking the shepherd—who was truly nothing like the stammering fool he'd appeared to Eleanon, but rather a courageous Outlander keen to aid Georgdi and the Lord of Elcho Falling.

She moved swiftly, anxious to escape any detection, sliding through the calm waters about the southern walls of Elcho Falling. Her way was clear for the moment, but Inardle wondered how long it would remain that way: the black roots of the Dark Spire now filled almost the entire lower half of the lake, lying there coiled and waiting.

Inardle reached the entrance to the tunnel and moved up it, only to find that partway through, her progress was hindered by debris.

Nonetheless, there were tiny spaces between the rocks and masonry that had fallen when the Dark Spire had pushed its way through this chamber in its journey upward, and Inardle managed to find her way through.

When she emerged into what was left of the chamber that had held the pool, it was to find the space almost filled with the bulk of the Dark Spire.

Inardle stood still a moment, once more in her Lealfast form, pressed against the wall, the spire not an arm's length distance from her.

The spire was looking more and more like Elcho Falling, with clearly defined windows and doors, and many balconies and turrets.

Axis sensed Inardle the instant she'd moved past the Dark Spire. He was in the command chamber with Isaiah and Maximilian—Maximilian had been telling them how he and Ishbel meant to untether the Twisted Tower—when he jumped up from his seat.

"Inardle is back," he said, then he was out the chamber and running down the stairs to meet her.

"You're back," he said.

She grinned. "Obviously."

"What news?"

"Not much . . . but I need to tell it. Is Maximilian . . . ?"

"In the command chamber. Come."

They started to climb, Inardle looking about. "Axis? What

has been happening? Elcho Falling looks as though a rampaging army has been through it. And what has Eleanon been doing outside?"

Axis sighed, and told her all the dire happenings since she'd been gone.

It was a heavy weight of bad news for someone who had only been gone a relatively short while.

"I hope your news is better," Axis finished up, opening the door into the command chamber for her.

Inardle didn't reply.

She walked into the chamber, greeting Isaiah and Maximilian, shocked at how tired they all looked. She'd thought Axis had looked terrible, but Maximilian particularly looked as though he'd spent the past few days fighting demons.

"The Skraelings?" Isaiah said as they all seated themselves.

"They are not far south of here," Inardle said. "Isaiah, they are becoming beautiful. I can describe it no other way. They are losing their vile, frightful appearance and they are becoming beautiful."

She paused. "And thoughtful."

Isaiah gave a small smile. "That is good news. It means they are moving in the right direction mentally. Did they tell you what decision they are likely to make?"

"They knew I had changed into River Angel form. They questioned me closely. They wanted to know if I had murdered as a River Angel."

"Ah," Isaiah said, knowing that she had.

"I explained to them *why*," Inardle said, "that it was justified, but they were deeply unhappy. Disappointed in me, and even themselves, so it seemed."

"And then?" Isaiah said.

Inardle shrugged. "Then they just vanished. I did not see them again."

"What do you think is happening, Isaiah?" Maximilian asked.

"They're already changing," Isaiah said. "The process

has begun. They need to drown themselves to completely change back to River Angels, but they're on their way."

"Which means . . ." Axis said.

"Which means they will be driven to come here," Isaiah said.

"But they seemed so disappointed in me," Inardle said.

"As they were," said Isaiah. "You had killed, and that saddened them. But think . . . these were once Skraelings, but are now creatures who are disappointed at one who kills. That gives me hope."

Isaiah paused, the fingers of one hand tapping away at the table. "If you want a prediction, then here it is. The Skraelings will come to Elcho Falling's lake. They will dive in and drown and complete their transformation. They will be driven to it. Whatever discussion they've been having over the past weeks has altered their mentality so greatly the change is now inevitable. But what will they do as River Angels? I am hopeful that what they will become will be a different incarnation of what once was. They hated that Inardle had killed as a River Angel. I suggest that they will not lift a finger to harm anyone when they become River Angels."

Maximilian smiled. "Then that's good news."

"Not quite," Isaiah said. "It means they will not lift a single finger to aid you against the Lealfast. They will not touch them."

There was silence about the table, and Inardle realised that the three men had somehow, perhaps even unconsciously, been pinning their hopes on the Skraelings. It was a strange world indeed, she thought, when men such as these were frustrated that the Skraelings would not ally with them.

"Maximilian," Inardle said, "you can do nothing about the Lealfast, or the Dark Spire?"

"No," Maximilian said, without looking at Axis, who was trying to catch his eye. "Ishbel and I have spent sleepless nights—thus our somewhat bedraggled appearance—trying to remember what we could of the contents of the Twisted Tower, in case there was any hope there . . . but no hope and little memory. The Twisted Tower must be drifting farther and farther from this world, and with it goes all its knowledge."

"Then we need to discuss StarDancer's—" Axis began.

"No," Maximilian said. "There is one further thing Ishbel and I can do."

Before Axis could press him for more information, Georgdi came into the room. "The Lealfast are winding up for the day," he said.

"I wonder what tomorrow will bring," Ishbel said quietly into the thoughtful silence.

Maximilian stood, Ishbel with him. Axis rose as well, wanting to speak with Maximilian, but he and Ishbel were gone before Axis had the chance.

In the cold depths of the night, Ishbel and Maximilian ventured to the edge of the Otherworld.

There, waiting for them according to the call Maximilian had sent out earlier in the night, stood Boaz.

"You face a dilemma," Boaz said. "Infinity has moved close to your world."

"The One, yes," Maximilian said. "Boaz, we need to ask how you managed to trap the demon Nzame when he waited in Threshold, and to drag him into Infinity. I—"

"Want to do the same with the One?" Boaz said, his face incredulous. "You can't."

"We *must* be able to do it," Ishbel said. "I, as your descendant, or Maximilian as Lord of Elcho Falling."

Boaz gave a slow shake of his head, holding both Ishbel's and Maximilian's eyes. "What I did to trap Nzame," he said, "was to use the power of the One which I commanded as a Magus, and then drag Nzame through to Infinity."

"And then you escaped," Ishbel said.

"And then I escaped by transporting myself to the very edges of the Otherworld—which at that time I called the Place Beyond—where I lingered until my wife Tirzah could pull me into the world of the living. Ishbel, Maxel, you cannot do this with the One."

"But why not?" Ishbel cried.

"Because I used the power of the One to do it," Boaz said. "Neither of you command that power and even if you did you cannot use it against the One himself. He would toss it back in your faces as a useless and broken thing. The One is infinitely more powerful than Nzame. The One *is* Infinity. I could not touch him. Neither can you."

Ishbel and Maximilian shared a look.

"StarDancer has given you the only plan that can possibly work," Boaz said softly. "I am sorry."

"You would see the end of the Lords of Elcho Falling?" Ishbel said.

"I would prefer to see that than see the One step through the Infinity Gate into the world of the living and decimate it. No one could stand against him. No one. There is only going to be a moment when he can be trapped, and Ravenna is the one to do it."

"The Land of Nightmares will hold him?" Maximilian said.

Boaz gave a nod. "It will hold him."

Maximilian looked at Ishbel, and saw his own desperation reflected in her expression.

They sat in their chamber atop Elcho Falling, not speaking, communicating only through their silence and shared concern.

"How can we trust Ravenna?" Ishbel said finally. "*How?*"

"You can almost certainly trust her in this," said a strange voice, and both Maxel and Ishbel sat up, swivelling toward the sound.

A tall well-built man stood a few paces away. He smiled and walked to stand before their chairs. Thick cobalt hair fell down over his brow, and his eyes sparked with blue fire amid fine, almost ethereally beautiful, features.

"My Lord of Dreams!" Maximilian said, rising to his feet, Ishbel only a moment behind him.

"Drava, please," the Lord of Dreams said. He gestured to Maximilian and Ishbel to sit again, before he took a chair opposite them.

"You think you have a terrible choice before you," Drava

continued, "but in reality it is an easy one. Ravenna, via StarDancer, offers you a good solution to your dilemma."

Ishbel wanted to say something, but she didn't know the Lord of Dreams, so left it to Maximilian to lead the conversation.

"You think we *can* trust her?" Maximilian said.

"Yes," Drava said. "She has learned well from the ruin of her ambitions, and her learning has sickened her. She will not prove disloyal again."

"I can hardly believe that," Ishbel said, forgetting her decision to leave the conversation to Maximilian.

"You are jealous of her—" Drava began.

"Jealous?" Ishbel said. "She murdered Maximilian— only *my* magic returned him from the gates of death!—and sought to destroy his authority as Lord of Elcho Falling so that she might have it for herself! She has led armies against Elcho Falling, she claimed *I* would be the citadel's doom, and—"

Drava waved a hand dismissively. "All that is behind her. Ravenna yearns for her mother Venetia and her little hut on the edge of the marshes in Escator."

"She will never have either of those again," Maximilian said.

"No, she will not," Drava said, "but she also seeks redemption. She is sick of betrayal. She will not betray you again."

Ishbel's mouth tightened and she looked away from Drava, unwilling to concede the possibility.

"I need to talk through the problems," Maximilian said, and Drava gave a small nod.

"Ishbel's ancestor said that the Land of Nightmares will hold the One," Maximilian continued. "I need your reassurance on this point."

"It will hold him," Drava said. "It could contain all of roiling Infinity and not weaken."

"If we agree to this plan," Ishbel said, "then Ravenna will carry the Lord of Elcho Falling in her belly into the Land of Nightmares. What will that do to the baby?"

"It will corrupt him beyond knowing," Drava said.

"Then my next question," Ishbel said, "is . . . what will happen if this corrupted Lord of Elcho Falling ever escapes from the Land of Nightmares?"

"As the One cannot escape, then neither will the Lord of Elcho Falling," Drava said.

"Are you *certain*?" Maximilian said.

"Totally."

"But *Ravenna* can come and go?" Maximilian said.

"Once she has trapped her son and the One in the Land of Nightmares, she will retain that ability," Drava said, "but I do not think she will do so. She will stay there. She knows what she risks if she tries to leave—that either her son or the One will travel on her coat tails."

Ishbel sat back in her chair, sighing and rubbing at her brow. "Again it comes back to trust in Ravenna."

"What choice do you have?" Drava said. "The Dark Spire grows and the One sits within, waiting to emerge. No one in this world has the power to contain him. You have heard the consequences of allowing the spire to reach maturity— would your distrust and jealousy of Ravenna truly mean you'd allow the One to oversee the destruction of this world? Or is this only about maintaining your own power?"

Maximilian winced at the brutal question. "No." He glanced at Ishbel, and saw resignation and acceptance in her eyes.

"Drava," Ishbel said quietly, "we really need to know we can trust Ravenna."

"Trust her," Drava said. "You could not up to a month ago, but you can now. She has completed her own journey over this past year."

They sat in silence for several minutes, Maximilian and Ishbel both coming to terms with what they must do, before Ishbel spoke again.

"What will happen to this citadel," she said, "if its lord remains trapped in the Land of Nightmares?"

"It will continue," Maximilian said, "its magic intact, but largely untouchable by anyone. It will wait, wondering if one day its Lord might return."

Something in Ishbel's face relaxed then, as if knowing the citadel would remain in its beauty and power gave her consolation.

"And us?" she asked quietly.

Maximilian gave her a small smile. "Our decision, sweetheart. Whatever we want to do. Stay here, without our powers, or—"

"Wait," Ishbel said. "I control powers as the Lady of Elcho Falling, largely in my own right through blood and training. What happens to these if Ravenna traps her son as Lord of Elcho Falling and the One in the Land of Nightmares?"

"I don't know," Maximilian said. "The possibility is that you might retain them. I don't know. We will have to see."

Ishbel nodded, and Maximilian could see that she had finally accepted the necessity of StarDancer's plan. Ravenna would get her powers back and be trusted to trap the One.

"It will not be long now," Maximilian said quietly.

Ravenna sat in her chamber. She had only been here a matter of days, but to her it felt like decades.

She hated being confined.

Suddenly a tall, beautiful man with cobalt hair materialised before her, and Ravenna gasped as she recognised the Lord of Dreams. She rose, then bowed her head. "Drava."

They had been lovers a long, long time ago, before Ravenna thought to return to the mortal world in pursuit of her ambitions.

"I have been speaking with Maximilian," Drava said without preamble.

Ravenna raised her head, looking at him with barely concealed hope.

There was only one reason Drava and Maximilian would have been conversing.

"I told Maximilian you could be trusted," Drava said.

Ravenna drew in a deep breath, holding it. Her eyes gleamed in hope.

"He is going to accept StarDancer's plan," Drava finished.

Ravenna closed her eyes briefly, letting out her breath in a long, slow exhalation. "Thank you," she whispered.

"Ravenna," Drava said, and Ravenna looked at him again.

"Ravenna, I hope my trust in you has not been misplaced."

"No, my Lord. It has not. I will do this, if only to make amends for what I have done in the past."

"You *will* trap the One in the Land of Nightmares?"

"Yes."

"And you *can* do this?"

"Yes. Easily, once Ishbel removes her curses."

Drava studied her. He had taken a gigantic risk in recommending Ravenna to Maximilian, and he needed to be very sure. "You will need to stay within the Land of Nightmares, Ravenna. You cannot leave. To do so might mean that—"

"I know the implications, my lord. If I left I might leave the way open for either my son or the One to leave, too. I will stay there. My life and the life of my son is enough. We can manage within the Land of Nightmares." She set her face in a tremulous smile, reaching out a hand to rest lightly on Drava's arm. "Your trust in me is not misplaced. I will do this for Maximilian, and I will do it for my mother, Venetia, whom I murdered."

Drava's face relaxed. He laid his hand over hers, then he smiled and allowed his hand to fall away. "Thank you, Ravenna."

Ravenna sat motionless for a long time after Drava had gone. She could barely believe that Maximilian had decided to trust her, or that Ishbel would remove her hateful curses.

She would have her power as a marsh witch returned.

Her son—Ravenna rested a hand on her belly—would have his rights as Maximilian's heir restored and, once Ishbel stripped Maximilian of his power, would *become* the Lord of Elcho Falling.

From horror and despair . . . to this. Ravenna drew in a deep breath, closing her eyes. She had thought her son would have nothing, but instead he would have everything.

Albeit trapped in the Land of Nightmares with the One.

"But even that . . ." she whispered. "Even that . . ." Her hand patted her belly, where her son now grew healthy with the good food provided Ravenna over these past days.

Surely he would not need to stay forever.

Not when Elcho Falling waited for its lord.

CHAPTER FIFTEEN

Elcho Falling

As they had previously, the Lealfast assembled into their circles in the hour after dawn, Eleanon moving to his usual spot on the small hill a little distance to the north.

And, as usual, Maximilian, Isaiah and Axis stood on the balcony of the command chamber, watching the Lealfast file into their circles.

Georgdi had just joined them, and now Maximilian addressed him.

"Report?"

"Most of the cracks have widened and spread overnight," Georgdi said. "Maxel, within a few hours, if they continue at this rate, the cracks from all the different sites will join up and encircle Elcho Falling. When that happens the citadel will not survive for long."

He stopped, waiting for Maximilian to respond, but Maximilian said nothing, continuing to regard Georgdi with bleak eyes.

"The Dark Spire burst through three more levels overnight," Georgdi continued, knowing this, at least, Maximilian must have suspected. The noise from the breaking masonry floors had reverberated throughout the entire citadel. "Its summit is now in the floor directly below the main ground level. By tomorrow . . ."

He didn't need to spell it out for them.

"Maxel," Axis said, "we must—"

"*Do* something?" Maximilian said. "Do you think I am holding something back just for the heck of it? Don't you think that if I'd had some magic solution I might not have used it already?"

He sighed, and apologised for his ill-temper. "I have been up all night—again—but it is no excuse as I know none of you have had much sleep, either." He paused. "Last night Ishbel and I talked, between ourselves and with Boaz, who once fought with the power of the One, and with Drava, Lord of Dreams. We have reached a decision. As neither Ishbel nor I can find any way of countering the power of the One ourselves, we have decided to accept StarDancer's plan. We will return Ravenna's power, and we will trust her to use it to drag the One through to the Land of Nightmares. It is all we can do, and we pray it will be enough."

Axis exchanged glances with Isaiah and Georgdi, then gave a nod. "Good. When will Ishbel remove her curses on Ravenna?"

"Today sometime, I think. We dare not hesitate any longer."

Axis gave another nod, relaxing within himself. *Better than good. Now he could concentrate entirely on the Lealfast and not worry about what happened at his back.*

"Excellent," said Isaiah. "Now all Axis and I need do is to stop the Lealfast while you, Ishbel and Ravenna work on trapping the One. You may be dealing with the power of Infinity, but I think Axis and I have almost as hard a task, for the Lealfast, if not capable of destroying this entire world, are certainly capable of razing a significant portion of it."

"Principally the portion we are standing on," Axis said. "Maxel, we are constrained by the fact we have hundreds of thousands of soldiers inside Elcho Falling and can't get them out. True, we'd face a savage battle with the Lealfast if we could get them out, but it would be something. Maxel, I ask again, are you certain we cannot use the transference method?"

Maximilian chewed on his lip, staring out at the Lealfast, and Axis sensed a weakening of his resolve. He prayed it would go the same way as his resolve not to trust Ravenna.

"Maxel, we *must* try," Axis continued. "Elcho Falling cannot take much more of this. Between them, the Lealfast and the Dark Spire will destroy the citadel within a day or two. I don't care that the odds are appalling. I don't care that I might die in the attempt. *We must try this, Maximilian.*"

"Axis is right," Isaiah said softly.

"You said that you and Ishbel could only transfer ten thousand," Axis continued, pushing his case. "Ten thousand is enough."

"Against a quarter of a million?" Maximilian said. "Against a race that can—"

"We are desperate," Axis said, "and we have nothing else."

"I will think about it," Maximilian said, and Axis hissed in frustration.

"How many of your plans for the defence of Elcho Falling have gone disastrously wrong in the past few days?" Maximilian snapped. "I will think this through, and you and Isaiah need to work out what every single possible implication might be. Wipe that look of impatience from your face, Axis. *If* I agree, then this one we do *my* way."

They stood silently on the balcony, watching. The Lealfast had formed themselves into their usual circles, and as Eleanon began his clapping (Axis wishing desperately for a single clear arrow shot), they began the same march they had employed for the past four days.

But, seven claps into the sequence, the entire mass of Lealfast suddenly raised their hands and clapped a single time, leaping a little into the air as they did so and landing down with a significant thump.

"Stars!" Axis said as he felt the balcony literally jump under his feet.

Another seven claps, another seven paces, and then again all the Lealfast leapt sightly into the air, clapped, and then thumped down.

Again the balcony shuddered, and this time something inside the command chamber toppled over and broke.

"Shetzah!" Isaiah said.

"Check those cracks," Maximilian said. "Now!"

Within an hour of the Lealfast beginning their new routine the additional tremors had extended the cracks from the many epicentres in the walls until Elcho Falling was completely ringed with cracks.

"They're extending right through the walls," Insharah said to Maximilian, who had come to one of the mid-level outer wall chambers to see for himself.

Maximilian crouched down and put his hand against the wall. One of the resounding Lealfast claps and thumps came from outside, and he felt the wall vibrate.

And shift. Only a tiny fraction, but it had shifted.

"Maxel . . ." Axis said, his voice tight.

"When?" Maximilian said.

"Tomorrow," Axis said. "I will need to spend some hours to handpick men and practise some manoeuvres." He didn't voice the thought that if only Maximilian had given permission earlier, they could have been ready to go right now.

Maximilian stood up. "Axis—"

He stopped as a gigantic shudder ripped through Elcho Falling, making everyone in the chamber reach for support.

"The Dark Spire," Axis said, but Maximilian was already out the door.

It had torn through the main ground level and up through the great staircase. Now its summit reared halfway to the next level.

The lower parts of the great staircase were all but ruined—several unlucky men lay injured on the floor by the sides of the spire, sent tumbling when it had pushed its way through the floor.

Georgdi was already there, organising ladders to be brought so they could bridge the gap between that part of the staircase that was still usable and the floor below.

Maximilian stared at the spire. He could feel the One inside, feel him throbbing in excitement and expectation, and knew then that they had a day, maybe less. He remembered the power that the One had sent seething down the path toward him from the Twisted Tower, and shuddered.

The One would not hesitate to destroy him the moment he had the chance.

Maximilian gave Axis a long, cool look. "Go then, organise your men and practise your manoeuvres, but I still want you and Isaiah to report to me at dusk with every single complication you can think of. *Every* conceivable complication, and then a hundred or so of the inconceivable ones. This is so dangerous, Axis, that it could as easily destroy us as aid us. I want this—"

"Thought through," Axis finished for him. "I understand. Maxel, I won't fail you."

"Meet me at dusk, Axis."

The One crouched underneath the tip of the spire, his hands splayed against the outer wall just above his head. He could see out, but his power shielded him from any prying eyes spotting him.

There stood the Lord of Elcho Falling, looking worried, and looking as if he were considering some plan.

What? the One thought. What could Maximilian throw at him now?

There was nothing. Infinity waited at the One's back, and it wanted Maximilian dead.

The One reached out his senses for an instant to Eleanon and the Lealfast.

Good. Eleanon intuited nothing about the One's presence. Eleanon would need to die as well—the One did not like the man's ambition—but as for the rest of the Lealfast . . . oh, they would be good and faithful servants to the One in the new world of destruction.

Dark winged warriors of death.

The One grinned.

"Ravenna?"

She rose from her chair at the sound of the unlocking door. "Maximilian," she said as he came into the chamber.

"Hello, Ravenna."

Ravenna clenched and unclenched her hands at her sides, wanting to look nervous and unsure. "You have come to a decision."

"Aye." Maximilian hesitated. "We have decided to trust you."

Ravenna gave a tight smile. "No doubt with much agonising."

"Yes. With much agonising."

"When?" she managed.

"Ishbel and I will come to you later tonight," Maximilian said. "Ishbel will remove the curses which bind you then."

"Thank you," Ravenna said, and Maximilian nodded, held her eyes for a long moment longer, then left the chamber.

Ravenna sat down, and smiled.

CHAPTER SIXTEEN

Elcho Falling

"Well?" Maximilian said. "Your thoughts?"

He and Ishbel sat once more in the command chamber, together with Isaiah, Axis, Inardle, Georgdi and Egalion. It was dusk, and the balcony doors had been closed against the cool evening air.

It was deceptively peaceful in the chamber. Outside, thousands of men scurried about the citadel, propping up and reinforcing walls with whatever they had.

Axis glanced at Isaiah, then addressed Maximilian. "Isaiah, Georgdi, Insharah and I have sat through the afternoon talking. We have addressed every possibility we can think of, and, while we believe we will lose men, we think the losses remain acceptable . . . so long as you can answer some questions we have about the procedure."

"Go on," Maximilian said.

"There are roughly a quarter of a million Lealfast outside," Axis said. "Only a fraction of that number are trained fighters, but they are *all* Enchanters and they have all been changed somewhat by their old alliance with the One. We are assuming they will be powerful opponents."

Maximilian nodded. *Good.*

"We, on the other hand," Isaiah said, taking over from Axis, "command many hundreds of thousands of trained soldiers within Elcho Falling. They're all good—Isembaardians, Outlanders, the Emerald Guard. I'd say we have roughly the same force as the Lealfast—and the fact that *all* our force are trained and experienced battlemen must put us on a par with the Lealfast."

Maximilian started to speak, but Axis interrupted whatever the Lord of Elcho Falling might have said.

"Whatever the Lealfast may brag about, Maxel, they've not had any extensive battle experience. Inardle?"

"No, they don't," Inardle said. "We did far more than 'shoot at rabbits' in the frozen wastes, and there were minor skirmishes here and there, but Axis is right. The men in this fortress have the fighting edge."

"But the Lealfast are a winged force," Maximilian put in. "And the Strike Force is effectively dead."

"For years I commanded the most powerful winged force in this world," Axis said, leaning forward, his eyes fierce, emphasising each word. "Do you think I don't know just how to bring one *down* from the sky?"

"The Lealfast command the power of Infinity," Maximilian said.

"Eleanon best of all," Inardle said, "but the others? I am not sure. Eleanon would have been jealous of that power. He may not have shared it beyond his immediate captains. Bingaleal was as powerful as Eleanon . . . but Georgdi killed Bingaleal easily enough."

"Surprise and cunning," Georgdi said, grinning. "Outlander specialities."

Maximilian had to laugh. "Point taken." Then he sobered. "But I cannot transfer hundreds of thousands outside for you. You *know* this. Even with Ishbel's aid I can only manage ten thousand."

"But it will be ten thousand of the absolute *best*," Axis said.

"If you use your ability to transfer these ten thousand," Isaiah said, "then we swap our men for Lealfast. We can transfer a fighting force beyond the walls of Elcho Falling, but it will also mean transferring Lealfast inside in counterbalance. Axis told me that you'd suggested one thousand Lealfast for ten thousand of our soldiers. Is this correct?"

Maximilian gave a nod.

Isaiah looked at Egalion. "A thousand is no problem," Egalion said. "The Emerald Guard will dispose of them efficiently enough."

"You are certain?" Maximilian asked.

"Can you pinpoint where they will transfer to?" Egalion asked.

"To within a chamber or two, yes," Maximilian said.

"Then we will be ready," Egalion said, and Maximilian accepted his words, for he remembered how the Emerald Guard had slaughtered so efficiently that night when the Lealfast had attacked within Elcho Falling.

"Is there any trauma associated with the transference?" Axis said.

"Not particularly," Maximilian replied. "Not if you are expecting it. So . . . presumably you would warn your men what to expect, which would be a moment or two of disorientation at the end of the transference. But the Lealfast may experience a little more disorientation, because they will *not* be expecting it."

Axis and Isaiah exchanged a glance and a shared grin.

"I think it has a chance of working, Maxel," Isaiah said. "The Emerald Guard can deal with a thousand Lealfast within this citadel. Axis, is ten thousand men enough?"

"It will do," Axis said. "Give me your best bowmen, Isaiah, and your most cunning Outlanders, Georgdi, and if I contribute one eagle and my own knowledge, then even a mere thousand is more than enough."

There was a momentary silence. No one believed him for an instant. Even ten thousand would more than likely be slaughtered.

But what else was there?

"Then we do it," Isaiah said, looking at Maximilian.

Maximilian held Isaiah's gaze a long moment, then nodded. "When?"

"Late morning tomorrow," Axis said. "I contacted my friend eagle an hour or two ago. He is far away but is returning. He will be here tomorrow morning. I need his eyes in the sky. So we will go tomorrow morning before noon. The Lealfast will be concentrating on their encircling dance . . . they won't know what's happening."

"And inside Elcho Falling?" Maxel said.

"I can position everyone within Elcho Falling early

morning," Isaiah said. "Egalion will marshal his men to where you say you can transfer the Lealfast, and, just in case the Lealfast don't materialise quite where we expect them, then every fighting man and woman left in Elcho Falling will be sitting ready with arrow fitted to bow."

"And the Dark Spire and the One?" Ishbel said, speaking for the first time.

"We have to risk it," Isaiah said, looking at Maximilian rather than her. "We *have* to."

Maximilian hesitated then gave a reluctant nod. "Tomorrow morning, then."

Isaiah, Georgdi and Axis spent several hours asking for volunteers from the best archers and soldiers in their combined forces, then Axis and Isaiah spent a further six hours organising the men into the vast central area of the citadel, which was the largest 'chamber' they could find to practice their manoeuvres as a single team.

First, Axis spent an hour getting the men to practise moving from a prone position straight into squads of fifty men which could instantly form a shield cover about themselves.

Then, once that was perfected (and this didn't take long, as the men were already so well trained) Axis organised the men who were not actively engaged in holding the shields, into individual pairings of one archer and one 'arrow keeper'. Axis wanted the archers to be able to fire as quickly as they could without having to scrabble for arrows from quivers on their backs, so the 'arrow keeper' part of the pair had to be able to slap an arrow into the hand of the archer smoothly, firmly and in the precisely correct manner—and the archer had to trust the arrow keeper to do just that.

This was not such a smooth procedure, and took two hours to sort out to Axis' satisfaction.

In the final few hours Axis had the men become accustomed to seeing through someone else's eyes . . . and trusting that vision.

They would not be seeing with their eyes tomorrow, but with the eagle's vision. The shield covers would be almost perfectly tight, save for tiny slits where the archers could fire their arrows.

Axis sent Isaiah to the top of the staircase and then, in the same manner as he did with the eagle, Axis allowed himself to see through Isaiah's eyes, looking down the staircase. Axis then had to twist the vision about, translating it to what a man on the ground would see, and it was this vision he shared with the bowmen.

This was difficult for both Axis and the bowmen. They had to shoot blind, or, at least, shoot their arrows by trusting implicitly in the vision that Axis gave them.

It was such trust that was the hardest thing to achieve, but in the hours before dawn, they finally managed it.

In the meantime, arrows had peppered the inside of the stairwell's ceiling, down the walls and into several sections of various squads' shield covers, but finally the arrows had shot well and truc.

They were ready, and Axis sent everyone off to grab a few hours sleep.

He met with Isaiah at the top of the staircase before he went to his own chamber.

"Ten thousand won't be enough, Axis," Isaiah said, very quietly. "Not really. You know it and I know it. You'll surprise the Lealfast initially, but they'll fight back instantly. And they'll fight back with Infinity."

"We have to do something, Isaiah," Axis said. "And I am willing to risk Infinity's wrath to do it. All these men know in their hearts what is at stake. They are all volunteers."

Isaiah nodded, rested his hand on Axis' shoulder briefly, then left him to his rest.

CHAPTER SEVENTEEN

Elcho Falling

A xis sat on the edge of StarDrifter's bed and looked at his father. StarDrifter was still very weak and his vision was poor, but at least he was alive and improving.

"What is happening?" StarDrifter said, his voice hoarse.

"Elcho Falling continues to crumble," Axis said, "but Maxel has agreed to my plan to attack the Lealfast. I am having men stationed in here later, just in case some Lealfast wanders in."

"The plan is shaky," Salome said.

"So is Elcho Falling," Axis said.

"And the One?" StarDrifter said.

"Maximilian and Ishbel have agreed to StarDancer's plan," Axis said, glancing across to the cot where his infant brother lay.

StarDancer was awake and lay smiling at Axis, and Axis could feel the boy's satisfaction emanating out in great waves.

He was already thinking of the day when he would be Enchanter-Talon.

"Good," said StarDrifter. "Good." Then he reached out a hand and fumbled for Axis'. "Be careful," he said.

"Being careful was never my great strength," Axis said. He rose from the bed. "The Lealfast are gathering. I must join Isaiah and Maxel." He gave his father's hand a squeeze, then kissed Salome's cheek. "Be well."

Maximilian and Ishbel hesitated before the locked door to Ravenna's chamber. Maximilian nodded at the guard to unlock it, then spoke to him. "You can leave the lady unguarded and unlocked from this point," he said.

Are you sure that is wise? Ishbel said in his mind, and Maximilian gave her a slight nod.

We must. We must trust her now.

Ishbel sighed and nodded herself, and then the door was open and Ravenna stood waiting for them within her chamber.

"This won't take long," Ishbel said, moving to stand by Ravenna.

Ravenna could feel the other woman's tenseness. Ishbel didn't want to be doing this.

Ishbel raised a hand to the top of Ravenna's head. "Turn about slowly," Ishbel said, and Ravenna complied, revolving on her feet.

As she moved about, so Ishbel began to twist her hands in a complex dance, occasionally moving them close to Ravenna to snatch at the thin air.

And Ravenna could feel the triple curses Ishbel had bound her with begin to unravel. It was if a constriction about her brow and her chest began very slowly to fade. Ravenna felt a sense of warmth and wholeness creep back into her being, as if she had been locked for a long, long time in a cold and barren place.

As she had, indeed.

Then, very suddenly, Ishbel made an abrupt movement with her hands and Ravenna felt, *smelt*, her connection with the marshes restored and power flood back into her being.

Almost instantly, certainly well before Ravenna could say or do anything, a goblet materialised in Ishbel's hands.

"I am sorry," Ishbel said, "but I need to be sure," and with that she dipped the fingers of one hand into the goblet, and she flicked dark, dank blood over Ravenna.

None of it stuck, and Ishbel and Maximilian shared a look.

"I will not betray you," Ravenna said quietly. "Not this

time." Within herself, she smiled. The blood test had not worked, because the betrayal, if such it could be called, had not yet been effected.

And might not. At least, not for decades. Ravenna knew she would need to watch for her and her son's chance with the utmost care. Then Ravenna looked to Maximilian. "But you still control your powers as Lord of Elcho Falling? You will need to—"

"Those he shall have until the last moment," Ishbel said. "*You* may think yourself trustworthy, witch, but *I* am leaving nothing to chance."

"But you may leave it too late!" Ravenna said. "What if the One emerges and Maximilian still controls his powers as—"

"Not yet," Ishbel said and, stiffening her entire body, she turned on her heel and left the chamber.

A moment later Maximilian followed her and Ravenna was left staring at the open door.

She rested a hand on her swollen belly.

"Soon," she whispered. "Soon."

The Lealfast assembled into their circles. Eleanon began his clapping. Today, as yesterday, after every seventh clap all the Lealfast clapped, leapt and thudded down. The small group on the balcony waited for something new, but there was nothing.

"Elcho Falling barely survived yesterday's attempts," Maximilian said. "I don't know if it will survive the day. Axis, where is this eagle of yours?"

"Still flying in," Axis said.

"Can you fight without him?" Isaiah said.

Thump and another shudder ran through Elcho Falling; somewhere in the distance the three men heard a slab of masonry fall into the lake.

Inardle, who had been inside the command chamber, came out to the balcony and peered over the railing.

"If I have to," Axis said.

"I'll ask Egalion to—" Isaiah began, then was halted by Inardle's cry.

"Look! Below, below!"

The three men peered over.

The lake's surface churned. For a moment none of them could make out what was happening. Axis looked briefly at the Lealfast to see if they'd reacted, but they were continuing their encircling march.

He looked below again, then reflexively reeled back from the railing as one of the Dark Spire's roots reared high into the sky, paused, then slammed into the wall of Elcho Falling about a quarter of the way up, burying its tip into the heart of one of the bloodied web of cracks.

As it pulled back, so a large piece of masonry materialised out of the water wall and fell into the water.

"There's another!" Inardle cried, pointing, and then suddenly, appallingly, hundreds of the roots were rearing out of the water, seeking cracks within the walls of Elcho Falling, burying themselves inside and tearing out large chunks of masonry.

"This is going to tear apart in an hour!" Inardle said, and Axis whipped about to Isaiah. "Fuck waiting for the eagle," he said. "We've got to go as soon as we can!"

"Are your men ready?" Isaiah said.

"They'll be ready within a heartbeat," Axis said. "All they have to do is to pick up their weapons. They're already assembled."

Isaiah looked at Maximilian, who gave a nod. "Go," he said. "Elcho Falling is not going to withstand this onslaught."

Axis and Isaiah turned as one, striding toward the door leading to the command chamber.

But in the instant before they reached it, Inardle cried out again, more urgently this time.

"No! No! Wait!"

They halted, turning to stare at her.

Inardle was back at the balcony railing, but this time she was staring wildly out at the countryside beyond the Lealfast circles.

"The Skraelings are here," she said. "I can't see them but I can feel them. I—"

"Look!" Maximilian said, pointing toward the hill on which Eleanon stood.

Eleanon, who had to this point kept perfect time with his hands, now faltered, looking about as if confused.

Then, in the next heartbeat, millions upon millions of Skraelings materialised out of nowhere, filling the landscape as far as the eye could see.

CHAPTER EIGHTEEN

Elcho Falling

One moment Eleanon was standing clapping rhythmically, grinning as he watched the roots of the Dark Spire begin to tear apart Elcho Falling, the next moment he was being jostled by scores of Skraelings, packed tightly together. It took Eleanon several heartbeats to overcome the sense of disorientation and shock, then another several to free his wings from the packed bodies and manage to lift into the air.

What was happening? What were all these . . . millions . . . of Skraelings doing here?

Eleanon could not believe it. Where had they come from? How had they materialised right within the midst of the Lealfast circles *without anyone realising?*

And what were they doing? Why did they look so different? Were they here as friend, or as foe?

Eleanon's mind buzzed with unanswerable questions and a growing sense of perplexity mixed with anger. He rose a further ten paces into the air.

He could see that the majority of Lealfast had managed to get airborne, although Eleanon wouldn't have been surprised if a few had managed to get themselves crushed underneath the sheer weight and volume of Skraeling feet. Stars, they were everywhere! *Everywhere!* Encircling the entire lake, packed tightly together, all facing toward the lake, forty, fifty, sixty deep.

Eleanon hovered, trying to recover his wits, trying not to allow his temper to scream forth and precipitate him into some unhappy action.

"What is happening?"

It was Falayal, hovering nearby.

"How the fuck am I supposed to know?" Eleanon said, then realised it was the wrong thing to say as he watched Falayal's face close over.

"I am about to find out," he amended, then flew away, searching among the Skraelings for some kind of leader.

"Gods," Maximilian muttered, hands on balcony railing, staring out at the scene.

"Maxel?" It was Ishbel, hurrying onto the balcony.

"Skraelings . . ." Maximilian said, extending a hand. "Everywhere."

"What are they going to do?" Ishbel said.

"Change back to River Angels," Isaiah said, "but whether or not that will help us, I do not know."

"They say they will not harm us," Inardle said, and everyone turned about to face her.

"You are speaking with them?" Maximilian asked.

"With Ozll, who speaks for all the Skraelings," Inardle said. She had a distracted look on her face, as if she found it difficult carrying on two conversations at once.

Axis opened his mouth to say something, but Maximilian waved him to silence. *Wait*, he mouthed.

"Ozll says they will not become who they once were," Inardle said. "He means, that while they will change back to River Angels, they will not be the River Angels of old. They will defend themselves, but they will never seek to harm or to murder without provocation. Ozll says they have sworn themselves to peace."

Inardle blinked, as if Ozll had stopped speaking and she now found the time to concentrate entirely on the conversation with those standing about her. "They will do nothing to aid us, I am afraid. They just want to change, to slip into the water and let death do to them what it wants, but after that . . . nothing. They will simply exist within the water. Whether Elcho Falling remains or falls, it is of no matter to them."

"Do they not know what Elcho Falling will become under Eleanon's guiding hand?" Ishbel cried. "Do they not understand that—"

"They understand," Inardle said. "They just do not care.

It is not their fight. It is not their matter. But they wish us well and they wish us happiness."

Axis turned away, muttering a curse. "We should never have trusted them, or thought them allies. I am not surprised that they should now seek to murder us through their inaction. Stars! They could slaughter the Lealfast within moments . . . *could* have done if they had acted immediately when they materialised. Why couldn't thcy have—"

"Axis," Maximilian murmured.

Inardle gave a little tilt of her shoulders. "I am sorry, Axis. If it wasn't for me . . . if I hadn't murdered . . . They were so distraught by what I had done in my River Angel form they swore a vow of peacefulness. They will not attack for any reason, save if they are attacked themselves. They will self-defend, but never do harm for others, however glorious the cause."

"They swore that vow just to see us dead," Axis hissed.

"You! *You!*" Eleanon drifted lower to the ground, toward a Skraeling who seemed to have a slight aura of command.

At least, there was the tiniest of spaces about him and those Skraelings closest seemed to defer to him.

Eleanon landed. "Your name?"

"Ozll," said the Skraeling. "Hello, Eleanon."

Eleanon was in no mood for the niceties of polite social interaction.

"Are you here to fight for the Lord of Elcho Falling?" he said, using his elbows to shove aside any Skracling who pressed too close.

"No," Ozll said.

"To fight for *me*?"

"No."

"Then what *are* you doing? The One is gone. There is no need to trail about looking for him. There's no reason for you to be here. Go. *Go!*"

"We won't take long," Ozll said. "Then we'll be out of your way."

Eleanon felt like striking out in his frustration. "You won't take long to do *what*?"

"Drown ourselves," Ozll said.

Then, before Eleanon could make any response other than an incredulous look, Ozll gave the most heart-rending moan that carried over the entire mass of Skraelings about Elcho Falling's lake.

Eleanon looked around, then at Ozll. "Drown yourselves? You want to *drown* yourselves? Then go right ahead. Would you like me to push you? Eh? Just do it, Ozll, *and get the fuck out of my way!*"

The world, he decided, had gone completely to madness.

They saw Eleanon lift away just after Ozll had moaned, and then, as Eleanon rose higher, the entire mass of Skraelings echoed Ozll's moan. It reverberated through Elcho Falling, causing more than a few pieces of masonry to fall into the lake, and making Inardle groan in sympathy.

"Gods, gods," she muttered, sinking into a squatting position on the floor of the balcony, her hands over her ears. "They are so sad!"

Everyone else only had eyes for the Skraelings. Immediately after that collective moan, the mass of Skraelings surged toward the water. As soon as the first of them entered the water, they began to scream, and then every single Skraeling was screaming, and all on the balcony and in the air and within Elcho Falling groaned and turned away from the horror.

"They are so scared!" Inardle said. "So terrified . . . can't you feel it? Can't you?"

Axis had reeled back against the outer wall of Elcho Falling. He had his hands against his ears and his face was contorted by the agony and fear he felt rising in great waves from the mass suicide below him. The Skraelings might have been terrified, but they were scrabbling over their comrades in order to reach water, wave after wave of them, rushing into death as fast as they could.

The lake began to seethe and bubble with their dying.

Eleanon hovered above the tangled, writhing mass of dying creatures, unable to believe what he was witnessing.

What had got into them?

And in the end, who cared? They'd all be dead soon enough and, apart from the stink of their decomposing bodies, they'd be no trouble to anyone ever again.

Eleanon could certainly do without them. They'd never been anything but a trouble.

He waved to Falayal. "Start to reassemble our fellows. This shouldn't take long, and then we can get back to the matter at hand."

Bodies of Skraelings sank deep into the lake. They wanted to float, but there was such a dense mass of dead and dying bodies above them that they were forced toward the bottom of the lake.

On the shores, the final few, desperate Skraelings had managed to trample over the corpses of their comrades and throw themselves into the lake.

Water began to fill their lungs.

Memories resurfaced. Memories of the water, and how it felt to be one with the water. How it had felt to dance through sun-dappled and storm-darkened rivers, and how it had felt to have the life-force of the water run through their entire beings.

How it felt to have the power of water in their hands and hearts and minds.

How it felt to sing with the water and to manipulate that song.

As they sank through death the Skraelings remembered, and as they remembered, so their corpses twitched and breathed in deeply of their element.

As they remembered, so they changed.

The watchers from Elcho Falling saw it first, but Eleanon was not far behind. One moment there was nothing but deep-packed Skraeling corpses extending far into and under the lake.

The next . . . the next there were rivers of light running through the water as one by one the Skraeling corpses metamorphosed.

Eleanon had alighted on the (now gratefully uncrowded) shores of the lake and stood, looking on with a frown.

What was happening now?

He took a step forward, then another, then more, until he was but three or four paces from the edge of the water.

The water was seething, but Eleanon could not quite make out what it was. It looked almost as if . . . as if . . .

Then, in one heart-stopping, shocking moment, a column of water reared up from the lake a pace or so away. It had eyes and features, although none of the features were clearly distinguishable, but Eleanon recognised it instantly.

It was what Inardle had turned herself into when she'd attacked Eleanon and his small group.

And Eleanon realised, as more and more columns reared up before plunging back under the surface of the water, that *all* the Skraelings had transformed themselves into these terrifying creatures, and that there were millions upon millions of these things in the water, and they would undoubtedly attack him as Inardle had once attacked.

With stunning, deadly force.

Ozll, or whatever he was now, had tricked him. He had only claimed to be peaceable so that Eleanon would grant the Skraelings free access to the lake.

No, they would attack, and they would do it within moments.

Eleanon panicked.

The One, watching, almost panicked himself. He realised what Eleanon was about to do, and knew that it would be the death of him if he were caught.

Damn it! Why hadn't he killed Eleanon a long time ago, when he'd had the chance? The man was incapable of responsible action!

The One had no choice now but to leave the comfort and safety of the Dark Spire. It was earlier than he'd planned, but needs must.

His hands pressed against the tip of the spire, bringing the full force of Infinity to bear on the structure.

He may as well make a grand entrance.

CHAPTER NINETEEN

Elcho Falling

E leanon stumbled backward, one small part of his mind
petrified that the water creatures would murder him as
Inardle had murdered his fellows, but the major part engaged in the one activity he was certain would save him and
the rest of the Lealfast.

He communicated with the Dark Spire, screaming at it,
demanding that it attack the creatures now within the lake
surrounding Elcho Falling.

Ozll might want to murder the Lealfast, but the Skraeling
had severely underestimated the power now at Eleanon's
disposal.

The Skraelings had always been stupid.

The River Angels frolicked in the water. They had been reborn
only a short while, but they felt that their life as the Skraelings
was so far behind them it was scarcely a distant memory.

The lake was deep and wide, and it contained the millions of River Angels easily, but even so, the River Angels
began to whisper among themselves about perhaps investigating some of the small streams that fed into the lake . . .
and if those streams might somewhere connect with larger
rivers . . .

Their reborn lives were filled only with happiness and
relief and hope, and that was all they desired.

Until something rose from the lake bed.

At first the River Angels ignored it, this dark-tentacled
creature that reached toward the sunlight, but then the tentacles began to snatch at the River Angels and squeeze them
and pain them.

Many of the River Angels so caught managed to slither free, but some did not, and they died crushed within tightening dark coils and then left to drift broken and lifeless in the lake's currents.

The reaction of the River Angels was instant and it was as if they acted as one entity. They were under attack for no other reason, it seemed, than that they existed and this dark creature wanted them dead. They had done nothing to provoke or warrant such an attack.

And so, they defended themselves.

Tens of thousands of them clung to each of the Dark Spire's roots. The roots cracked through the water, trying to dislodge the River Angels, but to no avail. The River Angels clung with tenacious purpose, running their strangely-shaped hands along the surface of the dark roots, further and further along, and everywhere those hands touched, so the dark root crumbled.

As the dark roots crumbled one by one, so the River Angels slithered further along, seeking as yet untouched parts of the roots to destroy.

"What is happening?" Maximilian said, leaning as far as he dared over the edge of the balcony. "What in the gods' names is happening?"

Below, the surface of the lake churned. The roots of the Dark Spire broke the surface, each covered with some sort of gelatinous substance. As those within Elcho Falling watched, it seemed that every time the roots broke the surface, they were just that little less . . . intact.

"Eleanon commanded the Dark Spire to attack the River Angels," Inardle said. "He panicked. He remembered the time I had attacked his group and thought the River Angels would thus attack the Lealfast."

Axis stared at her, then actually grinned. "He thought *what*? He had no idea that the River Angels were harmless?"

Inardle shook her head. "I don't think so. They must not have told him."

"*Maximilian!*"

Everyone turned. It was Ravenna, breathing heavily from her rush to reach Maximilian.

"The One is on the move," she said. "If you want this plan to succeed, Maximilian, then Ishbel needs to—"

She was interrupted by the arrival of Ishbel herself, who put a hand on Ravenna's shoulder.

"Get down to the spire," she said. "I will do what needs to be done while you run down the staircase. Go, Ravenna, *go!*"

Ravenna gave Ishbel one hard look, then turned and ran.

"Gods pray we can trust her," Ishbel muttered. She walked over to Maximilian and put her hands on his shoulders. "I am sorry this can't be done with more ceremony, my love."

Then her hands tightened on his shoulders, and her eyes narrowed in concentration.

Axis, watching, thought that Ishbel would weave some mighty spell, speak words of heavy portent and bleak enchantment. But all that he saw or heard was Maximilian's widened eyes, his staggering backward a step before catching his balance.

Tears welled in Ishbel's eyes and she caught Maximilian in a brief, tight embrace before she whipped about to Axis.

"Axis," she said, "I will need to be the one to transfer you and your men now and it comes with a condition. I am coming with you."

"Ishbel!" Maximilian and Axis said together, but Ishbel forestalled any further protest.

"*I must go with him!*" she said to Maximilian. "If you have any sense, Maxel, you'll damned well know why!"

The River Angels seethed along the roots, their determination only growing the more they destroyed. They understood now that these tentacles were only a small part of something much larger and darker, and it was this larger entity they now attacked.

They wanted to live their lives in peace in the water, and to achieve that, this jealous, hateful creature which had launched such an unprovoked attack upon them needed to be negated. So they seethed up the roots, millions of them, covering every available surface of every last one of the roots, and as they destroyed the roots, so they worked their way into the unprotected underbelly of the Dark Spire.

Ravenna came to a breathless halt, grabbing at a piece of broken handrail just before her momentum plummeted her into the space just above the tip of the Dark Spire.

The Dark Spire was slowly collapsing in on itself as if it were being destroyed from within. Its sides were deflating inward, and the very tip of the spire tilted to one side, as if it were losing whatever structural support was needed to keep it upright.

But that tip was also bulging and glowing ominously red, and Ravenna felt a pang of true dread.

The One.

For a moment she considered running, but then she forced herself to tighten her hands on the handrail and to summon forth every last piece of power she commanded as a marsh witch.

It was almost time. The baby within her now throbbed with the power of Elcho Falling.

Ravenna closed her eyes briefly, visualising the paths into the Land of Nightmares, then she opened them again, concentrating on the very tip of the collapsing spire.

It was now seething with dark shadows.

The One was not far distant.

What is happening, friend Axis?

Axis' head whipped up. *I am about to need you very badly, friend eagle. Are you ready?*

I am, Axis.

Axis lowered his eyes. "Ishbel, I need to move now. And I hope you can look after yourself, because I cannot spare a single man."

"I will not need your help, Axis." Ishbel and Maximilian exchanged a brief glance, sharing in that glance all they needed to say, then Ishbel turned back to Axis and placed a hand on his shoulder.

"It is time for us to move."

CHAPTER TWENTY

Elcho Falling

Axis bounded up several flights of stairs, moving through the massive gathering of fighting men.

Ishbel followed close behind, her movements sure and certain.

"We go in a few minutes," Axis shouted, the shout being taken up and passed further and further up the stairwell. "Prepare! Prepare!"

He ran up two more flights of stairs. "Egalion?"

Egalion shouldered his way through the packed soldiers. "The Emerald Guard stand ready, StarMan." He gave Ishbel, standing a few paces behind Axis, a curious glance but Axis ignored it.

"Ishbel will transfer a thousand Lealfast into the Common Room. Are you—"

"Ready? *Yes*, StarMan."

Axis gripped Egalion's shoulder. "Good."

"What are the Lealfast doing now?" It was Ishbel, coming to stand at Axis' shoulder.

Axis closed his eyes a moment, communing with the eagle. "They are still around the lake, still somewhat scattered and confused, but Eleanon is organising them. We have to go soon, Maxel."

"I need to see, too," said Ishbel. "I need to know where we need to go."

Egalion gave Ishbel a startled look at the "we".

"Then watch," Axis said, and Ishbel's mind was filled with a vision of the outside.

She saw with the eagle's eyes, high above Elcho Falling. There was the citadel, great gaping holes in its walls, and she saw the lake, its surface still churning somewhat with the activity of the River Angels deep below; she saw the Lealfast, now clearly gathering into their twelve groups.

I have no idea what Eleanon hopes to do from this point, Axis said into Ishbel's mind. *But I do not wish to give him the chance to execute it. I need to strike now.*

Where do you wish to go? Ishbel asked Axis.

There, and there, and there, and there, Axis said, showing Ishbel four points that would give his troops best advantage.

You need the Lealfast in the air, Ishbel said.

Once they know we're there, they'll take to the wing instinctively, Axis said. *Any winged race would do so.*

The vision faded.

"You are ready now?" Ishbel said.

"A moment," Axis said. "Egalion—"

But Egalion had already gone to join his men in the common room.

"Let me just share this vision with the men," Axis said. "They need to know where we go and how I wish to deploy them."

Ishbel waited, watching the faces of the men glaze slightly as vision filled their minds, then watched them nod, just slightly, as they responded to something that Axis said. Ishbel felt the first real frisson of hope that she'd felt in many, many months.

Maybe, maybe, *if* Ravenna could be trusted, then this would be the final act.

Axis reopened his eyes.

"Now," he said, and Ishbel drew on all her power as Lady of Elcho Falling, and did as Axis asked.

Axis felt as though a giant had squeezed his midriff and forcibly expelled all the air from his lungs. He had no sensation of moving, or of being transported. He just suddenly found himself face down in the dirt by the lakeside of Elcho Falling, heaving breath into his lungs.

He rolled over, forcing himself to move, desperate to get his men positioned before the Lealfast could do much more than rise into the air in panic. He rose to his knees and was

relieved beyond measure to see all the men rising and forming themselves into their practised, shield-protected squads.

Ishbel was there as well, crouched low to the ground, and
she gave a small wave at Axis' concerned look. *I am all
right. Do what you must without thought of me.*

Axis risked a quick glance upward—already the air was
filled with startled Lealfast—then he was down on the
ground, rolling as fast as he could under the shield wall of
the nearest squad of bowmen. Once inside he rose to his
feet, bending over slightly at the shoulders, and grabbed the
shoulder of the nearest bowman.

"See what I see," he whispered. He communed with the
eagle, sharing the view from a height far above Elcho Falling, then, using all of his skill as an Icarii Enchanter, he
twisted the vision, translating it to what a man on the ground
would see, then shared this vision with the bowmen.

See, he whispered among all their minds. *See . . . and act.*

In the four different locations, bowmen slotted their arrows through the tiny openings between the shields, took a
breath, and, using Axis' vision as their only guide, let loose
their arrows.

Immediately each bowman's arrow keeper slapped a
fresh arrow into the bowman's hand, and a moment later a
second wave of many thousands of arrows skewered the air.

And again.

And again.

And again.

The tip of the Dark Spire, now leaning precariously to one side
as the structure beneath it continued to crumble, had turned
completely black. It was also covered in cracks which were
opening wider and wider with every breath Ravenna took.

Behind them she could sense, if not actually see, a terrible darkness awaiting.

The One, crouched directly beneath the cracking skin of
the pinnacle of the spire, took a deep breath and then his
form began to change. His green glassy flesh melted away
and the One transformed himself into pure power.

In essence, it was not the One who now lay waiting beneath the top of the spire, but the pure power of Infinity. Beneath the roiling power the spire collapsed, but the top of the spire continued to hover in the empty space at the top of the destroyed chambers.

The One, now unadulterated Infinity, withdrew all power from the destroyed spire, concentrating it entirely inward and to his own purpose.

He could no longer "see" as such, as his physical form was destroyed, but he could sense the Lord of Elcho Falling, waiting just beyond.

High in the air, Eleanon reached for the power of Infinity.

And found it gone. Whatever had once allowed him to touch the power of Infinity was now destroyed.

The Dark Spire, he thought, eaten by the water creatures. Infinity was lost to Eleanon and his kind.

The gateway had vanished.

Already variously frustrated, enraged, disorientated and panicked, Eleanon lost his nerve and composure completely. All about him Lealfast were falling from the sky, pierced by arrows from the archers below. Eleanon knew he should call out an order, *knew* it, *knew* the Lealfast were waiting for something from him, then he cried out in pain and shock as an arrow thudded into his right thigh.

"Flee!" he cried. "Flee!"

Then another arrow, two, *three,* thudded into his right wing, and Eleanon began to fall from the sky.

"You know," Isaiah said, almost conversationally, on the balcony where he stood with Georgdi, "I'd heard stories of how good Axis was, how he could command men and how he could manage a battlefield, but this . . . this is extraordinary. I'd not want to meet him across a divide of hatred."

Georgdi only grunted in reply. He wished quite desperately that he was down there with Axis, helping to bring down the Lealfast Nation.

Maximilian had left Isaiah and Georgdi on the balcony. He'd crept down to a spot where he could observe the space above the spire where it had broken through into the ground chamber of the citadel.

Ravenna stood motionless at the handrail, just before the section where the staircase had broken free and tumbled down in pieces.

Maximilian halted, partly hidden by a corner of a wall. He watched with desperation—not that Ravenna would fail him, but with the need to go to her.

How could he let her do this alone?

"Don't," a soft voice said behind him, and Maximilian partly turned his head.

Garth Baxtor.

"This has been a long and terrible journey," Garth said, his voice very soft, "from the moment you were snatched on your fourteenth birthday, through your seventeen years of darkness in the Veins and the troubles Ravenna and I needed to endure to rescue you, to this now. A long and terrible journey. The least we can do, Maxel, is to bear witness for Ravenna."

Ravenna and my son, Maximilian thought and then he suddenly thought of Ishbel, and he realised *why* she had needed to transfer out of Elcho Falling with Axis.

Pray gods keep her safe!

"Look," Garth whispered, and Maximilian turned his eyes back to Ravenna and what lay beyond her.

The Emerald Guard were ready. The instant the Lealfast materialised inside the Common Room the Guardsmen moved smoothly into action. It only took five minutes. Five minutes of smooth, coordinated, almost dance-like movement on the part of the Guardsmen. Five minutes of screaming incomprehension and fear on the part of the thousand Lealfast, who were the balance of transfer, as they all died.

Not a single Guardsman had so much as a scratch.

It was time. The One exploded through the remnants of the pinnacle of the Dark Spire—not in physical form but as pure, bleak power.

Infinity, come to visit the Lord of Elcho Falling.

The One could feel him, standing not too far distant, and he hurled his power in that direction, ready to not waste a moment in winking the Lord of Elcho Falling out of existence.

This time he would leave nothing to chance.

But the Lord of Elcho Falling was moving, faster than the One could have thought possible, twisting along a path that confused the One.

But—the Lord of Elcho Falling was just ahead, only a step or two, and the One seethed forward . . . to find himself blinking in surprise.

"They're escaping," Georgdi said, pointing to the north, and Isaiah nodded.

Five, six minutes, and virtually every arrow fired by Axis' bowmen had found a mark. There were a few thousand Lealfast not dead and they were escaping.

Let them go, Axis, Isaiah said and, finally, the barrage of arrows from the squads of bowmen positioned about the lake ceased.

For long minutes the only sound that broke the silence was of the River Angels, heaving out onto the lake's shore the bodies of Lealfast who had fallen into the water.

The siege of Elcho Falling was over.

Maximilian and Garth stood watching as Ravenna turned and ran directly toward them. They both gasped, taking a step back, but in the moment before Ravenna reached them her form wavered, then vanished.

Directly behind her came a bolt of pure black power that Maximilian recognised from the time the One had thrown it at him down the path from the Twisted Tower. Maximilian grabbed Garth and pushed him to the floor, tumbling after him, but the instant before that black power consumed them it vanished. Maximilian and Garth were left gasping for breath on the floor.

Garth moved immediately to rise, but Maximilian lay still, remembering Ravenna running toward them and the moment their eyes had met.

And the instant after, when that long terrible journey which had brought the three of them together, and which had precipitated so much adventure and pain, was suddenly, horribly, over.

CHAPTER TWENTY-ONE

Elcho Falling

Eleanon slammed into the reed beds, swallowing his cry of pain instinctively so that any enemy nearby (the creatures in the water!) might not hear his voice. For a moment he was so winded, and in so much pain from the arrows, that he could not move. Then, achingly slowly, he rolled over, hiding himself deeper within the reeds, and trying to evaluate his position.

He was terribly vulnerable. He could not fly, although perhaps if he wrenched those arrows out of his wing . . .

Worse, though, was his total lack of the power of Infinity. It had ceased abruptly the moment the Dark Spire had died.

And even worse than that . . . even his powers as an Enchanter seemed warped, as if the constant contact with Infinity had damaged them. The Star Dance was dulled, fractured, he couldn't quite grasp it . . .

Eleanon could not think. He simply could not think. He had been so in control, and Elcho Falling so close to collapse . . . and now everything was ruined and his powers all but gone. He divided the reeds slightly, carefully, peering at Elcho Falling across the lake, hoping against hope that somehow it was still about to tumble into the water and that some good might come of this total disaster.

But what Eleanon saw pushed him even deeper into hopelessness—while the bloodied cracks still encircled the lower water walls of the citadel, they were very slowly closing over, almost coagulating.

Elcho Falling was healing itself now that the Dark Spire was gone.

I have to escape, Eleanon thought. *I have to get as far away from here as possible.*

Then, just as he was about to move, Eleanon heard the sound of someone moving through the reeds.

Axis did not bother to dampen the noise he made. He wanted Eleanon to know he was coming, and wanted him to despair hearing the strength and purpose of Axis' footsteps.

Through the eyes of the eagle Axis had known Eleanon was not dead, and that he was lying injured within the reed beds. He had set his men to mopping up among the Lealfast lying injured on the ground, then he'd headed straight for the reed beds at a jog, sword in hand.

This was something he'd promised himself in the ice hex.

Eleanon—wounded, in pain, helpless—panicked yet once more. He scurried through the reeds, desperately seeking a hiding place, not thinking that both the noise and the frantically waving reeds were a beacon to Axis. He moved as fast as he could, pushing through stand after stand of reeds, cutting his hands and shoulders on their sharp edges as he forced his way through.

Not thinking to look behind him.

Axis paused, watching Eleanon just eight or nine paces ahead, blundering his way through the reeds. He thought of all the enemies he'd faced over his lifetimes—Borneheld, Gorgrael, the Timekeeper Demons—and then he looked at Eleanon and felt contempt.

He could not even be bothered making a last defence.

Feeling sick to the stomach, Axis hefted his sword in his hand, and ran lightly over the reeds, catching Eleanon in just seven long strides.

Ravenna coursed through the Land of Nightmares, consumed with pure joy.

Behind her, very far behind, she could hear what remained of the One, screaming—or what passed for screams from a formless, helpless bundle of pure energy.

He was not doing well amid the Nightmares.

He could not touch Infinity here.

Ravenna slowed her plunge. The Nightmares reached out for her, too, but they did not harm her, only caressed her as she passed.

She was safe, and her son—the Lord of Elcho Falling—was safe, and close to birth.

This was not where she'd hoped to bring him into life, but it would do, and it would serve to teach him a few extra tricks with which to tackle life.

She smiled, and the Nightmares about her laughed at her joy.

CHAPTER TWENTY-TWO

Elcho Falling

Axis walked around the lake to the causeway.

His sword, freshly cleaned, rested in its scabbard against his hip. The gates of Elcho Falling stood open, men moving in and out on their business, and such was the air of normalcy that Axis thought that the citadel looked much like any castle or fort on a sunny day.

He stopped halfway across the causeway, peering into the water.

Deep below he could see ribbons of light flashing here and there and, just occasionally, the larger figure of a River Angel as it came closer to the surface, peering curiously at the man who looked down upon them.

It was a strange fate for the Skraelings. Axis stood there a long time, watching them, remembering all the hatred he'd harboured for the creatures, all the battles, all the friends lost to their ravenous jaws.

And here they were, flashing about in some mysterious, beauteous form, as if none of the horror and terror they'd caused had ever existed.

As if none of Axis' friends and countrymen had died.

As if Insharah's family had not died.

As if most of Isembaard had not died.

Axis straightened eventually, stepping back from the edge. All he could feel for them now was sorrow, both for them and for all the grief they'd left behind them.

He resumed his walk along the causeway, slowing as a column of horsemen emerged from the arched gates.

Georgdi.

The Outlander General halted the column as he reached

Axis. "You did well, Axis," Georgdi said, grinning. "Isaiah is sitting inside fair seething with resentment that you won the glory all by yourself."

"You're leaving? Already?"

"I need to see what has happened to the Outlands, Axis . . . and someone has to clean up the mess of wounded and dying Lealfast scattered across it."

"Did Ishbel make it back inside safely? What has happened with the One? Is Maximilian—"

"All is well Axis. Ishbel is inside, with Maximilian. Ravenna did what was needed. The One has gone."

"I . . ." Axis drifted into silence, not knowing what to say. He was glad that Ishbel and Maximilian were safe, that Ravenna had trapped the One, but was saddened to see Georgdi go, at the same time understanding why the man and his men wished to leave.

How many Isembaardians and Escatorians would be streaming out off Elcho Falling within the next day or two?

Axis' sadness deepened. How many other goodbyes would he need to say over the next few days?

And where, oh stars, would *he* go?

Georgdi looked down at Axis' face. He rested a hand on Axis' shoulder, caught his eyes, gave a nod, then kicked his horse forward.

There was no need to say more.

Georgdi had a deep sense that this was not the last he would see of Axis SunSoar.

Axis stood back and watched in silence as the Outlanders rode past. They took a full hour to ride out of Elcho Falling, and when they were done Axis trudged inside the citadel.

He'd expected there to be someone inside to meet him, but there was not, and so Axis climbed the ladder to the first usable landing on the great staircase, then climbed ever upward.

He went first to his father and Salome's chamber.

StarDrifter was half sitting up and looking cheerful, if not much better physically.

Axis sat on the bed, taking his father's hand.

"You have won another great battle," StarDrifter said. "A new feather for your legend."

"It was hardly a battle," Axis replied. "A sickening rout more like."

He looked over to Salome, cradling StarDancer. "My brother was the one who truly won the day. If he hadn't realised what could be done about the One . . ."

Axis drifted off, feeling exhausted physically and emotionally after the events of the day.

"We can rebuild the Icarii race, now," StarDrifter said. "We have peace, and a home within this lovely citadel . . . and we can rebuild the Icarii."

Axis had nothing to say. There were so few Icarii left, a handful of thousands perhaps, and so much lost. What to rebuild, and into what?

"You will stay, and help me," StarDrifter said.

Again Axis had nothing to say. He knew he couldn't stay. He and his father loved each other, but they made bad companions, and Axis knew the tension would see him leave sooner rather than later.

"Of course," he said, and bent and kissed his father's brow.

From his father's rooms, Axis went to the chamber he had once shared with Inardle. How long had it been since he'd slept in here? The past few weeks had been spent everywhere but at Elcho Falling, and when here, Axis had virtually lived in the command chamber.

It was, nonetheless, no surprise to find Inardle waiting for him.

Axis looked at her as she stood watching him, so beautiful, and felt nothing but sadness, too. He stepped forward, folded her in his arms, and held her close, rocking her a little.

"Eleanon is dead," he said softly.

"I know," she said.

"I'm sorry."

"I know that, too."

"Everything has gone for you, Inardle."

"And for you, too."

They paused, awkwardly. This was the moment where

one or both of them should say, *But, together, we can forge a new life.*

Instead they allowed the moment to draw out, then Axis leaned back, feeling uncomfortable.

"Don't say it," Inardle said, resting a finger briefly on his lips.

"What will you do, Inardle? You have no one left."

No one, she thought. *Not even you, Axis.*

"I loved you, Axis," she said, and again he took her in his arms.

"I know," he whispered.

They stood a long while, saying nothing, just holding each other, then Axis turned and left her.

"It has been a hard journey up to see me," Maximilian said to Axis when the StarMan emerged into the topmost chamber of Elcho Falling. Above them the roof lay open to the sky, Icarii tumbling through the revolving rings of the citadel's golden crown, the sun shining, the sky deepest blue.

Ishbel stood to one side, looking lovely in a gown of silver and rose. Axis went to her first, taking her hands and kissing her hard on the mouth.

"I always wanted to do that," he said.

She smiled. "I always wanted you to."

He leaned back, regarding her thoughtfully, still holding her hands. "You're pregnant," he said. "It is why you needed to transfer out of Elcho Falling with myself and my men."

Ishbel nodded. "I had only just realised in the past day. The child has barely been conceived."

She shared a look with Maximilian, and both smiled. "It is another daughter, and this one we hope will be born safely and live her life in peace."

"What does this do to the succession of Elcho Falling?" Axis said.

"We have not had the time and space to talk this through properly," Maximilian said, "but . . . it is possible that the succession of Elcho Falling can carry through the female line. Probably will, in fact, as Ishbel enjoys her own rights as Lady of Elcho Falling."

Axis' brow furrowed slightly in thought. "So there could be two lines of succession? One, the male line from you, Maxel, trapped in the Land of Nightmares and slowly being corrupted by both Nightmare and the trapped power of Infinity, and now a female line from Ishbel."

Maximilian gave a small shrug. "It appears so."

Axis hissed his breath out softly between his teeth. *Gods, he was glad it wasn't he who was going to have to deal with the consequences of this. It had the potential to become a true catastrophe if Ravenna's son ever escaped from the Land of Nightmares.*

"And you, Maxel," Axis said. "How does it feel, to be stripped of the power of Elcho Falling?"

"Both sad and joyous," Maximilian said. "Sad, because I can no longer sense the magic of the citadel, but joyous because I feel I have a weight lifted off my shoulders." He smiled, putting an arm about Ishbel's shoulders and kissing her softly on the cheek. "And I have a feeling that this was always Ishbel's mountain, both when it was Serpent's Nest and as Elcho Falling."

"You are going to leave, Axis, aren't you?" Ishbel said.

"I must," Axis said. "I can't stay here."

Maximilian nodded, understanding. "Isaiah waits on a balcony just a few levels down. Waiting to speak with you," he said.

Isaiah's hands rested on the balcony railing as he surveyed the lake and the surrounding landscape. He did not look up as Axis joined him.

"You left a right mess out there for my men to clean up," Isaiah said.

Axis leaned his weight on his forearms on the railing, looking out. Below, squads of Isembaardian soldiers were cleaning away the corpses of the Lealfast.

"Many escaped," Axis said.

"They won't be a trouble," Isaiah said. "Not for many generations yet."

By which time, Axis thought, *they'll have had the time to breed up and rekindle their anger and resentment. The Skraelings have gone, but in their place . . .*

"Not for many generations," Axis echoed.

Isaiah finally turned to look at him. "What are you going to do?"

Axis returned the look, then his heart lifted and he smiled. "I was hoping you'd tell me that, Isaiah."

CHAPTER TWENTY-THREE

The Salamaan Pass

E ight weeks later.

Axis pulled his horse to a halt, peering through the southern mouth of the Salamaan Pass into whatever was left of Isembaard. The sun burned bright overhead, and Axis was grateful he'd changed into lighter clothes the day before.

He was in the hot southern lands now, the ice and snow of the north a long way behind him.

There was a crunching of the land's sandy grit, and Axis looked over to where Isaiah, Insharah and Zeboath had pulled up their horses.

"It will not be much of a home for any of you to return to," Axis said.

"Nonetheless . . ." Isaiah said.

"There are family to be farewelled," Insharah said.

"And family to be found, perhaps," the physician Zeboath said.

Axis nodded. The past two months had been vastly healing for all four of them as they trailed slowly down through the Outlands, staying here and there with Outlander friends as they travelled—including Georgdi, who was fascinated to hear of Axis and Isaiah's destination, and looked as if he might one day decide to join them.

Insharah and Zeboath kicked their horses forward, but Axis and Isaiah waited a few minutes.

"There goes the future of Isembaard," Isaiah said, quietly.

"It will grow again," Axis said. "It might take generations, but it will grow again. The Lhyl runs, the soil will be fertile, and whoever is left from among this once mighty population will return from their hiding places."

Isaiah gave a nod. Already many tens of thousands of Isembaardians had returned from the northern lands through the Salamaan Pass into Isembaard. They carried news that almost all of the settlers that Isaiah had dragged north would eventually return.

As would the Isembaardian army. It had stayed a few weeks longer with Maximilian at Elcho Falling, but now the eagle, who constantly soared overhead and who communicated with his brethren further north, told Axis and Isaiah that Kezial was leading it south.

Kezial and Insharah would need to battle it out for the Tyranny, but Axis and Isaiah hoped they'd do it peaceably enough.

Meanwhile, the far, far unmapped south, and further adventures, awaited.

Axis caught Isaiah's eyes, and they grinned simultaneously.

"There is a long road ahead of us," Isaiah said.

"Then let us ride it," Axis said, and booted his heels into his horse's flanks.

EPILOGUE

The Land of Nightmares

Ravenna screamed, and the Nightmares closed in about her.

She screamed again, and the Nightmares reached out their hands.

One more time, and then the Nightmares were cradling Ravenna and Maximilian's son in their terrible hands, loving him a little, before laying him down in Ravenna's arms.

Ravenna cradled her son, tears streaming down her face. For so many months she'd thought that her son would be denied her or that, if he did make it to birth, his heritage would be denied to him.

But he *had* been born, and he *had* been born with all his heritage his to take as he wanted.

Lord of Elcho Falling.

She kissed his brow, marvelling that, even newly-born, she could clearly see Maximilian's features in his.

Maximilian's son.

Ravenna wept in joy.

She cradled their son against her breast and was delighted when he began to nurse. He would grow strong here, learning from her and from her nightmarish midwives.

"And one day," Ravenna whispered to him, "one day I will take you home to Elcho Falling, which is your right."

She smiled yet again, then, in a soft voice, began to tell her son about Elcho Falling and all it would mean to him.

One day.

GLOSSARY

Alaric: a nation in the extreme north.

Aqhat, palace of: the home of Isaiah, Tyrant of Isembaard.

Armat: one of Isaiah of Isembaard's generals.

Axis: see SunSoar, Axis.

Baxtor, Garth: a physician who employs the Touch (the ability to determine sickness through touch). Garth was primarily responsible for freeing Maximilian Persimius from the Veins eight years before this tale begins.

Bingaleal: one of the Lealfast leaders.

BroadWing EvenBeat: an Icarii, and friend of Maximilian Persimius.

Central Kingdoms: a loose term incorporating Hosea, Pelemere and Kyros.

Coil, Order of the: an order which once lived in Serpents Nest, now Elcho Falling. They worshipped the Great Serpent and used the bowels of living men to foretell the future.

Coroleas: a continent to the west, renowned for the immorality and cruelty of its peoples, former home of Salome.

DarkGlass Mountain: an ancient pyramid originally built to provide a pathway into Infinity. Once it was known as Threshold.

Doyle: A member of the Emerald Guard and former assassin.

Drava, Lord of Dreams: the Lord of the Land of Dreams. Once Ravenna's lover. He was also instrumental in rescuing Maximilian from the Veins many years previously.

Dreams, Land of: magical dream world ruled by Drava, Lord of Dreams.

Egalion: captain of the Emerald Guard, and friend to Maximilian Persimius.

Elcho Falling: a magical and mysterious citadel of legend.

Eleanon: one of the Lealfast leaders.

Emerald Guard, The: Maximilian Persimius' personal guard, composed of former prisoners of the Veins.

Escator: a poor kingdom on the coast of the Widowmaker Sea. It is ruled by Maximilian Persimius.

Ezekiel: Isaiah of Isembaard's most senior general.

Falayal: a Lealfast elder.

First, the: the top caste of Corolean society comprising Forty-Four-Hundred Families. The First commands virtually all of the wealth and power within Coroleas.

Georgdi, Chief Alm: general of the Outlander forces.

Gershadi: a nation in the extreme north.

Hairekeep: a fortress standing at the southern entrance to the Salamaan Pass.

Hereward: former kitchen steward of the Palace of Aqhat in Isembaard and companion of Isaiah on their escape from Isembaard.

Icarii: a mystical race of winged people who once lived in the mountains of Tencendor. The Enchanters among them wielded the Star Dance to produce powerful enchantments. Now, a scattered remnant from the destruction of Tencendor live about the Central Kingdoms.

Inardle: one of the Lealfast, lover of Axis.

Insharah: captain of a band of Isembaardian soldiers. Friend of Axis SunSoar.

Isaiah: Tyrant of Isembaard and God of the Waters.

Isembaard, Tyranny of: a massive empire below the Far-Reach Mountains, currently ruled by Isaiah.

Josia: see Persimius, Josia.

Kalanute: one of the Lealfast elders.

Kezial: one of Isaiah of Isembaard's generals.

Kyros: a city state within the loose alliance of the Central Kingdoms. It is ruled by King Malat.

Lamiah: one of Isaiah of Isembaard's generals.

Lealfast: an Icarii-like race of the frozen north.

Lixel, Baron: a trusted baron of Maximilian Persimius, currently ruling Escator in Maximilian's absence.

Lord of Dreams: see Drava, Lord of Dreams.

Malat: King of Kyros.

Margalit: the major city of the Outlands, and Ishbel Brunelle's childhood home.

Maximilian Persimius: see Persimius, Maximilian.

Nightmares, Land of: a terrible bleak world beyond the Land of Dreams.

Nzame: an ancient demon who once controlled DarkGlass Mountain in that time when it was known as Threshold. He was trapped in Infinity by Boaz Persimius, then a Magus of the One.

One, the: DarkGlass Mountain and Infinity incarnate in flesh.

Outlands, the: a province to the far east, renowned for its wild nomadic culture.

Pelemere: a city state within the loose alliance of the Central Kingdoms.

Persimius, Avaldamon: an ancient Persimius prince, now dead, who had fathered Boaz on an Ashdodian princess.

Persimius, Boaz: an ancient Persimius prince, as also Magus of the One, who lived in Ashdod two thousand years earlier. He was the ancestor of Ishbel Persimius and husband of Tirzah.

Persimius Brunelle, Lady Ishbel: orphan from Margalit, raised to be archpriestess of the Order of the Coil and wife of Maximilian Persimius.

Persimius, Maximilian: King of Escator and now Lord of Elcho Falling. Maximilian endured seventeen years in the gloam mines as a youth and young man when his cousin Cavor seized the throne.

Persimius, Josia: an ancient Persimius prince, now guardian of the Twisted Tower.

Ravenna: a marsh witch woman who patrols the borderlands between this world and the Land of Dreams, and is the only person able in walk the Land of Nightmares. Her mother was Venetia. She is cursed by Ishbel after trying to murder Maximilian Persimius.

River Angels: an ancient, magical race.

Sakkuth: capital of the Tyranny of Isembaard.

Salamaan Pass: a great pass which is the only easy access through the FarReach Mountains into Isembaard.

Serge: a member of the Emerald Guard and former assassin.

Serpent's Nest: a great mountain on the coast of the Outlands.

Skraelings: wraith-like creatures of the ice and snow of the northern frozen wastes, they now ravage over Isembaard and owe their loyalty to the One.

Sonorai: one of the Lealfast elders.

Star Dance: Enchanters among the Icarii wielded the music of the stars (the music made as the stars move about the heavens, and which the Icarii called the Star Dance) in order to create powerful enchantments. The Star Dance is no longer available to those Icarii remaining alive as the Star Gate, which filtered the Star Dance through to them from the heavens, was destroyed during the final Tencendor wars.

Star Gate: a magical portal which once existed in Tencendor, the Star Gate filtered into Tencendor the magic of the Star Dance, which the Icarii Enchanters used to create their enchantments. Demons destroyed the Star Gate during the final wars of Tencendor.

StarHeaven SpiralFlight: a member of the Strike Force.

Star Web: an Icarii, and lover to Maximilian Persimius.

SunSoar, Axis: formerly a hero from Tencendor and a member of the Icarii race, Axis once reigned over Tencendor as its StarMan before relinquishing power to his son Caelum. Axis died some five years previously during the destruction of Tencendor but was brought out of the Otherworld by Isaiah, God of the Waters.

SunSoar, Salome: former Duchess of Sidon in Coroleas, now wife of StarDrifter SunSoar.

SunSoar, StarDrifter: Axis' father, and a powerful Icarii prince and Enchanter. He is now Talon of the Icarii.

Tencendor: a continent which once lay in the western regions of the Widowmaker Sea. It was lost five years before this tale begins in a catastrophic war with demons.

Tirzah: wife of Boaz Persimius. Long dead.

Twisted Tower, the: a palace of memories belonging to the Lords of Elcho Falling.

Veins, the: the gloam mines of Escator where Maximilian Persimius was imprisoned for seventeen years.

Venetia: a marsh witch woman who patrols the borderlands between this world and the Land of Dreams. She was murdered by her daughter, Ravenna.

Viland: a nation in the extreme north. The Vilanders often have trouble with Skraelings.

Wayward, Abe: a sailor from the Outlands.

Weeper, the: a strange but immensely powerful Corolean bronze deity. It had once harboured the soul of Josia, a Persimius prince.

Yysell: Axis SunSoar's body servant.

Zeboath: an Isembaardian physician.

Turn the page for an excerpt of
Sara Douglass's newest novel

THE DEVIL'S DIADEM

A standalone historical fantasy set in a
12th-century England very similar to our own, in
which a deadly—some say devil-sent—plague
ravages the country, and a young noblewoman
may be the only one who can stop it . . .

Maeb Langtofte That Was, Her Testimony

In the name of our Saviour, the heavenly Lord Jesu, and of his beloved mother, the blessed Virgin Mary, greetings. Pray hear this testimony from your humble servant, Maeb Langtofte that was, on the eve of her dying. May sweet Jesu and his Holy Mother forgive my sins, and let me pass in peace, and forgive me the manner of my passing.

My faithful servant and priest Owain of Crickhoel writes down these words and in some places will speak for me when I no longer have the breath. Brother Owain has taken my confession and offered me Godly advice these past thirty years. He has been a good and faithful friend to me and I pray that his reward in the next life will reflect this.

My life has been one of sin, but no sin has been greater than that of my young womanhood. Pray sweet Jesu forgive me, forgive me, forgive me. I did what I thought best and yet I am stained with mortal sin. Pray sweet Jesu do not apportion blame on Brother Owain for what he writes. His pen may wield the words, but it was I who wielded the sin.

Sweet Lord forgive me my lack of trust, and forgive me my lack of learning, for in both I have failed you in this life. I pray that in my next life I can redeem both sins and failures to you. I thank you from my heart for the gift of the Falloway Man, for without him I could have no hope of redemption. Your grace and love of this sinner, this womanly fool, is unending.

But I waste time, Owain, for I do not think I have long left in this mortal life. So we shall begin, and it is fitting I begin with that day I met he without sin, the one, shining, uncomplicated love of my life, Lord Stephen of Pengraic.

[Part One]

Rosseley Manor

CHAPTER ONE

His footsteps tripped down the great stone staircase as if from Heaven—their passage rich with joy and authority. Their lightness and pattern told me he was tall, athletic and undoubtedly young; happy, for those footsteps surely danced in their delight of life; confident, and therefore a member of the great nobility who lived in this manor house, for no one else would have dared to so skip through the majesty of the central vestibule.

He would be one of the older sons, a prince in bearing if not quite in rank.

There was a flash of gold and silver as he passed the doorway of the little shadowy alcove in which I sat, waiting. He was tall, and golden-haired, bedecked with jewels and vibrant fabrics and with a glint of steel at his hip.

I was dazzled, even by this brief glimpse of a member of the Pengraic family.

Then, unbelievably, he was back at the doorway, and stepping into my alcove.

I rose hastily from the rickety stool on which I had waited and dipped in brief courtesy. I kept my eyes down, and surreptitiously pressed my hands into my skirts so that they may not betray my nervousness.

I prayed my French was gentle enough to sound sweet to his ears. I had spent too much of my childhood practicing my English with the village children, and not enough perfecting my courtly French with those of more seemly rank.

"What have I found hiding in the doorkeeper's alcove?" he said, and the warmth in his voice made me dare to raise my eyes.

He was of my age, perhaps nineteen or twenty years, and therefore must be the oldest son, Lord Stephen. His hair was light wheaten gold, his fine beard similar, his eyes a deep cornflower blue. His clothes were of a richness I had never seen before, his tunic all heavy with gold and silver embroidery that his noble mother must have stitched for him.

"Rumour has it that doorkeeper Alaric has only rats in here for company, not beautiful young maidens."

"My lord, I am Mistress Maeb—"

"Mistress Maeb Langtofte!" he said, and I was amazed that he should know of my name. "My mother told me she expected a new woman to attend her. But what do you here? In this dark hole? Has no one announced you yet?"

"The man at the door—"

"Alaric."

"Yes, my lord. Alaric. He asked me to wait here while he sent word to your lady mother."

"Alaric has always been the fool . . . or maybe not, for if *I* had found you suddenly at my door I, too, might have secreted you away in my bedchamber."

I glanced at the tiny cramped bed nestled into a hollow in the thick stone wall—the alcove had not the floor space for both bed and stool—then met Stephen's eyes.

And then, the Virgin help me, I flushed deeply at the import of his words.

"I only jest, Maeb," he said gently, and at the care in his voice, combined with my overall awe at his presence and kindness, I felt my heart turn over completely. "My mother has been resting this afternoon and thus you have been kept waiting, for foolish Alaric must not have wanted to disturb her. Had he told any of us you were here, we would have seen to it you were welcomed far more warmly, and far sooner. Alaric is a fool, indeed."

Lord Stephen paused to study me, and the gentleness in his eyes and face increased even more, if that were possible.

"You cannot wait here," he said. "I shall escort you to my mother myself—"

"Stephen," said a voice, and we both jumped.

"My lord," Stephen said, and half bowed as he turned.

A man stood in the alcove doorway—he could not have entered unless he had wanted to completely fill the tiny space of this alcove with the crush of our bodies—an aged and wearied form of the youthful vitality which stood before me.

It could only be Lord Stephen's father, Raife de Mortaigne, the Earl of Pengraic.

Unlike his son, Lord Pengraic's tone was hard and devoid of compassion, and my eyes once more dropped to the floor while my hands clutched within the poor woolen skirts of my kirtle.

"You have no time to waste in idle chatter," Lord Pengraic said to his son. "The bargemen await and we must be away. Have you said your farewells to your lady mother?"

"I have, my lord," Stephen said.

"Then to the barge," the earl said.

Stephen inclined his head, managing to shoot me an unreadable look as he did so, then stepped past his father and disappeared from my sight.

The air felt chill and the world an emptier place without him close. I was amazed that so few moments in his company could have made so profound an impression on me.

To my consternation the earl did not turn immediately and follow his son.

"Who are you?" he said.

I dipped again in courtesy, and repeated my name.

"Langtofte . . ." the earl said. "Your father was one of the sons of Lord Warren of Longtofte, yes?"

"Yes, my lord. Sir Godfrey Langtofte." A son left poor, with little land, and who left me yet poorer in worldly goods and hope when he gave what he had to the Templars at his death five months ago. My mother, might the Virgin Mary watch over her always, had long been in her grave. My father had left me with the name of minor nobility, but nothing else of any worth, not even brothers and sisters to comfort me.

"And so now you are here," the earl said, "waiting upon my wife, which doubtless you think a prettier life than one spent at your devotions in a nunnery, which must have been the only other choice available to you."

His tone hurt. I kept my eyes downcast, lest he see the humiliation within them.

"Mind your ambitions do not grow too high, Mistress Langtofte. Do not think to cast the net of your aspirations over my son—"

"My lord!" I said, now stung to look at him too directly. "I did not—"

"He would think you nothing but a dalliance and would ruin your name yet further, and you would grace whatever nunnery I banish you to with a brawling infant of no name whatever, for do not expect *me* to allow it the de Mortaigne—"

"My lord! I—"

"Think not to speak over me!" he said, and I took a step backward, pushing over the stool, so wary was I of the contempt in his face.

Pengraic was one of the greatest nobles in England, not only the most powerful of the Marcher Lords, but also close confidante of the king. He could destroy my life with a word.

"Be careful of your place here, Mistress Langtofte," he said, now very soft, "for it rests only on my sufferance."

With that he turned on his heel and was gone, and a moment later I heard shouting as the earl's party moved down to the great barge I had seen waiting earlier at the pier on the Thames.

I stood there, staring at the empty space which still seemed to me to throb with his anger and contempt. My heart thudded in my chest, and I bit my lip to keep myself from tears.

The earl's unfairness knifed deep, particularly since it contrasted so brutally with the warmth of his son. I eased myself with the notion that Lord Stephen must have received his gentleness and kindness from his lady mother, and that she would keep me under a similarly gentle and most noble wing, and shield me from the unjustified anger of her lord.

Thus began my life in the Pengraic household.

CHAPTER TWO

I waited in that wretched little alcove for what felt like hours. I felt its cold and dampness seep into my joints, and I wondered how the man Alaric managed to sleep in here at nights.

I hoped the Lady Adelie believed in braziers, or maybe even a fire, in the family's privy chambers.

I hoped Lord Pengraic was no reflection of his wife, and I thought surely not, for Lord Stephen had been so sunny and warm, and as that was nowhere in evidence in his father, it must have come from his mother.

It was a nerve-wracking wait. Pengraic had struck to the heart when he'd said I had but two choices—enter a nunnery or take the only other offer open to me: serve Lady Adelie, Countess of Pengraic, who was a close cousin of my father's mother. I loved my Lord God and all his saints, but I did not think I would manage well with the isolation and rigidity of a nunnery. Besides, I wanted a home and family of my own one day. After the death of my father I had little choice left in my life. I had stayed some months with a distant cousin, but she and I did not settle well together and she resented the cost to her household of the small degree of food I ate at table. It was a relief to leave her house. I felt keenly the loss of my home on the death of my father; I was well aware that alone, and with no dowry, I was but a hair's breadth away from destitution despite my noble heritage.

How unhappy then, that in this single household prepared to offer me shelter the resident lord appeared determined to despise me.

I sat there and tried to fight back the despondency. I

wondered why it took so long for the lady of the house to send for me. Was this a test? Had she forgot me? Should I say something to Alaric who occasionally slid by the door, glancing in as if he, too, wanted me gone?

Finally, as an early evening gloom settled over the house, I heard more footsteps on the staircase, and a moment later a woman appeared at the door.

"Mistress Maeb?"

I stood up, a little too hastily.

"Yes."

The woman stepped closer, holding out her hands to take one of mine. She was older than me, perhaps by ten or twelve years, and even though her face and eyes were weary she offered me a smile and her hand's clasp was warm.

"I am Evelyn Kendal."

"Mistress Kendal," I said, and dipped in courtesy.

She patted the back of my hand. "No need for such formality with me, Maeb, though you should always show Lady Adelie respect. We have kept you waiting long. I am sorry for that. My lady has been feeling unwell and she asked us to sit with her while she slept. But now she is awake and feeling more cheerful, and has remembered you. Is this your bag? So little for all your belongings! Follow me and I shall bring you to my lady."

I picked up my bag—truly only a heavy cloth wrapped about my few remaining possessions—and thankfully departed Alaric's alcove. A few steps beyond it I heard him scurry inside, a shadowy spider glad to have his home released to him once again.

This was my first good look at the interior of Rosseley manor house. I had been awestruck when I rode up, for the entire house was of stone, a great rarity for its expense and thus only an option for the greatest lords. Inside it was spacious and well appointed—the hangings on the walls were thick and colourful and there were large wooden chests pushed against walls. As we passed the doors that led into the great hall of the house I saw a glimpse of the colourful pennants and banners hanging from the walls and ceiling, and I was much impressed.

But what should I have expected? The Earl of Pengraic was one of the Marcher Lords, almost completely independent of the king, wealthy beyond most of the Norman nobility, and a great man for the influence of his and Lady Adelie's families and of the extent of his lands, lordships and offices.

"This house came to the earl as part of Lady Adelie's dowry," Evelyn said as we began to climb the staircase. "We use it during the winter months when the Marches become too damp and cold for my lady to bear. We sometimes spend summer here, also, for the earl often needs to attend court and it is but a day or two's barge ride along the Thames to the king's court at Westminster."

"Is that where the earl and his son have gone now?" I asked. I had spent a moment envying the Lady Adelie for the wealth of her dowry, and then the envy evaporated as I thought on the marriage it had bought her.

Evelyn nodded. "King Edmond has asked the earl's attendance upon some difficult matter, I believe. Have you travelled far, Maeb?"

"A long way," I said. "All the way from Witcnie."

Evelyn stopped on the stairs and laughed in merriment. "A long way? Oh, my dear! The distance from here to Witenie is but a trifle compared to that which we will cover when eventually we go home to Pengraic castle in the Marches. *That* is a long journey!"

I flushed, feeling myself a country bumpkin. I had thought the four day ride along the roads from Witenie—just west of Oxeneford—to Rosseley manor on the Thames south of Hanbledene, a grand adventure in my life, but when I compared it to the vast distance this household needed to travel from the Welsh Marches to this lovely spot in Bochinghamscire . . . I felt the fool.

Evelyn smiled kindly at me. "It is always an entry to a vaster world, Maeb, when you first join a family such as this. I forget sometimes what it was like for me, eleven years ago."

I nodded, feeling a little better for Evelyn's compassion, and we resumed our climb up the staircase.

* * *

The upper level of the house comprised the family's private quarters. There were a number of smaller chambers, and one large, the solar, and it was to the solar that Evelyn led me.

My first question about the family was answered when Evelyn opened the door, and I felt the warmth of the chamber.

Lady Adelie did like a fire, then, or braziers. At least I should be warm.

We paused just inside the door and I looked about hastily, trying to spot my lady. The chamber was well lit from a window to the east and, indeed, warmed by several charcoal braziers. There was a richly-curtained bed at the far end of the chamber, several stools and benches positioned about, a cot or two, and what seemed to me to be a great horde of children standing in a group looking at me curiously.

To one side in a beautifully carved chair, alongside the largest of the braziers, sat a woman who, by the richness of her clothes, must be the Lady Adelie, Countess of Pengraic.

I dipped hastily and dropped my eyes.

"Mistress Maeb," she said, her voice thin with exhaustion, "come closer that I might speak with you more easily."

I walked over and took the stool that Lady Adelie patted.

Her hand was bony and pale, and when I finally raised my eyes to her face, I saw that it was thin and lined, her eyes shadowed with weariness.

"I am sorry I kept you so long waiting. The day . . ." She made a futile gesture with her hand. "Well, it has escaped me. I should not have so delayed you, for you are family, and welcome here."

She managed to put some warmth into that last and I smiled in relief.

"Thank you, my lady," I said. "You have greatly honoured me by asking for me to be here. I am immensely grateful, and shall do my best to serve you in whatever manner you ask."

"It will be a thankless task," Lady Adelie said. "I shall try, myself, to be of little labour to you, but, oh, the children."

The children . . . The words echoed about the chamber, and I glanced at the six children who had lost interest in me and now talked or played amongst themselves. They all had Stephen's look—fair-haired and blue-eyed—and ranged in age from a crawling infant to perhaps thirteen or fourteen for the eldest girl.

Lady Adelie must have seen my look, for she managed a small smile. "And this is not all, for there is my eldest son, Stephen." She sighed, and placed a hand over her belly. "And yet another to come later in the summer."

"My lady has been blessed," said a woman standing behind Lady Adelie's chair, "that she has lost only two of her children to illness or accident."

"Blessed indeed," Lady Adelie said. Then she nodded at the woman behind her. "This is Mistress Yvette Bailleul. She, Mistress Evelyn and yourself shall bear the burden of my care and that of my younger children still playing about my skirts. But you look cold and weary . . . have you drunk or eaten? No? Then we must remedy that. Evelyn, perhaps you can take Maeb further into your care and make sure she is fed, and show her to the cot you will share? We will all sup together later, but for now . . ."

Lady Adelie's voice drifted off, and I saw discomfort and weariness in her face. No wonder, I thought, having spent her marriage bearing so many and such healthy children to the earl. I hoped he was grateful for his wife, then felt a little resentful on my lady's behalf that he should burden her with yet another pregnancy at an age when most women were thinking to leave the perils of childbirth long behind them.

I rose, curtsied once more, told the countess again how grateful I was for her offer to call me to her service, then Evelyn led me away.

THE EPIC DARKGLASS MOUNTAIN FANTASY TRILOGY BY

SARA DOUGLASS

THE SERPENT BRIDE

978-0-06-088214-3

Rescued from unspeakable horror, Ishbel Brunelle has devoted her life to the Order of the Coil, a sacred cult. But the Serpent has loftier plans for the archpriestess—and an eerie, eldritch warning: *Prepare for the Lord of Elcho Falling . . .* In a realm beset by treachery, the DarkGlass Mountain looms above all as the terrible Dark God Kanubai prepares to break free from his prison in exile.

THE TWISTED CITADEL

978-0-06-088218-1

In a dread time of magic and peril, three unexpected heroes have emerged—Ishbel Brunelle, priestess of the Serpent Coil; Isaiah, the Tyrant of Isembaard; and Maximilian, the Lord of Elcho Falling. Yet they could not prevent the rising of the Dark God Kanubai. And now, backed by the malevolent DarkGlass Mountain, hordes of insatiable Skraelings ravage the land as war inevitably approaches.

THE INFINITY GATE

978-0-06-088220-4

Ishbel Brunelle and Maximilian have raised the magic of Elcho Falling and found a new ally in former god Axis SunSoar. But their enemy grows stronger through blood and betrayal, the mysterious Lealfast have their own agenda, and when unexpected treachery threatens, Axis SunSoar must face a darkness greater than any he has ever known.